<u>The Necessary Path Series</u>

Book One:
The Orbit Scrolls

<u>The Necessary Path Series</u>

Book One:
The Orbit Scrolls

Bruce W. Davis

Inara Publishing

An Imprint of GCRR Press
1312 17th Street Suite 549
Denver, CO 80202

INFO@GCRR.ORG • INARAPUBLISHING.COM

Inara Publishing
An imprint of GCRR Press
1312 17th Street Suite 549
Denver, CO 80202
www.inarapublishing.com

Typesetter/Copyeditor: Alexandra Hademenos
Cover Design:

www.shanealmgren.com

Library of Congress Cataloging-in-Publication Data

Book one : the orbit scrolls / Bruce W. Davis
p.   cm. – (The necessary path series)
Includes glossary references and maps.
ISBN (Print): 978-1-959281-08-5
ISBN (eBook): 978-1-959281-09-2
I. Title.   II. Series.

PS3573.O52.D38   2023

CＳ

To God, Creator of all that exists.
To Jesus Christ, Savior of all who ask and believe.
To my wife Annie, who never gave up on me.
For the sunrise of your smile each day.
To my daughters, Heather and Nikki.
I have loved and cherished you from your first breath of life.
To my sons-in-law, Brent and Shawn.
Honorable men. Trustworthy husbands. Exemplary fathers.
To my grandchildren: Kelci, Blake, Caleb and Jackson.
Intelligent, respectful of those they meet on their life paths, and oh so eager
to charge headlong into life.

May *The Orbit Scrolls* furnish a glimmer of what makes Poppy tick.

Acknowledgments

Heartfelt gratitude to John Davidson, friend and brother-in-law, for your expertise in computerizing the initial cover design and the maps of the Wraithian world. For all your patience, for all our back-and-forth changes, I thank you very much, bro'.

Sincere thanks to Inara Publishing's Dr. Darren Slade for your noteworthy critique of the manuscript, and to Alexandra Hademenos for your precise copyediting.

To the late Professor Venkatesh Srinivas Kulkarni of Rice University: in a veritable sea of hyper qualified writers and aspiring authors, you noticed me. Then, you encouraged me.

Contents

*Character is the sculpture you create,
from the choices you make,
and from the values you cherish.*

*Reputation is the shadow cast by your sculpture,
as Life shines upon it.*

Prologue:
Introduction to the Treatise

Pelanjia—Empire and Myth

Investigating legends invites risk, for the passions of skeptics and believers alike run soul deep. Consider just these few:

Wraithaven—reigning for eight millennia at least, is humankind's most enduring myth.

Legend declares that a yet undiscovered mountain range—the Shield—is both a desolate abode of eternally warring "gods" and a vast mountain prison for demonic spirits bent on exterminating all human life. Location: Somewhere beyond the continent of Tripada's western horizon.

The *Mascarene Treasure Caverns*—secret mountain lairs filled with gold and gems plundered from ancient kingdoms by mythical dragons. Locations: Unknown, but for enough gold coin, "authentic" maps can always be secured.

Glynac—the living sword that kills or heals at its owner's discretion. Forged by the gods (of course), but stolen by a legendary boy-king. (But are not "magic swords" always stolen by some prophecy-linked waif?) Location: Unknown, but sworn to exist by "credible," albeit long-dead, eye witnesses.

And let us not forget the *Spring of Perpetual Youth*. Location: Either deep in the unexplored heart of Mascarene, insolently labeled the Dark Continent by most Embricans, or in the vast Unknown Region of unmapped western Tripada, where it competes with the equally evasive Wraithaven. The common thread running through all legends is that they always seem to exist in the allegedly pestilent, forbidden interiors of unexplored regions.

How convenient. With barely one-third of our planet's surface mapped, and with no explorer intrepid enough to circumnavigate our world, most legends will continue to enjoy their unenlightened sanctuaries for centuries more.

One enduring myth, however—second only to Wraithaven—can now bathe in the light of at least some measure of reason. I speak of the Pelanjian people, extinct now for over two thousand years. Colleagues caution me to avoid the subject, lest it taint my academic credentials. I appreciate their concern. Yet, I contend that no human legend, myth or superstition, however fanciful, is without some grain of truth. No legend springs into existence unfounded. No superstition creates itself from nothing.

Within that context, lies both the audience of skeptics who decry most of the unfounded embellishments attributed to the legendary Pelanjian Empire, as well as the fewer, but equally fervent defenders claiming that Pelanjia was the most superior empire in human history.

As for me, having researched and listened to the oftentimes deafening opinions of both sides, I find I must align with the defenders of Pelanjian myth, despite the skeptics and their superior numbers. In that regard, I confess to being swayed by fragmentary legends over equally fragmentary history.

Despite often fantastic embellishments that twenty centuries of unchallenged history have added to the Pelanjian myth, some original truth must remain of what we know, or what we *think* we know, about Pelanjia today.

The eleven-island archipelago of Pelanjia does, in fact, exist. That it was once inhabited is also without question. Sakora's dig at Erytheia nine years ago, Gaetano's at the re-discovered Port of Salacia on the Itherian Peninsula five years ago, and my own dig (underwritten by this university) at the Isthmus of Gianna four years ago all confirm through clay tablets that Pelanjia was the ancient world's primary hub for the spice trade.

Logically, as a spice hub, Pelanjia might well have been the wealthiest nation of its time, as legend declares. Another myth assertion, that the island nation was unsurpassed as a military force, is highly likely. Wealth breeds jealousy; and given humanity's history of greed-inspired warfare, how could a small, wealthy nation, especially an island nation, *not* have been a target of larger, aggressive nations? Yet, Erytheian tablets confirm that Pelanjia remained at the peak of world influence for over four centuries—an impossibility for a weak nation.

Tablets at Gianna and Salacia both document thirteen invasion attempts in those centuries—roughly one per generation. In all translations, the invaders were "crushed," not just repelled. Does this confirm that Pelanjia was a population of battle-hardened, fanatically trained warriors, as legend declares? Quite possibly, yes. But were the invaders slaughtered by "ghost warriors who killed in cold silence and with supernatural stealth and skill"? Not likely.

History is also unsure from whence came the art of glass-making, the firing of ceramics, the invention of the telescope, the invention of the compass or the sextant. Legend, without hesitation, credits the artistic, inventive Pelanjians.

For a moment, allow reason to lean in the direction of legend. Would not island dwellers be skilled mariners? Could Pelanjian mariners have actually created the Pelanjian spice hub by establishing new trade routes, rather than waiting for the rest of the world to find *them*? That alone suggests an adventurous, collective purpose as a people. National intent at this level pushes the boundaries of exploration, of invention. How could such a master sea-faring people *not* invent the instruments of seamanship—the compass, the sextant? Why would glass-making not evolve into lens-making, and thus make way for the invention of the telescope or of ceramic firing?

Could our modern seaports today, and rediscovered sites shrouded by the dust of millennia, have been seed colonies of the Pelanjian expansion? Legend declares an emphatic "yes!" An interesting, but unproven theory thus far.

Did vastly superior Pelanjian "dragon" ships fly across the waves as myth enthusiastically contends? Certainly not, yet Sakora's unearthing last summer of the north wing of the Caladian central palace in Erytheia offers a tantalizing consideration. A huge, magnificently wrought mosaic, nearly fifty feet in length (but damaged) depicts a harbor scene—Caladia at its presumed peak. Thick-bellied, blunt-bowed ships of verified Caladian design are depicted berthed at docks and under sail.

What tantalizes Sakora's team most, however, is the damaged lower portion. Fragments of remaining tiles suggest a single ship of outlandishly streamlined design in comparison to the ungainly Caladian vessels. Possible remnants of wing-like horizontal sails augment much taller masts adorned with unconventional sail design. Expert opinions on site are as diverse as they are heated.

The first proof, defenders declare, of a Pelanjian ship under sail. Not so, equally qualified skeptics counter. Not a ship at all, but a fanciful depiction of a mythical sea beast entering the harbor. I reserve my personal opinion, for now.

The sea-faring aspect aside, rabid supporters of Pelanjian superiority assert that Pelanjians valued education above all, including their famed military prowess. They allegedly held to a strict code of honor of some sort, and their knowledge of the healing arts, of medicinal herbs, and surgical techniques was unsurpassed even to this day. Their life spans were allegedly three times the average of the day, perhaps more. They were splendid artists, poets, and musicians. They allegedly invented the concept of libraries, which were superb and numerous, despite the fact that not a single known Pelanjian scroll or book survives today.

I view such hand-me-down embellishments without evidence as fanciful wishes by folk so un-empowered by current existence that they dream of perfect worlds beyond past horizons. Yet, even the lack of evidence has justification. The legal and business transactions of that era were etched upon clay tablets or wooden slats. Such artifacts are relatively common today, but only under perfect archeological conditions.

And what of Pelanjian records, skeptics ask? Easily explained, proponents argue. Pelanjians used neither method. Pelanjians invented not only parchment writing, but paper as well. Allegedly. If so, only a miracle would preserve such fragile evidence for two thousand years. Thus continues the perpetual loop of argument—logic versus the fanciful.

The struggle to separate truth from Pelanjian legend may well prevent the world from ever knowing even a fraction of the complete story; but at the very least we must consider these points: We know historically that after the Pelanjian disappearance, humankind declined into the era history labels the Dark Millennium.

It was during the Dark Millennium that unmeasurable damage was wrought to civilization. Entire tribes, nations, even empires ceased to exist when ejecta from simultaneous volcanic eruptions somewhere in the uncharted Void Region west of Mascarene blanketed the globe for decades. Under sunlight-robbing skies that seemed blood red at sunrise and sunset, agricultural output and its international trade was essentially eradicated worldwide.

Once-thriving Embrican and Mascarenean nations (many allegedly spawned by Pelanjian explorers) dissolved back into warring tribes bent on slaughtering each other over this fertile valley or that strategic mountaintop.

The last official assembly of the then fifty-five-nation World Trade Conference achieved but one objective as the coming one hundred year Starvation War began to ignite its horror. The delegates elected to replace the two regional calendars of that era, the Valerian Record (V.R.), and the Imperial Chronical (I.C.), with a worldwide calendar designated the Year of the Red Sun (R.S.).

Yet, from that new starting point, one cannot help but conjecture whether our current level of technology is nothing but an incomplete re-emergence of that which the ancient world once enjoyed pre-Dark Millennium. Is the level of advancement we boast of today only a shadow of what once was? Defenders of the Pelanjian myth declare emphatically, *yes!*

For example, Embrican historians credit the invention of paper to Altherian monks five hundred years ago. Does this support the argument that the art of making paper ceased *exactly* with the Pelanjian disappearance? Did it really take the world—and the Altherian monks—fifteen hundred years to *recreate* it?

Also, if Pelanjian explorers had truly circumnavigated the globe and thoroughly mapped it two thousand years ago, again as legend claims, why have we not done so yet today? Does our vaunted level of human civilization today retain naught but flawed remnants of the greatness that was the Pelanjian Empire?

Lastly, how, by all that is logical, could such an allegedly advanced race disappear so completely from the face of the earth? What was the chink in their armor? Did Blood Plague exterminate them, as legend proclaims? If so, why have we not found even a shred of their everyday existence, their artistry, or their power? No shards of Pelanjian pottery exist. Archeologists have unearthed no broken Pelanjian sculptures, no corroded Pelanjian weapons.

Yes, modern civilization still has just cause to fear Blood Plague. Every few centuries, different seaports reignite the devastation again as in 742 R.S., 938 R.S., and in 1312 R.S., when one in three Embricans died. And true, a small island nation serving the world's shipping trade would be most vulnerable to a ship-borne outbreak. Our terror remains fresh thanks to the outbreak only eighty-four years ago that killed hundreds of thousands along the eastern coast of Mascarene.

Still, no human being has dared set foot on the Pelanjian Archipelago for two thousand years! Historical assumption of their demise has devolved into an ingrained generational fear paralyzing academic curiosity to this day. Myth declares that the deadliest form of Blood Plague still awaits the unwary after defeating even the legendary healers of Pelanjia. Did the entire population die in their beloved islands? Did their advanced dragon ships rot into nothingness as would lesser vessels left moored and unattended in their berths? Has twenty centuries of time, storm, and tide dissolved what must have been a vast wharf complex back into the sea?

Consider the possibility if we were brave enough to explore the Pelanjian Archipelago. Might we find Pelanjian bones overgrown by twenty centuries of unchecked jungle growth?

By the gods, what really happened to these people?

In closing, I submit below an engraved quote from a small marble tablet unearthed on the Isthmus of Gianna just over two years ago, on 24 Andril, 2034 R.S. The language is definitely Caladian. The syntax is definitely not.

The site is what remains of a small Caladian monastery leveled by an earthquake during the approximate time frame of the Pelanjian extinction. I have reproduced the quote in its exact form and presentation, and have translated it as accurately as our Embrican language can interpret it. Is it truly "Pelanjia's Prayer," as the first line declares? Or is it merely a supplication raised by a monk sympathetic to the invasion-beset Pelanjians? As of this date, 19 Mairche, 2036 R.S., we simply do not know.

<u>*Pelanjia's Prayer*</u>

We teach our children what our fathers taught us.
We teach them the ways of war as centuries of fathers have taught
before us.
To survive, our children's children must do the same.
We pray for your deliverance from war, oh Lord.
We pray for peace.
Teach us how a seed begins life, how to glean a poet's vision.
Teach us the mysteries of Your tides, not how to slay an armada.
What might our people become, oh Lord, if the slaying was no more?
If our honor was not tainted by constant warfare?
If the energy of our people created instead of destroyed?
Show us please, Great Creator, another path.

Sincerely,

Mezentius Telemon
Professor d'Antiquities' du Literatum
Académie' d'Embrica d'Lang-Sha

Part One:
Readers

We are all individual threads of varied hues woven into Wraithaven's collective tapestry. Threads of Pride, of Honor, of Discipline reinforce the threads who are: Teachers, Healers and Guardians. Our historical threads, our cultural intentions, bind our Scientists, Artisans and Priests to our Pickets, Mariners, and Farmers. Our Warriors and Poets, our Youth and our Elders, are all integral to the same dynamic tapestry.

Yet, of us all, our culture's strongest threads are Readers. They reveal the Orbit Scrolls to our children. They guide us all upon the loom of Nung-Cha. They blaze the trail that is our Necessary Path.

—Wraithian Adage

Reader

Early autumn 4287 M.C.
Scimitar Province, Wraithaven

Five hundred years old, the cottage, nestled within a sloping copse of blood-red flame maples, was relatively new compared to many in the province. The large hay barn and smaller outbuildings common to properties cultivating vineyards and orchards were centuries older. Walls of fitted limestone blocks anchored them all fast against Wraithaven's fierce winter blizzards. Gray slate roofing tiles clad each structure like a warrior's armor.

The instant Taggart Kayne awoke, he knew the day would not follow its normal routine. Having awakened two hours before dawn was the only thing typical.

He lay still at first, absorbing the subtleties of the morning. A chilly autumn breeze out of the northwest whispered through the half-opened window in the north wall of his bedroom. His breath frosted into faint clouds before dissipating. The small cast-iron stove in the bedroom's corner rested dark and silent now. No oak logs burned, crackling orange and happily behind the grating of the little hinged door. The wood had cooled to ash hours ago, leaving naught but a hint of oak coal scent to ride the breeze to his nostrils.

Faint rhythmic ticks of the mantle clock in the adjacent gathering room sought his attention. A great-horned owl hooted in the forest beyond the hay barn. The weight of the heavy quilt drawn up to his chin conspired with the scents of wool and the cedar-lined trunk it had lain in to keep him warm and comfortable right there. But on the seventy-one-year-old man's left side where Alina, his wife of forty-seven years, should still be cozying next to him, his left hand sensed only her residual warmth clinging to the mattress. She had started their day without him.

He slipped out from under the warm quilt and donned simple leather sandals and his *dra-ki*—a black-streaked, light gray martial arts uniform consisting of a heavy, long-sleeved, cotton jacket and loose-fitting trousers. He looped a long black cotton belt twice around his waist, securing the belt with a square knot at his navel. Both ends of the belt hung precisely twelve inches below the knot. An embroidered, six-inch-long red dragon decorated the left belt end, signifying Master Dragon rank in empty-hands combat and in seventeen different martial arts weapons. A similar dragon wrought in gold and blue thread graced the right belt end, a second Dragon-level rank in stealth and covert tactics. Wraithaven had no higher martial rank.

Upon leaving the room, Taggart took his scabbarded *Dai-ryu* (Great Dragon) single-edged long sword and his *Kai-ryu* (Small Dragon) dagger from the oak wall pegs above the headboard on his side of the bed. He slipped the weapons into his belt, but despite the darkness of the room, he noted the empty pegs on Alina's side.

At the back door, taller even than Taggart's rangy 6'4", stood the weapons cabinet of burled oak. Inside the exquisitely carved 850-year-old heirloom, all seventeen pairs of weapons, from spiked war hatchets to chained wheat flails, hung neatly on wooden pegs.

We were to practice staff and scon-ki, (wheat sickles), *this morning,* Taggart thought, shutting the double doors. No moon hung in the cloudless, black sky, but the backyard was dotted with a dozen, knee-high, seemingly randomly spaced points of yellow light—tiny candle lanterns obviously lit by Alina. The scent of eight-foot-tall dwarf apple trees, their supple branches heavy with ripening fruit, silently welcomed him. Two different gravel paths led from the back door to a waist-high stone wall fifty paces away.

Two paces wide, the main path meandered with a shallow *S*-curve to a low cedar gate in the wall. A narrow meditation path branched to the left off the wider path, before looping tightly back upon itself, crossing the main path seven times until blending with it again at the gate. In places, the little path crossed over tiny gurgling springs on low teak bridges. In others, flat slate steppingstones served as crossings.

Beyond the wall, a diffuse yellow glow backlit the fruit trees just enough to define their shapes. Even in total darkness, Taggart could have negotiated either path without a misstep.

This time of morning, only one path would do. Taggart paused to appreciate the aroma of apples wafting through the orchard, noting tonal differences where the light breeze hissed through distant spruce needles, or shouldered past the stouter apple leaves. Then, clasping his hands at his belt, he bowed his head, and stepped reverently upon the narrow, winding trail. His mind entered *Nung-Cha, The Necessary Path.*

Past the stone wall lay the Kayne arena, a twenty- by thirty-pace rectangle of flat, perfectly joined slate pavers. At the northern edge, precisely at the center, rose Enkia-Entae, the Prayer Stone. The seven-foot-tall natural obelisk of gray granite was so named in the ancient Mindocean tongue meaning "to reach." Crowned with patches of gray lichen, its northern side be-robed with delicate dark-green moss, the great stone loomed like a vigilant, eternal guardian. Calloused feet of thirty-five generations of Kayne warriors had worn the slate smooth from boundary to boundary.

Spaced evenly around the perimeter, a faint yellow glow from oil lanterns washed just enough light across the slate to define the boundaries. On any other day, Taggart and Alina would have lit them together.

The slender, six-foot-tall woman knelt in silence before the Prayer Stone. Her legs were folded beneath her. Her back was straight. Her head was bowed with eyes closed. Her slender hands rested on her thighs.

She was, in Taggart's artistic mind, as perfect as a marble sculpture. He absorbed the flickering lantern light as it played across her gray-streaked brown hair drawn to her mid-back in a single warrior's braid. His own brown hair, just as long and just now beginning to streak with gray, was plaited into an equivalent shape. Where path met arena, Taggart stepped out of his sandals next to

Alina's. He placed his sheathed sword and dagger in the wooden rack next to her weapons. Fists at his sides, he bowed toward the Prayer Stone and entered the arena.

Alina's breathing was slow and calm. She did not acknowledge Taggart when he knelt precisely two paces to her right and mimicked her pose.

Silently, Taggart began his meditation.

I revere the truth this stone symbolizes. As it is bound to the earth. So too am I. As it reaches toward my Maker. So too do I.

Father Creator, with gratitude I begin this day, Your gift of life to me. May the orbits of my soul honor You. May I commit no harm to Your creation this day.

I give thanks for . . .

Taggart envisioned his life's treasures: Alina, their marriage, their children and grandchildren, their health, his profession as master sculptor, his apprentices so bright with promise laboring at the quarry miles away, the latest crop of Twelfth-Harvest children who anxiously awaited his and Alina's arrival, and many other blessings. Completing his prayer of gratitude, he stopped and began to exhale slowly and softly.

Detecting the end of his meditation, Alina matched her breathing to Taggart's. Eyes still closed, they raised their heads to synchronize into the *Final Eleven.* They inhaled for a slow count of four, held for four, exhaled for four, and held again for four before beginning the next cycle. Completing eleven such cycles, they touched their foreheads to the slate before the Prayer Stone.

Then, as if joined by invisible bonds, the couple stood up, and executed a precise about-face before walking in step to the south end of the arena. Only when Alina stood did her martial rank reveal itself. One red dragon and a second blue-and-gold dragon emblem stood out in bold relief against the black of her belt.

Silently, for a quarter hour, they followed a progressively intricate routine of stretching and warming-up exercises. Upon completion, they bowed to each other, turned to face the stone, and then snapped into aggressive combat stances, fists raised, knees flexed and ready. What followed fused grace, power, and extraordinary fluidity based upon the characteristics of seven different animals.

The millennia-old, advanced Dragon-level combat forms of Wraithaven's martial arts system, known as *Nung-Cha*, began with *Ice Cat Slaying*, a powerful dance of low crouching movements characterized by quickly executed, lengthy stances. Hands clawed in tight, blurred defensive circles too fast for an untrained eye to follow. Bone-crushing hammer-fists mimicked the killing strikes of Wraithaven's most dangerous predators—saber-toothed felines as large as oxen.

The perfect synchronization of the couple was made possible only by a half century of disciplined practice, by having pushed their bodies to fifty thousand repetitions of the advanced forms. Both remained silent, not punctuating the more explosive points of the form with loud shouts as Outsider martial systems taught. Climactic strikes, killing blows, were punctuated with explosive exhalations of breath at the focused, pantomimed strikes of fist, foot, or elbow.

To a non-Wraithian observer, the strenuous ritual might be perceived as overzealous acts by rare adherents to such an activity. This was not the case here. Across the length and breadth of Wraithaven, the morning entry to *The Necessary Path* started the day's activities. School children and the elderly, tradesfolk and militias, healers, teachers and families all began their days thus. Villages and schools held mass *Nung-Cha* gatherings. It had been so for over two thousand years. To do otherwise was unthought-of.

With the final strike of *Ice Cat,* they paused for a count of four. Rising to the attention stance, they took three measured breaths.

Descending Crane followed, allowing them to recover from the vigor of *Ice Cat* through deceptively graceful spins and the narrower stances of the form. High snapping kicks to the front and side, blurring spear-hand jabs, and axe-like chops of the hand's knife-edge mimicked the hunting techniques of the silver crane. The only obvious noise was the whip-like snaps of their trouser cuffs and jacket sleeves.

The beguiling subtlety of *Hunting Serpent* immediately followed. Tight, looping blocks and wide, circling deflections masked iron-fingered strikes to the throat, eyes, and heart of imaginary opponents, delivered so quickly naught but advanced practitioners could differentiate the moves.

The fourth, *Wolf Pack Playing*, simulated defense and attack against multiple opponents. Strikes of fist, elbow, and feet were three times as numerous as any other form and demanded unfettered speed during execution. The rigorous form taxed both practitioners, but decades of practice made the intricate violence seem easy. In not one strike, parry, or leap did they break their fluid synchronization.

But that was not to say the moves were performed mindlessly. Even after decades of practicing *Nung-Cha*, Taggart was never unaware of the origins of the *Wolf Pack* form. *It was created to epitomize the predicament plaguing our ancestors,* he thought. *Multiple nations often declared simultaneous war upon our Pelanjian ancestors. Combined fleets attacked multiple times in every Pelanjian generation intent on invading the home islands, determined to exterminate every man, woman and child. Always outnumbered. No allies to help. Always alone. Learn to fight! Or die!*

His reverie came and went quickly. It had to.

Iron Shark followed, the most fluid form of all. They spun from low, sweeping crouches, lashing out an extended leg in one direction then another to sweep an imaginary opponent's feet out from under him. Killing blows of knife hands and crushing blows from a foot heel always followed such "iron broom" techniques. They delivered deadly strikes from upright stances, from low crouches, and lastly even from flat on their backs. Upon ending, they kicked back to the upright attention stance like acrobats.

Awakened Dragon, significantly slower and less flamboyant, was the most demanding of all. Straightforward fist strikes, rising palm heel "neck breakers," and forearm blocks were delivered with slow, exaggerated tensing of every muscle possible. *Awakened Dragon* was a strength builder, designed to reinforce the speed of a strike delivered in actual combat. The final strike, a low, kneeling stance punctuated by a straight downward blow of the right fist, left sheens of sweat glistening on their brows.

The two rose for what should have been a ten count state of preparation for the seventh and final form, *Crag Lord Defender*. Without a word, Alina typically led the form by distancing herself two additional paces from Taggart, which he would then match. This morning Alina didn't move. The ten count came and went. So did another.

She's distracted, Taggart surmised, not looking at her, just waiting her out.

A sneering voice whispered in Alina's mind. Again. *Two thousand years of peace and still we enter The Necessary Path as if it was needed.*

And it isn't! She threw back. *Hasn't been for centuries! Our cultural paranoia feeds upon itself!*

Forgotten about Cathmore? The Voice sneered. *So soon?* It was ready for her reply. Again. As always.

How could I forget? Ever! And then, as quickly as it had appeared, the Voice abandoned its playground.

Silently, Alina forced herself to move the required two paces. Taggart followed.

Crag Lord was the most elegant form of them all, combining the swift, circular clawing techniques of *Ice Cat* with high aerial spins and kicks more flamboyant than the confined movements of *Descending Crane.* The entire arena was required for the wide, circling arm blocks and the long-distance attacks unique to the form.

It was no accident that *Ice Cat* began the seven forms or that *Crag Lord* ended them. When ancient explorers first set foot on Wraithaven's pristine soil, two of the many wonders of the New World had made lasting impressions.

No predator in the known world matched the size and unparalleled ferocity of the immense saber-fanged felines that prowled Wraithaven from her glacier regions to her fog-shrouded valleys. As for the crag lords, no other name seemed appropriate for the huge, golden-brown eagles that patrolled the timberline country on twelve-foot wingspans.

After studying both creatures for a hundred years, ancient *Nung-Cha* masters created the two complex forms for the Dragon rank. As the New World had absorbed the folk who began to call themselves Wraithians, the two new forms were absorbed by the ancient five first created millennia before in the home archipelago. That meant little to Taggart and Alina. The two "new" forms were nearly two thousand years old before either of them were born.

Crag Lord was a favorite of the couple. Falling back into the lead, Alina found the sublime rhythm of the form after the first few moves, abandoning the Voice as completely as it had abandoned her. Sheer pleasure from executing the precise, demanding movements began to radiate from the pair now. Eyes sparkled, smiles refused confinement, surfacing despite, or perhaps *because* of the concentration, the effort. *Crag Lord* was beautiful, as much dance as martial art, and the beauty of dance begets joy. It simply does.

At the last movement, a strongly executed, low front stance, accentuated by snapping, double-fisted strikes to the front, the pair stood up, bowed to the Prayer Stone, then to each other before relaxing. Only then did they speak.

"Good morning, my sweet," Alina said, catching her breath enough to greet Taggart with a lingering kiss. "Captured by the quilt this morning?"

"Hardly, love," he said, cupping her face with big, calloused hands. "More like a poor husband abandoned by his impatient wife."

"I never sleep well before a Reading."

Taggart slipped his arms around her. "I attribute that to your youth, girl," he said with a grin.

Married when he was twenty-four and she was nineteen, the five-year difference inspired occasional quips.

"Old men certainly don't seem plagued by restlessness."

"It's not our first Reading," he said, stroking her lower back.

"I know, Tag. I just sense an unclear darkness awaiting us this time." Taggart did not dismiss Alina's apprehension. She possessed an uncanny knack to sense danger, or something beyond normal routine. He could only surmise that her inherent eye for detail that characterized her complex tapestry designs, empowered her during the traditional mounted stag hunts of late summer. She was often the first rider in a stag pack to detect game sign.

At age fifty-nine, citizens who seek Wrathaven's most honored social rank as a Reader may apply for an intensive, year-long course of study in the national capital of Conclusion Bay. Once qualified, the now Sixtieth Harvest Readers conduct the annual threshold-crossing ritual known as a Reading. For Twelfth-Harvest children, the three-day autumn campout in Wraithaven's remote valleys introduces them to the *Orbit Scrolls*. For married couples who wish to serve as a team, a younger spouse can enter Reader training with the older one, as did Taggart and Alina.

After returning from their two-year tour of duty as Pickets in northern Cathmore, Taggart had reached sixty-three harvests, and Alina, fifty-eight. They have Read twenty-one times thus far, occasionally conducting multiple Readings in a single year when the number of eligible children in their sector required it. They live for the Readings now, marveling each time "transit children" shed their child's mantle.

Upon the completion of a Reading, the wooden practice sword carried by every Wraithian child from the age of seven is replaced by a real, but shorter version of the steel sword carried by adults. A Twelve-Harvest child can own property, and virtually always receives a first acre as a gift from family the week of the Reading. In return, Twelve-Harvest young ones are expected to choose more sober adulthood over childish behavior.

⋏　　　⋏　　　⋏

"So, love," Taggart said, "we don't seem to be sparring." On any other day, one-on-one sparring followed two full cycles of the seven forms. Weapon drills then followed, with a five-mile run to the quarry and back completing the exercise for the day.

"No, we don't," Alina whispered huskily against his ear.

"Then dare I predict that we shall not run, either?"

"I think not, old man. Readers and Dragons need their rest, especially *old* Dragons." She ran her fingertips slowly down his chest. Her left hand took the ends of his belt as she backed slowly away from him, her hazel eyes holding his of gray. As his right hand slid over hers, the intricate dragon tattoo looping around his thick wrist and hand covered an identical tattoo on her smaller hand.

Rest indeed, he thought as they strolled back to the cottage, using the most direct path.

2

The Road

F alcon's Road is two wagons wide where it traverses thirty-one miles of mountainous terrain between the Kayne family quarry and the village of Falcon's Aerie, but no straight portion is longer than two hundred paces. Like a great tan serpent, it pours gracefully over gentle hills when it can, yet it tightens radically around the harsher slopes when it must.

Untold thousands of roads snake among Wraithaven's hamlets, towns, homesteads and ranches, matching the mosaic of intersecting mountains and glacier-fed streams and rivers that define Wraithaven. From Conclusion Bay on the west coast to the eastern border nine hundred miles away, over a million Wraithians populate Wraithaven's eleven provinces. The most lightly populated, and the most rugged is this, the extreme northeastern province of *Scimitar*.

"Ah, my favorite part of Falcon's Road," Taggart said. He and Alina reined their identical brown, white-stockinged mares from a light canter to a steady walk. The riders were well seasoned and well provisioned travelers of the road and certainly of their destination. The saddlebags of each carried their Mission Robes, emergency rations of hard tack, jerky, and cheese, plus oiled canvas ponchos – "rainers."

On a lead behind Taggart, a pack mare named "Five" bore a pair of large panniers, strong willow-framed baskets encased in oiled canvas to protect freshly inked Scrolls for presentation to this year's Initiates, and the long, white ceremonial robes of Scroll Night.

The last bend had ended eight miles of tight loops winding through dense stands of pine and spruce. Now, the landscape opened panoramically. Here, the towering, ice-crowned peaks of the Shield commanded attention, looming over travelers in breathtaking silence.

Ancient, long extinct nomadic tribes migrating across the vast steppes outside the Shield believed that imprisoned evil "wraiths" battled jailer gods to escape and feast upon human souls. Thus did the seeds of Wraithaven germinate in the local human minds, then eventually propagate worldwide in that part of the human soul that so easily welcomes myth and legend.

That humankind's greatest evil still lurked behind the Shield seemed seared into the genetic code of the human race. Myth had always prevented bold attempts to explore either reality or root cause behind the Shield.

To the actual inhabitants of Wraithaven, however, the impregnable, brooding peaks have meant consummate peace and sanctuary for over two thousand years. While the rest of humanity cowered under fear-spawned myth, Wraithians lived with fact-based reality. That reality, despite its splendor and seclusion from humanity's propensity to wage war, was not without danger. That many large, territorial-driven predators roamed every province of Wraithaven answered why no Wraithian went unarmed beyond the confines of town or village. By habit, Taggart and Alina wore powerful long bows strung across their chests, while scabbarded *Dai-ryu* long swords and quivers of arrows hung at the ready from their saddle horns.

Here at Taggart's favorite spot though, their weapons held no more significance than the boots they wore. The road seemed to enjoy itself as it headed for Falcon's Aerie twelve miles away. Travelers felt invited to pause before continuing. The view was a kaleidoscope of colors and textures.

One sensed that same soul-deep insignificance one feels when standing upon a desolate ocean beach, knowing without any doubt that the crashing breakers *have* always been, and *will* always be. The eternal, jagged slopes here contrasted as much with these temporary human beings as they did with the temporal forests that knelt in homage before them.

Stately emperor spruces disperse in random formations throughout the mid to lower slopes. Aloof as the crags, they seemed like disciplined, warrior monks who take their roles as valley sentinels seriously. Autumn winds teased the riders with fleeting scents of horse and spruce and forest loam, but the down-swept, silver-green branches of the great sentinels barely moved.

Contrasting such staid elegance, deciduous hordes erupted across the valleys in brilliant splashes of colors. At times, the flame-red maples and golden-leafed birches brazenly trespassed in small stands near their aloof elders. At other times, they crowded the great ones in mischievous, uncountable numbers. They waved leaves of flamboyant crimson, sun yellow and pumpkin orange in even the slightest breeze.

"I like the birches the best," Taggart exclaimed, as the road swept near a large stand of the peeling, white-barked trees. The delicate golden leaves waved in the late autumn breezes like a billion delicate handkerchiefs. "I should write poetry about such places and events, my lady," he said, enjoying the scenery immensely.

"And what would you write, love?"

"I think I would pen that each of these exquisite leaves seems to cheer travelers on, as if we were their personal parade."

"And?" she prompted.

"*And*, that leaves ticking against their neighbors sound like a million elfin hands applauding the passerby."

"A splendid analogy, love," Alina said, "but I think mallets and chisels fit your hands better than a feather quill might."

"These?" he asked, holding his veiny, calloused hands palms up with mock innocence.

"Those," Alina grinned back.

Even against his tall, rangy frame and broad shoulders, Alina felt his hands seemed out of scale. As if the Creator had meant them for an even larger man.

When they gripped mallet and chisel to liberate Taggart's latest vision from the raw stone blocks, they seemed to exude life of their own. When formed into "knife hands," or "hammer fists" during *Nung-Cha* practice, they became focused weapons, and had, in fact, been lethal on five occasions against marauding highwaymen during their two-year Picket tour-of-duty in Cathmore. But her hands had been just as lethal during that tour, despite her preference to create exquisite tapestries with them upon her loom.

For Taggart, broken nails, ridges of yellowed callus, and countless scars from flying shards of marble and granite had taken their toll over the decades, but when he touched her, the gentle artist always restrained the warrior within. During a Reading they unrolled the Orbit Scrolls with a reverent touch that set the tone of the event more eloquently than words ever could. For Alina, Taggart's hands exemplified the complex nature of the man. In truth, the hands of each served two masters—the artist's outwardly expressed accomplishments, while the warrior's deadliness was hidden and restrained by internal shadows.

"We should visit Mairin this time," Alina said, changing the subject. "It's been six weeks now."

Taggart grinned a wide *oh really?* at her. With a mock pout, she slapped at his shoulder. Any time spent away from their grown children, and especially the grandchildren, bordered on disaster from Alina's perspective, which often meant trading quips with Taggart over the subject. In truth, Taggart missed chasing about with the little ones as much as Alina did.

Their eldest son, forty-four-year-old Mannis, and his thirty-four-year-old wife, Caleigh, had four children: two sons, Bowyn and Devlyn, age seven and ten, and a daughter-and-son set of twins, Bredon and Donia, age four. Even by Wraithian standards, the couple had married late. Mannis had completed his stonemason apprenticeship under Taggart by the age of twenty, yet, despite an obvious talent for intricate stone detailing, he never acquired Taggart's passion to liberate visions imprisoned within blocks of marble and granite.

With Taggart and Alina's reluctant blessing, Mannis had sought a mariner's life instead, serving aboard several coastal freighters, and ultimately as the captain of a swordbill schooner. After six years at sea, Mannis returned to his landlocked birthplace, *Scimitar*. In time, he found the true passion of his life: Caleigh, their four lively children, and the two-thousand-acre cattle ranch and pear orchards they had built with their own hands.

Their second son, thirty-nine-year-old Baran, and his thirty-four-year-old wife Leah, Caleigh's twin sister, had three children: daughter Tyra, age twelve, son Maccus, age six, and two-year-old daughter Brina. Like Mannis, Baran, Leah and their children had carved their twenty-two hundred acres of cattle ranch and peach orchards out of a remote, mountain-surrounded valley in the spectacular Spear Blade range.

Being the oldest grandchild, Tyra had benefited from six years of equestrian advice from Taggart, whereas her sibling Maccus had just begun his lessons. He had taught her to ride and shoot the recurved Wraithian longbow. In turn, Tyra had taken to the sport of mounted archery as if born to it, winning six straight tournaments in various age groups. Having just turned twelve, she gave special meaning to this particular Reading. Tyra would be Taggart and Alina's first grandchild to be initiated into Scroll Night.

As Alina had pointed out, they owed their third child, thirty-five-year-old Mairin a visit. Mairin and her thirty-seven-year-old husband, Edan, had a son, Fynn, age seven, and a daughter, Oriana, age four. Both were primarily academy teachers but also held roles as survival instructors at Falcon's Aerie's Central Academy. They lived just outside the village on a small vineyard of over one hundred acres.

For the prior four weeks, Taggart and Alina had conducted three separate Readings for the villages of Raven Creek, Jannock's Falls, and Torchwood. Now they returned to the fourth of six total villages in their four-hundred-square-mile SOR (Sector of Responsibility). Timing had been poor during their last trip to Falcon's Aerie. Week-long summer maneuvers for the Falcon militia had taken Mairin, Edan, *and* the grandchildren to the rugged Black Creek Pass area twenty-three miles distant.

Each summer, village militias engaged in mandatory war games against neighboring villages. Over the years, the exercises familiarize local militias with terrain surrounding at least ten other villages, thus preventing confusion if called upon to defend a given region.

Post autumn harvest, larger winter operations combined company-sized village militias into battalion-sized groups of four to six companies. Sometimes lasting two weeks, the operations pitted units of one province against those of a neighboring province.

Maneuvers so late in the year extended terrain familiarity and tested the toughness of each man, woman, and child. Night or day, in waist-deep snow or in powder barely dusting the forest floor, the large units ran, and outflanked, and defended positions. Mountain-hardened senior commanders, most aged 70s to even 90s, pushed the units to their physical limits.

Warming fires were rare. Shelters were canvas lean-tos, or wind barricades of snow blocks if the snow was deep enough. Food is jerked venison or beef, dried peaches, apples, raisins and nuts.

And always the units run, covering mile after mile in areas of light snow, or bulling their way through waist-deep drifts by breaking trail for each other, until exhaustion of the point runner gave the next person in line his or her turn.

The extreme conditions toughened Wraithians, instilling the mindset to overcome any adversary no matter the severity of the environment. To participate in the winter maneuvers was an honor, a test of self. To be too young, too old, or too infirm to wargame was considered personally demeaning.

For over two thousand years, the rhythm of Wraithaven has been thus: First come the short, local maneuvers of late summer. Autumn Readings for those reaching their twelfth harvest immediately follow, with communal celebrating of the adulthood transition. Harvests and preparation for the winter maneuvers follow. Then, due to the brutal Wraithaven winters, and the distances between many homesteads and village schools, the week preceding the winter maneuvers also signals the end of the school year. During this week, books and Learning Duties are assigned to the children for completion during deep winter in preparation for the spring tests and grade promotion for the new school year.

Learning Duty assignments become collectively shared responsibilities for families. Honor and duty perpetually link personal and family conduct.

As for Taggart and Alina, this last Reading of the year at Falcon's Aerie would be as bittersweet as are all last Readings.

All Readers experience seasonal depressions, for the gloom of winter signals a twelve-month wait until the next autumn Readings. For the Kaynes, Tyra's presence would sweeten this year's event, certainly, but the pride and contradictory disquiet of watching a child cross one of Life's thresholds will be in attendance as well.

Duty, however, would allow the Kaynes little time for melancholy. Within weeks after this Reading, Taggart would lead the six-company-strong unit, Scimitar's First Combat Battalion, in the grueling winter games as commander. This year, they would face an aggressive and wily opponent, Dark Forest's Third Battalion from the neighboring province of North Gale.

Alina would command First Battalion's Healer Corps, a unit of highly skilled medical specialists who tended to be *very* busy during the harsh conditions of the maneuvers.

3

Playground

Three miles outside of Falcon's Aerie, Taggart said, "Let's take Lookout Trail. Maybe we'll get lucky."

Ample time remained to meet the children and their families at the academy by noon. Off the main road, Lookout Trail was barely a footpath snaking through a dense stand of fire maples. Beyond the trees, it dissolved into a secluded rise overlooking a shallow valley. Tethering their mounts well inside the tree line, the Readers pulled compact brass telescopes from their saddle bags and crept quietly to the rise.

Low, bushy junipers mixed among pines ranging from the height of a child to over two hundred feet, randomly dotting slopes and ravines. Boulders and low rock outcroppings surfaced throughout the pines. Where the sun washed over thin, rocky soil the longest, patches of brown tufted grasses waved in the light breezes. Where shade prevailed, the soil lay exposed and unadorned.

The valley had the feel of an obstacle course. A low, tree-dotted plateau arose four hundred paces away as if it commanded valley center. Less than thirty paces across, the plateau looked like a military outpost, which was no illusion—today. The scene granted Taggart's wish to "get lucky."

"That's Calder and Enid Halwyn up there," Alina whispered, focusing her telescope upon four figures atop the plateau.

"Aye," Taggart whispered back. "Best trackers in *Scimitar*, even in their nineties."

"Best stealth mentors too. And they can outrun folks a third their age."

The Halwyns were both six feet tall, whip lean, and had by no means been crippled by age. Owners of vast apple and peach orchards, they moved with the casual strength of farmers who've learned how to pace a hard day's work from sunrise to sunset.

"Recognize the other two?" Taggart asked. "They're younger is all I can tell."

"I believe so. The big man is one of your apprentices from twenty years back or so, Blayne Maddox. The woman is his youngest sister, Moyna, Moyna Sarid since marrying Bodyn Sarid a few years back. The helmets make it impossible to be sure, but I remember the duty roster posted at the academy on our last Reading. This is their month."

Blayne Maddox had been one of Taggart's most adept apprentices in his time, a strong, energetic young man who excelled in fine detailing on any stone, be it limestone, marble, or granite. He had since moved to North Gale Province, established a fine name as a stonemason, and now had a wife and three stout sons.

All four wore Wraithian militia uniforms: light canvas, sleeveless, stiff-collared tunics cut just below the waist, canvas belts, and long, loose-fitting trousers. Coloration matched the splotchy dark and light gray of the surroundings. Thin streaks of black and tan slashed in random diagonals across the uniforms. Hints of dark, juniper green appeared at random. Exposed flesh of face and arms mimicked the color pattern via skin paint.

Only the younger pair wore traditional, gray camouflaged war helmets. Calder and Enid favored simple brown leather headbands to secure their long, thick manes of white hair. All wore single-edged long swords strapped diagonally across their backs, a dagger in a shoulder sheath, and a second belted at the small of the back. Four longbows and quivers of arrows were stacked precisely against a tree.

The four strolled casually atop the plateau, conversing occasionally, but eyeing the terrain as if watching for the approach of an enemy. They guarded a mound of reed baskets holding apples, loaves of dark-crusted rye bread, and wedges of the dark yellow cheese known locally as *Scimitar Gold*. Near four tethered mounts, an oak water cask cooled in the shade.

The sentries and their supplies were not the real show though. What slithered quietly from all sides toward the plateau, moving stealthily from boulder to tree to juniper bush was what the Kaynes had hoped to see. That, and the tapered willow branches, riding crop long, that each sentry carried. A white flag about the size of a man's outstretched hand waved from the tip of each branch. There seemed to be no connection between the combat-clad sentries and the willow branches, but Taggart and Alina just held the four in their scopes and waited. They didn't wait long.

Without warning, Calder's branch whipped out and stabbed downslope toward a large boulder partially hidden by a low juniper. The bush barely shook, but a small tan cloud of dust erupted behind it before dissipating in the wind. Calder's branch skewered the dust cloud forty paces from the plateau.

"She moved too fast," Alina whispered with amusement. "Caught old Calder's eye." Both Readers aimed their telescopes at the source of the little dust cloud.

An eight-year-old girl had tried to crawl too quickly from the base of a large pine to the bush. For camouflage, she had attached pine boughs and tufts of long grass to her arms and legs with virtually invisible black silk thread. Streaks of brown mud upon her face, neck, and hands even carried over to her smaller version of the sentries' camouflaged uniforms. Her body outline was broken even further by weaving grass and small twigs into her long, honey-colored hair, also streaked with brown mud.

"Her camouflage is superb," Taggart said. "I can barely make her out."

"Just needs a little work on her timing," Alina added.

"Flow *like* smoke!" Calder's raspy baritone demanded from the plateau. "Don't *make* smoke!" The child knew exactly who Calder's target was. The white flag at the end of the Elder's pointer made her wish she could melt deeper into the acrid soil her left cheek rested upon.

"I count eleven," Alina said, sweeping the uneven terrain surrounding the plateau. "Plus two teachers, one upslope to the left and the second downslope on the right." The teachers were as camo-dressed and fully armed as the sentries. Each also carried a quiver of arrows and a longbow.

"You missed two upwind behind the plateau. They're goners soon, I'll bet," Taggart said, touching his right finger to the side of his nose.

"Ha!" Alina chuckled. "Only a matter of time."

All told, thirteen eight-year-olds and their two teachers had run the one-league distance to this "playground"—one of five within a two-league radius of Falcon's Aerie. The objective: Arrive as a single unit, make final adjustments to camouflage, spread out, and then maneuver to within striking distance of the lunch without being detected. The run had been brisk, breakfast was long ago. The children were hungry.

"They look good," Taggart said, inspecting each widely dispersed child. Beyond the camouflage, each child wore a short wooden sword strapped across the back, and a single, double-edged steel dagger belted at the small of the back.

"Aye," Alina said, her scope seeking each camouflaged lump. "Good discipline. Quiet as spiders."

"Blayne is up to something," Taggart whispered. "He's not moving now. Someone is about to learn a lesson." The thick-shouldered young warrior stood still, feet apart, his sinewy, stone-mason arms folded across his chest. His blue eyes just stared at one portion of the valley.

A slap barely carried from valley right, but it was enough for Moyna Sarid's flag to snap in that direction.

"Congratulations!" she barked loudly across the course. "You just killed your entire unit! Let the mosquito bite! It's inconvenient—not deadly! A mosquito is only deadly if you slap it and expose your team! That is how Shadow Cadres die!"

Enid Halwyn chimed in. "Ignore the sweat stinging your eyes! Don't move! The itch goes unscratched. Don't move!"

"Bleed! . . . In! . . . Silence!" Moyna shouted for all to hear. "When the cocklebur pricks you! The wasp on your arm, the scorpion on your hand—leave them be! Let the snake crawl where it will!"

About that time, Blayne's unmoving pointer snapped once to his right and twice to his left. Three children had tried to move with extreme caution even though Blayne had obviously chosen to focus on their sector.

"Impatience! . . . Will! . . . Kill! . . . You!" he bellowed harshly at the three offenders. "Stealth goes beyond camouflage! Stealth is a state of mind *and* body! Remember that!" he shouted. "Become the shadows! Flow like smoke!"

The lesson that Taggart had predicted earlier came within moments of Blayne's lesson on patience.

Calder had his back to the two children upwind of the plateau, who thought they had chosen a better strategy to reach the objective. The Elder turned just enough to snap his willow pointer at the two "attackers." He didn't even bother to face them. "I can *smell* you!" he snarled loudly. "I've *been* smelling you for an hour! Hunt like that and you'll starve to death! You don't hunt deer or stags from upwind! Don't do it with a human either!"

Moments later, Enid whistled the three-note warble of the cliff wren's danger call. In return, both teachers whistled the *skree-skree* cry of a scissor-tailed kite gliding on patrol. After many hours in the dirt, class was over. The children could now relax and eat lunch with the sentries and teachers in the shade atop the plateau.

In another hour, the class would run the three miles back to the academy to finish the day.

Taggart grinned, remembering the eternal mantra instructors intone as they ran. The ubiquitous *flow like smoke*, of course. *Feet should caress the skin of the earth, not pound it. Ree-laaax. Feel the forest shadows, the carpet of silvertip needles. Sip the air. Don't gulp it. Run loosely. Flow. Forsake established trails. The forest is your path.*

Taggart started to turn away, but Alina still held her scope to her right eye. "One is still down," she said, tension in her voice. "By that stump next to the flat outcrop."

A tall, lanky, red-headed boy still lay stretched flat on his stomach. His chin rested on the dirt. His pale-blue eyes stared straight over his left arm, bent to guard his face. The boy's right hand slowly drew out the dagger sheathed at the small of his back. He lay as still as a stone. Sweat drenched his body despite the cool breeze and ran into his unblinking eyes.

Alina drew in a breath of horror. "My God," she whispered as Taggart reopened his scope.

Two feet from the boy's face, a brown-and-black banded snake, seven feet long and as thick as a man's forearm, lay coiled to strike if the boy so much as blinked.

"Pine viper," Taggart whispered with disgust. "Don't move, son. Don't . . . move."

The venomous creatures were known for their aggressiveness. Pine vipers preferred to strike repeatedly with inch-long, hypodermic fangs, rather than to slither timidly into underbrush. A victim's chance of survival, or the loss of a bitten limb, depended on how quickly one found a healer for treatment.

Enid Halwyn sounded a sharp double whistle—*whit-whit*—as she nocked a heavy stag-killer arrow and drew her longbow. The twelve children, already moving toward the lunch cache, stopped instantly. A single *whit* answered from Taggart's left and below him. Another echoed from fifty paces to his right. Both teachers had seen what the sentry had and had drawn their bows to full draw.

Another single whistle came from the sentry. Three razor-sharp broadhead arrows launched from three bows simultaneously. Three gray blurs whispered through the air like lightning bolts, striking the coiled serpent in virtually the same instant.

At the strike, the boy leapt to a low crouch, whipped his unsheathed dagger from behind and slashed the blackened seven-inch blade in a wide arc. The arrows had pinned the snake's body too far back. Three blurred feet of brown and black lashed out. Even faster, the boy's dagger blurred behind the snake's gaping mouth.

The snake's triangular head and six inches of its body dropped in the dirt at the boy's boots. For a long moment, he watched the arrow-pinned body writhe obscenely, watched the severed, be-fanged head open and close, reflexively biting again and again. Drenched in sweat, the boy finally composed himself with an obvious shudder. He wiped the blade clean on his trouser leg, sheathed the dagger, and joined his classmates as they once again headed uphill for lunch. Several boys laughed and punched his shoulders good-naturedly.

Closing their telescopes, the Readers gave the plateau one last look. Their mission complete, all four sentries and both teachers waved and acknowledged them with honor salutes—closed right fists touching their left breast while bowing slightly at the waist.

The Readers responded in kind, silently adding applauding gestures because of the distance to thank the instructors for their service to the children.

"A fine class," Taggart said, as they returned to their mounts.

"Indeed," Alina said, "a very fine class."

4

Village

Wraithaven's towns and villages avoid the congested, haphazard sprawl that characterize most hubs of human activity on other continents. Twisting, confined goat paths that evolve into streets simply do not exist. A main road might wind through a town, but the streets and boulevards that define that town are orderly, wide by design, and arranged with growth in mind.

At Falcon's Aerie, the graded dirt of Falcon's Road ends at the village welcome sign. From there, it flows through town center with shallow, respectful curves, as perfectly stone-paved as the streets and boulevards that branch from it.

Centuries-old flame maples line the main road, their autumn leaves providing a brilliant canopy of scarlet. Each tree reaches for its counterpart across the street, even as it shades raised sidewalks of yet more brick pavers. With every wind gust, great sheets of crimson leaves cascade down to jostle with yesterday's leaves, growing evermore crispy and brown.

Limestone and granite are favored building materials for the shops and larger emporiums, with frequent accents of darkly stained timbers and stucco. Slate is the preferred roofing material, though many of the larger buildings are crowned with verdigris-accented copper sheathing. Thatch roofs are shunned.

"We're still early," Taggart said as they dismounted at Athdara's Livery and Stables. "Let's board the mounts, bring Five, and take an early lunch at the inn."

The six-hundred-year-old Crescent River Inn covered an entire block on the northwest side of town. Famous for a huge variety of breads and exotic cheeses, its real reputation was for uniquely marinated meats and an outstanding wine cellar. A third of an hour away, another third would take them to Falcon's Aerie's Central Academy, and the rendezvous with this year's Initiates.

As expected, the leisure walk took longer. Townsfolk saw to that, hailing them from open-door shops, or greeting them with honor bows as they walked down the street leading Five. Readers are venerated everywhere in Wraithaven, but Readers give back as much respect as they receive. And at this time of year, thousands of Readers conduct the Scroll Night rituals throughout the nation.

"Me second nephew is in this Readin'," a burly wheat farmer blurted out, approaching them with an outstretched hand in greeting. "A fine son to me brother he is," the man added, grinning with pride. "Whip smart too."

"And what would the lad's name be?" Alina asked, taking the fellow's meaty hand with both of hers.

"Marcus," the uncle said. "Marcus Riordan."

"Ah," Taggart said, "son of Killian and Eryn, the furniture makers."

For a moment, the man was speechless, surprised and flattered that such honored folk would know of his family. Taggart followed quickly with, "Then you must be Killian's younger brother, Curran. Those are your wheat fields on the west side of Saber River. We saw them two weeks ago during the Raven Creek Reading. You've a magnificent crop this year, my friend."

"Aye . . . thank you," the young farmer stammered. "The Lord's rains blessed us this year. We're watchin' me brother's place during the Readin'."

"Then you've brought Kyla and baby Tara along?" Alina asked.

"Aye," Curran said, "but how . . . ?"

Taggart smiled and patted Curran's thick shoulder. "Readers listen—a *lot!*"

Curran just shook his head in amazement.

The couple left him after exchanging a few more pleasantries. Recalling such details never failed to amaze people, but there was nothing magical about the skill. Reader training emphasized connection with the *autumn children,* and that took highly detailed research and a good memory. For Readers, such research preceded a Reading by many months and was as deeply ingrained in them as their daily *Nung-Cha* practice.

Time at Crescent River Inn was more greeting than eating. Bites of the inn's fiery mutton stew and the dark Binoccan rye bread were taken sporadically as various patrons pulled up empty chairs to greet and exchange regional news. A rockslide had closed Spear Peak Road in North Gale Province, and twin grandsons had been born to the Slevyn clan outside Black Creek, making a total of thirteen now. A lightning strike had started a fire east of Dark Canyon and had burned over a thousand acres of prime silvertip forest before being contained.

Sopping the remaining broth from their bowls with the last of the rye, Taggart and Alina managed to take their leave, still shaking hands with patrons and waving to others across the room.

"A good thing we beat the mid-day crowd," Alina said as they unhitched Five. "We'd never have gotten out of there."

"True, love," Taggart chuckled. "Too many friends and acquaintances. A fine problem to have."

"Aye," Alina agreed, "but after this Reading, promise me we'll stay in town for a few days. We're too far behind on the news."

"As in baby news?"

"Yes, as in new babies. *And* crops, *and* marriages, *and* folks coming and going."

Of the two, Alina was by far the most gregarious. Taggart absorbed himself in work at the quarry. As master sculptor with thirty to fifty young apprentices at any given time, he had to communicate with others, but subjects tended to be quarry related: stone cutting, tools, or the use of them.

Alina, on the other hand, just loved being *with* people, talking with them, absorbing opinion and events with equal relish. The more the merrier. Taggart often said she could enter a room full of strangers, her smile beaming fairly, and leave an hour later knowing the names, family histories, and interests of most of them.

Taggart tried to mingle, but it was an uncomfortable effort. Even after forty-seven years of Alina's help, Taggart believed that not even *another* forty-seven years would cure him.

"We'll take up a room at the inn after the Reading," Taggart said. "I promise. We'll spend a few days here—to catch up—then stay at Mairin and Edan's. While they shut down their classrooms for the year, we can watch the little ones."

"The inn is always full this time of year," Alina said with disappointment. "Finding a room will be impossible."

"Not when one has a husband who makes reservations two months in advance during a supply trip, like *you* have." Immensely pleased with himself, Taggart grinned from ear to ear.

"If you died this instant," Alina said, raising an eyebrow, "they wouldn't be able to remove that silly grin with a mallet and a chisel."

Taggart laughed and shifted Five's lead behind his back to his left hand. He curled his right arm around Alina's waist and pulled her close. "Then how about a kiss of gratitude before I die, old woman? We're almost there."

5

Academy

In Wraithian communities, the first building constructed for communal needs is always the academy. The tradition is deliberate. Wraithian mindset prioritizes education over every matter beyond basic survival. Illiteracy in Wraithaven is nonexistent. Should a newly founded community consist of little more than tents and covered wagons, the first log structure to be communally raised is the academy. As a community prospers, the first log structure to be replaced with stone is *always* the academy.

Communities lack town squares. Government buildings are kept intentionally small. Communal gatherings requiring communal decisions are deliberately held on academy grounds.

The Kaynes' rendezvous with the Reading Initiates and their families would take place in the academy's main courtyard, the central hub of other low-walled, slate-paved assembly areas linking dozens of classrooms, workshops, and storage facilities into a single complex.

"Ah," Taggart said, tying Five to a hitching rail and water trough, "our host."

A tall, slender, gray-haired man of sixty-two waved from the shade of the portico at the main entrance—Blair Herne, Prime Mentor of Falcon Aerie's Central Academy for seventeen years. His wife of fifty-nine, Morna, taught math and Wraithian history to Tens. Friends since their late twenties, the Kaynes and the Hernes shared a common interest for the rigorous, mounted stag hunts of late summer. Alina and Morna also shared an artistic passion for the design of intricate wall tapestries.

Waving acknowledgment, Taggart and Alina pulled short, hooded gray mission robes from their saddle bags, donned them over their clothes, and tied them at the waist with horsehair belts. Worn only during the formal greeting of Reading Initiates, the simple, mid-thigh-length garments would be replaced by full-length, hooded robes of white, coarsely woven wool on Scroll Night.

"You're early," Blair beamed, as the three exchanged handshakes and hugs. "I'd hoped you would be."

"Ran into more folks than expected," Alina said. "Lunch was shorter."

"Even *without* the mission robes, I notice," Blair laughed.

"Not wearing them didn't help," Taggart said. "Guess we're too notorious."

"Ha! That you are, my friends, Blair said with a grin. "That you are."

"We missed you on our last supply trip," Alina said. "A field trip I believe?"

"It was," Blair said. "Took a class of Eights and Morna's class of Tens to Mt. Trahern observatory. Our two-day overnighter turned into five, thanks to a blizzard that blew in."

"Happens often enough up there," Taggart said. "No predicting them."

"True. Had a few worried parents and grandparents, but the kids took it in stride."

Trips to local mines, to working ranches or farms, or to the observatory atop Mt. Trahern always go prepared for emergencies. Each child brings a hunting bow, a backpack, emergency rations, a canteen, and sleeping bag. Open wagons that can quickly convert to canvas-covered shelters carry two weeks' supply of dried fruit, jerked venison, first-aid supplies, and casks of water. Should thunderstorms or blizzards occur, the group simply shelters in place until conditions improve.

Given Wraithaven's rugged terrain and the abundance of aggressive wildlife, no less than six mounted outriders armed with bear lances and war bows accompany any field trip. There is never a shortage of parental volunteer escorts because autumn is Wraithaven's most dangerous season. Immense silvertip bears prowl for food, preparing for winter hibernation. Stag bulls as large as draft horses, and wielding man-long antlers claim breeding territories. Packs of huge dire wolves roam the more remote areas, and though rare, the largest, most feared of Wraithaven's predators—the saber-toothed wraiths of the timberline cannot be ignored. Over the centuries, even though wildlife has learned to avoid contact with humans, deadly encounters still occur.

"By the way," Alina said, knowing full well what was coming, "we heard about the tournament during our Wind River Reading weeks ago."

"So, you know then? We trounced them *and* Raven Creek soundly, my friends. Soundly!" The Prime Mentor's grin could not have been wider. Falcon's Aerie's Central had not only hosted the annual event but had earned first-place bragging rights for the three-day, three-school academic and sports competition, greatly honoring the community.

Last year, with the competition held in Wind River, Falcon's Aerie had drawn to an exact second place tie with Raven Creek, each having scored 8,586 points out of a possible 10,000. Wind River had taken first place with 8,647 points.

"To say that Wind River is chafing a bit is an understatement," Taggart said. His and Alina's smiles betrayed their loyalties. Their grandchildren attended Falcon's Aerie Central.

"Let 'em chafe," Blair said. "They'll be ready for us next year for certain—especially since it'll be Raven Creek's turn to host the games."

"Just for the record, how bad *was* the trouncing?"

"It was 9,837 for us, 8,716 for Raven Creek, and 8,682 for Wind River."

In such annual competitions, scholastic scores for the tests taken in classrooms are secured by the tournament committee under lock and key. Spectators cheer the physical competitions held outdoors, where results are obvious, but no academy knows exactly where it stands on a given day. Final standing is only posted once academic and physical scores are tallied on the fourth morning.

On the first day of the annual competition, every age level is tested in geology, chemistry, astronomy, biology, and earth sciences. The second day—testing in math, geography, world history and Wraithian history. As many as 7,000 points out of a possible 10,000 can be earned on these two days.

On the third day, physical competitions are held. No more than 3,000 points can be awarded in *Nung-Cha* empty hands bouts, in weapon drills, in five-league foot races, in long-range archery, and in the grueling *mounted archery* combat courses.

From the moment academy standings are posted until the early hours of the next day, boisterous celebrations erupt throughout the hosting town. Feasts and dances seem endless, choral groups and mandolin-wielding balladeers perform, and congratulatory speeches are applauded until sheer weariness finally sends locals to their homes, and out-of-towners to their rooms at the inn or their campground tents.

"You would have been thrilled with Tyra's performances," Blair said. "As a Twelve, she was allowed a maximum of two academic and two physical competitions."

"And?" Alina asked, anxious to hear how their granddaughter had performed.

"Her academic choices were navigational computations and geology."

Taggart groaned. "Nav comps was brutal for me at twelve. I made it through, but it took five times the study of any other subject to do it. And geology you say?" He grinned at his granddaughter's choice. "A natural subject for those who work with stone and chisel. My favorite subject at academy."

"And her physical choices?" Alina asked.

"Mounted combat archery and empty hands bouts," the mentor said.

"And her scores?" Taggart asked.

"Perfect scores in all four competitions," Blair said. "Only one other Twelfth-Harvest child in our academy's history has ever scored perfect scores in four competitions in the same year."

"Leah!" both Readers exclaimed in unison, "Her mother!" Every day, Tyra grew more like the Kaynes' daughter-in-law. Tall, athletic, and bright, when mother and daughter stood side by side, the resemblance was uncanny.

"She won all twelve bouts in empty hands, besting eight boys and four girls. Then proceeded to shoot two perfect rounds on two different equestrian combat courses. Twenty-four targets, twenty-four hits."

"She *is* deadly aboard Shadow," Taggart agreed. "She and that stallion are matched as well as any competitors I've ever seen."

"Aye," Blair said. "I was able to watch part of her second ride and three of her hand-to-hand bouts. She has, let us say, a certain . . . *intensity* at times. I remember her mother that way at Tyra's age. Must be the green eyes."

"Could be," Alina said. "When Tyra focuses on a task, it *will* be done!"

"After the hand-to-hand bouts, some of the boys called her *Snake* under their breath. When I asked why, they said they never really saw her hand or foot strikes until they felt them. *Quick as a snake*, they declared."

"Ha! That's my girl," Taggart beamed. "Smart, beautiful and quick."

Empty hands bouts for Twelves pitted one competitor against another single opponent. Competitions for ages sixteen through eighteen, the last years spent at primary academy, pitted a single defendant against up to three attackers. Even with cotton-padded arm and body armor, bloody noses, black eyes, and cracked ribs were commonplace in all age groups.

"And tough," Blair said. "She was as tall as anyone in her category, but the boys always outweighed her. Their extra muscle didn't help much. Her speed nullified that, and her techniques were flawless."

"It's too bad we missed this year," Alina said. "Reading dates in other villages conflicted. Two years hence, when she can compete again, we'll be in the audience. We'll schedule the Readings around the tournaments better."

In either the academic or physical competitions, only four students from each age class can enter in any one year. The next year, different students are chosen to represent their academy. If selected again in their next eligible year (two years later), a student must choose different academic and physical competitions. Skills balanced over a variety of subjects is encouraged in primary academy. Specialized expertise is only nurtured in later university years, or during trade apprenticeship.

"Come," Blair said, "let's roam the halls a bit. We'll drop in on the Elevens, of course. You might be interested in a new tact we're trying in pre-Wraithian history. Traditionally a senior-level technique, we are curious how younger levels respond."

"Lead on, my friend," Taggart said as they pushed open the leaded-glass oak doors and entered the slate-paved main corridor.

6

Curriculum

To enter an academy as a town citizen is one thing; to do so as a mission-bound Reader is quite another, for a Reader's mission robe is a thing of diverse weights. The shoulders sense the physical weight of subtle padding across the upper back and upper chest, even though clever tailoring and precise stitching deny any obvious embellishment to the garment. By design, the padding's sole function is to remind.

Over their year-long retreat, cloistered Reader candidates are reminded a prescribed one thousand times that one's shoulders should sense *the weight of duty, the weight of responsibility.*

"Embrace the weight," Elder trainers intone, "the instant you don the robe. Allow it to humble you, even as it inspires you. Honor the weight, even as the weight honors *you.*"

And it does. Readers meditate upon the intent of the robe at sunrise and at sunset for three days leading up to a Reading. This calls forth the robe's spiritual weight. By linking the Reader's soul with the weight of duty, it ignites the coming bond with the Twelfth Harvest children.

The mere presence of a robe-clad Reader not only transfers the weight of spiritual anticipation to the children of a given Reading and their loved ones, but also to those still awaiting *their* Twelfth Harvest, and *their* Scroll Night.

To a culture immersed since birth in the concept of honor, the robe inspires the weight of respect for its wearer. All Readers are volunteers, with one tenet of the Reader's Creed being, *No compensation shall be accepted from society save that of friendship, food or shelter.* A common axiom declares, *Even the poorest Reader is venerated by the wealthiest Wraithian.*

Spiritually, Readers exemplify the tenets of the Pelanjian Beacons, the Orbit Scrolls, and the formal crossing of the Wraithian threshold separating childhood from young adulthood. That is the final weight brought forth by the robe. A Reader's conduct literally sets the behavioral standard for Wraithian culture itself.

Entering the main building of the academy complex only heightened the Kaynes' sense of privilege for their current mission. The heavy doors opened to the twelve-foot-high Greeting Wall, which was constructed of precisely cut blocks of light-gray limestone, a match to most hallways, offices, and classrooms. Floors were dark-gray slate tiles. Man-long glass skylights lit the Greeting Wall, the rooms, and all hallways sufficiently on clear, bright days as today. On overcast or stormy days, wall-mounted oil lanterns cast their soft yellow glow to supplement the natural light.

While large, colorful tapestries, oil paintings commemorating noteworthy moments in Wraithian history, or portraits of famous historical figures decorated corridor walls, all Greeting Walls in all academies are devoid of such ornamentation. Greeting Walls display but one thing.

Upon Falcon's Aerie's wall, a glass and oak display case six feet high by four feet wide protected a copy of the Pelanjian Beacons—the twenty tenets declaring Wraithian core values. The same values had once anchored the pre-Wraithian ancestral homeland—the Pelanjian Archipelago. Twin lanterns illuminating the Beacons were lit first thing each morning and extinguished at each evening.

Classrooms and offices held smaller framed copies, but this copy, hand-wrought in the exquisite calligraphy of the Pelanjian mother tongue, had hung here for over eight hundred years.

The artist who designed the Beacons for the Raven Creek Academy centuries earlier had used real gold leaf from local mines to embellish the calligraphy of the piece. The Wind River artist had worked threads of pure silver into the Beacon tapestry displayed on his academy's Greeting Wall.

The largest, most ornate of all such displays in Scimitar Province, however, was the twenty-foot-wide Beacon mosaic at Jannock's Falls Central Academy. Each letter of each word consists of hand-carved slivers of obsidian embedded in one-inch squares of poured amber-hued glass. The masterpiece had required the talents of two successive generations of renowned glass makers, two generations of jewelers, and had taken forty-one years to complete.

After twenty-one Readings over the years, the Kaynes have seen every Greeting Wall in their SOR, and still, Taggart preferred the exquisitely inked penmanship of the Beacons at Falcon's Aerie. Minutely detailed roses in red, white, and yellow sprouted from thorny, intertwining vines bordering the piece. The first letter of each tenet was three times the height of the rest of the text.

The ancient calligraphy—as much a work of art as penmanship—drew the heart of the Reader-sculptor renowned for his fine stone detailing each time he and Alina visited the academy. With each visit to each academy, the Kaynes bowed before the ancient Beacons and tapped fists to chests in honor salutes. Then to properly set the tone to rendezvous with their latest Twelfth-Harvest children, they began to read each of the twenty Beacons softly aloud with the same smooth synchronization that characterized their daily *Nung-Cha* practice. Oblivious to all else, the Kaynes read each word as reverently as if they were doing so for the very first time.

BEACONS FOR THE PELANJIAN PEOPLE

1. *Honor Father Creator above all else. He bestows the gift of life one heartbeat at a time.*
2. *Revere how the Prayer Stone mimics humanity. Both are anchored to the earth. Both reach for our Creator.*
3. *Respect all life as you do your own.*
4. *Honor your parents.*
5. *Honor your family name. It is your bond.*
6. *Respect yourself. You are a creation of our Maker.*
7. *Respect your neighbor's path. Do not hinder it.*
8. *Honor and protect our Elders. They have led us from horizons past.*
9. *Honor and protect our children. They will lead us beyond horizons yet unseen.*
10. *Honor the Orbit Scrolls. They show us ourselves—as well as others.*

11. Covet neither your neighbor's possessions nor spouse.
12. Never steal. The thief dishonors self.
13. Never lie. The liar dishonors all.
14. Never murder. The murderer dishonors Life.
15. Govern through open doors.
16. Choose moderation over excess.
17. Honor Nung-Cha daily. It unites us, protects us, and liberates us.
18. Discipline the body to strengthen the soul.
19. Choose death before surrender. Choose death before dishonor.
20. Fight no enemy twice. Wage war totally, or not at all.

Blair and his guests then continued down the main corridor leading to the central courtyard. They stepped lightly, taking care to minimize their boot falls against the slate.

"Interesting," Alina whispered, "how one feels the same sense of awe in academy halls as one does in a temple."

"Aye," Blair agreed. "I sense it every morning before the students arrive, and in a different way every evening after they leave."

"One senses the intent of each place, I think," Taggart said. "One dedicated to the worship of one's Creator, the other to cultivating the gifts from that Creator. Each place is sacred in its own way."

The twelve-foot-high walls, the sunlight streaming through skylights, and invisible dust motes *did* create a temple-like atmosphere. The walls felt protective, nurturing, and eternal. One could imagine them being willed into existence by some all-powerful cosmic force, not built by the calloused hands of mere human beings.

Blair stopped them outside a classroom of seventeen Ninth-Harvest children. He pointed in silence first to the "9" sign just left of the open doorframe, and then to his right ear. The teacher, a tall, twenty-eight-year-old brunette woman, Eryn Tierney, did not react to her silent visitors. She simply continued the lesson. The children's backs were to the hallway door.

The subject this hour was Wraithian culture. Topics ranged from which products or crops came from Wraithaven's eleven provinces to the hierarchy of provincial and national-level government. The instructor was about to move into the subject of national defense.

Wraithian formal primary education begins at age seven and lasts until eighteen. On day one of a student's first year, the child is expected to speak, in addition to native Wraithian, the most common language spoken on Wraithaven's continent of Tripada—Tertian. Halfway through the "year of eights," the second most common language along Tripada's eastern seaboard is introduced—Senaldan.

It is unclear whether one language is the historic root of the other, but both sound similar and are catalogued by Wraithian linguists as "hard languages." Meaning that speakers of either pronounce "k" and "ch" words from the back of the throat, yet without overt emphasis. To non-fluent listeners, most words in either language seemed clipped, creating the supposition that the pace of either is hurried.

In comparison, the Wraithian language, after 4,000 years of development from its Mindocean and Pelanjian roots is considered a "soft" language. There are more vowels than consonants in spoken Wraithian, and generally sentences are longer in both verbal and written forms. Pace and rhythm are considered melodic and smoother, spoken more from the front of the mouth than the back of the throat.

Only two other settled continents exist: the largest, most populous being Embrica, and the second being the resource-wealthy but poorly explored Mascarene, labeled the *Dark Continent* by

Outsider nations. Both Polar Regions, Shaitan to the north and Bakula to the south, are barren of human life.

By the time students reach age level eighteen, and complete its courses a year later, they will be able to speak and write five additional world languages beyond their native Wraithian.

At age eleven, High Embrican, the formal version of the most widely spoken language on the Embrican continent is introduced. Considered the language of more wealthy and educated folk, High Embrican is characterized by a melodic, singsong rhythm and a large vocabulary, having assimilated over the centuries many words native to local languages. In contrast, Low Embrican is a coarser, less complicated version favored by tradesfolk, rural workers, and the generally less educated social classes.

Interestingly, given the tendency of Embrican to shy away from the more guttural hard languages, it is thought to actually have evolved from Old Mindocean roots similar to those of Wraithian speakers.

Basilian, another common Embrican language is introduced to students reaching the age thirteen level. Its roots are unknown, but given the commonality of it and Tapargese, the most widely recognized language across the Mascarene continent, Basilian is very probably the root of what amounts to a sister language.

Both are languages of sea traders which in itself points to Mindocean influence. Mariners, dock facility folk and merchant traders of land *or* sea revert to Basilian and Tapangese easily when communicating wither others in common with their livelihoods, no matter their native languages.

Both are spoken with a speedy cadence, short sentences, and both liberally share many common words. Once Basilian is mastered, the addition of Tapangese comes easily. To non-speakers of either language, the slight slurring and "th" sounds make both seem the same, and indeed if one speaks only Basilian, one can at least grasp the meaning of Tapangese with little problem.

The one thing that differentiates the two is that Tapangese speakers are more prone to emphasize facial expressions which further define their spoken narrative. Anger, happiness, sorrow, compassion, are easily identified by watching a Tapangese speaker.

Language fluency is emphasized at every age class, given that any question in math, science, history or the arts will be asked using languages learned from preceding levels.

By age eighteen, question and answer sessions use all five languages. Native Wraithian is used only as a summation tool for any given class level. The class of "nines" that held the Kaynes current attention, were already two-year veterans of the immersion of language and varied scholastic courses. The skill by which Eryn Tierney transitioned between national defense and language instruction was admirable. She was obviously a veteran of the technique as well.

"Class, she began, "Wraithians recognize four levels of strategic defense. Anant, what is the first level? Answer in Tertian, please."

"Our Pickets are Wraithaven's first line of defense," the boy answered.

"And Pickets are what exactly?"

"Spies, ma'am. They serve tours of duty in other countries to monitor their intentions."

"Why?" the instructor countered.

"Because thanks to our Pelanjian ancestors, we are isolated from the Outsiders. But to ignore them or their intentions is foolish."

"Very good, Anant. Your pace is brisk enough, but remember the uvular fricatives, the back-of-throat noises. Expand on that, Carbry, and in Senaldan please. On their missions, do Pickets live as Wraithians?"

"No ma'am. Outsider nations don't even know that Wraithians exist. To them, Wraithaven is still a legend of mythical evil. Pickets pose as itinerant tradesfolk from countries other than their mission target."

"Can anyone become a Picket?"

"No, Lady Tierney, the young cannot. A Picket must reach at least their sixtieth harvest."

"And why is that, Aphina? In Tertian, please."

"Pickets must be invisible," the girl answered.

"And what does that have to do with one's age?"

"Outsider cultures revere youth and strength. Elderly are ignored, set aside. They become invisible to their own people. Pickets take advantage of that."

"Coalan, what other qualifications must Pickets possess? In Senaldan."

"Pickets hold Master Dragon rank in armed and unarmed combat techniques," the boy responded, then quickly added, "they're *double* Dragons, ma'am. They also hold Master Dragon rank in stealth and tactics. Oh, and most are married, and serve together."

"Very good, Coalan. Now, Shylah, the second level? In Senaldan, please."

"The second level of defense is distance, Lady Tierney," the girl answered.

"How so?"

"Wraithian territory begins on the west coast of Tripada and ends eleven hundred miles east at the Shield. The Desolate Region begins at the foothills of the Shield and extends sixteen hundred miles east to the western bank of the Lost River. The thirty Outsider nations along the eastern coast of Tripada avoid the Lost River. They won't even extend their settlements to the eastern bank."

"Very good, Shylah. Continue, Cinnia, in Tertian this time."

"The Outsiders fear the Desolate, ma'am," the girl said. "To them it's a dead place of sand dunes, rocks, and no water."

"And is it?" Lady Tierney asked in flawless Tertian.

"No. All Wraithians are taught where the major springs are. Pickets learn of many more."

"Is that all?" the instructor asked. "All there is to the distance factor? Edan, continue in Tertian, if you will."

"No, Lady Tierney," the boy answered. "Tripada's southern coast is uninhabited also, because the Desolate extends down that far."

"Excellent diction by the way, Edan. Continue."

"The northern coast of Tripada melds with Shaitan, the North Polar Region, and that isolates us further. Also, from our western coast to the sparsely populated eastern coast of Embrica is over five thousand miles of ocean, still uncharted by the Outsiders. Wraithian maps call it the Western Ocean."

"Thank you, Edan. Now, Ailis, what is the third level of Wraithaven's strategic defense? In Senaldan."

"Our terrain, Lady," the girl answered. "The Shield contains the highest mountains in the world. Our Pelanjian ancestors were the first to discover an opening through the Shield from the sea on the west coast. The Shield encompasses Wraithaven, and inside are thirty-one peaks over twenty thousand feet. The Guardian's Spear on the Shield's eastern ring is over thirty-one thousand feet high. Only we know all the passes, rivers, and intersecting mountain ranges throughout Wraithaven. Outsider invaders from the east could never penetrate past the Shield's Outer Ring."

"Excellent, Ailis." The girl had spoken confidently, if not defiantly, of the Outsiders. Her classmates sat a bit straighter, alight with defiance to possible invasion. "Now Class, together, in Wraithian. What is our fourth and final level of defense?"

"Us!" The children shouted. "The Wraithian people! The Wraithian sword!"

Eryn gave a quick wink to her silent audience before continuing.

"Excellent, class. Now let us discuss how weather patterns differ across our eleven provinces, and how that affects agriculture in each. Open your books to page 232. Airell, translate and read aloud, in Tertian, pages 232 through 237. Iona, continue aloud in Senalden from page 238 through . . ."

Blair and his guests continued down the hall, pausing every few moments to listen in on classes in geometry, world geography and writing communication. Tradition called for them to visit Elevens, those children who would experience their personal Reading next year. The Readers would not share details of Scroll Night, just meet the children to inspire anticipation. Coincidently, the new method to teach pre-Wraithian history was about to be introduced to the Elevens. The Kaynes' married daughter, Mairin Tanguy, taught Elevens and had helped create the advanced course.

As the three reached Mairin's room, the class was completing its study segment of world geography. She would now present the new subject. She smiled at their appearance, but Blair gestured to continue. The Reader visit could wait a bit. With a barely perceptible nod, she began.

"Class, today we are about to try something new. Something considered a senior-level course of study—until now."

That got the students' attention. In but one more year, they would cross the child-to-adult threshold at their Reading. Adults would expect more of them after that, but now it seemed something *very* adult was being offered *before* experiencing Scroll Night. This was an honor.

"Under each of your chairs is a box. Please open it and take out the two books inside."

The children did so. The books were brand new, and each was nearly two inches thick—considerably thicker than most other study volumes.

"The first volume, *The Mirror Resolution*, is a collection of entries from the personal journal of Fleet Admiral Rhys Balgaire, supreme commander of Pelanjia's renowned Northern Fleet."

"The second volume, *The Pelanjian Extinction*, is a collection of essays and theories by numerous Outsider scientists, thinkers, politicians, and similar observers who declare their suppositions of the Pelanjian Empire's passing."

A boy on the first row, Macklyn Keir, raised his hand. "Lady Tanguy, why study these books? The writings are old, and one is by Outsiders. We already study Wraithian history."

"A fair question, Macklyn. This study compares ancient Pelanjian history directly against ancient world history. Yes, the selected works in both volumes *are* old—over two thousand years in fact. You will note that all entries are dated using the Red Sun Calendar as R.S. or B.R.S. (before Red Sun). Remember, the Red Sun Calendar was created at this time in history. The admiral's entries include our Mindocean Chronical year as well.

"This morning we will see how reality often clashes with superstition. Admiral Balgaire's writings record Pelanjia of his day. The *Extinction* volume records misconceptions about the Pelanjian Disappearance.

"Your winter assignments will include written essays comparing various dated entries in both volumes and answering questions for each comparison. To introduce you to the volumes, we will move quickly and read aloud in Wraithian only. Our classroom desks are numbered one to thirty. This year, there are only twenty-one students registered for our class. Therefore, you will find slips of paper numbered one through twenty-one which mark a particular entry in both books.

"Macklyn, your desk is number one. You will read aloud entry marker one. Carryl, your desk number is two. Read immediately wherever the next marker resides. Iden, you will conclude the reading with marker number twenty-one."

"There will be no breaks between readings. Discussion will follow at the end of the last reading.

"Macklyn, please begin. Let us delve into the realms of fact versus myth."

7

Vengeance

[Book Marker 1—*The Pelanjian Extinction*]
Stroud Thatcher-son. Scribe
Royal Household of Melchior Bahrom Majied the Light
12 Septombray 2038 M.C. (8 B.R.S.) Shahnaz, Cytheria

I am neither warrior nor mariner. I am but a humble scribe to His Majesty. In twenty-seven years of life, I have only seen the *Light* twice, and just barely.

Both times, boisterous, cheering throngs forced me behind them as he passed through flower-bestrewn boulevards of our capitol, Shahnaz, astride a magnificent white stallion.

I never saw his seven children, his three wives, or the five hundred retainers who rode in his wake in gilded carriages on those two parade days. I just cheered as the crowds did, knowing only by the rising volume that another royal coach had just passed by.

Today, there are no cheering, jostling hordes. I am alone and I fear for my life. I record my thoughts in this journal because that is what scribes do. We record. I do so in the simple two-room cottage of my father, in the countryside outside Shahnaz. Father is a thatcher of cottage roofs. Only my chance visit to him yesterday saved me last night.

The Pelanjians have come. A neighbor whispered such to my father as if those fearsome folk might come for him as well. The king, his grown children, his wives, retainers, and personal guard contingent are all dead, slain in the royal palace under the shroud of a moonless night. Only the three youngest royals survived—all under the age of nine. All three were rudely thrust upon a fishmonger and his wife asleep in their crude hovel near Central Market.

Rumors claim the couple awoke just past midnight to the cold touch of sword blades against their throats. A half dozen assassins, huge despite being unarmored, surrounded their bed.

They were too tall to stand upright in the hovel it is said. Further proof that they were Pelanjian. Clad in clothing of shadow black streaked with faint stripes of gray, they kept silent, save for two words from the one who yanked the husband from his bed. "Protect them," the dark shape growled in Cytherian, pointing to the three blindfolded and gagged youngsters. Pelanjians, it seems, do not slay children.

The assassins left then, without further word. Only the boiling yellow flames consuming the royal palace a mile away and the burning ships and wharves a quarter mile away gave any shape at all to the killers who seemed to dissolve into the shadows.

The royal barge, *Golden Splendor*, lies a smoldering, burned-out hulk now, sunken at the royal wharf after burning all night. The imperial yacht burns even now, still tethered in its berth. Every royal schooner has burned and lies at the bottom of the harbor. So does every one of the navy's seventeen three-masters that survived the failed Pelanjian incursion four years ago.

I remember the cheering throngs of those patriotic days. His Majesty promised to end the Pelanjian stranglehold on the world's spice markets forever by *putting every Pelanjian man, woman, and child to the sword*. The invasion lasted but two and a half *days*! We sent our entire 211-ship navy. Only seventeen returned to home port.

The Pelanjian force last night might have numbered a hundred, or ten thousand. No one can say. No one—no one alive— saw any of the famed Pelanjian dragon ships. Even by the boiling yellow flames that are still eradicating the entire wharf and warehouse complex, no witnesses have come forth. Witnesses cower in fear, I suppose. As do I.

Only after the flames die today will the casualties be counted: in the palace, the wharves, and every other target the raiders attacked. Rumors already declare that thousands were slain, that the heart of the Cytherian economy, and indeed, the entirety of Cytheria's government were *all* destroyed in less than a single hour.

⌃   ⌃   ⌃

[Book Marker 2—*The Pelanjian Extinction*]
Personal Journal Entry—Captain Fendric Tilson
23 Mairche 2040 M.C. (6 B.R.S.) Port Salacia

Yesterday, the Conclave of Salty Nomads met again at the venerable Mariner's Roost in Port Salacia. Hard to believe three years have passed since our last reunion. We numbered thirty-two only a decade and a half ago. We were younger, leaner, fire-breathers all back then, daring, bold, and aggressive ship captains who faced any tempest on any horizon.

We number but twenty-three now, nine of our finest ship masters less, taken by storm, by pirates, by war, or by revenge in the case of the five lost to Pelanjian executioners in the Shahnaz Raid two years ago. In our private dining hall, we avoided *that* subject. We quaffed kegs of ale. We gnawed mutton bones and pork ribs. We spoke of lighter matters. Anything to hold the spirit of our eleven-nation assembly, to keep us full of ourselves. Anything to keep the laughter booming and the ale flowing.

At every three-year conclave, we swap tales of sons and daughters spreading their wings, of wives passed on, of new wives to a few. The eldest of us speak of grandchildren. We tried. But by deep evening, we grew somber. Getting too old for our own good, I suspect. Seen too much life. Seen too much death.

John Tinkerson, master of the Andorean-registered *Sea Rover*, started the evening's mood slide by mentioning pirates. He knows the subject well, having been held captive for fifteen months after the sinking of his *Wave King* by Malaiken pirates who demanded, and got, two thousand Andorean gold sovereigns for his release.

Talk of pirate atrocities naturally followed: of captured seamen hanging upside down from yard arms as their ship burned. Malaikens preferred that particular amusement for common prisoners unworthy of a company's ransom. Jafuran clans preferred beheading crews en masse. Takalans goaded their children to slice naked prisoners with razor-sharp oyster shells until they bled head to foot from a hundred shallow wounds. Only then would the proud fathers loop the victims with ropes and troll for sharks. "Dancing with sharks," they called it, and depending upon the number of prisoners, a captive festival could last for weeks.

But now, the three huge pirate clans that once ruled the Makara Archipelago, the Chantrea Archipelago, the Solvann Islands, and terrorized the dozen shipping lanes that once dared those waters no longer exist.

Most of us have refused contracts in those regions for years. But one of our number, Captain Mablevi of the Cytherian-registered *Resolute*, claimed to be making an outrageous fortune sailing those deadly waters. Again.

I didn't believe him at first. He's an excellent seaman and a worthy captain, but he is a notorious braggart as well. Still, he commanded our attention when he spoke of witnessing burned-out ghost towns that were once boisterous pirate sanctuaries. Every pirate stronghold in both archipelagoes *and* the Solvanns is gone, erased by fire. Every pirate-crewed vessel lies a burned-out hulk wherever it was moored. The few that tried to flee lay broken on island reefs.

No one knows how many active pirates the three clans once boasted. Five thousand? Ten thousand? Fifty to sixty odd ships all total. No vessel survived. Terrified pirate wives, children, and slaves who fled into the jungles surrounding the strongholds told similar tales on every island. "Great dragons" came by sea. "Dragon warriors," both men and women, overwhelmed the defenses. They killed in cold silence, many witnesses claimed. They held no trials, spared no prisoners, save those captives held by the pirates. When a dragon unit passed, only death lay in its wake. They slew unmercifully, as a man would do to a nest of vipers under his house.

For three days and nights, the operation—the slaughter—continued. The so-called dragon warriors vanished in their sleek dragon ships without uttering so much as a single word of warning or demand to the women and children they spared. The invaders took no prisoners. They took no booty, no silver bars, no gold coins, and no chests of precious stones. They disdained the stolen treasures around them as something unclean.

Pelanjians. We all knew. Absolutely. No other nation or king's army wages war so precisely, so totally, so damned lightning quick.

A thought occurs. As far as any of us know, no Pelanjian vessel in history has ever been attacked by pirates. If Captain Mablevi's tale is true, I would say that we know the reason.

8

Mirror Resolution

[Book Marker 3—*The Mirror Resolution*]
Rhys Balgaire, Flt. Adm. (Ret.)
12 Janobraan 2041 M.C. (5 B.R.S.)

Mirrors do not lie, I am sad to say. I wish they did. They reflect truth, not wishes. Reality, perception, procrastination or problems left unsolved cannot hide. Mirrors show us the fitness or the unfitness of our bodies, the need to shave or not, the boundless joy of youth, the weariness of age. They also show fear.

The fear in mine is that my reflection reveals the unspoken truth of Pelanjia. The weariness in my eyes is the same weariness I see in the eyes of our people. The grim set to my jaw matches the same encroaching bitterness that stains the faces of our children, their parents, and their grandparents.

The rigid squint of my gray eyes, the forehead creases seared bone-deep by ten thousand suns, the crow's feet clawed into existence by the fury of countless storms testify of my life at sea. It is the ruthlessness that smolders within that squint that troubles me. That same ruthlessness smolders in the eyes of our people.

We are growing more intractable, more resentful of the Outsiders' jealousy with each new generation. We cannot continue to frequent the realm of battlefield hatred and still expect our capacity for love to remain unscathed. Love and hate are not mutually exclusive in the human heart. They do not necessarily cancel each other out, but eventually one dominates the other—either by active choice or by acquiescence. I fear that our ability to choose one or the other is weakening by the violence of the battlefield, by our preoccupation of the next wave of violence under sail from the next invasion fleet.

We are losing our capacity to gaze in sheer reverence as morning breaks upon the eastern horizon to declare our Creator's glory. We no longer admire as the first pink of sunrise transforms into the radiant blue of day. We are losing our awe as He ends each day in even greater glory to the west. We no longer bid our Maker good-night, as He does us from His palette of deep crimsons and fiery oranges.

The horizons hold naught but menace now. We ignore the colors to watch for the black spikes of ships' masts targeting us. Hating us. Thinking us a people unworthy to live in peace. Thinking of us as nothing but a ripe target.

We are learning to hate—as a people. To our shame, we have mastered the art of warfare. More to the point, the sin of slaughter has mastered *us*!

This cannot be!

This will *not* be!

We have the eyes of cornered predators now. Either we act boldly to save our national soul, or everything we've labored for centuries to achieve will be for naught. I must bring my concerns before the Grand Council and present my case.

I have a plan that many will consider audacious.

The Haunted

[Book Marker 4—*The Mirror Resolution*]
Rhys Balgaire, Flt. Adm. (Ret.)
9 Fenobraan 2041 M.C. (5 B.R.S.)

Today might prove to be the most dramatic turning point in the history of the Pelanjian people. More unique, more unprecedented than even the Survival Quest three and a half centuries ago.

Nothing like the Survival Quest had ever been attempted by any culture in human history. Pelanjia had endured four major invasion attempts prior to the Quest; we had survived, but barely! Those who had attempted to invade our shores were bloodthirsty and well indoctrinated in the brutality of warfare. Warfare was, and still is, an integral part of every Outsider nation. To survive as a nation of peace in a world of war, we had to not only learn the craft of war but excel in it. And do so quickly! Island Nations do not have enough acreage to engage in battles that last months or years. We were a nation of eleven islands. Any Outsider Commander would not have to be a military genius to design a war plan to attack and overwhelm each of our islands one at a time until our whole archipelago was conquered.

We had to be more efficient at defending ourselves, at killing! We needed the power of a surgically precise lightning strike. Nothing of the sort existed on the planet. Our ancestors had to invent it. They had to invent something else as well. Something that did not come easily to the sons and daughters of our Mindocean ancestors. To our shame, then as well as today, our ancestors had to invent, no *learn,* the necessity of ruthlessness. Peaceable folk could only survive as a culture by being more vicious than their attackers. As the old adage goes, it takes two to make peace, but only one to make a war. This applies to individuals as well as nations unfortunately.

Thus did the insanity of warfare manifest itself to a people so instinctively reluctant to acknowledge it.

Pelanjia was in its infancy then, a nation central to relatively few, emerging Embrican and Mascarene trading states. Pelanjians literally invented themselves as the central hub for the fledgling spice trade between the two continents.

Did those Pelanjians envision the immensity of what would one day become the Pelanjian Empire? Probably not, but who is to say? What can be said is that as of the Survival Quest, those islanders survived and prospered even in the barbaric times awaiting them for the forthcoming centuries.

The completion of the Survival Quest and the subsequent absorption of the combat techniques gleaned worldwide and codified into what would one day be known as *Nung-Cha,* resulted in the most permanent change to our culture. Prior to the Quest, ancient Mindoceans and early Pelanjians tried to live by the *Beacons,* all sixteen of them. After the Quest mission, the sixteen became twenty, courtesy of a seemingly endless string of invasion attempts which put new-found war skills to the test.

The new number seventeen honored combat skills while number eighteen called for physical discipline. Number nineteen declared "death before dishonor," while number twenty espoused to "fight no enemy twice!"

Thus did the last four *Beacons* achieve permanence in Pelanjian culture. Thus did our transformation begin.

The Survival Quest sent one hundred scout teams of ten men and women each to scour the planet for the most skilled warriors from every culture. Ninety-three teams returned within that ten-year mission. Not all were intact. Seven disappeared completely without a trace. Whether lost at sea, or slain by animal, men, or disease in their target regions, their fates were lost to history.

Those who returned brought masters of the deadly arts back with them. They also brought team members scarred or permanently injured from skirmishes in their regions. Survivors spoke of temperatures hot enough to bake the human brain, of sea storms too vicious to describe, or northern regions so cold livestock froze to death standing in snow drifts. Family stories maintain that fewer than one in fifty mission veterans ever bothered to speak again of their experiences once their reports were recorded.

From the perpetually war-torn city-states of Alcinia and Kratos along the northwestern shores of the Andorean Sea, we learned the art of combat grappling. From the isolated island nation of Usagi off the northeastern coast of Mascarene, we learned the deadliness of the single-edged long sword, the dagger, and the empty-hand attack. From the wind-swept steppes of Tabansi, we learned the feint, the encirclement, and the death stab from the fiercest mounted archers on the planet—the Kohansan nomads.

The Kohansans closely resembled their Pelanjian visitors. Tall, with slightly more slender builds, probably due to their rugged uncentralized lifestyles. They were dark tan of skin, with almond-shaped eyes almost as black as their long, unbraided hair which flowed behind them in splendid symmetry with their mount's tails when warriors flowed over those hills and plains in full charge. Interestingly, the Pelanjians learned the word "Kohan" meant *two tails.* Their cultural pride centered on equestrian skills and the legendary stamina of their stocky mounts. The group our explorers contacted was actually an accumulation of eighteen once-warring tribes into a single horde ruled by the iron hand of the Great Khan Nimka-Sha.

Hundreds of individual tribes roamed the steppes of Tabansi, raiding each other, hunting prairie deer, wild sheep and the elusive stelnaks. It was Nimka-Sha who saw the conquest potential of en massed tribes better fed by domesticated flocks of sheep and stelnak. Prior to Nimka-Sha, the concept of "domestication" did not exist. He literally willed the concept into existence by the sheer power of his vision.

Curiously, it was the skill of the longbow-wielding Pelanjians that got his attention and respect. That, and the fact that he had never seen skilled women warriors until he met the Pelanjians.

We learned of the great siege engines and catapults so necessary to the huge land armies of the Embrican continent. Our warrior scientists improved them, multiplying their power by factors of ten. We watched, we studied, and we learned. War axe, iron mace, and shield skills came from the savage North Sea raiders of Basilia.

From the birth-trained warrior society of Palemon in central Embrica, we absorbed the legendary, collective discipline of the shield wall.

The swarthy, bull-shouldered Palemons were totally absorbed by their warrior ethic. Dark-eyed and black of hair, during wartime they routinely shaved beards, mustaches and their heads to deny an enemy a handhold. Training for combat began as soon as a male child could walk and that brutal lifelong training bordered on cruelty. Sadly, their culture seemed bereft of cultural art or of any propensity to express themselves architecturally. Buildings, temples and homes were of quarried, but unadorned stone blocks. War was their only cultural art. And they were good at it. *Very* good!

We bred giant war stallions to carry fully armored knights like nearly every nation on the Embrican continent. The seemingly impenetrable long-lance phalanxes of Eastern Gianna and Entoria were studied and practiced and studied even more. The two most contracted assassin clans in all of civilization—the Shadow Hand of Shuang, and Usagi's House of the Blood Orchid—revealed their unmatched stealth techniques, the use of the darkened blade, the garrote, and the Iron Fist.

We incorporated the formation-shattering power of en massed longbow battalions favored by the armies of Northcliffe and Ganelon. From tribes inhabiting the nigh-impenetrable jungle swamps of Chiamalka and from the Jahzara-Ni clans which prowled the forested peaks of the Mount Zhenga chain, master hunters taught us the arts of stealth movement, of camouflage, of patience, and of the hunter's discipline to track and kill in absolute silence.

The Chiamalkas were, on average, a hand taller than the Pelanjians and more slender, while the Jahzara-Nis people were generally a hand shorter and more thick-set. Both were charcoal-dark in complexion and when they addressed each other, or even a stranger, they stared directly eye-to-eye, uncomfortably so. Their golden-tinged brown eyes seem to bore right inside the listener.

Interestingly, it was the Chiamalkas who taught us how to run as effortlessly as their hunting parties did when literally running antelope and wild deer to ground.

We learned from them all, and from many rarer forms of combat as well. Then we taught ourselves how to defeat each one, how to exploit the weaknesses that only Pelanjians found.

In the end, masters from the divergent groups of warrior monks, the House of Akiyanan and the Dewei-Zhu sect influenced Pelanjia the most. Both ardently pursued lives of isolation and peace. Both valued pre-sunrise meditation periods to begin the day, with entire families up to entire villages participating as one. The quiet of those times was unbroken save for the whisper of synchronized breathing emanating from the collective individuals.

Synchronized breathing allowed them to join the rhythm of Nature, they humbly explained. Time spent with them convinced the Pelanjians it was so.

As for individual and cultural manners, no other group found on either of the two continents could match their almost servile comportment. To the unobservant, it would be dangerously easy to misjudge politeness for weakness. The Pelanjians made no such mistake. They arrived on all those shores, unnamed valleys and jungles of their missions with wary but open minds. They arrived with respect.

The Akiyanans developed superb sword and weapon-making skills, while those of Dewei-Zhu believed *religiously* in empty-hand fighting techniques based on various animal species. The Dewei-Zhu also eschewed typical weapons of war, preferring to defend themselves with astonishing skill using nothing but common farming implements: the shoulder pole, wheat flails, rice pounders, hay sickles, and others.

Both groups were radically polite, even to strangers—as long as those they encountered meant peace. Those who meant them harm, however, whether an individual or an army, found a defensive, virtually savage response greater even than the legendary berserker rages of the Basilian Sea raiders.

A cultural philosophy of balancing a lifepath of gracious courtesy and honorable peace with the lightning stroke of an enemy-provoked violence suited the Pelanjian mindset perfectly.

Inadvertently, it was a Dewei-Zhu monk, Huang Shen Zhi, who named our unique system of collected war skills. One day he told one of our most skilled combat instructors, "In your quest to survive, you Pelanjians have embraced the path of *Nung-Cha*, even more completely than my own people."

When asked the meaning of *Nung-Cha* the warrior-monk replied in his people's humble fashion, "*Nung-Cha*. The Necessary Path."

Within thirty years of the initial Survival Quest, every Pelanjian man, woman and child was trained in *Nung-Cha*. We still tread the Necessary Path daily three hundred years later.

But even such a drastic turn to ensure our culture's survival pales alongside what will, what *must* occur today. I intend to convince the Pelanjian Grand Council that Pelanjia must embark upon a *new* Necessary Path.

Before our eleven island governors, I will present a single question: "What might we become if our honor was untainted by constant warfare, if the energy of our people created, instead of destroyed?"

I will wait as long as it takes for the answer.

I must know the answer.

Pelanjia must know!

10

A Charted Course

[Book Marker 5—*The Mirror Resolution*]
Rhys Balgaire, Flt. Adm. (Ret.)
11 Fenobraan 2041 M.C. (5 B.R.S.)

Two days ago, I posed my question to the Grand Council. "An excellent and profound question, Admiral," Beathan Tearlach, Talon's council representative, answered. "Council will ponder your . . . cultural challenge, as it were, and reconvene two days hence."

I was crestfallen. I almost demanded an answer. I sought at least some acknowledgment of agreement. Uncharacteristically, I kept my silence, restraining a retort that would have been filled with outrage and outright indignation.

That was two days ago. Reappearing before the Council this morning, Representative Tearlach greeted me thus. "Admiral Balgaire, your question can only be answered by Father Creator."

My greatest fear arose. The Council would prefer to maintain *status quo* over bold action. Obvious disappointment clouded my face, but within heartbeats, he continued with, "We say, let us move forward with all haste. Let us discover what Creator already knows."

Eleven oak gavels unanimously agreed with a single resounding crash against the teak desks of all eleven island representatives.

Success! The concerns I noted in my own mirror existed in theirs as well, it seems. In one week hence, I will meet with the Council again, but this time behind closed doors. I will bring my twenty-member team of like-minded retired and in-service admirals, ships' captains, and naval architects. Behind those doors, we will present the plan to evacuate every Pelanjian man, woman, and child to a new, but as yet unknown homeland."

[Book Marker 6—*The Mirror Resolution*]
Rhys Balgaire, Flt. Adm. (Ret.)
18 Fenobraan 2041 M.C. (5 B.R.S.)

Today, the Council learned of the plan my team and I have dubbed "The Disappearance" for the last four years. From the moment I first posed my theoretical *what if* to these nineteen trusted friends and colleagues, we have all poured our hearts and minds, our time, and our personal fortunes into the greatest gamble our nation will ever undertake. The scope of the plan is immense, requiring discipline, iron will, grinding human toil, and unprecedented logistic complexity. The eight basic steps of the plan, however, are simple: Seek, Build, Find, Explore, Claim, Return, Deceive, and lastly, Disappear.

First, we must *Seek* out a new home land. Dubbed the Prime Mission, within two months, squadrons of dragon ships will begin to scour the planet for our new home. I will detail this effort more precisely the day the first explorer ship begins its mission.

As the squadrons *Seek*, we at home will *Build* the vessels necessary for Pelanjia to disappear. Only our two largest islands, Scimitar and Talon, allow warehousing and wharf facilities to Outsider shipping. The other nine smaller islands, despite having excellent wharf facilities, are strictly off-limits to foreign shipping. Business will continue as usual on Scimitar and Talon, but it is upon the nine smaller ones where the new shipyards and warehouses are already being raised in secret.

It is there where the huge hulls of the newly designed colony ships will be laid. There, warehouses containing thousands of miles of chain and hawser and line, forests of oak and teak planking, and untold square miles of canvas will await their day to adorn over eight hundred colony ships and escorting *dragons*.

We will build and conceal our great gamble until the explorer ships succeed. Once they *Find* a new land, they must *Explore* and *Claim* the territory, but only if it is uninhabited.

The next stage will be the *Return* of the Prime Mission dragon crews. Only after thorough examination of the explorers' discovery by the Grand Council will the decision be rendered to continue on with the next-to-last step—the *Deception.*

That step must *Deceive* the entire human race by convincing it of our demise. We intend to feign an archipelago-wide outbreak of Blood Plague, the most virulent plague known to humankind.

Once the *Deception* is successful, the final step will be to *Disappear* from our beautiful islands completely. We will leave not a single trace of our existence. Everything, however small or insignificant, will either be carried to the New World or be burned along with the villages, farms, and warehouses of our culture. We intend to leave no trail to follow, no clue to examine, no real evidence that Pelanjia ever existed at all. Without Pelanjian hands wielding axes, without human management and the unrelenting cultivation of Pelanjian jungle and forests for crops and livestock, any proof of human habitation will disappear under jungle canopy as completely as we will in our New World.

Let the jungle reclaim what the greed of Outsiders once coveted. Let the canopy overwhelm the blood of Pelanjian heroes who fought so bravely to preserve our culture. Let the forests reclaim the beaches where Pelanjian men and women died, refusing, with swords in bloodied, wounded hands, to retreat even one step against the greed of a planet.

Let the centuries pass. Let the name Pelanjia join other unprovable legends that dwell as little more than echoing ghosts within the misty realm of the human psyche.

11

Stalking the Nightmare

[Book Marker 7—*The Mirror Resolution*]
Rhys Balgaire, Flt. Adm. (Ret.)
13 Andril 2042 M.C. (4 B.R.S.)

Tonight, the Prime Mission begins. At 2200 hours, the dragon ship *Gale Sword* will cast off from Dark Point's berth number sixteen. She is honored to be the first ship of the first squadron to embark upon the mission to find our new homeland, but she is honored without fanfare. History books will record her name, but tonight she leaves in the darkness of a moonless sky. So will every ship of the Prime Mission that follows.

All 130 ships of the Prime Mission will disembark from different islands in the chain. They will rendezvous well over the horizon, and thus away from curious eyes, before assembling into squadrons for their assigned missions.

In all, twenty-six squadrons of five fully equipped ships each will be dispatched over the next five months. The Prime Mission of these 130 vessels is to seek a new homeland free from war, free of the need to relentlessly prepare for yet another invasion attempt.

The plan dedicates five years for the mission. The criterion is simple and narrow. The homeland must not be another island or archipelago. A mountainous, rugged, and defendable wilderness with access to the sea is preferred. The land cannot be inhabited.

This eliminates two thirds of western Embrica, the largest, most densely populated continent. The uncharted eastern third has potential. Group One, the five-squadron East Embrican Fleet, will investigate.

Like eastern Embrica, portions of the so-called *dark continent* of Mascarene have potential. Most of the eastern seaboard down to the southern cape—aptly named Cape Horror for the monstrous, ship-killing storms in the region—is populated by warring clans carving out regional tribal kingdoms. Mascarene's western coast is poorly mapped, as is the northwestern coast. Group Two, the six-squadron West Mascarene Fleet will set sail to explore that potential in two weeks.

The largest fleet, Group Three, is the Bakulan Fleet. Eight squadrons strong, the forty ships will fan out south and southwest, using Mascarene's southern Cape Horror as their starting point. The region south of the cape is vast, millions of square miles no doubt. Maps do not exist of this hostile region. Shipping lanes do not exist. The possibility of finding a hospitable homeland in that storm-ravaged expanse is remote. Even so, by the end of the five-year mission, every sizeable island, reef, and shoal will be charted right up to the ice cliffs of Bakula—the southern polar continent.

One month after the last squadron of Group Three departs, Group Four will weigh anchor from the secluded harbors of Mist, Pelanje, and Blade. For weeks now, those three islands have labored day and night to ready the fleet that might well be our greatest hope for success. It must be said, however, that the Group Four Fleet is also our biggest gamble, by far, of any of the other groups.

Designated the Wraithaven Fleet, Group Four is second in size only to the Bakulan Fleet. This seven-squadron, thirty-five-vessel fleet will follow the general course of the West Mascarene Fleet at first. However, once the Wraithaven Fleet reaches Mascarene's western coast, it will continue westward into what current charts, maps, and globes call the Void.

The fledgling nations and rising city-states along Mascarene's eastern seaboard are rapidly becoming major sources of the world's most desired spices and many of the finer teas, but they still have no deep-water merchant fleets. Pelanjian and Embrican vessels exchange manufactured goods of glass, bronze, and iron for the raw spices and teas. The untapped, unexplored western seaboard lies twenty-five hundred miles away; the two coasts separated by mountains, jungles, and sprawling expanses of rolling grassy veldt and hostile deserts.

What lies beyond that western coastline is unknown—the Void. That great unknown might well be Pelanjia's salvation. It sounds illogical to even write these words, but I feel almost summoned by that vast unknown. Humankind's most enduring and terrifying myth—Wraithaven—has always been described as lurking somewhere over the western horizon. There, as legend declares, towering mountains allegedly ring a nightmarish, inhospitable land. Impetuous gods supposedly war among themselves, even as they labor to imprison bloodthirsty wraiths bent on escaping their mountain fortress to feed upon human souls.

For ten thousand years the myth has tainted to some degree that deeply hidden attraction to superstition lurking at the core of every human heart. More than anything, that dogged millennia-upon-millennia persistence to still provoke nightmares in the minds of otherwise rational human beings is what attracts me.

For surely no superstition springs forth from nothing. Surely no enduring myth achieves generational perpetuity without containing some seed of truth, no matter how deeply that seed is buried in the dust of ancient history.

If an actual Wraithaven exists, our squadrons will find it. If the towering mountains of legend exist, so much the better. Given the fear the legend has perpetuated across time, the land should be considered forbidden, thus uninhabited by local tribes. Timidity, nourished by mythical terror, should keep it uninhabited. I pray for it, because Pelanjians are anything but timid.

A final note to this entry. My wife and I have two grown children: a son, Darach, and a daughter, Terrwyn. Both are captains of their own dragon ships, Darach of *Storm Breaker*, and Terrwyn of *Wave Lance*. Both volunteered for the Prime Mission. Both command vessels in the seventh squadron of the Wraithaven Fleet.

I wish them and all their shipmates Godspeed as they set sail for the Void.

12

Barren Odysseys

[Book Marker 8—*The Mirror Resolution*]
Rhys Balgaire, Flt. Adm. (Ret.)
27 Julaam 2043 M.C. (3 B.R.S.)

Disappointment. Last night, the first ships of the Embrican Fleet returned to drop anchor in the harbors of Crescent, Pelanje and Tempest. Over the next two nights, the entire fleet will arrive, save for one ship—*Moon Runner*. A rogue wave took her off the coast of Kratos on the return leg of the mission. Only three officers and twenty-nine crew members were rescued of the 205 souls aboard.

We grieve for the lost and for their families, of course, but the fleet brings back another kind of sorrow. As rugged and as inviting as the eastern coastline of Embrica had first appeared, the beaches and harbors for over a thousand miles gave ample evidence of human settlement. Over five dozen different tribes and clans were ultimately identified, most engaged in fishing and fur trapping. The rest pursued the great whale pods which migrate annually from the north polar region of Shaitan to the southern polar cap of Bakula.

The planned five-year mission essentially ended in fifteen months and lasted that long only because the crews stayed to thoroughly chart the waters, shoals, and islands along that wind-swept coastline

The clans were not warlike, even willing to peacefully interact and greet our ships, but they are living on borrowed time, I think. The only thing separating the little clans from the rest of the war-prone Embrican continent is the Embrican Divide, also known as the Eastern Wall. Once the perpetually snow-cloaked mountain passes are breached by one of Embrica's glory-hungry war lords, the idyllic peace that shelters the little clans will evaporate under the torch of war.

[Book Marker 9—*The Mirror Resolution*]
Rhys Balgaire, Flt. Adm. (Ret.)
7 Augustaam 2044 M.C. (2 B.R.S.)

The West Mascarene Fleet has returned—all ships and crew accounted for. The west and northwestern coasts of Mascarene differ drastically from the rest of the so-called *Dark Continent*. The fleet found that whether the coastline ended as beach or jagged cliffs, the hinterlands beyond are naught but desert. Spectacular towering dunes flow like slow, ocean waves in some regions. In others, harsh, rocky terrain suitable only for lizard and scorpion were declared by the scout teams as unfit for permanent human habitation, croplands, or adequate defense.

Many teams ventured hundreds of miles inland, only to confirm that the vast deserts reached even deeper by hundreds of miles. The northern one-third of the continent is desert, while the central and southern two-thirds fairly boil with forest and jungle and spice valleys jealously guarded by fierce, war-like tribes too numerous to count.

The whole Mascarene continent is out of the question for sanctuary. The thirty ships of the fleet will be dry docked for re-fit. Only the seventy-five ships of the Bakular and Wraithaven fleets remain on mission. Only they give us hope.

[Book Marker 10—*The Mirror Resolution*]
Rhys Balgaire, Flt. Adm. (Ret.)
8 Descombray 2044 M.C. (2 B.R.S.)

Yesterday, the remains of Squadrons One, Four, and Six from the Bakulan Fleet, our largest, returned. Four ships lost out of the fifteen that composed those three squadrons. All four ships are recorded AHL—*all hands lost*. Surviving crews describe the region's storms as the most vicious on the planet.

Lead-gray skies, waves towering fifty feet high, sixty, possibly more, and currents and winds spawned from the southern polar region took a deadly toll on all who braved those waters.

No land hospitable enough to support life was found, despite the concise quality of the new charts and maps. Five squadrons of the Bakulan Fleet still remain on station. We are now nearly thirty-two months into the five-year mission.

Progress continues on the colony ships, but I find it impossible today to pridefully record our gains. Will the Prime Mission be remembered by history as "Balgaire's Folly"?

Great Creator, help us. We have not heard from the seven-squadron Wraithaven Fleet since they sailed into the greatest unknown on the planet.

[Book Marker 11—*The Mirror Resolution*]
Rhys Balgaire, Flt. Adm. (Ret.)
4 Maja 2045 M.C. (1 B.R.S.)

Today marks our thirty-seventh month into the five-year Prime Mission. I fear I have become more actor than leader. Those under my command call me "Iron Eyes," but never to my face. Maira smiles when she overhears the name. She kisses my cheek and whispers that it is a term of respect, a part of my *warrior mystique.*

I was forty-three when I earned (or was branded by) the nickname. Two-and-a-half decades have now passed, since I commanded the Northern Battle Group. We intercepted the thousand-ship Basilian Alliance Fleet eight hundred miles north of our shores. The largest invasion fleet of the century intended to *end Pelanjian influence once and for all.* So pledged the royal families of Basilia, Gianna, Kratos, and Phaedra.

Before weighing anchor for the intercept, I met with my captains in Port Scimitar. The meeting lasted less than ten minutes. I quoted the well-documented threats made by each royal family. Each of our eleven islands would be attacked, overwhelmed by unstoppable numbers of troops, and burned one by one. They vowed to take no prisoners. Our adults would be nailed to wooden posts, burned alive, but only after watching the beheading of our children.

I ended the meeting by ordering the assembly to stand at attention and recite loudly with me, Pelanjian Beacon number twenty. *Fight! No! Enemy! Twice! Wage war totally or not at all!* We *shouted* it a second time—with fury! The rafters shook when we screamed it the third time. Then I dismissed them.

There were no questions. Their eyes, blazing like torches, declared what they would do. Then my captains stormed back to their vessels like silent avenging gods. Their boots hammered the slate tiles of the building. Their heels spurred the teak decks of the berthed dragon ships.

I did not command those captains.

I unleashed them.

Outnumbered four to one, our two hundred and thirty ship fleet sank over seven hundred Alliance vessels. We lost seven ships in the five-day battle. We took no prisoners. We struck the capital ports of each Alliance state. We hunted down and sank every ship we could find that had fled the main battle. The ports, the wharves and warehouses, the merchant fleets moored in presumed safety, the royal palaces, and their villages no longer exist. We burned it all. After fifteen months we returned. Our sins bonded us, even as they branded us all with haunted eyes of iron.

But I am no longer the ruthless commander of that time. I must force myself to make daily entries to this journal. It has been weeks since I have entered comments of any real worth. There are days when the human cost of the Prime Mission crushes me utterly. I weep alone in my study over the lost crews—my brothers and sisters every bit as close as any sibling could be. I weep for the widows, for the widowers, for the children left with such voids in their lives. I *am* the instrument of such loss.

Only Maira knows. My lovely, ever-patient wife is my anchor, my strength, my only sanctuary to soothe the daily wounding of my spirit.

I dry my eyes to attend the next of the endless construction and logistic meetings. I force the iron back into the gray. My military bearing, my voice of authority, my faith in the mission all seem like lies. Like affected things. I fear that I am but an actor wearing a mask of what I once was. Of what I must still be until this audacious mission is complete.

13

We Call It "Tripada!"

[Book Marker 12—*The Mirror Resolution*]
Rhys Balgaire, Flt. Adm. (Ret.)
23 Julaam 2045 M.C. (1 B.R.S.)

Three nights ago, vessels of the Bakulan Fleet's Second, Fifth, and Eighth Squadrons began arriving in the harbors of Mist, Dark Point, and Refuge. By week's end, all vessels of the fifteen should be accounted for. Only thirteen actual ships will physically arrive, but the crews of all will touch home soil, save for five lost to accidents and storms over the last thirty-nine months.

Squadrons Three and Seven intend to circumnavigate the southern polar region before returning home. Having failed to find any land of sufficient size or hospitable conditions to claim, the five remaining squadrons met in a secluded bay of a newly discovered island chain to decide their next step.

It was agreed that two full squadrons composed of five vessels each would complete the mapping of the Bakulan coastline. Those crews were all volunteers, which meant extensive shuffling of existing crews to replace gaps left by those choosing to return home. Two vessels, *Sea Shadow* and *Storm Warrior*, were cannibalized for sails, rigging, and any other useable equipment before being scuttled. They left no evidence of their exploratory passage, just as we intend to leave no evidence of our disappearance from the home islands. The returning ships stripped their own stores to properly outfit Squadrons Three and Seven, and immediately enacted a "half-ration" state for the voyage home. The volunteers reason they can complete their mission-within-a-mission in twelve to fifteen months before returning to Pelanjia.

Now only the Wraithaven Fleet remains unaccounted for. Seven squadrons. Thirty-five ships. Just over seven thousand men and women. They are our only hope.

‿　　　‿　　　‿

[Book Marker 13—*The Pelanjian Extinction*]
Ibycus the Blessed, Supreme Oracle for Typhon, the Storm Bringer.
The Jade Temple of Kratos
18 Janobraan 2045 M.C. (1 B.R.S.)

Lord Typhon whispers to me as he does to no others. In my meditations, in my daily readings of the ancient tomes, he warns of his building anger. The sacred leaves of the night flowers Palesa and Hanzila burn in the great copper Brazier of Insight. The sweet gray smoke writhes deep into my nostrils. It unlocks my mind to Typhon's glorious intentions.

I see visions of the gods, so regal in their golden armor. I hear their war cries as they unsheathe great silver swords to battle the shadow demons in the heavens. The hideous, be-fanged wraiths of legend rise from mist and earth to slay all that lives. Only Typhon and his heavenly warriors can stop them. Only the gods can keep them imprisoned, lest they break free to drink the blood of all humanity. I hear things no other priests hear. I see, I know of things unknown even to kings and their generals.

The heavenly war is beginning. Once again. The very sunsets and sunrises reveal this to me. They burn brighter each day with the blood the ancients spoke of in millennia past. The wraiths have gathered in force, I believe. The blood in the skies—of gods and wraiths alike—will only worsen as the battle rages. In the coming months and years, the crimson at sunrise and sunset will only deepen.

We must pray. Every nation, every people must offer sacrifices to the gods who battle to keep humanity safe from the demons of Wraithaven.

Humankind has sinned. Obviously. For it is sin that awakens the wraiths. Sin ignites their rage toward us all. But for Lord Typhon and his fellow gods, the wraiths would have broken free of the Wraithaven fortress long ago, and scoured the earth clean of every human being who draws breath.

I know the cause of the war in heaven this time. Typhon's smoke tells me this. Pelanjians have provoked this war. The deadliness of their armies, the reach of their vengeful fleets, the gold filling their coffers, the arrogance of their black sciences, are the sins Lord Typhon and the other Immortals must bleed for in the heavens once more.

Pelanjia is an affront to the gods, an abomination that provokes their anger even as the stench of Pelanjian existence rises to awaken the bloodthirsty wraiths. I pray, as we must all, that the gods will lose patience with the Pelanjian blasphemers. Once the gods have returned the wraiths to their mountain prison, may they strike the Pelanjian Archipelago a mighty blow. Let the gods crush their vile race as no human power has been able to do for four hundred years.

[Book Marker 14—*the Mirror Resolution*]
Tripada/Wraithaven Summary Report
From: Terrwyn Balgaire, Capt., Pelanjian vessel *Wave Lance*
To: Rhys Balgaire, Flt. Adm. (Ret.)
17 Andril 2046 M.C. (1 R.S.)

After thirty-eight months systematically exploring Tripada's eastern, southern, and western seaboards, the entire fleet now anchors in the largest bay found thus far along the mid-region of the west coast. We've named it Conclusion Bay. The collective observations of all surviving captains will be compiled into a single, condensed document. The survey of Tripada will be outlined in phases. Each phase will be summarized until our mission is completed.

Phase One—Survey of Tripada's Eastern Coast.
6 Andril 2043 M.C.—7 Septombray 2044 M.C.

1. Squadron One finds no western passage along Shaitan's ice shelf.
2. The rocky northern coast is sparsely inhabited due to violent winter storms and lack of arable land.
3. Squadrons Two through Seven discover indigenous clans along the southern eighty percent of the eastern seaboard. Our right to claim is denied, despite the magnificent Possibilities there.
4. No evidence of human habitation has been found deeper than eighty miles inland. Generational fear of alleged demons in the far west keep the clans huddled close to the coastline.
5. The presence of the widely scattered clans disappointed us at first. Now, it is their terror of what exists over the western horizon that gives us hope.
6. All crews will rest, re-fit, and resupply as best we can before beginning Phase Two, the mapping and exploration of Tripada's southern coast.

Phase Two—Survey of Tripada's Southern Coast
22 Septombray 2044 M.C.—3 Augustaam 2045 M.C.

1. The entire fleet rounds the southeastern Cape Tempest to resume our ten-mile segment mapping strategy along the southern coast.
2. Each segment requires only four to five weeks to complete now, compared to the nearly eight-week average on the eastern seaboard. Experience there has made our exploration teams more efficient.
3. The southern coast is far less formidable than the eastern one.
4. Dunes, low beaches, river deltas, and swamplands greet us now.

5. No sign of human habitation, even deep into the hinterlands.
6. It is true. Allegedly forbidden land equals an absence of indigenous folk. Beaches are unblemished save for tracks of gull, fox, deer, and Pelanjian boot soles.

Phase Three—Seeking Tripada's Western Coast.
3 Augustaam 2045 M.C.—19 Septombray 2045 M.C.

1. After nearly ten months, Squadrons One through Seven survey approximately two thousand miles of the southern coastline west of Cape Tempest.
2. Squadrons One through Five will complete this systematic mission. The coastline grows more mountainous as we continue westward. No evidence of human activity.
3. Squadrons Six and Seven are relieved of the coastal survey and dispatched to seek Tripada's western coast at full speed. Rear Admiral Grishian will command our two squadrons.
4. We are now forty-two months into the five-year Prime Mission. We are running out of time. We must push our vessels and ourselves as never before.
5. 2 Septombray 2045 M.C. (1 B.R.S.) We mourn the loss of two vessels from Squadron Six—*Squall Dancer* and *Gale Hawk*—upon the rocks of the treacherous, still unnamed southwestern cape: 412 total complement, 173 rescued. Savage, three-day storm. Sixty-foot waves. Incalculable wind speeds.
6. 19 Septombray 2045 M.C. (1 B.R.S.) We discover Tripada's western coast.

Phase Four—Survey of Tripada's Western Coast.
23 Septombray 2045 M.C.—1 Mairche 2045 M.C.

1. Squadron Seven and the three surviving vessels of Squadron Six sail north.
2. We calculate Tripada's east-west axis as 3,200 to 3,600 miles between coasts.
3. The southern one-quarter of the western coast is sparsely forested in comparison to the eastern coast, but is more foreboding and cliff strewn.
4. We continue the ten-mile segment mapping. The further north we explore, the more spectacular the coastline becomes. Forests grow heavier with each new segment. No evidence whatsoever of indigenous human life.
5. 11 Janobraan 2046 M.C. (1 R.S.) Deep explosive booms, originating in the open ocean to the west begin at eight bells.
6. Skies remain heavily overcast since the explosions first occurred. The distant rumbling continues day and night. Sunrises and sunsets have taken on what ancient folk might have described as a bloody cast.
7. Admiral Grishian dispatches *Night Arrow* from his Sixth Squadron and my *Wave Lance* and *Wave Dancer* of the Seventh to investigate. We believe we are experiencing part of the Wraithaven legend.
8. As suspected, the continuous explosions are volcanic, but not from just one volcano. Thirteen volcanic islands form a ragged line 1,300 miles long, and nearly 1,500 miles west of Tripada's western coast.
9. Seven of the thirteen cones are horrifyingly active, possibly having erupted within days of one another. Three smolder in preparation for yet more eruptions, we believe.
10. We name each of the thirteen cones individually. We name the entire group the "Grishian Fire Chain," in honor of our fleet commander, Rear Admiral Lander Grishian.
11. We can only observe the horrific phenomenon from extreme telescope range. We navigate among rafts of pumice many feet thick and acres in size, floating hundreds of miles from the cones. Atop the pumice lie decomposing bodies of sea

birds, fish, and seals. Bloated whale carcasses feed uncountable sharks.

12. Incalculable clouds of ejecta boil skyward, turning the day into night. Lightning bolts flash inside the immense plumes of ash and fire. Endless earthquakes churn the surrounding ocean into a chaos of filthy, hell-spawned waves.

13. In eras long past, when humanity's greatest achievements were the obsidian hide scraper and the hand-thrown spear, these volcanoes erupted. When a man's greatest aspiration was to provide an animal skin tent to shelter his family, the great fire chain had boiled awake, and became as gods to the terrified.

14. Ancient historians—both Outsider and our own ancient Mindocean scholars—have written of years without summers, of years with no spring at all, of year-long winters. Yet, despite the fervor of Outsider scholars, there is no link to Wraithaven at all. The dormant volcanoes of the fire chain simply erupt every few thousand years, we believe.

15. When they do, the skies of the northern hemisphere darken with the ejected ash. The earth is denied the warmth of sunlight. Crops fail. Structured societies collapse under the horror of starvation. Nations war over what food is left. We are about to witness this cycle of war and famine in our lifetime.

16. *Night Arrow, Wave Lance,* and *Wave Dancer* abandon the treacherous waters of the fire chain. On 1 Mairche 2045 M.C., we rejoin the fleet systematically progressing north along Tripada's western coast. We *will* find Wraithaven!

17. Towering, snow-capped mountains spear like craggy fingers into the sea, creating spectacular fiords in many places before disappearing over the eastern horizon.

18. We begin to refer to them by the legend name, the Shield of God. The name is appropriate. No mountain range on any continent can compare to such grandeur.

19. Our mapping strategy changes. Each survey ship carries twenty single-occupant kayaks. The eight surviving ships of Squadron Six and Seven total 160 kayaks. We blanket the waters with eighty kayaks per day while the other eighty rest.

20. Tripada's western coast is often deceiving. Where the fiords offer open passage to the land, we land our ships, or anchor just offshore. The kayaks discover that not all seemingly impenetrable cliff walls are true obstacles.

21. Hidden passages lie behind the forbidding cliff walls, many of them large enough for full-sized ships to pass. We have begun to find deep, cliff-sheltered harbors and bays behind the cliffs.

22. 17 Mairche 2046 M.C. (1 R.S.)

    <u>WE DISCOVER WRAITHAVEN!</u>

    An immense bay lies behind spectacular cliffs that conceal a wide, sinuous fiord leading for miles inland. The main passage is wide enough to accommodate fifty dragon ships abreast. A half-dozen smaller fiords lead into the bay that is many miles across. We credit the kayak crews for the discovery of this magnificent sanctuary of snow-white sand beaches. From offshore waters, the coastline looks like a wall of mountain and forest disappearing beneath the waves.

14

Discovery

[Book Marker 15—*The Mirror Resolution*]
Personal note to Tripadan/Wraithaven report
Terrwyn Balgaire, Capt., Pelanjian vessel *Wave Lance*
16 Junaam 2046 M.C. (1 R.S.)

Father's contention that territories deemed forbidden would, in all probability, be uninhabited, has proven correct thus far on Tripada. So has his belief that no myth or superstition springs forth from nothing.

That the *bloody skies* of antiquity were the result of volcanic eruptions, and not of gods battling demons, has been accepted as the most probable explanation for centuries in Pelanjia. That too has now been verified.

The Shield, thought of as a prison for demons by some cultures, or as a fortress for the gods by others, exists as well. I have seen all these things myself: the Shield fortress, the "bloody" skies, even the myths that have refused to die for ten thousand years.

The spectacular, snow-capped mountain ranges that collide to form the Shield are unsurpassed on the planet in height or in such formidable complexity.

The jagged peaks of Embrica's northernmost territory of Alcinia spear magnificently into the sea, creating fiords of seemingly bottomless sapphire blue. In comparison, here in . . . dare I say, Wraithaven, they are as foothills.

For nearly three months now, all thirty-three remaining vessels of the Wraithaven Fleet have anchored in the immense, mountain-sheltered bay we have named Conclusion Bay. Fifty such fleets could anchor here without crowding each other. This is truly the *conclusion* of the Prime Mission. I am sure of it. The entire Wraithaven Fleet is sure.

Our seven thousand surviving crewmen and women now witness the phenomenon called Wraithaven. As I record this report, three hundred twenty-member teams scout and map the interior of this vast land. They sweep across uncountable valleys, report of immense rolling prairies well-watered by spring-fed streams. Glacier-melt rivers weave like the Creator's own tapestry through immense forests of hardwoods and towering, red-barked evergreens. We have found not a shred of previous human activity. Human beings have never trod such forbidden soil.

Until today. Now, Pelanjian boot soles leave impressions in the snow-white sand of Conclusion Bay. They follow the game trails, leaving marks alongside the tracks of deer, wild sheep, wolves, and magnificently antlered creatures we call stags.

When father asks if we have truly found Wraithaven, we will answer, "yes," because of the proof I've written here.

But when he and the Grand Council ask if we are sure, we will tell of the mythical fog rivers that still flow down from the windswept peaks of the Shield as they did in ancient times to envelop and slay entire tribes of trespassers. Yes, the eerie fog rivers *do* flow down at dusk, only to return to the peaks at dawn. As for the invisible demons that hunt within the white, flowing vapors? The legends did not lie. The terrifying slayers still exist. Tragically, they have slain Pelanjian warriors in our day, just as they slew ancient nomads who trespassed too close outside the Shield millennia ago.

But Pelanjians slay also. Deaths of our own do not go unavenged. As I complete these final notes, a large wooden crate is being lowered into the hull of *Wave Lance*. In one week, we will depart for dear Pelanjia with news of our discovery. We will deliver the crate to the Grand Council Hall on Scimitar.

We will open the crate before them all and allow them to see the gift our taxidermists have prepared for them—a wraith of legend. No doubt they will pace off the twelve-foot-long monster. They will hesitate to touch the grotesquely muscled shoulders of the 1,600-pound cat at first. They will first touch the gray, white, and black splotches of the terror's pelt, before daring to touch the snow-white muzzle that blends so perfectly within fog and night shadow.

They will note that the huge yellow eyes that gleamed so ghostly green in the light of a nomad's legend, gleamed just as green in a Pelanjian explorer's campfire. And then I think, they will dare to touch the dagger-long claws and the twin incisors as long as a man's forearm that spear down from the muzzle of the great beast.

It is then, I think, that they too will finally believe.

[Book Marker 16—*The Mirror Resolution*]
Rhys Balgaire, Flt. Adm. (Ret.)
11 Augustaam 2046 M.C. (1 R.S.)

I make this entry today, nearly fifty-three months into the Prime Mission, with the first glimmer of hope I have felt in months. Many months.

Four nights ago, three ships of the Wraithaven Fleet's Seventh Squadron dropped anchor in North Gale's West Bay. At just past midnight, a night falcon brought news of the arrival to Mission Headquarters here on Scimitar. Moments later, a courier on horseback was dispatched to our cottage with a message officially sealed *For Admiral Balgaire's eyes only!* The message read: *Papa, please come to North Gale as soon as possible. You've done it, Father! Love, Terrwyn.*

Our daughter's ship, *Wave Lance*, was one of the three vessels.

This entry will be but a summary of Maira's and my meeting with Terrwyn and her two fellow captains By the time their full debriefing is complete at week's end, their field notes, the observations of officers and crew, and the hundreds of newly created charts and maps will fill many bound volumes. What I will record in these few pages is this:

As planned, the seven-squadron, thirty-five ship Wraithaven Fleet passed the West Mascarene Fleet as it began its survey of the continent. Once in uncharted waters, the fleet elongated into a scout line formation 140 miles long and headed northwest toward Shaitan, the northern polar continent. Once lead vessels reached Shaitan's ice shelf, the scout line intended to swing due west and seek the origin of the Wraithaven legend.

Beyond their most ambitious hopes, the fleet discovered an entirely undocumented continent, a land mass so vast it might eventually prove to equal Embrica in scope.

The seven squadrons systematically fanned out along the rugged eastern seaboard. Squadron One, at the northern extreme of the formation, sought a passage west along Shaitan's polar ice shelf. The thirty ships of Squadrons Two through Seven made landfall in ten-mile increments, exploring and mapping each segment as deep as two hundred miles into the hinterlands before moving southward to map new ten-mile segments. The squadrons continued this process until reaching the reef-strewn, storm-ravaged southern cape now named Cape Tempest.

The crews were awed by the rugged, defendable coastline, carpeted by vast hardwood forests. Crystalline rivers and streams poured from cliffs, from steep forest edges into sheltered bays longing to be turned into harbors for shipping and commerce. Shoals of krill and finger-sized serdons, horizon-vast, poured beneath the fleet like darkened storm clouds alight with untold billions of tiny, silvery flashes. Vast pods of whales followed, feeding at leisure upon the tiny creatures. Aggressive swordbills patrolled deeper waters, claiming the steep edges of the continental shelf. Schools of giant yellow tails and blue fins fed the meat-starved crews.

However, despite the superior defensibility and livable conditions of the region, every captain's log expressed disappointment—at first. The explorers found as many indigenous tribes along the two-thousand-mile seaboard as the East Embrican Fleet had. The criteria of the Prime Mission denied the fleet any right to claim the land. Yet, as communication with the various groups improved over the months, a common denominator came to light. Fear. No group lived deeper into the hinterlands than one hundred miles.

The tribes were there because a terrifying legend had driven them millennia ago from their ancestral homelands thousands of miles to the west. Pottery decorations, cave paintings, and ritual tribal dances all depicted campfires in the skies, with warrior spirits battling great tusked demons bent on slaying the earthbound tribes. Names for the distant terror varied: Place of Shadows, Demon Lair,

Prison of the gods, Fog Devils. The fleet now knew where the legend of Wraithaven lay.

The fleet learned something else as well. The single name over fifty tribal dialects gave to the continent itself meant *haunted*. To Pelanjian ears, the word sounded like *Tri-Pa-Dah*. Thus, our newly created maps now call the continent "Tripada."

Further recorded details in this journal have been omitted from this manuscript by the Pelanjian Council of Education to conserve space in this volume. Unabridged entries to this original journal are found in: *The Disappearance Journal* by Admiral Rhys Balgaire.

15

Deception

[Book Marker 17—*The Pelanjian Extinction*]
Assim Pakravan, Commodities Broker, Sapheldan Spice Consortium
11 Mairche 2050 M.C. (5 R.S.)

A s grave as the world situation is, I fear it has grown even worse *today*! I compose these words from the safety of my cabin aboard the Consortium vessel, *Resplendent*, which will (very shortly I pray) weigh anchor and carry me to the safety of my homeland, *Thesius*.

The crew is in full panic to cast off. Imagine the eyes of terrified sheep doomed by the arrival of a wolf pack. Officers scream for more speed, faster unfurling, faster knots. Eleven years through storm and wave with these men, and never have I seen such outright fear.

Resplendent is not alone. More than forty other ships are united in the same panic. Each ship scrambles to cast off. Pelanjian towboats arrive to tow us from the sprawling wharf facility. Captain Ansari waves them off. Panic-stricken mates interrupt their bellowing just enough to shake their fists and to scream curses at the towboats. *Resplendent* tows itself free from the captivity of the berth, using *our* lifeboats, *our* hawsers *our* sweat. The Pelanjians are cursed, every one of them. I know. I saw the arrival of that curse with my own eyes.

This morning, World Spice Guild agents from twenty-three Embrican nations and eight kingdoms of the barbaric Mascarene continent met with Pelanjian Fleet Admiral Rhys Balgaire. The agenda included facility leasing and berth reservations for the next year. This is an annual event. I have attended eleven such meetings.

We met under dire circumstances to begin with. Worldwide shipping has been in turmoil since the advent of the perpetually overcast skies. Sunsets and sunrises have been blood red for nearly five years now. Temperatures have dropped noticeably throughout Embrica and Mascarene. The sun never really shines. Thick, overcast skies hide it. Crops now fail in even the most historically productive regions. The spice valleys of the Mascarene interior produced a third less output this year than two years ago. Projections for next year are even worse.

Winter snowfall over the known world is heavier, begins earlier, and lasts longer than ever in recorded history. Brutal winter fronts stride through the northern hemisphere like conquering Frost Giants. Embrica's winter line has crept six hundred miles south, one hundred and fifty miles further than the year before. Starving Embrican nations attack equally starving neighbors for foodstuffs, for livestock. Pirates prowl once-safe sea lanes, overtaking the now rare grain and supply ships of nations that have not drawn bows in anger against one another for centuries. Four years of war have eradicated historic treaties *and* allies. Admiral Balgaire's enforcement of leasing increases by the Pelanjian Grand Council only exacerbates the world's suffering.

The admiral is actually a personable man, polished and elegant of manner. He is perhaps six feet four inches tall, wide-shouldered, and lean, as Pelanjians tend to be. His neatly trimmed snow-white hair and beard contrast with his sea-creased face and his dark, golden-brown skin. His dark-blue uniform, with its double row of golden buttons, is immaculately tailored. His movements, his energy, his quick intellect and commanding baritone all befit a man in his forties. Yet, rumors put him well into his seventies—an irrational claim surely. Embricans consider age fifty old. Few of us reach age sixty.

Rumor or not, the admiral presided over our meeting as always, as if he was the only adult in a room full of unruly children.

We met in the Aerie, a bold, two-story structure of stone and timber that from a distance seems more ship than building. A huge lower deck and a somewhat smaller observation deck above spear like prows of schooners under sail toward the jagged basaltic cliff jutting over the surface of Refuge Bay, 864 feet below. The building is the Scimitar Port Authority, and it is there on the mountainous, heavily forested capitol island of Scimitar that the best views of the Pelanjian Archipelago exist.

The real port authority is Admiral Balgaire, who sat calmly, ramrod straight at the head of the centuries-old burled table that accommodated fifty chairs. Two rows of twenty-five chairs each lined the glass walls surrounding the table. Each agent is allowed one assistant during a meeting. Many of the table and wall chairs were vacant.

Only thirty-one nations were represented this morning, about half of the total that trade eighty-five percent of the world's spices and commodities through Ports Scimitar and Talon, Pelanjia's two largest of her eleven islands. Few agents claimed their traditional places at the admiral's table. Most sat in the assistant chairs, their backs against the walls rather than by an enemy. Admiral Balgaire's iron-gray eyes noted the random vacant chairs. He allowed us to shuffle our papers. He seemed to record every shifty look exchanged by colleagues turned dire enemies. He allowed us to murmur under our breaths at acquaintances now too close for comfort.

At precisely 9:00 a.m., the commanding familiarity of his smooth baritone brought the meeting to order. He welcomed us as if the skies were clear, as if there were no famines, no declarations of war—as if the Pelanjian Grand Council had *not* increased leasing fees by three hundred percent! Oddly, his voice was soothing despite the world's predicament. My contentment lasted perhaps a third of an hour.

Just as we began discussing the new, outrageous facility fees, a young, uniformed Pelanjian ensign interrupted. He stepped quickly down one of two sets of interior stairs that led to the upper observation deck. Two other stairs outside led from our lower level to the same upper deck. Coming to ramrod attention at the foot of the stairs, he stammered, "Ad . . . Admiral, a moment of your time sir. Please!" The terror in the young officer's voice was as thick as sea fog.

The admiral nodded and the young man strode quickly to bend low and whisper in the admiral's left ear. The admiral's eyes went wide. Tense whispers were exchanged between the two men.

Admiral Balgaire abruptly stood up and said, "Gentlemen, let us recess a moment. We will reconvene shortly."

He and the ensign stepped outside to continue a very animated conversation. It was unprecedented to interrupt the aplomb of our gathering. When the ensign pointed toward the upper deck, the admiral broke into a run, taking the stairs three at a time. Our stunned silence turned into chaos. Admirals don't run!

We stampeded for the inside stairs, elbowing and cursing our way to get to that upper deck and claim one of a dozen telescopes mounted to the guard rail. The admiral's brass telescope was larger than the others and mounted to the pointed prow of the deck. The young ensign just watched us, his face a mask of worry. The admiral paid no heed to our thundering footsteps. His right eye never left the eyepiece of the scope. He just muttered a gasp that sounded like a man who had just received a death sentence.

"Great Creator!" he exclaimed. "Not that!" Something in that scope had shaken Iron Eyes Balgaire to his core.

Moments later, our scopes revealed what he knew. Humankind's ultimate horror had invaded Refuge Bay.

The admiral turned to face us. "Gentlemen," he said, his voice cracking, "we have a . . . situation. Please return to your ships and set sail for your homelands immediately. Containment is paramount."

"Situation?" A hideous understatement. We scrambled for our carriages. The stench of panic-induced vomiting by two agents wafted over our second stampede of the morning.

Two Pelanjian dragon ships, normally so elegant of line, so graceful of sail, so impossibly fast, lay at anchor in the middle of Refuge Bay. The bay is a magnificent deep blue two miles across. Huge granite blocks define the wharf facilities where a hundred ships of Pelanjian and non-Pelanjian registry lay berthed. Those two dragonships were the only flaws in an otherwise splendid panorama.

Both listed badly. The sails of both were shredded as if by the claws of some fearsome beast. A few had been repaired with patches. Thirty feet of bowsprit was missing on one ship. The aft mast of the other had been sheared off, leaving a jagged, ten-foot-high stump. I am no mariner, certainly, but I swear that the back of one of the ships seemed broken. That explained why the ship wallowed so gracelessly, but even a non-mariner must ask, "What could break the back of a dragon?"

Yet, that did not cause our stampede for town. That came from the hideous red-and-yellow pennants streaming from the masts and sterns of both ships. With their pale ivory-colored skulls in their centers, such pennants are the universal warning that Blood Plague is aboard a ship, a port, a town, or a garrison.

Even from our distance, our telescopes revealed bodies strewn in disorder across the decks of both ships. Some were covered with blankets, others lay exposed and still. A few remaining crewmen inched weakly for the lifeboats and dinghies shuttling to shore.

What fools! The dragons should be burning at anchor! Dead or alive, the crews should be burning! But no, the Pelanjians are evacuating those still alive for treatment ashore. What monumental arrogance! Blood Plague has no cure! The hideous plague pennants fluttered from the masts of each tiny craft shuttling from ship to shore and back again. The stampede started when the first pennant rose over warehouses and adjoining buildings where the sick must have been transferred.

The Pelanjians have allowed Blood Plague to infect the central hub of the world's lucrative spice trade. International trade and commercial shipping will wither. Fortunes will dissolve.

[Book Marker 18—*The Mirror Resolution*]
Rhys Balgaire, Flt. Adm. (Ret.)
15 Augustaam 2050 M.C. (5 R.S.)

Five months ago, the Deception officially began when I met with spice and commerce agents from thirty-one different countries. We've come a long way since.

The plan had always called for the Deception to be based upon a Blood Plague outbreak in Pelanjia. That morning, I played the role as bearer of the evil tidings in the same manner that I would have in calmer times. What caused us to deviate from our original timetable, and to accelerate the plan was, of course, the event that the rest of the world is bent on calling the Red Sun Disaster.

On the thirteenth day of the first month, Janobraan, 2046 M.C., the skies of the northern hemisphere began to thicken with overcast. From our Prime Mission explorers, we know this was the result of the Grishian Fire Chain eruptions on 11 Janobraan of that year. Sunrises and sunsets blazed so uncharacteristically red they were described as "bloody." Panic ignited, then eventually grew into a conflagration of its own—unchecked, fanned into superstitious terror by the ignorant, by the newly religious, and as always, by opportunistic warlords.

Ancient myths were resurrected. The gods supposedly warred in the heavens among themselves, or they battled hideous demons that had broken free from their mountain prison far beyond the unexplored western horizon. The gods were angered against humanity for—pick your favorite reason. Each newly sprouted religious cult proclaimed to know the answer. In no time it seemed, the gods were no longer angry with all of humanity, just part of it. Just certain blasphemous sinners. Just that portion of humanity most deserving of punishment. That eventually came to mean just Pelanjians. We have been invasion targets of the Outsider nations for centuries. Now, according to the flourishing new cults, we were targets of none other than the gods themselves.

The original mission plan had no contingency for the rebirth of a legend, or for a catastrophe of planet-wide crop failures. We had to adjust. We factored in the probability of civilization's breakdown. When war erupted on the known continents, we altered our equation to disappear.

The timing was superb. The eruptions resurrected the myth of Wraithaven as a place of terror (not that the superstitious world had the slightest idea where it actually was). Crop failures begat continent-wide wars throughout Embrica and the burgeoning kingdoms along Mascarene's eastern coast. Worldwide, shipping and land commerce was cut in half, then to half of that. Then we did what seemed both illogical and greedy. We tripled leasing fees for berths and warehouse facilities—even those that lay empty. To the disaster-beset Outsider nations, it made no sense. It drove away two-thirds of the shipping lines and spice conglomerates struggling to survive. The Blood Plague scare, allegedly brought to our archipelago by the two contaminated dragon ships wallowing at anchor that day, solidified the plan. By the end of that fateful meeting day, not one Outsider ship, not one non-Pelanjian human being remained in our islands.

Unknown to the world, we had stockpiled the essentials of shipbuilding for years before we launched the secret Prime Mission to seek our new home.

We built great warehouses deep inland on each island, well away from the eyes of foreign traders or casual visitors. We built them of wood, rather than of stone, for the plan dictated that the cavernous facilities would burn along with every other scrap of evidence that Pelanjians had ever existed. History would be left to scratch its head and wonder. Hopefully.

We stockpiled forests of oak timbers carved into ribs and keels for our new ships, and untold acres of canvas for the sails. We coiled thousands of miles of ropes, lines, and hawsers, and stacked the reels beside countless drums of forged iron chain, alongside oak barrels of nails, screws, and fittings.

What we did not forge, weave, or build ourselves, we imported through artificially created shipping companies operating under counterfeit flags of foreign ships. We were laying keels for the immense, newly designed colony ships before the Prime Mission dragons ever left port. We were going to leave. We just needed a destination.

With the advent of the Red Sun event, however, we accelerated the plan exponentially. Shipyards, carpentry shops, canvas mills, forges for chain and tools, for weapons and plows, all began working nonstop. Including the mission ships that had returned from their search missions, we would need over eight hundred ships to move every Pelanjian citizen, every head of livestock, every book, scroll, tool, weapon, herb, and boot lace to the New World.

The actual Disappearance is spaced over eleven two-week periods. Every two weeks, one of eleven fleets sets sail for Wraithaven. Each fleet consists of forty dragon ships with a compliment of 315 each, and thirty-five much larger colony ships, each with 520 souls aboard. Seventy-five ships, 30,800 men, women, and children in each fleet named after one of our eleven islands. Colonists of each fleet, no matter its name, will come from every island. We will not risk losing an entire fleet composed of all the citizens of a single island. Neither will we risk the loss of a family name. Family lines are dispersed over different ships in a particular fleet, as well as over different fleets. Basic family units will travel together, but we will not allow an entire lineage to be lost over the dangerous four-month voyage.

In the Disappearance phase, we will move eleven fleets totaling 825 ships and 338,000 souls from Pelanjia to Wraithaven over twenty weeks. The first fleet to sail will be the Dark Point Fleet. The next ten in order will be Mist, Refuge, Pelanje, Tempest, Blade, Ambric, Talon, Crescent, Scimitar, and finally, the fleet I will personally command, the North Gale Fleet.

In two months, we will complete the Deception phase of the plan by visiting the World Trade Conference in Masalah. When that mission is complete, the fleets will begin the Disappearance.

[Book Marker 19—*The Pelanjian Extinction*]
Halim Pavaka of Entoria, World Trade Ambassador
22 Orctombray 2050 M.C. (5 R.S.)

I write this entry on the fourth and final day of the World Trade Conference. Pelanjians have always been bold. The whole world knows that. They invent what others have not dreamed of. The mariner's sextant, the compass, and the telescope all came from them. Their fired porcelain is nothing less than art. They sail where others cannot, or will not (which no doubt explains their current plight). Their dragon ships have no match in grace of line, in speed, or in seaworthiness.

Their knowledge of medicine, of surgical techniques, of herbal use seems more sorcery than science. They are rumored to live longer by far than the rest of humanity, but we cannot prove it. Every Pelanjian man, woman, and child is a skilled warrior, and we don't know why that is either. They have never been defeated on the battlefield. But they have never warred against gods before. Perhaps at last, the mighty Pelanjian Empire has met its match.

We "Outsiders," as they refer to the rest of the world, can now afford to be smug concerning the fate of the Pelanjians. The scales of life seem poised to finally tip away from them, and back toward the rest of humanity. Predictably, the Pelanjians don't realize that. They've ruled the waves too long, controlled the trade routes too long, and been undefeated too long. Yet, even as the gods single them out under the same darkening skies above us all, the Pelanjians wave their banner of arrogance in our faces.

Four days ago, the World Trade Conference convened here in the ancient capital of Masalah, on the Isthmus of Corrigan, an event that occurs every three years. This year—the fifth full year of the Red Sun Disaster—actually united the world in one significant way, despite how war has utterly ruined the continents of Embrica and Mascarene.

The conference was scheduled to last thirteen days as always. It lasted but four. We were in turmoil. All of us. Panic at the looming specter of lost fortunes consumed us all. Accusations and threats from the fifty-six nations represented flew like arrow storms. We accomplished but one significant thing on the final day of the conference—the creation of a new world calendar— the Red Sun calendar (R.S.). It was decreed that the year the skies first darkened would become year 1 R.S. Prior to the universal change, the nations of southern Embrica favored the Valerian Record, and thus would have called that year 856 V.R. The Imperial Chronicle, favored by northern Embrica and Mascarene, designated that year 384 I.C. Pelanjia used its own calendar, of course. They claimed a continuous historical record from their Mindocean roots to the present day. According to their Mindocean Chronicle, the year was 2046 M.C. Even in calendars, they insinuated superiority.

The sheer arrogance, the brash challenge the Pelanjians displayed yesterday, however, stretched the bounds of logic. They disrupted the conference with their typical display of power, even as they sought the world's compassion.

The Pelanjian delegation arrived unannounced and uninvited. The Prime Amphitheater of Masalah, a city known for an abundance of such venues, is a splendid creation of white marble.

From the podium centered down on the wide "hub" floor, concentric levels of luxurious, leather-padded marble benches rise in wide arcs. The acoustics are as outstanding as the structure is elegant. A loud whisper at the podium can be discerned at the upper tiers. The theater can seat twenty thousand, though less than seven thousand were in attendance.

Yesterday, just before noon, Erus Theron, the Alcinian ambassador began leveling his nation's grievances of piracy against a once-peaceful neighbor, Medora. He had just begun to list the atrocities of the starving Medoran pirates, including rape and cannibalism, when the Pelanjian delegation arrived through the wide entrance to his right. No, I said that wrong. The delegation did not arrive. The delegation invaded!

Two hundred battle-armored Pelanjian Defenders, swords strapped across their backs, war spears riding upon their right shoulders, marched onto the podium floor in four arrow-straight ranks of fifty warriors each. Their iron-shod boots thundered against the marble floor in perfect cadence. Imagine two hundred aggressive iron hammers striking stone at the exact same instant, step after step. The contingent halted before the podium with a final, echoing stamp from those armored boots.

Without a spoken command, the two hundred executed a crisp right face toward the tiered audience, drew those eight-foot-long spears and snapped to attention. Spear butts struck marble at the exact instant the heels of their boots struck each other. Seven thousand delegates stared in shocked silence as echoes of boot and spear rose among us. *No wonder they've never been defeated in battle*, I thought. *They're machines! Huge, living machines!*

These men and women were not ceremonial palace guards. Their short helmets and armor were clean, but not polished. The basic color of gray was slashed with random diagonal strokes of black and dark ivory—a supposed match to the volcanic stone of their homeland. Armored from helmet to boot, they all stood nearly seven feet tall. No feathered plumes graced their helmets. They wore no flamboyantly colored capes. Sword sheaths, helmets, and armor were devoid of gilding. These troops were functional, war-seasoned veterans absolutely prepared for battle!

They did wear one thing that warranted special attention, though. Each warrior wore a black mask behind their gray helmet cheek pieces that covered their noses, mouths, and the front of their throats. Only their eyes showed. Hard, challenging, menacing eyes!

After a moment, the two rear ranks slid open to allow six Pelanjian Elders to ascend the podium stairs. The Alcinian ambassador had already disappeared to parts unknown.

The color of the Elders' long, hooded robes matched the gray-and-slash pattern of their Defender's armor. They too wore black masks under their hoods from nose to throat. The implied threat of Blood Plague contamination was so obvious I'm surprised any of the seven thousand of us remained on our tiers. The fate of the world's spice and trade hub and the matter of personal fortune overrode the inherent fear the masks inspired, I suppose. It did in my case, but the tension throughout the tiers to bolt for the exits was as taut as a bow string.

The speaker for the Pelanjians was none other than the renowned, retired Fleet Admiral Rhys Balgaire, Port Authority Commandant for all of Pelanjia.

His smooth, commanding baritone carried easily through the tiers. He actually thanked us for allowing them to participate in the conference. Jaws dropped at his audacity. "*Allowing* them?" Who could have stopped them? Seven thousand delegates had no doubt that had every soldier in Masalah's satin-clad ceremonial army barred their way, those two hundred Defenders would have simply carved a bloody path through them right up to the podium.

The admiral called us "fellow world citizens." He spoke of how the world spice trade had forged links between nations, of how it had fostered a spirit of wide-ranging cooperation, of how we should reach across our differences to help our fellow human beings. The man was deluded. No. He was insane. Desperate!

"We know you are aware of our plight," he said, beseeching with outstretched arms. "The ships that fled our ports the morning of the outbreak upon our shores carried word to your ports. More ships fled those ports to spread the news even further."

Yes, they had, which explained why Pelanjians had not been invited, why no Embrican or Mascarene ship had strayed closer than a thousand miles to Pelanjian shores since.

"All eleven of our islands are infected" he said. "We burn our dead every hour of every day. We scuttle death ships filled with the bodies of our families in the waters of the Carthyngian Deeps. Over eighty percent of our population is dead. We have few ships left. Every island burns. We have done the honorable thing. We have isolated ourselves from you, from the rest of civilization. We have buried our own, and encircled our islands with marker buoys flying Blood Plague pennants."

I envisioned such anchored buoys bobbing upon the offshore waves, their obscene red-and-yellow pennants announcing the death of an entire race. I wept no tears. Nor did any other delegate, as poised as I was for flight from my bench.

"We ask you, our neighbors, for but one thing," the admiral continued. "We ask that you allow us sanctuary—at a place of your choosing. Allow those of us who are yet well to start our people anew. We have fewer than thirty serviceable vessels. All others have been scuttled or burned as funeral pyres. Send us but twenty empty ships, that we might carry the living away from the dead, away from the smoke of burning villages and fields."

As if exhausted, he dropped his arms to rest upon the podium. He bowed his head and shook it sadly side to side.

Our answer? A seven thousand-delegate stampede for every exit *not* at podium level. Joining the mad flight, I looked over my shoulder. Once. The Elders spoke briefly among themselves; then rejoined the ranks. The two hundred brought their spears to port arms, executed a crisp right face, and thundered away like a single, hideous war machine. I was one of the last human beings on earth to see a live Pelanjian. An historic moment I suppose, but that was yesterday.

This morning, the fourth day of the conference, less than three thousand of the original seven thousand delegates reconvened. We immediately passed two resolutions—unanimously.

First, we declared a quarantine zone enveloping the Pelanjian Archipelago for two thousand nautical mile radius in every direction. Given how quickly the word of the Blood Plague had already spread, this formality quadrupled the current region of avoidance. Pelanjian vessels encountered on the high seas would be shunned. Pelanjian vessels in distress or sinking would disappear under the waves. Pelanjian crews would not be rescued.

Secondly, Commerce Way, the street the Pelanjian delegation used to travel from their ship's berth to the Prime Amphitheater was itself quarantined. That part of Masalah is a ramshackle assembly of thatched-roof wooden shops, taverns, and slums of the poor. For three blocks on either side of the Way, soldiers have now chained the doors and windows of every building shut, effectively imprisoning the area residents inside their shops and homes. Contagion must be contained. Shops and taverns can be rebuilt. There is never a shortage of the poor.

It is now late afternoon as I complete this entry. Soldiers have fired the quarantined zone. Inns, shops, shabby domiciles, *and* their captive residents all burn—for the good of us all. Two thousand archers ring the zone to cut down any who try to escape.

Wharf Zone A4, where the Pelanjian ship berthed, is not immune. A dozen berths on each side of the empty Pelanjian berth, most with ships still in them, now burn as well. More archers ring the zone to cut down escapees. A hundred tow boats carrying a thousand archers patrol the waters beyond the burning ships, killing those few who try to swim from the flames.

Immense columns of smoke and flames boil toward the overcast skies, mixing with the haze of countless altars offering sacrifices to mollify the terrible judgment of the silent, angry gods. Better that five thousand ill-breds die in the inferno, we all told ourselves, than to lose a city of eighty thousand. But even so far away in my apartment, tormented wails of the condemned reach my ears. I had raised my hand along with the other members of the conclave to seal their fate. Yet, I cannot silence the screams of those condemned to burn.

I think I shall hear them forever.

16

Disappearance

[Book Marker 20—*The Mirror Resolution*]
Rhys Balgaire, Flt. Adm. (Ret.)
7 Augustaam 2052 M.C. (7 R.S.)

End Day has finally arrived—the last day we will think of ourselves as Pelanjians. I can scarcely believe it is finally here. Just over ten years ago, the plan was a dim future veiled by the distance of uncharted horizons. Even as essential to the survival of our people as it was, it seemed surreal. Today, in every Pelanjian heart, the sadness of our departure, the sheer realism of doing what humankind has never attempted, wars with the optimism of dreams yet undreamed.

This fleet, the North Gale Fleet, will be my last command. The Council honors me so for designing the plan to save Pelanjia's soul. I am humbled to my core by their confidence in me. Over the last nine years, ten thousand doubts have assailed me. Fear has whispered scathing accusations against me in my mind. Ten thousand times, fear has demanded to know, *Who are you to engineer such audacity?*

Haunted, taunted by worry of all the things that could go wrong, yet prodded with a fanatical zeal for the possible future of our people, I've hovered over every aspect of the plan like a worried grandmother caring for an ailing child.

That question still echoes in my mind, although faintly now, because fine ships have been lost over the course of the plan, ships crewed by the finest mariners, both men and women, on the entire planet. Ships and families are still being lost as each fleet journeys for our New World of Wraithaven. In their honor, I will remain strong when doubts seek me out. I will defend my actions with reason, with logic.

Our ancestors came as Mindoceans in search of a permanent home. They chose this eleven-island archipelago deliberately. They named it Pelanjia—*beautiful sanctuary*—and so it was. They settled Dark Point first. In less than a century, all eleven islands were claimed. Within another century, the eleven settlements were united as a common people. They were crews no longer, tribes no longer. They began to think of themselves as Pelanjians.

Ultimately, they had to disappear as Mindoceans in order to embrace their maturing, collective power as Pelanjians. By sheer force of deliberate intention, they climbed from spiritual and intellectual darkness and into the light of Pelanjian dreams unimagined by their Mindocean ancestors.

As Pelanjians, we have raised fine libraries, exquisite artwork galleries, museums and academies of higher learning unmatched on earth. But to protect our culture, we have had to learn and excel in the art of war. Only so trained could we break the will of those who would invade our beautiful sanctuary. Anything less would have meant our extinction long ago. Yet, we cannot allow the beat of war drums to drown out the subtle rhythms, the poetry that we believe Creation to be. Pelanjia cannot lose her soul.

To prevent that, we must repeat our own history. As we have convinced the world of our demise, so must we convince ourselves. We must disappear as one people, only to resurrect as another. We are no longer Pelanjians. We will teach our children from whence they came. We will remind them of their roots, but by plan, by deliberate intent, we . . . are . . . Wraithians!

Today, this last fleet will weigh anchor and leave our beloved islands, never to return. We will take the longer, more hazardous southern route discovered by the Bakulan Mission Fleet when they explored south of Cape Horror. One thing is certain. No Outsider ship knows of the Bakulan route. Only Pelanjian charts exist of those remote and treacherous waters. None will witness our passage. None will follow. The quarantine mandated by the World Council of Trade guarantees this.

Ten full fleets have preceded us in two-week intervals. Survey teams from the earliest fleets are already dividing Wraithaven into eleven provinces, each one named after a Pelanjian island. Orchards and fields are being planted. Stone is being quarried. Breakwaters and wharf facilities and academies are being raised. Today, the skies of the Red Sun are the same color over Wraithaven as they are over the rest of this devastated world, but one day they will clear.

Under those clearing skies, Wraithian children will dream dreams beyond the imaginations of their Pelanjian parents. Their children's children will dream greater still. And one day, they will be able to answer what we, in this war-torn era, have so often asked of ourselves: *What might we become if our honor was untainted by constant warfare, if the energy of our people created, instead of destroyed?*

17

Concerning Gods and Men

[Book Marker 21—*The Pelanjian Extinction*]
Fariel Rashne of Thebis, Royal Historian
Court of His Supreme Majesty, Assim Kaveh III
55 R.S. (Exact Date Unverified)

The gods govern lowly humans by their own sense of time, not ours. They do not inform us of their intentions for our world. They do as they wish to us. Seldom do we ever discern their hidden purposes.

The human mind, with all of its limitations and potentials, either believes in the gods, or it believes in coincidence. It cannot cling to both. One negates the other. Such was the fate of the Pelanjian people. Their demise was not merely coincidental with the Red Sun disaster.

They angered the gods with their high-born ways, by their rigid code, or was it *codes*, of honor? They sought to become gods themselves by raising prideful libraries, cultivating allegedly curative herbs said to contain power that smacked of dark magic and sorcery. Their devotion to alchemy and the enchantments they called "science" separated them from the majority of gods-fearing humanity.

They lived well into their hundreds, allegedly, while the rest of humanity died of old age by their fifth decade. The gods were surely jealous of such arrogance. For the sin of extended life alone, the Pelanjian islanders paid the ultimate price.

The gods saw to that, even as they warred against the wraiths and turned the heavens to blood. They shattered the earth and it trembled and groaned in pain and agony. They sent great waves to erase coastal civilizations. They loosed the War Beast, with his famines and plagues, upon the rest of humanity.

From the assumed first day of the Red Sun Disaster, nearly seven years passed before the skies returned to pre-disaster clarity. It took that long, the priests declare, for the gods to subdue the wraiths. The earthly wars that accompanied the war in the heavens lasted much longer.

Crops began to fail less than a year after the disaster began. Starving street mobs tore apart their own cities in search of food, of anything that would burn to ward off the vicious winters that followed.

Kings and princes and dukes warred against once-allied neighbors. The word "ally" died in that first year. Immense Embrican and Mascarenean armies, all of them on the brink of starvation, marched across those continents to conquer those perceived as more fortunate. Desperate invasion fleets plundered once-elegant coastal civilizations centuries in existence.

When the kings and princes and dukes were all dead, local warlords rose to take their places. They too led unmerciful armies of starving survivors to crush yet more cropland under their boots, to eradicate even more of humankind's advances in industry and art and technology.

Untold millions died in the century that defined the Starvation Wars. Today, eight years after the assumed last nation-against-nation battle was fought, bandit gangs still roam the countryside, killing to survive. They do not roam alone. They hunt, as do the ever-present wolf packs that have long been the true rulers of Embrica's countless, now silent battlefields.

The gods did this to us all to eradicate the Pelanjian stench rising to their nostrils. They reminded us that wars, famines, and plagues come from them, not from happenstance.

We know this to be true, because over the decade following the Red Sun Disaster, the Pelanjian race was annihilated from the face of the earth by the gods. Not a single man, woman, or child survived. Not one. Their mighty dragon ships disappeared from the once-prosperous trade routes that were themselves dissolved by the Starvation Wars. Thus, we who survived by the mercy of the gods, were taught the price of arrogance and empire.

18

The Next

“Thank you, Iden,” Mairin said. “That will be all for today.”

“Lady Tanguy,” Baird Murtagh asked, raising his hand quickly, a smile wreathing his face. “Will we read more tomorrow?” His habitual boredom with history had vanished.

“Why? Did you find it interesting? Class?”

“Yes!” The boy answered. A dozen eager hands rose for attention. Baird’s enthusiasm was obviously contagious.

“It was fun reading how wrong the Outsiders were about the Pelanjians,” Erbin Brannoc, a red-haired son of dairy farmers said.

“Some of the things they believed were silly,” Tegan Argraff, the brunette daughter of the renowned Argraff weavers added. “So wrong about so many things.”

“Silly to us in today’s time,” Mairin said, “but their conclusions and suppositions made perfect sense to them. In . . . their . . . time.

“But what made them so wrong?” the burly lumberjack’s son, Angor Drystan, asked, his raised hand the first of a half dozen clamoring to ask the same question. “Were they that uneducated? Even these writers?”

Mairin hesitated briefly before answering. The fact was she was enjoying herself at the moment, enjoying the barrage of questions voiced by enthusiastic children chattering away like magpies on a fence post. *I helped design this course,* she mused. *Exuberance, curiosity, ignited by their curiosity for a new subject.*

She suddenly realized that she had uncharacteristically been moving about the room more than normal, taking steps up and down the aisles to acknowledge the latest question. *I can’t help myself.* She thought with exuberance of her own. It had been some time since she had seen such obvious interest. She could not restrain a smile as she finally addressed Angor’s question.

"In a way, they *were* uneducated," she replied. "They weren't considered unintelligent in their time, I'm sure. But understand that in the era preceding the Red Sun Disaster, certain legends passed from generation to generation were assumed to be factual. Unexamined, unverified beliefs I should add, because in many ways it was simply more comfortable to live that way."

"On the other hand, Pelanjians were *un*comfortable to just blindly accept generational myths. They required, as we do, real fact-based answers. To everything! That is what launched the 130 ships of the Prime Mission to disregard accepted myths and ultimately discover and *claim* the forbidden place called 'Wraithaven.'"

More hands raised, eager to continue the discussion.

"Unfortunately," she said, "we must end our discussion soon. Only a few more questions. We have too many core subjects to complete these last weeks of the school year. Our reading today was to introduce you to some of your winter assignments. Such opposing points of view should prove more interesting than most winter assignments."

That brought groans from the class. Winter assignments were completed when Wraithaven's savage blizzards closed most travel under impenetrable snow depths.

"Lady Tanguy," Dyfed Calum said. "did Admiral Balgaire survive the journey to Wraithaven?"

"He did, which brings up one last point before we move on. The *Mirror Resolution* is a systematic collection of the Admiral's thoughts and commentaries over thirty years. He describes Pelanjia's last two repulsions of invasion attempts, the creation of the plan, the execution of the Pelanjian Disappearance, and the founding decades of the New World, *Wraithaven*. The Admiral's attention to detail shows us the historical causes, their effects, and the final result, which is us!

"The *Extinction* volume is different. Its value is that it is *not* a collection of only one man's thoughts and opinions. The entries are presented in historical sequence but are from so many writers world over that we can begin to grasp the turmoil of that era. Admiral Balgaire's volume covers a thirty-year time frame. *Extinction* encompasses over fifteen hundred years."

"Why such a difference?" Bari Vaddon asked.

"Because we have our own works detailing the complete Wraithian history for that period. *Extinction*, being of so many sources, shows the degradation of Outsider civilization. The parts we read this morning are but a fraction of the overall volume. Eventually, over the millennia, Pelanjia became exactly what Admiral Balgaire had predicted, a forgotten nation, more myth than historic reality. The Deception, the plan by our ancestors, coupled with the greatest age of turmoil and destruction in human history, erased virtually all memory of Pelanjia. The wars ignited by the Red Sun event lasted over three hundred years *beyond* the initial century of conflict known as the Starvation Wars. Conquerors rose and fell endlessly. Maps changed drastically. National boundaries dissolved. New nations struggled into existence while others struggled *for* existence.

"The eleven Pelanjian fleets carried away every possible shred of evidence that our people had ever existed. They carried away the contents of our libraries, while libraries on Embrica and Mascarene burned. Knowledge collected in millions of scrolls and books over the centuries on those two continents, burned under the invader's torches, under the conqueror's spite, under the victor's contempt for the vanquished.

"So also went the contents, records, and musings once thought safe in the repositories of government buildings, temples, monasteries, and academies. To a conqueror, the stones of an ancient library or monastery were of greater value to construct a fortress than the parchment scrolls and volumes rotting away on shelves open to the elements. We cannot begin to estimate how much accumulated knowledge was lost in the turbulent centuries immediately following the Red Sun event.

The generation that suffered so much at the beginning of the Disaster was the last to have any direct memory of Pelanjia. The next generation had survival to concentrate on, not past history. The generation after that had probably burned any remaining history texts to stave of the terrible winters of the era.

"The Dark Millennia following the Starvation Wars defined the extinction of human civilization. Even today, only a handful of nations have rediscovered the level of advancement they had once attained—two thousand years ago! The wars, the famines, and the plagues that followed were so destructive to human development that many major inventions, from the printing press and the making of paper to the art of glass making were lost.

"When Pelanjia disappeared, the world lost those advancements. The art of making high quality steel is still lost to the Outsiders. Advances in health and longevity are still lost. Beyond Wraithaven, age fifty is old. Age sixty is ancient! Age seventy is virtually unheard-of.

"You will discover all this and more during your winter studies, but for now, I would like to introduce you to some special guests. Class, please rise and greet the Readers, Taggart and Alina Kayne: my parents."

As the Kaynes reached the front of the room and turned to face the class, Mairin and the children bowed slightly but crisply at the waist and tapped fist-to-chest honor salutes before returning to attention. The traditional formality given to any classroom visitor.

Taggart and Alina returned the formal greeting in unison but did so just a measure slower than the children. Thus does respect earned honorably over decades acknowledge the energetic courtesy of youth.

As the class returned to their seats, the three adults gathered at the front of the class.

Alina winked at her daughter before saying loud enough for the still settling students to hear, "So this is the class you've told us so much about."

"Possibly the best class of Elevens you've ever taught, I recall you saying?" Taggart ventured. "From what we've just heard, I believe it. Excellent. Simply excellent." Every child's face was wreathed in a smile. *Readers liked our reading! Readers!*

The Kaynes then began the annual ritual performed by Readers for the nation's classes of "Elevens." Knowing what was coming, Marin smiled and took a seat at her desk at the front of the room. Unbeknownst to the children, they were about to begin their bonding with the Readers who would greet them as next year's Twelfth Harvest Initiates and lead them to the next horizon.

"Who is Carryl Gamon?" Alina began.

A tall, slender girl raised her hand. "I am, Lady Kayne."

"Ah, I understand that congratulations are in order for your perfect academic scores in biology and geography during the recent competition. Well done. Very well done!" The little girl beamed.

Taggart immediately called for Dylan Gowyr. Seeing a stocky blond boy gesture in answer, Taggart said, "We've heard of your expertise with the mandolin your grandfather Berwyn made for your fourth birthday. No one makes a finer mandolin, or violin for that matter, than Berwyn Gowyr. We hear that you compose and sing ballads as well. Perhaps at your Reading next year, you might bring your instrument and allow us to enjoy your music."

The boy seemed awestruck to be so honored to entertain at the Scroll Night celebration. That his grandfather's craftsmanship was also recognized filled the boy's heart with pride.

And so it went. Each Reader moved around the room, identifying each child and mentioning something of note about them. Recognition meant the same to these children of next year's Reading as it had to a burly young wheat farmer from Saber River.

Despite having seen the ritual greeting of Elevens many times, Mairin smiled, amazed at the details her parents brought to the impressionable youngsters. The children beamed with pride. *These Readers know us. By name!*

The Readers' last acknowledgement was for an athletic little brunette girl on the front row, whose personality had changed noticeably that year. She exuded a guarded demeanor that had not existed before. Her neatly trimmed bangs and short brown hair could not hide the haunted stare her blue eyes sometimes took on. The corners of her mouth stiffened when she tried to concentrate on her studies or during playtime outside. Academy staff discussed the mystery, but Seren's parents had quietly revealed the cause to the Kaynes months before, essentially blessing the Kayne's next step.

"Children," Alina said, "we wish to honor Seren Caddoc for her courage last winter."

The children looked perplexed, as did Mairin. *Courage for what?* Seren's face reddened with embarrassment. She actually slumped in her seat, breaking eye contact with the Kaynes to stare at her clenched hands atop her desk. Her chin quivered as her winter memories attacked her yet again. Alina and Marin moved quietly to stand beside Seren. Each placed a comforting hand on her shoulders.

The child's entire body was a rigid ball of tension. The memory had owned her for too long. It fought to keep her even as her eyes began to glisten. It knew. She was no longer alone. Rescuers had arrived. The strong hands touching her shoulders, the strong baritone voice exposing her tormentor now fought for her. Fought her tormentor as she could not. The hands, the voice, reached deep into her soul, found the vile, squirming thing hiding in the shadows it had created. Then they dragged it into the light. They showed it no mercy, just as it had shown a little girl none.

"A pack of dire wolves broke into Seren's home late last winter as she cared for her baby brother, Trynt," Taggart said, taking a deep breath. He forced himself to voice the child's horrifying secret. "Her parents, Angor and Arial, were working in their barn when the wolves came. Only Seren stood between them and her one-year-old brother. She fought six wolves with her father's javelin and his war hatchet. Inside her house! She killed two and wounded a third before her parents and others came to the rescue."

The attack, though rare, was not unprecedented. On average, the huge animals weigh more than a full-grown man, yet they avoid human contact except under extreme circumstances. Most wolf attacks against human beings occur during deep winter, when scarcity of prey pushes the high-timber packs to the brink of starvation. The pack that attacked the Caddoc homestead had, in fact, never encountered humans before.

The long-legged creatures stood four feet tall at the shoulders, yet the snow that they had futilely hunted through was even deeper. The harsh, unrelenting winter had stripped all fat reserves from their bodies. Bulling through the deep snow drifts had burned fully thirty percent of their bodyweight away. When they chanced upon the relatively clear road passing the Caddoc homestead, it was a welcome relief. The gaunt pack simply did what came naturally. They loped along the easier path until the wind brought the scent of prey—Seren and Trynt, and the sound of the infant's crying. Had the wind been blowing from just a slightly different direction, the pack would have attacked Seren's parents in the barn.

The pack crashed against the narrow front door of the cottage in a terrifying cacophony of snarls and growls. With the day's activities well under way, the crossbar was not in place. Only a light wind chain high on the door kept the pack from bursting into the front room in one savage mass.

Seren did not hesitate in the slightest. She yanked her father's war javelin from its rack above the fireplace and hurled it at the leader, an immense, scarred creature nearly midnight black. The javelin took the creature in the throat, slicing through the jugular. With no time to reach the second javelin higher on the wall, Seren grabbed one of two long-handled war hatchets hanging next to the fireplace. The weapon was too heavy to swing one-handed as her father did so easily. Instead, she rushed for the door, screaming in fright and rage and hatred at the second wolf, a gray-and-tan monster that snarled like a demon in its efforts to scramble over the leader's body wedged halfway in the doorway. She swung the deadly weapon two-handed, as if chopping kindling.

The weapon's steel head had a wide axe blade on one side and a six-inch-long, armor-piercing spike on the other. Whether by instinct or chance, she struck the second beast right at the base of its skull with the spike end. The spike pierced the wolf's spine where it met the skull. The wolf died in that instant. A single yipe pierced the winter air as the spike struck bone. In a moment of confusion, the remaining four wolves milled about outside the door, frightened by the deaths of their leaders, but driven insane by the scent of blood and the prey inside. Starvation won out. Struggling to wrench the hatchet from the wolf's skull, and to hold the splintered door shut with her body, Seren's movements plus the sound of Trynt crying in the nursery down the hall incited the pack to resume the attack.

Seren wrenched the bloody weapon loose and swung it in a big overhead arc at the third beast forcing its way over the bodies blocking the door. The axe blade struck the wolf right in the face, destroying the left eye as it drove deep into the snarling muzzle. The huge gray beast jerked back with a painful yelp, only to meet the fangs of the other three. Crazed and distracted by the scent of more fresh blood, wolf fought wolf outside the now damaged door.

Seren screamed, "Daddy! Daddy!" as she broke free for the nursery. She reached the nursery and slammed the door shut, just as the four remaining wolves boiled into the house. The little girl jammed a chair under the door latch to secure it, screaming, "No! No! No!"

She never dropped the hatchet. The wolves threw their heavy bodies against the door. The door frame cracked. Each thunderous impact bowed the door more. Claws and fangs dug against the door, under it, trying to break through. Frightened by the hideous noise, little Trynt screamed at the top of his lungs. The snarls were insane now, furious at the meat so close. A door panel cracked. Wolf fangs gnawed savagely at the weakened oak. Iron hinges squealed in protest as the furious assault twisted them from the long black screws securing them to the door jamb. A second panel cracked. A single wolf paw exploited the thin opening, pushing claws through.

Seren kept screaming, "No! No! No!" but now it was from what certain tribes called berserker rage. Her face was a mask of hatred for the monsters beyond the nursery door.

Her blue eyes blazed with savage determination. Nothing would get to her baby brother. Nothing!

She looked quickly around the room for something to protect the baby. *The blanket trunk under the crib.* Fueled by adrenaline, she held the hatchet with one hand and wrenched the heavy oak trunk out with the other. The weight should have made it impossible. With a guttural shout, she threw the lid open. The trunk was empty. She threw the crib blankets into the trunk, and swiftly stuffed the squalling infant inside. Slamming the lid shut, she shoved the trunk back under the crib. The wolves threw their huge bodies at the door. Metal hinges screamed as they began to tear from the door jamb. Horrible, insane snarls filled Seren's universe.

Wielding the hatchet with both hands, Seren charged the door, chopping as fast as she could with the deadly weapon at every paw, foreleg, and muzzle that pushed through the cracks. When the spike struck home, a wolf yelp added to the din of growls and snarls and her own screams of rage to kill the monsters at her door.

Half-blinded by wolf blood splashed across her face, she no longer screamed for help. She and Trynt were alone! She would *kill* these killers. *All* of them! She threw her body against the door.

Again! Again! She brought the hatchet down on another wolf paw with a guttural shout, severing a toe of the beast. Behind her, a long, gray foreleg reached far enough inside to claw three deep slices down her right calf. She ignored the pain. A monster in her own right, a mindless killer with blood-stained teeth and hands, she reacted with blazing speed. The hatchet flashed downward, severing the attacking paw.

She was still screaming, still terror-blind to anything but the wolves, still standing her ground in front of the crib when her father and mother finally broke down the door. Her rage had deafened her to the battle beyond the door as her parents and three farm hands had slain the four remaining wolves with axes and pitchforks.

It took many moments of calling her name over and over to bring Seren out of her wild-eyed rage, to calm her down. Splashes of wolf blood stained the whites of her eyes, but eventually they lost their savage blaze. The blood-stained blue reverted back to terror as her battle rage died, then immediately transformed into pure fright for Trynt.

Angor and Arial moved to hug her, but Seren turned away as if they didn't exist and dropped the bloody hatchet. Muttering Trynt's name in a continuous, incomprehensible string under her breath, she fell to her knees and yanked the trunk out from under the crib. Nothing in her universe existed except Trynt. She scooped the squalling baby up in her bloody arms and crushed him to her even as his cries grew louder. When Angor moved to take the baby, Seren twisted away from him, held one hand up and virtually growled, "No!" There was not a shred of sanity in her bloodied eyes.

For the rest of the day she held the baby, refusing to give him up, refusing to wipe the blood away from her hands or face. Arial prepared a cup of warm porridge for the baby, but Seren would allow no one else to feed him. She stared at his tiny face and fingers, absorbing every detail. She had not spoken an intelligible word since her screaming had stopped.

She held Trynt in her arms all night as he slept. When he soiled his diapers, she changed them immediately. When he cried from hunger, her mother merely set a bowl of milk or porridge on the small oak table next to the battle-ruined door. Seren ignored her parents when they looked in on her. She just took the food silently and fed the baby. They stopped asking if she needed anything.

Angor and Arial left the damaged door open to at least watch their daughter pace the room with Trynt. Sometimes she rocked him back to sleep in the big oak rocker that Seren's grandmother had rocked Seren in years before. She wept randomly and often, sometimes in silence, sometimes muffling her sobs against the baby's blanket. She ate nothing, drank nothing. On the third full day after the attack, weakened by as many days without sleep, she stumbled and fell to one knee as she paced the room with Trynt. That ended her self-imposed ordeal.

Arial moved quickly to take the baby from her arms. Angor scooped his daughter up in his arms and cradled her against his broad chest, weeping in her hair as he carried her to her room. Seren knew nothing of that though. She had fallen asleep the moment Angor swept her off her feet.

When Seren finally woke the next day, she did so with a start, screaming, "Trynt! Trynt!" She ate sparingly, and then only because Angor and Arial forced her to. For the next two weeks, she doted on Trynt whenever she was allowed to be alone with him. When Arial carried the baby from room to room, Seren shadowed them, limping from the poulticed claw wound to her right calf.

It took nearly three weeks after the attack before Seren could get a full night's sleep. It took her another three weeks before she could concentrate enough to work on the assignments of her winter studies. Winter winds rattling the imperfectly repaired front door startled her.

Three months after the attack, Seren returned to the routine of the new school year. She attacked her studies with even more intensity than usual, but nightmares plagued her sporadically.

The yap of a town mongrel sometimes produced flashbacks of the attack, replaying in her mind the sounds of snarling wolves, of their claws and fangs digging into the nursery door. She stared into the distance at such times, oblivious to all else. If classmates asked her what was wrong, she replied, "Nothing," and forced a smile back on her face. She never mentioned the attack, never felt even a twinge of heroism for her actions. She only remembered how small, how weak she had felt in comparison to the monsters, how inadequate she would have been to protect her little brother had the wolves broken through the door. They would have killed him no matter what she did. That realization gripped her in its jaws every waking hour.

But the memory demon of that terrible day could no longer hide in the deep recesses of her mind and soul. Seren's barricade of silence that had protected it so well was now spider-webbed with cracks. The demon was vulnerable. The Readers had voiced its presence out loud, pointed directly at it. Now others knew it existed. The demon's power to torment one vulnerable little girl began withering under the understanding of Seren's friends and peers, under the tears of those who loved her.

"It was a terrible day for you, Seren," Taggart said. "We know this. Our hearts break for you even as we force such a terrible event into the light. We," the Reader emphasized with outstretched arms, "are your light. Your classmates, your teacher, your Readers. As terrible that day was for you, it was a day of triumph and victory as well."

"They . . . they almost killed Trynt," Seren stammered, her voice high, nearly a wail. "Almost killed him." She shuddered in remembrance, but saying the words aloud for the first time gave her the strength to look the Reader straight in the eye. She wiped her tears angrily away as she spoke. A gesture of defiance. *Anger at her tears.* Taggart thought. *A good sign. The start of healing.*

Still beside her, Alina and Mairin patted her shoulders, leaning down over the desk to whisper. "But they didn't, little warrior. They. . . Did. . . . Not! *Could* not! Because of you. You were there for your little brother."

Taggart crushed his own emotions. Doing what must be done. *Even with her parents' permission, this is tough.* He forced himself to echo those whispers aloud. "They didn't, little warrior, because Father Creator placed you exactly where you needed to be. Your *Nung-Cha* training gave you the strength and the reflexes to defend your little brother. Give Father Creator your gratitude for that. Your love for Trynt was the love expected from a sister. You demonstrated it with the strength in your arms, with your determination, with your courage. Know that. Remember that."

At that, Taggart gestured with both hands for the class to stand. As the children rose, Alina and Mairin gave the little girl a final pat to her shoulder before joining Taggart at the front of the class. "Courage and honor!" Taggart proclaimed loudly, reciting the ultimate Wraithian compliment, "courage and honor!" He bowed to Seren with an honor salute. Everyone else followed suit. Rising from his bow, Taggart smiled and began clapping his hands enthusiastically as he spoke. "Because of that day, Seren, you will have no better friend in your life than Trynt." The class joined him in applause.

"Because of that day," he said louder over the applause, "Trynt will have no greater friend in his life than his big sister." The applause of the class grew even louder, forcing Taggart to shout, "Much honor, little warrior! Much, *much* honor!" The entire class, Marin and Alina joined him word for word, applause for applause.

The applause continued until Seren rose from her desk, shyly raised her hand and smiled at everyone. The magnitude of what she had done began to pierce the darkness of knowing what *might* have happened had she not been there. "Thank . . . you," she said. "I . . . I love you all."

Alina and Taggart took Seren's "thank you" as permission to conclude their visit.

"Thank you for allowing us to visit your class, Lady Tanguy," Alina said with a formal bow to her daughter before addressing the class once more. "We eagerly look forward to your Reading next autumn."

Taggart joined her to honor salute the class one last time. "May Creator's peace go with you all," the Readers intoned. Rising from their bows, the children responded, "May His Great Hands protect you on your journey."

Leaving the classroom, the Kaynes waved good-bye, but could not help but making eye contact with Seren one last time. Taggart smiled and gave her a wink. The little girl smiled and wriggled her fingers in a playful good-bye. She would be fine. Eventually. The healing started today would continue. Her Readers would see to it.

Part Two:
The Gathering

"All hail…"

"This day, our mission is to gather seekers like ourselves."

"Are there any among you who would join us?"

—Traditional Reader Greeting

Rendezvous

“Thank you,” Blair said softly, shaking each Reader's hand once outside the classroom. “You've cleared up a mystery. No one knew. Poor little thing.”

“She has a long road yet,” Alina said, as they continued down the hallway. “She needs time to file the event properly in her mind. Exposing it was just the first step. She should also write about it. Not to share, necessarily, but to slay the demon that traumatic memories often become.”

“Yes, of course,” Blair agreed, “catharsis. I'll speak with Mairin. A personal essay would work, but in Seren's case, I think there is something better.”

“Which is?” Taggart asked.

“Poetry. She loves discovering underlying messages in classic verse. A poetry assignment might be a good second step in a day or so. But let us speak more of that later. We're here.”

At the end of the hall, a door on the right opened into the central, walled courtyard. Six paces outside the door, a ten-foot-high post supported a large bronze ship's bell. Against the west courtyard wall, knapsacks were neatly aligned. Each one carried flint and steel, an oiled canvas *rainer*, jerky, dried fruit, first-aid items, and a water-skin. Strapped to each was the weapon that Wraithians are taught to use since birth—the four-foot-long, single-edged long sword. Along that same wall, weapon racks of weathered gray cedar held assorted walking spears, javelins, and unstrung longbows.

Other weapon racks flanked the north gate, where the Reading Procession would exit. Here, shorter longbows, quivers of arrows, and walking spears suited to the children waited, as did two eight-foot-long walking spears reserved for the Kaynes.

The courtyard could easily hold a crowd of eight hundred. Today, less than fifty adults and children whispered in nervous anticipation around oak tables and benches. Eight children, their parents, and many grandparents awaited the arrival of the Readers.

Blair opened the door but did not announce the Kaynes. The group instantly quieted. With the Readers' first step into the open-air courtyard, the time spent there, the expanse itself, the adults, and the twelve-year-old Initiates created a unique world. Taggart and Alina walked hand in hand to the bell post as if they were all alone. They stopped, closed their eyes, and bowed their heads in silence. Those adults and children still seated rose immediately and joined the others in stances of attention. Robe hoods were thrown back and hats were doffed, as the group bowed their heads to join the Readers in silent meditation. Quietly, Blair returned inside.

Moments later, Alina pulled the bell rope and rang the bell four times, the formal greeting expected from a visitor to one's home. The group relaxed at the sound and stepped behind the children, maneuvering them into a single line facing the Readers. Inside the academy, classrooms across hallways emptied into classrooms with windows open to the courtyard. The jostling was obvious, but even more pointed was the respectful silence as over two hundred students ages seven to eighteen jockeyed for a good spot to watch the courtyard. The only thing more sacred to Wraithians than the event called Scroll Night, was the formal greeting of the year's Initiates.

"All hail the house," Taggart announced, his right hand raised in greeting. His rich baritone carried the traditional phrase easily across the expanse. "We are the Readers Taggart and Alina Kayne. This day, our mission is to gather seekers like ourselves." He and Alina walked toward the group as he spoke. Every adult already knew who they were and had heard the same words in their youth. The ritual words of greeting were ancient even before the Disappearance brought the Pelanjians to the New World of Wraithaven two thousand years before.

The adults intoned as one. "Welcome, Sir and Lady Kayne, Readers for our people. How might we assist your mission?"

"Are there any among you who would join us?" Alina asked in a clear, strong voice. She could never suppress a smile whenever she spoke the words. She loved this part of the Reading ceremony.

We call the Reading during Scroll Night a pivotal point for our youth, but this moment, this first greeting, is pivotal for all present.

Tears welled in the eyes of many of the men and women. Smiles of pride creased expectant faces. A few faces were more sober. The hands of parents patted the shoulders of the children as they waited their turn to answer Alina's simple question. The hands of grandparents patted the shoulders of *their* adult children in encouragement.

"Here . . . is . . . is one," the parents of a boy first in line said in unison, their words sticking ever so slightly with emotion.

"And who might this seeker be?" Taggart said, extending his right hand.

Shaking Taggart's hand as he bowed to the Kaynes, the stocky, black-haired boy responded as untold numbers of children had done in millennia past. He threw his shoulders back and recited clearly, "I am Marcus Riordan, Sir and Lady Kayne. The proud and loving son of the furniture makers, Killian and Eryn Riordan."

"Welcome, Marcus," Alina said, shaking the boy's hand. "Please join our mission."

After a quick hug from his parents, the boy picked up his knapsack and took his place at Alina's side. The simple act of walking away from his parents was as deliberate to the ceremony as it was heartfelt to everyone in the courtyard, as it was also to every pair of eyes that watched in silence through classroom windows.

The second set of parents responded. "Here is one."

"And who might this seeker be?" Taggart asked, as he would for each of the others waiting their turn.

"I am Leah Brenna, Sir and Lady Kayne," the willowy, blond girl answered with a bow and handshake with Taggart, "The proud and loving daughter of the tanners Cavan and Ailis Brenna."

"Welcome, Leah," Alina said. "Please join our mission."

The girl kissed her parents, slung her knapsack over one shoulder, and took her place next to Marcus. And so the ritual of greeting and initial separation went. Sons and daughters of stonemasons, potters, farmers, ranchers, goldsmiths, and sword smiths all waited their turn to step away from the life of a child and into the world of an adult.

When the last child, Brann Halwyn, son of the potters Lucas and Elsh, joined Alina, the mood of the group relaxed noticeably. Alina left the line of children to take her place beside her husband. "Thank you," she said, "for entrusting us with your wonderful children." She and Taggart bowed respectfully protracted honor bows to the parents and grandparents. The assembly replied in kind.

"Now then," Taggart said with an enthusiastic grin. "Let us applaud our newest seekers."

Grateful for the break in the solemnity of the ritual, the assembly responded with hearty applause, whistles, and whoops of joy. The two hundred students watching from the classrooms broke their silence with enthusiastic applause and with whoops of encouragement as well.

"By tradition," Taggart said in a deliberately casual voice, "we shall proceed in the Wraithian manner. Readings in ancient Pelanjia were simpler events. No dangerous wildlife prowled the home islands. Readers led Initiates unescorted to Scroll Night sites and returned three days later to a time of celebration.

"As Wraithians, we have to deal with wolf packs, bears, territorial stag bulls and Maker forbid—even the occasional wraith.

"Today, day one, we will hike eight miles to just outside of Big Calder Springs. We never camp right at the springs because of its attraction for wildlife.

"On day two, we will continue along the traditional path to the Reading Theater at the head of Last Trail Valley. We always take a short rest stop at the Kaynes farmstead seven miles from the theater. This time, however, we will also Gather the only missing member of our Reading, our granddaughter Tyra, who is home there recovering from a riding injury. Had she not been injured, she and her parents would be here at the academy today. The Reading takes place on the evening of day two, followed by the traditional celebration on day three."

Taggart's explanation was an important part of the greeting ritual. It reminded all of the origins of the Scroll Night Readings, yet indelibly stamped the difference between millennia past and the realities of the present.

Alina made sure that the Wraithian manner was in order. "Who speaks for the group? Are the Guardians assembled?"

"I do," Bodyn Marsali, the stonemason answered, "and yes, they are."

Bodyn then outlined how the children would be escorted to the Reading Theater. Traditionally, parents and grandparents served as armed Guardians, the grandparents being further distinguished as Elders.

"Eight Elders, including the Halwyrs, Riordans, Briacs, and the Berits, left yesterday by wagon and horseback to prepare the site. Ten more Elders will follow us: four by wagon, six on horseback. They will join the parents as additional flankers. Oran and Cailin Briac will take point today. On day two, we'll rotate at point every three hours. Your pack mare is already hitched to the supply wagon."

No Reading was held without wagons and a fair number of mounted riders. Readings were deliberately held in remote areas, with preferably at least a five-mile clear radius from a theater to the nearest settlement or homestead if possible. Yet, such remoteness required that Processions be well planned. Mounted riders were not only for emergencies. In some of Wraithaven's more dangerous regions, riders often took *extreme point* ahead of those on foot. Wagons carried survival rations, extra weapons and canvas shelters and could transport injured or sick if need be.

That aside, tradition declared that the three-day event be conducted on foot. Once the assembly left the academy grounds, Readers and their charges hiked as a single unit, using the time to get acquainted.

Those adults walking point, providing flank security, or following with the supply wagon and mounted riders would essentially disappear into the rugged, forested terrain. Guardians and riders do not speak or betray their positions in any way. Only if danger threatened the children would they show themselves. Even then, they would not speak, no matter how close their defensive perimeter might be.

"All seems well in order," Alina said. "Let us make ready."

The children slipped on their knapsacks as the adults made for the west wall. The adults quickly slipped sword-knapsacks on their backs and took up secondary weapons from the racks flanking the gate. War bows were strung.

Once everyone had adjusted their equipment, Alina walked back to the bell post. As point couple, the Briacs had already slipped away, breaking into a relaxed jog once past the courtyard wall to get further ahead. The parents and Elders who would take up flanking roles began moving through the north gate. There were no final waves or words of farewell between the Initiates and their Guardians. Only Alina spoke as she reached for the bell rope.

"By all means," she said, smiling, "let us begin." She rang the bell a full six times, the first gong being the signal for the fidgety students peering through the surrounding windows to let out a tremendous cheer.

The Twelves smiled and waved back at the applause, as each of their names was called out by the spectators. And then the traditional finale came, which sent the group toward the waiting mountainside on a high note.

A loud, metallic clanking began as every teacher and student above the age of twelve tapped an exposed dagger against the hand guard of their sheathed swords. Within seconds, the mass clanging took on a strong rhythm to match the chant that rose from over two hundred voices. "Burn the *wood*! Burn the *wood*! Burn the *wood*!"

In four days, when these twelve-year-olds return to complete the school year, they will wear very real steel swords. The wooden practice weapons currently sheathed across their backs will be burned the morning after the coming-of-age ceremony called Scroll Night.

20

Procession

The Procession group formed with Taggart in the lead and Alina assuming rear guard. Once past the manicured academy grounds, the trail became sublimely practical, created by centuries of traffic from human boot, from horse and oxen hoof, from wagon rim. Lacking the pavestone-defined perfection of Falcon's Aerie's boulevards, the wagon-narrow dirt road was the only link to the town for dozens of remote farmsteads and ranches carved out of the rugged terrain in Scimitar Province. Where the road could avoid deep ravines or major rock outcroppings, it did. Where it could not, it crossed upon lichen-encrusted stone bridges that had served for centuries. Where rolling meadow met ancient evergreen stands of dark timber, the road eased around trunk bases as wide across as a supply wagon. It challenged the stamina of all when the terrain rose or declined steeply, but even this served the Wraithian mindset. Physical exertion during one's Reading is considered an enhancement to the experience.

Taggart's long, effortless stride matched the rhythm of his oak walking spear as it touched the earth every few steps. The children kept silent until their shorter legs found their own rhythm.

The flank, point, and rear Guardians disappeared into the surrounding forest, never betraying their positions with so much as a snap of a broken twig. The assembly of children and Readers, however, was under no such restraint of silence.

During most Reading Processionals, questions from the children eventually break the ice. Less than two miles into the hike, the most common question came from Drystan Bradach, son of the vintners Ewan and Kiera.

"Sir Kayne," the boy said, "is it permissible to see a Dragon Master tattoo in its entirety?"

"It is," Taggart said. "Let us pause a moment." When Alina joined him, both Readers pushed the right sleeves of their mission robes past their elbows. The children drew close, inspecting the symbol of Wraithaven's most prestigious martial honor.

From middle knuckle to the wrist, a fanged and clawed dragon covered much of the back of the Readers' right hands. The long, sinuous tail of the beast coiled twice around the right wrist before spiraling around the forearm to end in a spiked club. Wrought in deep indigo, the detailing of claws, fanged jaws, and body scales was superb. Eyes, tongue and claws were subtly shaded in dark red.

"Do all Dragon Masters get tattooed?" Devyn Briac asked.

"It's not a requirement," Alina said, "but most eventually do. Those who intend to serve as Pickets when they get old enough, as Taggart and I did, wait to return from their Picket tour before taking the mark. Remember, a Picket on tour anywhere in the world must blend in with a local populace. Large tattoos draw attention. And questions," she added.

"They're the same," Seanna Berit noted, "in size and everything."

"Of course," Alina said. "Masters are masters. One's gender has little to do with skill, though in martial arts, males generally have more physical strength than females. Quinn, are not your parents, Corann and Briana, both master goldsmiths?"

"Yes, Lady Kayne, they are," the boy said, "but master goldsmiths are skilled in fine detailing, in the precise cutting and polishing of gemstones. Power is not needed as it is to attain Dragon Master rank in *Nung-Cha*."

"True," Taggart said, "brute power is not. The power of imagination *is*. So is the power to control the tools of their trade."

"Seanna," Alina said, "your father, Taran, is a master swordsmith, is he not?"

"Yes, Lady Kayne, he is."

"Are you aware that twenty years ago, he made our swords to commemorate our acceptance into the Society of Dragon Masters?"

"I know he has made special master swords before, ma'am, but I've never seen one. I help him in the forge sometimes, but never when he makes a master sword."

"Well then," Taggart said, "when we camp for the night, we will show you how a master craftsman combines the artistry of a goldsmith with the power of one who has mastered the working of steel. The dragons he engraved on our blades are true works of art. We consider ourselves honored by your father's skill. Until then, though, let us press on. The more difficult portion of this road still lies before us."

For the next few hours, the Readers and children questioned each other, exchanging personal details and experiences. How many sculptor apprentices did Taggart have? Who was Alina's mentor when she apprenticed to the Weaver's Guild? Who has been on their first mounted stag hunt? Who is the oldest of their siblings, and thus the first to experience a Reading?

A quarter mile from Big Calder Springs, the group came to an abrupt halt. On point, Oran and Cailin Briac sounded the triple whistle of the Twilight Shrike, signal of imminent danger.

The gray, crow-sized shrike had two unique habits. First, it impaled its prey, small rodents, amphibians, and insects still alive, on the two-inch-long thorns of crag sage bushes. Secondly, its territorial call, common throughout Wraithaven, was only heard at twilight. Thus, a natural sound to wildlife, became an excellent daytime danger signal for human beings.

Moments later, as the Briacs broke out of the tree line a hundred paces ahead, Taggart and Alina knew real danger lurked ahead. Oran approached in a low, crouching gait, holding his now unsheathed walking spear low in his right hand. Sixteen inches of double-edged steel blade glinted in the afternoon sun.

Cailin followed, imitating his low, crouching gait, but stopping every twenty paces or so to turn and cover their retreat from the tree line behind them. Her walking spear was strapped across her back next to her sword, but she held her powerful longbow at the ready, a heavy stag-killer arrow nocked to the string.

"Not good," Alina whispered. She gave a patting motion to the children behind her with her right hand. Instantly, the children stopped, pulled their bows from their backs, nocked arrows, and knelt in a tight defensive circle. Silently, each obeyed their training, focusing on their sector of the 360-degree perimeter as they formed it. Smiles and bright, cheerful eyes vanished with the danger call's first note. The young faces were set and grim. Eyes glinted hard, filled with resolve. Despite the spectacular, autumn-painted terrain, it was still . . . Wraithaven.

As to why the scouts had sounded the alarm, at fifty paces away, the mystery ended. Oran and Cailin stopped and finally stood up from their crouching sprint. They raised their right hands above their heads, forming them into claw shapes. They turned in place, to make sure the unseen flankers noticed, and just for good measure, whistled the danger call once more before dropping their arms.

The signal brought every Guardian in at a lope. Bows were pulled from shoulders. Arrows were nocked to bow strings. Spear sheaths were stripped from the blades and tucked into belts, all on the run. Guardians and Elders appeared like ghosts rising from the earth.

Waves of gooseflesh swept across Taggart's forearms as the claw sign summoned reinforcements. "No!" Taggart whispered as he stripped the leather sheath from his own walking spear and tucked it into his belt. "Anything but that!" Alina replaced her spear with the longbow slung across her back. She nocked a stag killer as she took her place at Taggart's side. The claw sign meant but one thing.

The ancient terror that had created the Wraithaven myth countless millennia ago lay directly in their path.

21

Legend

Oran pointed and made hard eye-contact with Taggart and Alina before dropping to one knee to brush an area of dirt free of stones and twigs with his left hand. Held vertically at his right side, Oran's once-pacific walking staff had now transformed by the exposed blade into an eight-foot-long weapon. Three paces away, Cailin stood with her back to him, silently scanning the forest from where they had just departed. Oran scratched a crude map in the dirt with a stick. Fear masked the faces of them both.

With the children now surrounded by a defensive ring of Guardians, the Readers moved quickly to meet the scouts.

"Haven't seen that sign for some time," Taggart whispered. "Are you sure?"

"Never saw one alive before," Oran said. "Just a partial skull and a few scattered bones on a stag hunt once when I was fourteen. But I'm sure."

"Here's the main pool," the scout said, scratching a large oval to represent the ten-pace-wide basin. "Fifty paces above, the springs pour out of a stone ridge in a double stream that converges here into the final stream emptying into the pool." Oran scratched one last figure to illustrate a large outcrop where the streams met as one. It's right under there," he said, pointing to the outcrop. "Even as huge as it is, I almost missed it."

The Kaynes recognized each detail of the crude map, having traveled the region on militia maneuvers, business trips, family visits, and Readings over the decades. The area near the outcrop remained in dappled shadow thanks to the dark timber and the large ferns that thrived in the perpetually moist soil around the springs.

"The fur is splotchy," Oran said, "gray and black and every shade in between. It blends so well with the shadows; we only saw it because Cailin noticed the white muzzle and the fangs."

The Readers let Oran talk. Unlike him, they *had* seen such creatures alive in the wild, had seen them kill. Both shuddered in recollection.

"We're lucky the wind is blowing upslope," Oran said with obvious tension in his voice. "Had it had been blowing from us down to the pool, we would have walked right into its ambush. I don't even want to *think* of what would have happened."

Nor did Taggart. The creature the Briacs had fortunately found before it had found them, was unparalleled in ferocity, the most dangerous predator on the planet.

To the long-extinct nomadic bands that once roamed the rolling prairies of ancient western Tripada ten thousand years ago, the creatures had inspired the Wraithaven legend. The region had never supported permanent human settlement, although it might have, save for the legend that grew around the mountain range that ultimately came to be known as the Shield.

Nomads then were of two basic types. Hunter-gatherer clans followed seasonal migrations of wild oxen, antelope, and ice deer. Herder clans followed emerging grasses to feed their shaggy-coated *stelnaks*, ancestors of current-era domestic goats.

The legend of Wraithaven was born in that surreal zone where sharp gray peaks spear through the soft, tan prairie swells like splintered bone shards through living flesh. To wanderers, the abrupt transition of prairie to steep, forested slope seemed fit only for gods. The dense forests clung to the land until the jagged peaks rose so far from the warmth of the earth that they brooded under eternal crowns of ice and snow and cloud. To such folk, the majestic Shield seemed more fortress than mountain range.

Yet, despite its vast expanse, the formidable Shield is a static thing, and while static things can inspire awe, even worship, it is movement that generates fear. Fear invades the human heart when that heart realizes that darkness and death are deliberately stalking it. And death is what the legendary fog-rivers of the Shield brought to those ancient nomads. They still do.

Except in deep winter, thick, white rivers of fog stream down from the towering peaks as the earth cools at eventide. They flow like the phantom serpents that ancient story-songs and story-dances once described. They collide and boil into each other in the foothills-to-prairie zones, blinding the human eye, swallowing even the most vigorous campfire. There, in that great sea of white, the human mind began to invent what it did not understand.

Death inhabited the fog-rivers and left no evidence, save for obscene splashes of blood made visible once the fog streamed back upslope upon the warming air currents of the new dawn. Survivors tried in vain to explain what they *thought* they had seen.

As generational recounts acquired embellishment over the centuries, the fog-rivers manifested into demon-gods posted to guard the Shield against human trespassers. To the logic of ancient storytellers, if one's clan avoided the Shield, the fog-rivers would not flow down from the peaks. They would not flow if trespassers did not draw attention to themselves by wandering too close to the Shield.

Thus, no clan had ever ventured *inside* the towering Shield. Centuries upon centuries amplified the terror. The region from the base of the great peaks eastward became devoid of human life. Fear pushed the nomads ever eastward until only a relatively narrow belt of land along the eastern coast of the huge continent held permanent tribal settlements. For over ten thousand years, the western eighty-five percent of Tripada past Lost River seethed with a mythical life of its own. To Tripada's indigenous humans, the forbidden region became the Desolate.

As for what inhabited the eerie *fog-rivers of the gods* to slay beast and human alike, that grew in the telling as well. Legends passed orally, the story-dances around tribal campfires, and cave art of the clans all described *mist demons*.

It mattered not, the stories declared, whether a lone hunter or an entire clan trespassed. Once the dense fog enveloped one's camp, the slaying began. Knife-long claws flashed out of the dense gloom, slaying herd beast, child, or the strongest warrior with equal impunity. The talons were the color of the fog itself, things of white and gray and shadow, and they shredded flesh and bone and leather armor with inhuman power. It was only when the demons claimed their prey that they showed their faces.

Huge, wide-set eyes appeared first, glowing pale green in a campfire's fog-muted light. Next, a snarling, mist-white muzzle transformed from mist-being into a solid, physical terror. The huge maw opened, brandishing two outlandish fangs as long as swords. In a heartbeat, the horror appeared, speared those grotesque fangs into the victim, and disappeared back into the fog with its prey.

On such details all renditions of the night terrors agreed. Over time, the legend found other continents, other civilizations, until Wraithaven became humanity's oldest myth, staining the fabric of the human soul planet-wide.

Over the centuries, the demons became evil spirits—*wraiths*. The name of the uninhabited mountain range, however, nearly disappeared from the memory of humankind. The term *Shield* appeared in only the most obscure surviving texts.

What did survive over the millennia, what did not fade from the human tongue and psyche, was the name *Wraithaven*.

22

When Monarchs Collide

*A*nd here we are, Taggart thought, *facing the same legendary horror that terrified folk ten thousand years ago. The tribes are long gone, yet the legend remains. The reason for its creation remains. Amazing.*

Despite Taggart's objections, Oran and Cailin led the Readers back to where they had first whistled the danger signal.

"Stay with your son," Taggart whispered. "We know the springs."

"Devyn is safe," Oran replied. "Nothing will get through that perimeter."

"He's Scimitarian," Cailin whispered, ending the discussion.

Oran nodded in terse agreement. The matter was settled. Wraithians take great pride in their home provinces. Residents of *Scimitar* believe themselves tougher and stronger than those of neighboring North Gale, who believe the same of themselves. Such provincial pride among the eleven provinces makes competitions in sports or militia maneuvers often quite *vigorous*.

Oran was right enough about the perimeter though. Any attempt by man or beast to break that ring of armed parents and grandparents would fail. The four teamsters had closed with the group, hobbled their team, and now stood atop the wagon, bows ready. The six mounted Guardians took positions well outside the perimeter, two armed with bows, four with twelve-foot-long bear lances.

As the scouts and Readers low-crawled through the tan meadow grass to disappear inside the tree line, the silence from the perimeter was almost tangible. Every eye focused, every ear listened . . . for anything.

Fifty paces inside the wood line, the shallow vale sheltering the springs sloped down to overlook the main pool of Big Calder.

Less than a hundred paces in any direction, the surrounding tightly packed evergreens gave the place a claustrophobic air. High on the slope, multiple year-round springs gurgled around tree roots and rocks before ultimately emptying into the largest pool below. At mid-slope, half hidden by the dark, shadowy ferns, lay the large boulder next to the granite outcrop the size of two supply wagons. The Procession road swept right of the main pool before meandering down through the trees.

Dozens of game trails threading through the forest to the pool proved why human travelers avoided camping there. The dense timber, tall ferns, and boulders provided perfect ambush sites for predators to take thirsty prey. Such as today.

Even knowing where to look, thanks to Oran's earlier map, the Kaynes had to strain to see what lay beneath the granite outcrop. Had the creature not adjusted its ambush crouch, it would have been virtually impossible to distinguish it from the dappled ferns and shadows. But once the eye caught it, the brain refused to lose it.

The great predator had been known by many names in the two thousand years since Pelanjian boots had first marred the pristine soil of the New World. "Crag lion," "ice cat," and "saber-tooth" were all adequate descriptions one way or another. The immense cats prowled above the timberline most of the year, shadowing the glacier regions to feed upon the curl-horned sheep or the black-antlered deer there. But it was the beast's eons-engraved instinct to hunt within Wraithaven's eerie fog-rivers that inspired the ever-practical Wraithians to simply call them, "wraiths."

Standing on all fours, the cat's thickly muscled, humped shoulders would have reached Taggart at mid-chest. From the tip of the snow-white muzzle to the bobtail on the low hindquarters, the creature measured nearly eleven feet long. Females averaged nearly eight hundred pounds, while mature males often weighed well over fifteen hundred. This eight-year-old male was in his prime. Evidence of the animal's savage life was clawed in grotesque white scar tissue along the otherwise handsome pelt of mottled gray, ivory, and shadow black.

The retractable claws were as long as assassins' daggers, but everything about the beast, its size, the tense musculature writhing under the pelt, the glaring yellow eyes, all paled in comparison to the great incisors. Twin ivory fangs swept down from the muzzle like scimitars. As thick as a man's wrist at the base, they bore a serrated edge along the back side. No other creature on the planet possessed more fearsome killing weapons. Wraiths killed by delivering a neck-crushing blow from its razor-clawed front paws or by driving the dagger-fangs through a victim's throat.

To the four observers, the choice was obvious. The Procession must backtrack to provide miles of separation from this danger, using an alternate trail system. Silence from the Guardians would still be maintained during the detour, but they would assume closer flanking positions and remain in sight. The tactic would change the mood of the trek, certainly, but it would create a unique memory of this Reading as well.

A sudden, preparatory move by the cat stopped the Kaynes and the Briacs from back-crawling away from the overlook. A faint, musky scent rode the breeze past the concealed wraith, before wafting up to the humans on watch.

The pungent odor suggested wallow mud and rank animal sweat tinged with blood, even a hint of decay. Yet as faint as the scent was to the human nostrils, it thoroughly energized the great predator. The cat kept low, but immediately shifted to align with one of the lower trails weaving through the forest. The great claws unsheathed, digging for better purchase in the damp soil. Fern fronds broke up the outline of the huge head. The ears twisted to hone in on the trail. An unidentified creature was approaching the pool.

A huge, shadowy mass moved deep inside the dark timber. Patches of dark brown passed momentarily across the narrow spaces between the tightly spaced evergreens. Taggart thought first of the grizzled, silvertip bears that roamed hereabouts, but the shape did not amble as if on a scent trail. Immense, hump-backed mountain bison were found at most elevations in all eleven provinces, but this shape did not move like a random grazer.

Whatever it was, there was no subtlety in its approach. The shape moved with challenge, with aggression. In the hushed silence, twigs and fallen branches snapped, crushed by heavy hooves—not paws.

Just before stepping into view, the creature abruptly whirled to attack a low scrub juniper. Heavy antlers stabbed into the unfortunate little evergreen. Stones clacked loudly as driving hooves dislodged them. Explosive, angry snorting accompanied the pointless attack. Taggart knew immediately what it was.

Waves of tension rippled under the wraith's pelt. The creature rose to spring, but nervously settled back low to await the appearance of the prey. The wind favored the cat, but it could barely hold itself in check. It was as infused with power as an arrow drawn full length on a strong bow.

Moments later, an immense bull stag burst from the shadows less than sixty paces from the hidden wraith. Driven nearly insane by the fires of his kind's annual rut, the bull was fifteen hundred lean pounds of muscle and sinew.

Every autumn the territorial stag bulls become Wraithhaven's second-most dangerous creatures, often fighting each other to the death for the right to gather harems of stag cows. Smaller sub-species existed on other continents, where the term "stag" referred to males only. Pelanjian explorers had made no such distinction, labeling the entire species "stags," while referring to the males as "bulls" and the females as "cows."

Like the cat, the seven-year-old bull was in his prime. Yet, despite the danger it represented, Taggart's sculptor's soul admired the majestic creature. Six feet high at the shoulders, the bull wore a magnificent antler crown of rock-sharpened bone. Two dark-brown main beams sprouted from his skullcap to sweep back toward his withers. Over seven feet in length, each main beam flaunted eight ivory-tipped tines the length of axe handles. Four vicious-looking tines speared straight out above the creature's eyes before hooking upwards. Wraithian hunters called them "wolf killer" tines for good reason. All four, plus the next two on each main beam, were stained with fresh blood. Something that resembled nearly twelve feet of pale, wet rope coiled obscenely around the tines of the left antler. Taggart recognized it as a length of intestine torn from the body of a recent challenger.

This bull was a seasoned veteran of such challenges and was as combat-scarred as the wraith. Jagged streaks of white scar tissue marred the bull's muzzle and thick neck on both sides, even extending past his heavily muscled shoulders.

Both creatures ruled as unmerciful tyrants in their respective domains, recognizing no other living thing as their superiors. They ruled. Period. Yet, of the two, only the great cat did so every day of its life. The stag, when not beset by the hormonal flames licking at its brain and its fight-or-flight sense during the two brief months of the annual rut, behaved as any herbivore. The sound of a falling branch, a dislodged stone, or the faintest scent of danger would send this creature into flight. But not today. On this day alone, this bull had crippled a smaller bull, and had slain a second challenger nearly as huge as himself. For the remaining weeks of the rut, no perceived challenge would go unanswered. By *anything*!

That became evident less than thirty paces from the pool, as an errant breeze swirled a faint scent of the waiting cat past his nostrils. The bull stopped in mid-stride. The hackles along his neck and shoulders rose threateningly. He stamped his front hooves in annoyance. His nostrils flared as he lowered his head for attack. His eyes glared with fury. A second breeze repeated the scent.

The bull lost all semblance of control. He shook his rack of bone weaponry and pawed the earth in the threat display of his kind, bellowed a deep-pitched roar of challenge to the unseen predator. The bull's hot breath hurtled forth as an exploding fog in the crisp autumn air.

The challenge severed the last of the wraith's patience. With a screaming roar, the cat launched from the shadows like an arrow shot from a war bow. The attack was a lightning-like blur to the watching humans, but even so, they noted a flaw in its execution. The cat was wounded. His left front leg had been ripped to the bone from just above the shoulder socket past the first joint of the foreleg. Weeks old and healing poorly, the injury explained the cat's presence at this lower elevation.

The fog-rivers flowed, but they did so currently only as thin streamers. They would thicken over the coming days, and that would provoke the wraiths to follow them. When the fog-rivers were thin, though, the huge predators remained above timberline to hunt. That was not an option for this cat. His wounds had prevented him from hunting the nimble sheep, deer, and goats of the upper realm. A half-ton wraith required a large amount of meat every few days to survive. This cat was now into his fifth week without meat of any kind, having missed a dozen kills in that time. Gnawing hunger pangs drove him mad. Starvation had dropped his normal fifteen-hundred-pound bodyweight by three hundred pounds.

Yet, even wounded, his initial leap was a perfect blur of speed. Upon landing, the leg faltered slightly, but held well enough for the longer second leap. The leg still held on the second landing and the launch of the third leap. At the third landing, the cat would launch upon the back of the fleeing stag, a proven tactic when hunting such prey.

But the shock of that landing proved too much for the injured leg. The bone did not break, but the damaged tendons could not bear the force of twelve hundred pounds of enraged wraith attacking at top speed. The left shoulder collapsed. In stunned surprise, the enormous carnivore somersaulted in a furious cloud of dust and forest detritus.

The cat knew a full heartbeat of confusion as earth blurred into sky in his graceless roll. His rage was immeasurable. The stabbing agony of starvation, the proximity of this meat, the pain of his wound, all combined with the indignity of his body failing him at this supreme moment. His roar of frustration echoed back over the children and those manning the perimeter around them. In mid-scream—in mid-roll—the upended cat was met by the full-speed charge of the prey that should have fled at his first scent.

The battle-ready stag's crown of bloody, sharpened bone smashed full-bore into the cat's snarling face and injured left leg. With a vicious twist of his powerful neck, the bull raked his antler tines along the left ribcage of the wraith, tearing open long, hideous wounds. Another furious thrust picked the cat fully off the ground even as he clawed savagely at the unfeeling bone sabers that sought to impale him. The charging, bellowing bull upended the screaming, struggling cat for the second time in its life, tossing him to one side, although his knees buckled in the process.

The instincts of both combatants were in full flame. The cat instantly righted himself and crouched low. The bull immediately launched a second charge. Taut with bloodlust, the cat was ready. With a blur, the cat feinted to his left. The bull veered to impale his shifting enemy, leaving his thick neck exposed to the cat at last.

Taggart's vivid imagination froze the epic battle into a singular vision. *Monarchs*, he mused. *I'll title the piece "Monarchs." Done in white marble, I think. Full size certainly to capture the fury, the magnificence of such superb creatures.*

His mind registered every detail: the whiskers flaring from the wraith's ridged and snarling muzzle, the gaping jaws brandishing the great canines. The musculature of the bull, writhing like grotesque iron serpents from neck to shoulder to flank. The antler-weapons spearing for the cat, driven by instinctive hatred of this ancient enemy.

The cat rose on its haunches to meet the charge. The huge right paw rose higher than a man, poised to slay this ancestral prey. *Descending out of the gathering fog enveloping a nomadic camp, slaying herd beasts, ancient warriors, or children equally as the legends declared.* Taggart imagined ancient tribes venturing too near the Shield, imagined how such a paw must have looked flashing out of that dense white river of Wraithfall.

The killing blow was unstoppable. The bull was doomed. Save for the capriciousness of fate. Save for the instincts of wraiths.

Untold thousands of wraith generations had perfected the killing technique. The great cat pushed forward with its hind legs as the right front paw flashed down toward the bull's neck. But the power of the killing blow was enhanced even more when the left front paw speared its claws into the earth, a final foundation melding speed, power, and twelve hundred pounds of muscle into a single bone-crushing impact. He obeyed instinct.

The instant the wraith's left paw hit the forest loam; a bolt of white-hot agony lanced from his re-injured left shoulder directly into the brain of the furious cat. The torn ligaments and muscle tissue could take no more. His second attack was over the instant it began. The wraith's roar of triumph transformed into a high-pitched shriek of pain as he backpedaled to flee. The bull would not be denied his victory. The wolf killer tines speared the chest and snarling muzzle of the half-upright, retreating cat.

Instinctively, the wounded predator's good right paw flashed out in a defensive slash. The blow was half power at best, more slap than killing strike. Even so, the claws raked deep, bloody furrows along the length of the stag's neck, literally driving the head of the bull into the earth. Momentum somersaulted the bull's huge body atop the fleeing cat, sending even more scathing waves of pain through him. That blow ended the battle.

In all his seasonal battles for dominance, this stag monarch had never been defeated, never been overpowered by another bull, never been driven to his knees and upended. He had always been the strongest, the most cunning, and the most savage in any contest until this day. This lucky day. Yet, just as the wraith's painful wounds had overpowered his agony of starvation, this tremendous blow drove the combative fire from the great bull.

The bull recovered quickly and reverted to his normal survival state. His great hooves thundered against the earth as he fled back along the same forest trail that had brought him.

The cat did not pursue; indeed, *could* not. He simply snarled at the fleeing stag as if the prey had meant nothing. Chest heaving from the battle, he tried to lick his wounds, but pain prevented him from reaching the major ones on his left side. For a few moments, he licked a few of the newest ones on his chest and left leg but stopped suddenly to raise his muzzle to the breeze still wafting from downslope. He craned his neck to better taste the scents, to collect and register them in his brain.

The scents only teased the giant cat at first, until his brain absorbed them, recognized them, and decided to follow them. With his left paw held off the ground as if in a sling, he abandoned the churned earth of the battlefield to take the easiest path toward the new scents—the well-worn Procession road. Even with only three good legs, he could travel faster than a human could along such an obstacle-free trail, and many hours, many *hunting* hours, remained well after sundown.

As the predator disappeared down the road twisting through the dark timber, the four observers arose to head back to the others.

"Last blow probably ended the stag's season," Taggart said.

"Aye," Oran said. "He's had his last fight, maybe his last female for the year."

"The season isn't typically over for a few more weeks, though," Cailin said. "He could still recover enough to get back into the rhythm of things. Most likely, if he does, he won't be so . . . ."

"Energetic?" Alina finished. The four chuckled at that.
"The cat is a different story," Taggart said. "He's starving because of that old wound. Hunger pangs are pushing the pain of his injuries aside."

"What about the Procession?" Oran asked. "Do we backtrack? Take an alternate route?"

"We'll put it to a vote," Taggart said, "but I say proceed as is. The stag wants no more of this place, that's certain, and the cat is on another scent trail."

"Besides," Alina added, "when taking this route, we always camp away from the springs for just this reason. Where the perimeter is right now is close to where we normally make camp the first day anyway. We should stick to the original plan."

Every Reading Procession in Wraithaven follows the same tradition. Days one and two, the Procession days, gather the twelve-year-old Initiates. Meals for Initiates and Guardians alike those days are cold—jerky, dried fruit, cheese, and bread without a campfire. Initiates and Readers eat together, while the Guardians do so out of sight. When the children bed down at dark, the Guardians move in closer to stand fifty-percent watches—meaning that every other adult is either awake or asleep in two-hour rotations.

On the second evening, the Readers light a single campfire for the Reading. The Guardians remain in the darkness, ensuring that nothing disturbs the event.

The morning of the third day, the Guardians reunite with their children to congratulate them, to feast on a sumptuous, *hot* breakfast, and to burn their wooden swords in the traditional coming-of-age ceremony.

"We'll stay much closer to the children this night, I'd think," Oran said. "They might actually have to see us."

"No harm there," Taggart said, "given the circumstances."

Despite his wounds—old and new—the wraith kept a brisk pace down the road. Instinctively, he would have avoided such a smooth, open path so devoid of cover. Exposure made him nervous, but thus far, none of the hated Two Legs, or their horse- or oxen-drawn wagons used the road. What overpowered his instinct for concealment was the plethora of scents wafting from downslope, promising him warm flesh swimming in hot, rich blood. They filled his nostrils with unprecedented intensity, for he had never experienced such prolonged starvation before.

With every additional mile further from the site of his battle with the stag, the new scents grew stronger. Memories of the battle faded with each step closer to quenching the fire in his belly. Only the scents of the Two Legs and the myriad creatures that herded with them on the Kayne farm mattered. Home to Taggart and Alina's son Baran and his wife, Leah, the farm exuded two scents in particular that carried to the fast-closing predator.

One was that of a prey animal known as a Swift-Runner to the cat clan—a superb hunter-mount bred from an ancient line of champions, the stallion named Shadow. The other was that of the wraith clan's only true enemy, a female of the Two Leg clan. This enemy was the last twelve-year-old the Procession would gather—Taggart and Alina's granddaughter Tyra.

23

Hunters

"Twelve arrows left, Shadow," twelve-year-old Tyra Kayne said, leaning in her saddle to pat her gray stallion's thick, arching neck. "Twelve targets before supper."

Tall, even for a Wraithian her age, the girl was destined to reach at least the height of her mother, Leah, just under six feet, perhaps a bit more thanks to her father, Baran, at six feet, three inches. Tyra favored her mother the most, though, with the same long, slender legs, arresting green eyes, and shoulder-length light-brown hair that tended to honey-streak in the summer sun. Still willowy, genetics promised to bless her with a few more pounds of muscle than Leah, thanks again to Baran's wide-shouldered brawn.

Horse and rider had been training for over two hours on the five-acre hunter's course Baran had built for her. As always, Baran signaled to Tyra that it was time to stop practice by placing a lit oil lantern atop the corner corral post at the northeast corner of the main hay barn.

The course had few rocks or tree stumps, but still was not grazing-pasture smooth. Baran had designed gentle hills and shallow swales into the course to better prepare Tyra and her mount for Wraithaven's demanding mounted archery tournaments. Thus far, Tyra and Shadow had won all six regional, pre-Reading competitions they had entered. Post-Reading competitions ages thirteen through seventeen would be more difficult. Master Drills—national adult competitions—ages eighteen to one hundred, followed, reaching insane levels of stamina and complexity.

The girl's passion for competition explained her presence on the Kayne homestead today. A hard fall during practice the week before had injured her right knee and ankle. Bed rest, followed by crutches, finally allowed the bored-to-tears rider to take seat aboard her beloved Shadow once again.

She walked with barely a limp now, but with her Reading only a day away, her parents had allowed her to skip the last days of school. Had she not fallen, she and her parents would have joined the Reading procession at the academy. They would have taken the alternate route to the Reading site, shorter by three miles. Now, she would be gathered in the traditional, house-to-house manner and follow the centuries-old route that swept past the Kayne ranch and on toward Last Mission Valley.

Yet, as important as the Reading was to her, Tyra focused today on the course targets that challenged her more with each practice run.

The twelve targets were arrayed near railed hurdles, behind strategically placed boulders, or within clumps of bushes growing along the stream that meandered through the pasture. A few even twisted in the wind, hung by hemp cords from low branches of the flame maples that dotted the course. The last two were the smallest—and the hardest. Simple oak posts, four feet high and as thick as a man's forearm, stood on opposite banks of the stream at the last hurdle. Number eleven stood on the left side of the path just before the hurdle. Number twelve was on the opposite bank, and to the right *after* the hurdle. Each target was a knot the size of a man's thumb. To complete a perfect run, Tyra had to fire one arrow with Shadow at a gallop *before* the jump, then re-nock to fire a second in mid-air as Shadow cleared the obstacle. She had not hit both targets all day.

Tyra glanced at Staghorn Peak to the west, gauging her time left. The sun caressed the slope at timberline, and darkness fell quickly here. Her father's lantern meant she had barely enough time for one last run. Then she would lead Shadow to his stall, grab the lantern to signal that she was finished, and head back into the barn to groom Shadow for the night. With luck, her parents might even give her a hand.

Nocking an arrow for the first target, and gripping a second vertically against the bow's grip, the girl touched the big stallion's flanks with her heels and whispered near his left ear, "Go, Shadow! Go!" The well-trained mount bolted from the starting point as if his life depended upon it.

The huge saber-toothed cat limped steadily downslope toward the domain of the Two Legs. That he was so near to the repulsive, deadly little creatures proved his desperate hunger. Over the millennia, wraiths had learned to avoid the Two Legs. They were weak in comparison to the cat's normal prey: the thick-bodied, curl-horned sheep of the timberline, the black-antlered deer of the mid-slopes, or the powerful stags that grazed at all elevations. Unarmed, Two Legs were as easy to kill as stag calves, but the slaying of one of their number always brought armed packs of them on the trail of retaliation.

In that regard, Two-Leg packs were more savage than stag bulls during the rut. Once on the trail of the killer of one of their own, the Two-Leg packs killed every cat they found: males, females, even cubs in their dens. The savage, territorial nature of the great cats was enough in and of itself to keep the species, numbers low, but confrontations with Wraithian hunters over the centuries had driven them to the status of "rarely sighted." Had the immense predators not preferred to prowl the inaccessible glacier regions, they would have been hunted to extinction centuries before.

At full gallop, Shadow was perfectly attuned to each subtle nudge of Tyra's knee or foot, by each shift of her weight. To him, each touch, each shift, each whispered word was a command to execute or to anticipate, to slow down or to speed up, to jump, or to race the wind. No other rider alive could so blend with the rhythm of this mount. So it is with all mounts and riders who bond as completely as these two had.

From the day of his birth in the Kayne barn, the then six-year-old Tyra had loved him, playing with him from the day the beautiful little colt could walk. She loved the white blaze down his face, and the four white knee stockings that emphasized the dark gray of his coat. She had gamboled with him in the pasture like a colt herself. In turn, the now six-year-old Shadow still followed her around the Kayne ranch like a puppy.

On a low hill, the great cat crouched within the shadow cast by a large, tan boulder and a prone, winter-slain spruce, weathered gray and denuded of bark and needles by three brutal winters. The hill overlooked Tyra's course a few hundred yards away, but it was also within sight of the Kayne farmhouse.

The failed attack on the stag had drained the predator badly. His debilitating wounds had come from a she-cat the month before. Hunger now lanced his belly like malignant, twisting thorns. Even in times of plenty, the notoriously short-tempered cats needed little provocation to ignite their rage. The unfamiliar pain of starvation had driven this cat to the edge of his control.

The light breeze wafting from the barn and pasture was perfect for an attack. There was ample prey to bring down here, even in his wounded condition. The scent of a dozen milk calves corralled inside the barn mingled with the scent of chickens foraging near the large open double doors. The scent of a few free-ranging goats competed with the scent of mature cattle in the railed pasture beyond the barn. The repugnant scent of his kind's hereditary enemies, the Two Legs, polluted the cleaner prey scents, but above them all, he focused on the heady scent of the dark Swift Runner.

The stallion was tired after so much training. Flecks of foam flew from his great, straining shoulders and powerful neck—undeniable prey signals to the waiting predator. Slaying such a tired beast would be much easier than fighting a rut-crazed stag bull in his prime.

Leaning low over Shadow's straining neck, Tyra nocked her ninth arrow, drew quickly and fired at the target low and to her left, barely visible behind a large boulder. Shadow was at a full gallop, but not at full speed—yet. The solid *thunk* of her bodkin point told her she had scored nine-for-nine this run. Still low in the saddle, she reached to the quiver across her back, her father's words whispering in her mind.

Stay low in combat, Tyra. Be a small target. Shadow needs you alive!

She nocked the tenth arrow, her body still low and to the left of Shadow's neck. His great nostrils flared with each explosive breath, with each thunderous hammer of his hooves against the earth. For her, he would run until his last heartbeat. For her, he would fly. She had but to ask.

The tenth target, a hand-sized plaque, hung head high from a maple branch by a single hemp cord. Tyra rose quickly upright in the saddle and fired.

An errant gust of wind twisted the target the instant she released the bow string. The arrow flew past the target without even nicking it—a clear miss. "Curse you, damned wind!" she screamed, then immediately tried to force her disappointment aside.

Missed targets don't exist! Only the next one does!

She dug her heels into Shadow's flanks, sending him to near top speed. In one smooth motion, the girl dropped the reins across the saddle horn, emptied her quiver of its two last arrows, grasping one against the bow grip, while nocking the other upon the arrow rest. Her green eyes blazed with fury for missing the last target, but with even more ferocity to kill the last two. She held to Shadow with knees, feet, and balance only now. The jump and both targets would be taken with hands free of everything but her bow and arrows.

"Fly, Shadow! Fly!" she shouted as he thundered toward the eleventh target, low and left of the five-foot-high rail fence. She drew her bow hard, angrily, and fired straight into the knot before Shadow even slowed to make the jump over rail and stream.

By the time Shadow left the ground for the jump, Tyra had nocked the last arrow, twisted to the right, and drawn the bow to the corner of her mouth. The twelfth target, low and to her right on the opposite bank, had to be taken while Shadow was airborne. The shock of landing would ruin the shot.

The great stallion cleared the top rail as if it was his first jump of the day instead of the last. Tyra's arrow flew from her bow, a gray streak propelled by her intensity, enslaved upon its course by the sheer force of her will. The last thing she saw before she grasped the reins again and yelled in triumph was the arrow slamming into the post, a thumb's width from the knot.

24

Trapped

For a quarter-hour, Tyra trotted Shadow between the barn and the course, allowing him to cool down and regain his breath. "You have wings, my beautiful giant," she said, "wings! No steed in Wraithaven can match you. I love you, Great One."

At the corner post holding the lantern, she was all smiles as she waved to Baran and Leah, watching from the stone porch.

"She must have nailed the last two," Baran said, waving back with Leah.

"She's better than I was at that age," Leah beamed, "and Shadow is twice the mount that I ever rode."

True enough, Baran thought. *But Tyra has a long way to go to equal her mother's three national championships before the age of twenty-two.*

"Good days," she said.

"So are these," he said, stepping behind her, wrapping his thick arms around her waist, and nuzzling her neck.

Leah loved the feel of his sturdy embrace, the seemingly impossible tenderness such a broad-shouldered man could exhibit.

"Let's help her with Shadow tonight," came her soft whisper. "Then a quick dinner and off to bed."

"A very quick dinner," he chuckled, meeting her gentle mouth with his.

The cat remained still as the prey with the Two Leg on its back trotted slower and in ever-smaller circles, yet still hundreds of yards away. Frustration at seeing such easy meat so close pushed him to the breaking point. The impulse to shriek in rage and charge for the Swift Runner threatened him with every heartbeat. Piercing shards of hunger sent waves of agony through his immense body, but the discipline of the consummate hunter held him in check. *Barely*. The Swift Runner would escape if he attacked across so much open ground, even if he had not been wounded.

The lengthening shadows of the rapidly descending evening helped to settle him into the attack-state. Beyond his pain and injury, the habitually nocturnal creature felt exposed, and of all things, vulnerable. In the desolate, slate-gray regions above timberline, the gray, white, and black splotches of their fur made wraiths virtually invisible against the lichen-crowned boulders and remaining patches of snow. So unfit for humans, the windswept realm virtually guarantees minimal contact between Wraithaven's two top predators.

Only the phenomenon known as Wraithfall lures the great cats into patterns of behavior most likely to bring human and cat together. Year round, except in deep winter, dense fogbanks form in the valleys of Wraithaven's rugged mountains. Each morning, as sunrise warms the earth, the shrouds of white tear into smaller patches of fog and float ghostlike up through the forested slopes. Above timberline, the fog collects again into dense cloud banks that often hide the peaks.

As the earth cools at sunset, the process reverses. The cloud banks lose cohesion and pour like low streamers of white smoke down through the slopes to resettle again in the valleys.

For millennia, the cats have used their mottled coloration and the eerie movements of Wraithfall to deadly advantage. As the fog patches stream downslope in the evening, they are accompanied by the most savage predators ever known to humankind. As the patches rise in the morning, the nocturnal hunters follow.

Wraithfall, and the giant killers that hunted within it, were, in fact, the reasons that Wraithaven was taboo long before the Pelanjians came. The deadly combination of weather phenomenon and huge predators extinct on every other continent except Tripada became the seeds of the Wraithaven legend. Nomads who survived Wraithfall began telling, singing, and dancing their memories of the white river horrors. The demonic long fangs that materialized from within the fog to kill with impunity became the seeds of legend.

Tyra dismounted to pat Shadow's neck and shoulders. He breathed normally now and nuzzled her in return. Reins in hand, she led the stallion through the large double back doors of the barn, then into his stall before hurrying down the length of the barn to collect the lantern waiting on the post. Tyra noticed her father kneeling next to her mother on the porch as he prepared to light another lantern.

Good, she thought. *I'll have help tonight.*

The ears of the great cat swiveled toward the barn. The creak of Shadow's tack carried back to him, as did the nervous clucks of two hens moving quickly out of the way of the tired stallion's hooves. Pigeons fluttered softly into the open hayloft above the door, cooing as they settled to roost for the night. The high-pitched squeaking of the Two Leg grated as abrasively upon his sensitive hearing as the shrill alarm whistle of a timberline marmot did.

Saliva pooled under his chin, triggered by the scent of the tired Swift Runner and by a similar scent of weakness emanating from the smaller Two Leg. The two creatures entered what was to the cat a great hill and den entrance. He would kill them both inside as he had slain the fully grown silvertip bear trapped in its hibernation den that spring. The month before, he had slain two half-grown wraith cubs cowering in their den awaiting the return of their mother out hunting. For two days, he had fed upon them.

Then the big female returned.

This male had never been as close to death as when the she-cat attacked him inside her den. He outweighed her by four hundred pounds, but her ferocity made up for that. There was no scale to judge the savagery of the battle. Saber fangs slashed deep, hooked claws tore into snarling, screaming faces, into flanks and bellies and throats. The fight was a blur of unparalleled ferocity inside the den. Once the combatants spilled outside, the deadly battle became a dizzying cloud of torn fur and blood and late-summer dust.

In the end, he had wounded her more grievously than she had him, though the difference was not obvious until he managed to limp away. As the moon rose past the silhouetted trees that night, a final spasm of pain washed over the she-cat. She died less than a body length from the remains of her cubs.

His memories of the epic battle were but vague images now. Only this prey mattered, only this promise of living meat. He snarled a low, rumbling growl and raised his head a bit higher. He extended his huge right foreleg slowly. Muscles writhed under the fur. Dagger-length claws unsheathed, then reflexively dug into the rocky soil of the hill. He rose to a higher crouch but did not scream and charge at this prey as he had the stag bull.

Just as Baran lit the second lantern, Leah's right hand squeezed his left shoulder—a signal, not a loving touch.

"Baran!" she whispered. "Look at the hill!"

Baran rose slowly to his feet, his eyes focusing on the distant boulder and downed spruce. At first he saw nothing unusual. The deepening gloom interfered, but he finally noticed something odd about the shape of the prone tree trunk. The uniform gray of the weathered trunk seemed splotched with ill-defined hues of gray, white, and black—or so it seemed at this distance. Then the splotches moved.

"I . . . I can't quite . . .," Baran began, then gasped, "Father Creator! Wraith!" Then louder, "*Wraith*!"

"Tyra!" Leah said, looking quickly toward the barn.

The great cat poured low from the shadow of the boulder like a streamer of smoke. Even limping, he moved quickly in the deepening gloom, stealing between the boulders and trees of Tyra's pasture. He did not slow down his low crouching pace even when he entered the long shadow cast by the barn. The time for caution was gone. The wraith of legend entered the prey's den to slay as his nightmare ancestors had for twenty thousand generations.

Tyra waved at her parents, but they were looking away from her and toward the hill with the dead tree. She just shrugged because the corral fence and corner of the barn obstructed her view of the hill anyway. She took the lantern from atop the post, hung her bow and empty quiver on a nail, and grabbed the pitchfork leaning against the fence.

As she turned back to the barn, her mother screamed her name, something she never did. Tyra turned as Baran grabbed the two heavy war javelins from their pegs above the door and jumped from the porch in a frantic run toward her. Two strides behind, her mother grabbed the strung *ready bow* and the quiver of stag-killer arrows. Their looks of deadly purpose startled Tyra to immobility.

Still saddled and bridled, Shadow stood quietly, casually nibbling at hay on the floor, enjoying the familiar comfort of his stall. The stallion did not even scent the wraith until the immense cat leaped atop the six-foot stall wall.

Stout enough to contain a passive horse, the stall could not support the half-ton of savagery that attempted to use it as a launch point. The boards splintered under the wraith's weight, forcing a clumsy, imperfect leap upon Shadow's back. The stallion screamed in terror and back-kicked the flailing cat. One hoof caught the cat squarely in the chest; the other struck the cat's wounded shoulder. It did no good at all.

The cat was too strong, his attack too savage. His hind claws tore through Shadow's leather-and-wooden saddle as if it was rotten cloth. A tremendous blow from the cat's unwounded paw stunned Shadow even as the two struggling creatures crashed through the remaining stall wall and into the main aisle of the barn. Kicking frantically as the weight of the wraith threw him on his side, the stallion managed one last pitiful scream before the great fangs stabbed deep into his throat and jugular.

Baran and Leah were still a hundred paces away, yelling for Tyra to run for the house when Shadow's agonizing scream pierced the moment. The thunderous roar that overwhelmed the stallion's scream was like nothing Tyra had ever heard. Lantern and pitchfork in hand, she bolted into the barn.

"Shadow!" she screamed. "Shaa-dow!"

Shadow's last conscious sight was the face of legend—a huge, bloodied muzzle of white, ridged and snarling, baring outrageous fangs and eyes glowing pale green. But tonight the eyes glowed not from the light of an ancient nomad's tribal campfire. Tonight they glowed from the light of Tyra's lantern, as she rushed to Shadow's aid.

The girl's headlong rush into the dark barn came to a sudden halt thirty paces from the immense wraith atop her beloved stallion. Tyra's twelve-year-old mind could not absorb what her lantern illuminated. She had only heard of such nightmarish creatures, never seen one. Dust clouds from the deadly struggle reflected in the yellow light as they settled around the killer and his prey.

The stallion's body and hooves convulsed hideously as the fangs ended his life. The little girl heard her beautiful mount's final choking breath, but her numbed mind could not logically connect Shadow's gasp with the wet, ripping sound as the wraith tore through the last bit of flesh. Under the crouching monster, Shadow—her giant friend, so invincible, so beautiful, seemed almost colt-sized. The shock was simply too much to grasp.

The wraith looked up from his kill, directly at Tyra's lantern. The glow confused him, for he had never seen such a thing before. But monarchs do not tolerate invasions of their realms, and this great den now belonged to him. He crawled atop the stallion's body, focusing on the strange light that challenged him. His immense shoulders bunched to charge. His rear haunches tensed. Bloody claws dug into the dirt floor for the attack.

Despite Tyra's horror, an overwhelming rage grew to challenge the towering monster. Rage hardened her eyes. Rage clenched her jaws. Setting the lantern down, she gripped the pitchfork with both hands and pointed it forward like a spear. Her movement ignited the cat to charge. Tyra screamed with hate-filled defiance, refusing to take even a single step backwards.

The charging wraith's roar shook the rafters of the barn. Dust and bits of straw floated down into the lantern light and onto the honey-streaked hair of the child with less than two heartbeats to live.

"Yeeeee-aaaah!" Baran's gut-deep bellow behind her so startled Tyra from her state of shock that she flinched. In the eternity between the wraith's deadly charge and Baran's war shout, a long, tan blur flew over Tyra's right shoulder, straight for the beast. The eight-foot-long, steel-shafted war javelin resembled a whaler's harpoon. Five feet of leather-wrapped oak handle encased the bottom portion of the shaft. Beyond that, three feet of exposed steel shaft ended in a razor-sharp, double-edged blade a foot long.

The weapon took the cat straight on between the neck and left shoulder. Baran's powerful throw buried all three feet of the exposed shaft into the killer's chest and lungs. The savage roar of the cat changed instantly to a choking, high-pitched scream of pain. The cat flipped onto its back, clawing furiously with all four paws at the enemy slicing deep inside him.

Before Tyra could react, the twang of her mother's longbow behind her sent a smaller gray streak over her left shoulder. The arrow penetrated to the fletching behind the cat's right shoulder. A second arrow buried in the center of his chest. A third blurred deep into his neck. Arterial blood sprayed from the stricken beast with every heartbeat.

The screaming cat clawed savagely at the arrows and javelin knifing through his vitals. His wounds were mortal, but the savage nature of his kind that in one way had doomed his species was, paradoxically, the very thing that had allowed such creatures to survive so long. He splintered the arrow shafts, but the razor-sharp broadheads only sliced deeper through veins and organs. Even after bending the steel javelin shaft nearly double, the great cat managed to right himself to face his Two Leg enemies.

Dark gouts of blood gushed from his gaping mouth. Red mist sprayed from his nostrils, turning his roar of hatred into a horrid, gurgling snarl. His jaws were wide open, brandishing the bloody sabers. His eyes gleamed demonically in the lantern light. He charged to destroy the invaders, pushing grotesquely with his unwounded hind legs only.

Ten paces away, Baran charged the beast with a bellowing roar of his own. He held his second javelin under his right arm as a mounted knight would hold a lance and drove for the cat. Either he or the beast would die. Right *here*, right *now*.

To Tyra, the battle became a blurred maelstrom. Her mind registered frozen instants of the fury but could not assimilate the entire event. Her father rushed headlong into that surreal horror of sound and dust and slashing claws. He stabbed the javelin deep, then held on with all his vaunted strength as the raging cat thrashed him about like a rag doll.

From the swirling dust, claws appeared, disappeared, reappeared again. Baran's left leg collapsed. Driven to one knee, he still held on, cursing the beast, screaming with soul-deep battle rage, driving the weapon even deeper as he struggled to regain his feet.

Leah tried to take another shot but could not release for fear of hitting her husband. The wraith forgot all else save his immediate adversary. Twelve hundred pounds of legend clawed for the two hundred and thirty-pound rancher fighting for his family at the other end of the second javelin. No mercy existed in either creature. No weakness. For both, only an insane, bestial instinct to kill boiled in that storm of dust and fury.

Baran regained his feet enough to drive the weapon deeper, to try and sever a vital artery or vein. Wraith blood and rancher blood alike splattered across stall walls, upon Leah, upon Tyra. Dark droplets sizzled upon the glass of the oil lantern. Driven to his knees, thrown on his side again and again, Baran roared with hatred, refusing with every scream of battle rage to let go of the javelin. To let go meant death for them all.

Tyra's mind never registered the launch of Leah's fourth arrow. The weapon blurred past, pierced the cat's right eye and drove straight into his brain. A single, ear-piercing shriek later, the battle ended.

The intense violence had lasted less than two minutes, yet it shook Tyra to the core of her soul. The discipline required for the daily rigors of *Nung-Cha* practice was one thing. The unfettered savagery of actual life-or-death survival was another.

Dazed and in shock, she turned to her mother, but what she saw virtually slapped the pitchfork from her hands. The lantern light showed a tall, immovable woman in a warrior's stance. Her sun-streaked brown hair pulled to a single warrior's braid down the center of her back framed her lean, tanned face like a war helmet. Leah's green eyes sighted hard and mean down the shaft of a fifth arrow drawn to the right corner of her mouth. Blood drops running into her eyes and down her cheeks went ignored.

The loving, nurturing mother on the porch just moments before had transformed into a stone-faced slayer of her family's enemies. Tyra's father was no less transformed. And that was what finally freed the tears to flow down her cheeks.

She turned just as Baran rose painfully to his feet and finally released the javelin protruding from behind the wraith's left shoulder. His right leg was strong, but not the left. Four claw marks slashed through his heavy canvas trousers from mid-thigh to below his knee. Blood ran down upon his left boot, black like tar in the lantern light. He ignored the wound.

His shoulders seemed to fill the barn through the mist of Tyra's tears. His thick, veiny arms were bloody, killing weapons in this place, not gentle havens of comfort or play. His teeth were bared, soiled by wraith blood, by his own. His jaws still clenched with battle rage. His brown eyes were alight, made hateful and menacing by the blood he didn't bother to blink away. They pierced past his short brown hair and trimmed beard as if he too wore a war helmet. Somehow, his right upper back had been clawed. His brown plaid flannel shirt hung in tatters, stained now a glistening crimson. By itself, that single wound made the gentle man seem even more savage, even more brutal.

In cold silence, Baran limped backwards to a support column and grabbed the big double-headed axe from its pegs without even looking at it. His enraged eyes never left the still form of the wraith as he approached it painfully. He ignored Leah and Tyra. He ignored his own blood seeping into the dusty floor. An inhuman growl propelled the axe as he struck the wraith at the base of its skull with all his might. Only then was Baran sure that no life remained in the beast.

At the muffled crack, Tyra dropped to her knees, covered her eyes with her hands and wept as hard as she ever had as an infant. "Please . . . Daddy," she sobbed. "Please . . . s-s-stop."

It might be argued that the abnormal ferocity of her parents was the final straw that brought Tyra to her knees. Yet, equally true, her tears were what broke her defenders from their savage war state and brought them back into the humanity of family.

Leah returned first. The threat over, she released the tension from her bow and dropped it and the fifth arrow in the dirt. She fell to her knees beside Tyra, hugging her with the desperate strength of a frightened mother, sobbing into her daughter's hair.

Moments later, Baran dropped the big axe and limped to them as quickly as he could. In obvious pain, he sank clumsily to his knees, sweeping the treasures of his life in a crushing hug. He wept explosively, briefly, as strong, quiet men do. Tears of fright at what he nearly lost mingled with tears of gratitude. More flowed from knowing that his strength, his resolve, had almost not been enough.

Lost in their tiny world of three, the rest of the universe simply did not exist until they stood up. Dozens of lanterns surrounded them. Kayne wranglers and orchard men were there. Baran's older brother Mannis and his wife Cayleigh, Leah's twin sister and a renowned healer, were there. Tyra's older teenage cousins, Caydyn and Riane, stood at the ready, as did Leah's parents, Marcus and Elsha Halwyn, there to serve as Guardians for the final leg of the Procession. The battle in the barn had drowned out the furious ringing of the alarm bell by Mannis. It had drowned out the sound of pounding feet as every soul within earshot had grabbed bows, hatchets, javelins, and pitchforks to help.

The lanterns parted as Baran scooped Tyra into his arms to limp back to the house. Leah looped her arm around the crook of Baran's left arm and leaned her head against his shoulder as they made their way out of the barn. Hands reached past the lantern light to pat them on the back as they passed. Murmured words tried to offer comfort, tried to express gratitude for their safety.

Barely able to speak, Mannis choked out, "I'll . . . we'll take care of . . . of things . . . out here." Shaken, Mannis knew as surely as he drew breath that he and the javelin he held would have been too late to save his younger brother and his family.

"Fine," Baran whispered. "I . . . I . . . thank you."

25

Tracks

Two hours past sunrise on day two, Oran and Cailin Briac again took point, but did so with the only change voted for by the Guardians.

Traditionally, Reading Processions arise at first light the second day, take a quick, cold breakfast, then proceed to gather any remaining candidates on the way to the Reading Theater. The wraith changed that.

After the children had bedded down the night before, most of the adults met out of earshot in the darkness. At least one family member for each child remained on guard while the rest voted on the next step. The brief whispered discussion was unanimous for continuing on the same trail, rather than backtracking and taking an alternate route. General consensus favored leaving the campsite later than normal in order to gain more light. Tempting fate in pre-dawn gloom that a wounded wraith might use to full advantage was out of the question.

It was also agreed that only two point guards could now be in greater danger than the Procession. Without reinforcement, the two Briacs might be perceived by the instincts of the wraith as stragglers in comparison to the larger "herd" of the larger Procession. By mutual agreement, the parents of Marcus Riordan, Killian and Eryn, took leave of their posts as flankers to join the Briacs.

Remaining flankers then condensed to fill in the vacated positions and maintain the integrity of the columns. As heavily armed as the Briacs, the Riordans added two unsheathed walking spears, plus two fully strung longbows with quivers of heavy "stag killer" arrows.

The morning's delay meant that the Procession would reach the Kayne farmstead nearer to noon instead of early morning, but that could not be helped. The Procession would maintain its measured pace, keeping its intent to acquaint Readers with Initiates. Tyra Kayne's gathering would not be rushed, but the pace for the final seven-mile leg to the Reading Theater would definitely have to make up for the late start.

The Procession assumed a war footing since sighting the wraith. Every walking spear brandished an unsheathed, gleaming blade. Bows were carried, not slung across backs. Razor-sharp stag-killer arrows were held at the ready against the bow's grip. The children were just as prepared as their Guardians, now carrying their bows as they walked. Conversation between them and the Readers continued as it had on day one, but it centered on wraiths now, on their place in Wraithaven's legend, of their effect on the first unsuspecting Pelanjian settlers.

Well ahead of the main group, the scouts stopped to hold a whispered discussion. Thus far, the two couples had spaced themselves only a few paces apart and had stayed on the road because the predator had.

"His tracks are plain," Oran said, "but wraiths will backtrack to set an ambush if they're being followed. They're damned smart that way."

"Not this one," Killian whispered back. "He's starving, too severely wounded, and he's avoiding the terrain off-road. Too rough on his injuries. The road is smoother, more comfortable."

"Walking point in the open is uncomfortable enough for us," Oran said. "It must be a hundred times more so for the cat."

"No doubt," Cailin said, "but hunger is forcing this animal to break his instincts. Uninjured and well fed, we would never have seen him in the first place."

"And he wouldn't have left tracks like this on an open road," Eryn added.

The pads of the cat's hind legs left obvious depressions in the dirt as expected of such a heavy creature, but the cat was traveling for the most part on three legs. He held his wounded left leg off the ground, which meant that the right pad took all the weight of the front-heavy body. Each depression of the right paw was twice the depth of the rear paws. *The pain must infuriate this beast each time his right paw catches his full weight*, Oran thought.

Clearly, the cat had not stopped for rest after the battle at the springs. The stag's antlers had torn long, gaping wounds from his left shoulder to his rib cage—ghastly but not fatal. The good news was that the cat's spotty blood trail was dried, not fresh and glistening. The cat had stayed on whatever scent trail had attracted him the day before and still remained well ahead of the Procession. That was as good as the group could hope for right now. *God help whatever is drawing the starving cat*, Killian mused.

Two miles out from Big Calder Springs, the tracks changed. At random intervals, the imprints of the rear pads were smeared as if the creature had been startled. Long, deep furrows from instinctively unsheathed claws further defaced the tracks. "The cat is testing his left foreleg now," Cailin said, "The pain of touching the ground makes him flinch."

Four miles out from the springs, the tracks changed again. All four pads were in use now, although the track of the left pad was noticeably shallower than the other three. The cat was forcing himself to use his wounded leg.

"Desperation pushes this animal," Eryn said. "If he hadn't been starving, he would have found a tight copse of spruce and laid up a week while he healed. The pain in his gut is worse than the pain from his wounds."

"The distance between the pad marks is growing," Cailin pointed out. "He's gutting through the pain to get to whatever he scented yesterday."

26

Wounds

The night of the attack was sleepless for the Kayne ranch. Only after tucking Tyra into bed did Baran allow any attendance to his injuries.

Carrying torches, Leah and Cayleigh first accompanied Baran to the creek-fed bathing pool behind the house. They made the trip in silence, save for a few painful grunts from Baran. His hard, vacant eyes and chiseled face masked his pain somewhat, but nothing escaped the notice of Cayleigh the healer.

Genetics and the work-filled life of a rancher made Baran's body averse to storing body fat, despite his size. Had he been a softer townsman, his twinges of pain under a layer of fat might not have been as obvious. To Cayleigh's professional eye, though, Baran's stoic silence hid nothing.

The musculature across his upper back and shoulders tensed like straining cables every few steps toward the pool. The wraith's claws had cut deep into his upper-right back. Even the slightest swing of his right arm caused his entire back to spasm.

The claws had done the most damage down the front of his left thigh and the side of his left upper calf. He had no wounds to his front torso, but as he eased into the pool, his eyes took on a steely glare as every muscle across his chest and shoulders reacted to the frigid water streaming over his open wounds.

The battle had rendered his trousers and shirt beyond repair. He hobbled back to the house wearing only his torn and bloodied boots and a brown towel wrapped around his waist. Cayleigh walked closely at his right side, ready if his wounds caused him to stumble. Carrying his bloodied, ruined clothes, Leah stayed close on his left.

Cayleigh was concerned. The swift, cold creek water had washed the wounds on his left leg, upper-right back, and the lone, deep slash across his right cheek, but Baran's leg was quickly stiffening up. The icy water accelerated that the process, and the sutures and poultices she was about to apply would certainly increase the stiffness.

"You'll be needing a cane or a crutch to get around once you're able," Cayleigh said as they arrived back at the house. "The leg will stiffen more over the next few days."

Baran said nothing as they entered the house.

The sisters helped him settle on a plain oak chair for treatment, expecting at least *some* response. His only comment was, "Leg or back first?"

Cayleigh made eye contact with her twin and shrugged. Leah mimicked the gesture. "I'll be in Tyra's room if you need me."

Leah kissed Baran's cheek and left the room. Both knew Baran well. He would bottle up every painful wound, every heartbeat of the attack and brood about it all properly. In cold silence, he would imprison and relive without end the horror of what could have happened to Leah and Tyra.

It's already started, Cayleigh thought.

"Drink this," Cayleigh said. "It will lessen the pain. Somewhat."

Baran sniffed the offered mug of hot tea before tasting it. The aroma of the bitter concoction made his eyes water. "Smells like a dung heap," he muttered.

"Tastes even worse," she said with a Healer's knowing smirk, "but it works. Drink!"

She waited for him to gulp the contents of the mug before applying the medicinal ointments to his wounds.

"This ointment will sting," she said, "a lot."

"Damn!" Baran hissed through his teeth at the first dab.

"Infection follows animal-inflicted wounds," Cayleigh said, "*always*. This is the best thing to stop it before it starts. After the sutures, I'll poultice the major wounds to draw out any drainage."

By the end of the two-hour procedure, the tea had taken the edge off his pain, but it had also made Baran drowsy.

"No more," he said, refusing a second mug of the noxious brew. "Getting sleepy."

"Which is the point," Cayleigh said, biting through the last horsehair suture.

"I'll sleep later," Baran muttered, rising painfully to return to Leah and Tyra. "Can't just yet."

"My sister married a very hard-nosed man," Cayleigh said, packing her herbs and instruments back into her satchel.

"And her husband married a hard-nosed woman," Baran returned.

"So did Mannis, I've heard," Cayleigh said. Both smiled and gave each other a peck on the cheek, she with a sister-in-law's concern, he with a stiff grimace of the pain he could not deny.

Throughout the night, when horrid nightmares jolted Tyra awake, she always found her mother on one side of her bed and her father on the other. They remained seated on the floor until dawn, their heads resting on the edges of Tyra's mattress, available for her to feel their presence before dozing off again.

Only once did Baran leave his post. Just past midnight, Tyra mumbled, "Daddy, Shadow should be buried on the hill."

Whether she had been fully awake, fully asleep, or in some half-dream state did not matter. Baran limped out to the barn to relay the message to Mannis and those moving the carcasses of Shadow and the wraith.

"Seems only right," Mannis said. "We'll pick the best spot overlooking the course and have it done by daybreak. Now get back to Tyra and Leah. And here, take this with you," he said, handing him a crutch.

An hour past dawn, the family and a dozen Kayne ranch hands crowded around Shadow's grave for Tyra to bid farewell to her beloved stallion. She slouched brokenheartedly between Baran and Leah, weeping silently. To her uncle Mannis and those who had helped him, she managed to stammer, "Thank you all . . . for working so hard for . . . Shadow." It was nearly impossible for the little girl to mention her beloved steed's name. Many wept with her. Others wept for her. "You've picked a nice spot for him," she added, forcing a wan smile through her tears. The wildflowers she had picked trembled in her small hands, making her seem even more fragile and wounded. Tossing them gently upon Shadow's side, she said, "Good-bye my beautiful friend. I love you. I'm sorry," she added, turning away, "I wasn't there for you."

Afterwards, Tyra essentially disappeared as the ranch tried to resume its normal rhythm. Baran and Leah allowed her time to grieve and to decide about today. When the Procession arrived, Tyra would still have to choose to be gathered or to postpone her Reading until next year. If she decided to go, they must be ready.

Baran was already bathed, sutured, and dressed. Only Leah needed to bathe and change into clean clothes to greet the Procession. Then Tyra's test would come.

Meanwhile, Mannis and his crew moved the wraith's massive body outside to the side of the barn. A decision about the carcass had been made. They would allow the Procession to see the creature whole before skinning it to show in an exhibition at the Falcon's Aerie museum. The skeleton would be painstakingly stripped of flesh and cleaned before mounting as well. Given the remoteness of the predators' range, the chance of a hunter or traveler ever finding more than a few scattered bones, a skull, or patches of a weather-ravaged pelt was extremely rare. The new exhibit would draw visitors by the thousands from surrounding provinces.

"Should we hold her back?" Leah asked, as Baran limped back to the porch. An oak crutch, complete with a thick cushion of old saddle blanket strips for his armpit, now leaned against the split-rail fence defining the barn pasture from Tyra's hunter course. Baran had replaced it with a walking spear. Leah withheld her obvious assumption.

"It's her Reading," Baran said, "her transition. She decides. Seems only right."

"True. She's taking it hard, though."

Unable to keep silent about Baran and his crutch any longer, Leah said with a knowing smirk, "You've managed to lose your crutch already, I see."

"Didn't lose it. Just found something more . . . practical."

"A spear? A *walking* spear?"

He tried flashing his signature rogue's grin that had first attracted her twenty years before, but the pain of his wounds crushed the grin's feeble attempt to rise. To Leah's concerned observation though, it was the pain burning through his eyes that betrayed him the most.

If Tyra chooses to go, no force on earth will keep Baran at home to nurse his wounds, Leah mused. *He'll go. And from the looks of things, he's planning to walk as a flanker, not ride in a wagon at the rear.*

"And what of *those*?" Leah said, pointing to the poultice bandaged around his left thigh. His knee was not bandaged, but below his knee another smaller poultice covered shallower, ten-inch-long slashes.

"An inconvenience," Baran said, forsaking all pretense to rely on logic instead. "Besides, the leg will only stiffen worse if I lay about waiting for it to heal."

"And Cayleigh's stitches? Two hundred and thirty by her count, wasn't it? She's an artist with needle and suture. Takes pride in her work."

"She should. A man couldn't ask for more handsome stitches." His feigned light response was unmasked by the clench of his jaws against the pain. His cold stare should have warned Leah of his impatience with their conversation. It didn't. She tried logic of her own one last time.

"And if . . . no, *when* they pull open, what then?"

"They'll hold!" he said, tightly. "If they don't, I'll ride in a wagon."

"But . . . ."

"Leah! Drop it! I'd go if the wraith had torn the leg *off*!" he virtually snarled. His eyes did not twinkle. At all. No hint of a grin softened his tan, lean face.

The matter was closed.

27

Concerning Loss
and Determination

The Briacs and Riordans arrived ahead of the Procession at mid-morning. The Kayne ranch bustled with obvious tension. The cat had made good speed using the obstacle-free road the afternoon before. Once the ranch came into view, though, his tracks had swung off the road and disappeared among young pines and boulders scattered across a series of low rises. The scouts noted how the tracks led toward a hill overlooking a panorama of sprawling pastures and peach orchards below. A huge, winter-slain spruce lay prostrate there. *A good hiding place*, Oran thought.

"Wonder what that's about?" Oran said, pointing to a large mound of dark soil near the fallen tree.

"Looks recent," Killian said.

Caitlin and Eryn both muttered the same thought. "Hope it's not a grave."

They dog trotted to the center of the activity, a gated fence on the west side of the big hay barn.

The scouts already knew Mannis Kayne and those helping to return the barn to normalcy. At the body of the wraith, Mannis gave them an account of the battle in the barn. In return, the four took turns describing the battle at Big Calder Springs. It was obvious now what scent trail the cat had followed.

"And Baran's injuries aren't life threatening?" Cailin asked.

"Not as long as he does what Cayleigh says," Mannis said. "She's a master healer. The claws cut deep into muscle but missed the tendons. His whole torso is one big bruise too, but infection is the worry. He'll stiffen up and won't walk right for weeks, but he'll tough this out."

"And Tyra?" Eryn asked. "She wasn't injured?"

"Her body wasn't," Mannis said. "Her spirit is another matter. Haven't seen her since Shadow's funeral."

The scouts glanced toward the hill and the obvious mound of earth.

"We left Shadow uncovered," Mannis said, gazing there too. "After Tyra leaves—if she does—we'll fill in the grave."

The Procession arrived about then, which meant that Mannis had to repeat the events of last night to the crowd of curious Initiates and their Guardians.

Attracted to the unusual activity near the barn, Taggart and Alina expected to find Baran, as well as Leah and Tyra there. That was not so.

The crowd quickly circled the body of the wraith. Several children gingerly touched the outlandish canines of the cat. Some patted the thick, wiry pelt, remarking at the density of it.
Others examined the jagged white battle scars that spoiled the splotchy gray-and-white pattern from muzzle to rear haunches.

Taran Berit, the swordsmith, pulled his right sleeve up, then knelt to compare his bare forearm with the great killing fangs. From gum line to the tip of the bloody fang, the tooth reached from Taran's elbow to his wrist.

Upon hearing Mannis's recounting of the carnage and of Baran's injuries, the Readers anxiously pushed through the onlookers and headed for the main house. Nothing of such magnitude had ever interrupted a Reading in all the years the Kaynes had served. That their youngest son was injured put everything else in their lives, work, the Procession, the children, and even the Reading itself, into a distant second place.

Halfway to the cottage, Baran and Leah rounded the southeast corner. Leah had obviously just bathed in the creek. Her hair was damp and combed straight back. The pair wore fresh gray woolen trousers and comfortable flannel shirts: Baran's a dark indigo, Leah's a light tan. Both wore sturdy hiking boots, implying that they would accompany the Procession. On any other day, that would have been a given. Baran's wounds, however, were obvious. The left leg of his trousers had been cut off to allow room for the poultices and bandages. He said nothing, but his clenched jaw betrayed his pain, as he limped toward the house using a walking spear.

Another poultice bilged under Baran's shirt at his upper-right back. Stitches closed a five-inch cut across his right cheek.

The couple did not wait for Taggart and Alina to reach them. They acknowledged the Readers with nods, but continued walking. Bewildered, Taggart and Alina stopped. Kayne greetings were always boisterous hugging events.

Alina cocked her head and gave her son a quizzical look. *Where's Tyra?* Baran shrugged his shoulders and gestured slightly with open hands. *We don't know if she is going or not.*

Still without a word, Baran made hard eye contact with his father and nodded toward the bell post at the foot of the short path leading to the house. Taggart nodded back, as Baran and Leah continued into the house.

"We play the ritual out," Taggart whispered, "as if nothing's happened."

"And Tyra?" Alina asked.

"It's up to her now," Taggart said. "We'll all find out when the bell tolls." He took Alina's hand and said, "Come, my lady. We have a bell to ring."

By the time the Readers reached the bell post, the Initiates and Guardians had formed a quiet, respectful throng behind them, just as they had in the academy courtyard.

After a moment of quiet contemplation, Alina rang the bell the prerequisite four times, and waited as the peals echoed over the valley of pastures and orchards. On cue, Baran and Leah emerged from the house to stand formally on the porch, almost at attention.

Taggart's baritone rang out. "All hail the house," he said, raising his right hand. "We are the Readers Taggart and Alina Kayne. This day, our mission is to gather seekers like unto ourselves."

Baran and Leah recited the words a hundred generations old. "Welcome, Sir and Lady Kayne, Readers for our people. How might we assist you?"

"Are . . . are there any among you who would join us?" Alina responded, her voice quivering slightly.

But Baran and Leah could not utter the next line of the ritual. Tyra had disappeared and taken her grief with her. For long moments, silence blanketed the waiting Procession and Tyra's disappointed parents. A few in the crowd looked down with embarrassment for the Kaynes standing so tall, so expectant, so very ready to be proud on this special day.

The gathering ritual provided a formal exit line, though it was rarely used. Should an Initiate fail to appear at the greeting, Readers would simply smile and reply, "Then we thank you for your time, neighbor. Let us greet one another again next year." That would be the signal for a Procession to continue on to the Reading Theater.

Taggart waited for a few more long moments, but then cleared his throat and began, "Then we thank . . ."

"Wait!" a clear young voice rang out from the southwest side of the house. A trail there meandered deep into a stand of emperor spruce. "Here is one!"

Like her parents, Tyra had bathed and changed into clean clothes, but she had done so by her favorite secluded pool a quarter mile away. Her damp hair was braided in a simple warrior's braid that reached the middle of her back. She wore a knapsack, and she carried her bow and a quiver of arrows in her left hand.

A great sigh of relief from the crowd transformed the hushed disappointment into joy. Heartfelt applause erupted. The faces of Baran and Leah beamed as broadly as those of the Readers. Tyra took long, purposeful strides to reach the porch, giving her parents exuberant hugs. Pride fairly blazed from Baran's and Leah's faces, as they stood even taller. A tear broke free, running down Baran's right cheek into his new wound.

"Here, Sir and Lady Kayne!" they both repeated loudly. "Here is one!"

"Ah," Taggart said, smiling broadly. "And who might this seeker be?"

"I am Tyra Alina Kayne, Sir and Lady Kayne," the little girl announced loudly, "the proud and loving daughter of the ranchers . . . of the *warriors* Baran and Leah Kayne."

"Welcome, Tyra Alina Kayne," Alina said, smiling as Tyra strode forward. "Please join our mission."

Tyra wrapped her arms around Taggart's neck and whispered, "A wraith killed Shadow, Poppy."

"I know, child," he said, voice quivering. "I know. I'm so sorry." He hugged her tightly, his eyes misting with sadness for Tyra's loss, but with even more gratitude that the wraith had not slain his son and family. It had been so very, *very* close.

Alina hugged her and whispered, "Are you sure you still want to do this, child? You can wait until next year. No one will think less of you."

"I'm sure, Nammy," she said, hugging her grandmother fiercely. "The wraith stole Shadow's life. It won't steal mine! It won't steal ours!" she said, looking back at Baran and Leah. Her grim smile, the hard intention of her eyes was as focused as when she sighted and drew her bow from Shadow's back.

28

Sacred Ground

Travelers agree that the Last Mission Trail is as visually spectacular as any in Wraithaven. Wide enough for a horse-drawn wagon in most places, the rambling trail still feels more like a game trail created by generations of hoof and paw than a human path carved through the rolling hills with axe and saw.

Seven centuries ago, an army of cartographers descended upon the sparsely settled Scimitar and North Gale Provinces to create a detailed map of Wraithaven's last uncharted territories. That mission, as others had already done in the nine other provinces, precisely identified every path, creek, river, hilltop, valley, cave, and mountain peak. One discovery was the major game trail to the remote glen that has served as one of Scimitar's Reading Theaters for over six hundred years. Maps named the game trail as Last Mission Trail. The beautiful little valley containing the Kayne's Reading Theater became Seclusion Glen.

With whimsical grace, Last Mission Trail threads casually over the crimson splashed, flame maple-crowned hills. It then swoops, eagerly it seems, down through golden groves of white-barked birches. It meanders nonchalantly past stands of towering emperor spruce, a special guest invited to Nature's royal palace. Majestic, snow-clad peaks crowd shoulder to shoulder, giving the impression of sentries posted to guard the intersecting valleys below. To a traveler, the trail with its palette of autumn colors and the looming peaks all conspire to whisper the word, *sanctuary*.

A random breeze hisses high in the rigid, silver-blue spruce tops, passing through with speed, then whispers softly through fluttering birch gold to tug at a coat sleeve. In crystalline skies, huge golden eagles—crag lords—orbit the trail and its valleys like scouts walking point.

The Kaynes walked close to Tyra at first, ready should she choose to open up about Shadow. She avoided the subject, though, except to express concern for Baran's injuries.

"There was so much blood everywhere. I didn't know which was . . . Shadow's, or Father's, or the wraith's. I've never seen Father badly injured before."

"Your father is strong, child," Alina said. "He will heal. He'll fight the pain like men do, but your mother will put her foot down when it's time for him to rest."

"Plus," Taggart chimed in, "your aunt Cayleigh is the finest healer in Scimitar. Your father is in the best of hands. But I do know this about my son: If he thought you were fretting about him instead of experiencing your Scroll Night, he would feel guilty about tainting your Reading."

"He would feel guilty because of his wounds?" Tyra asked.

"If they distracted you," Alina said, "yes."

Alina recalled the Procession as it left the farm. Her son, followed closely by Leah and Cayleigh—all armed with longbows and walking spears—took flanking positions on the left. Just before disappearing into the forest with the other Guardians, he made eye contact with her and Taggart. Too distant for words, Baran merely nodded curtly and struck his left chest briskly with his right fist. *Battle ready!*

Until you collapse face down in the dirt, Alina thought, motherly pride clashing with a mother's concern.

"Love can drive logic from the human heart sometimes," Taggart said, "especially from a parent. Parents value their children above themselves as well they should."

"And you are doing the same thing," Alina added. "Right now, your main concern is your father. A natural and honorable reaction."

Tyra didn't respond immediately. She didn't stop walking, but her attention was obviously elsewhere. The way she bit her lip as she stared far beyond the trail spoke volumes of something . . . yet unsaid.

Shadow's death? Taggart mused. *The horror of facing a monster with only a lantern and a pitchfork?*

"What else bothers you, Tyra?" Alina asked. "We truly believe your fa . . ."

"Faces!" Tyra blurted out. "Their *faces!*"

"Whose faces, child?" Alina asked, perplexed.

The Procession halted with Tyra's outburst. The other children backed quietly away from the Readers and their grandchild, averting their faces lest they be perceived as eavesdropping.

"Nammy, Poppy, I've waited all my life to hear you read from the Orbit Scrolls on my Scroll Night. I promise you that. But . . ."

"Ty," Taggart began, "we too are . . ."

"I can't get Mother and Father's faces out of my mind!"

The Readers exchanged quizzical looks.

"I've never seen them like that. So angry. So hate-filled! I've never seen *anyone* like that."

"Explain please," Taggart said gently, almost a whisper. *Something hidden can be drawn out here and now. Something dark can be exposed to light. A shadow is about to lose a measure of its power.* For an instant, he thought of Seren defending her little brother from the wolves.

"Go on," Alina coaxed. "Tell us about their faces."

"The . . . the look on Mother's face was so cold, so . . . hard! She seemed like one of your marble sculptures, Poppy. She wasn't Mother anymore. She was something else. I can't explain it very well."

"You're doing fine," Taggart said, patting her shoulder. A tear poised on the edge of Tyra's left eyelid, deciding whether to fall or not. Taggart quickly whisked one of his own away with his right thumb. "Don't hold back, Ty."

"The look on Daddy's face was worse. It frightened me. He never looks like that. Never. He smiles at things I do. He laughs with Uncle Mannis and the men of our family. He hugs Mother and kisses her hair. He plays with little Maccus and Brina like he did with me when I was their age. He's never mean. Never like that, Poppy. He . . . he's like *you!*"

"Yes, he is child," Taggart said, and this time he didn't whisk his tear away. A few had made their decision. He let them fall. "We raised him like he and your mother are raising you."

"He was savage, Nammy. Like a beast. He wasn't. . . He wasn't Father." Tyra wept softly, unlike the shattered way she had in the barn.

"He was still your father, child," Alina said, "but you are correct, at that very moment he *was* something else, just as your mother was something else, because something else was needed. At such times, the only thing that distinguishes the human from the beast is that the human has a soul."

"Hopefully," Taggart said gently, "you will never see such things again. Personal survival of oneself, of loved ones, resides quietly at the core of every human being by the Maker's design. When the need for it arises, everything good and gentle and loving about us all disappears, leaving only a raw, *very* savage, *very* beastlike entity."

"Consider, Ty," Alina said. "Every Wraithian incorporates *Nung-Cha* training into their daily routine. Despite enjoying an unprecedented 2,000 years of peace, we train as if war was eminent. And why when "war" is the most despised word in our vocabulary? Because our Pelanjian ancestors survived the last five hundred years of their existence only by learning the savagery of warfare. Savagery saved them, yet it changed them after the survival beast arose generation after generation. No Wraithian has ever fought in war, but two thousand years of Picket reports remind us all of its reality. The common thread of all returning Pickets is to pray that our culture will never need to see the survival beast arise in us."

"Ty," Taggart added, "Readers are honor-bound not to reveal what is covered during a Reading before its time, but I will tell you this. The Reading will introduce many new characters to you tonight. They will tell of themselves, but one in particular might be of interest to you."

"Strangely enough, he calls himself Shadow, and after tonight you will know that every human being is capable of reaching the same level of ferocity and absolute commitment for personal survival that your parents reached in that barn."

"Even you, Poppy? And you, Nammy?"

"Yes," Alina said, making subtle eye contact with Taggart. "Even us. Even *you.*"

Both Readers would take to their graves memories of road bandit attacks on remote byways during their Picket tour in Cathmore. They had survived five separate attacks during that two-year tour of duty. Seventeen axe and sword-armed bandits slain. Only five escaped unharmed. Three severely wounded highwaymen had escaped as well, their fates of death or survival unknown.

For the Kaynes, the occasional nightmare or daytime flashback reminded them of how the savage attacks had been repelled—nay, how they had been *ended*—by the fists and feet and weapons of *Nung-Cha.* Both still shuddered in memory, in shame.

Ugly memories scarred their minds and the satin of their souls, but their bodies bore scars as well. A thin, four-inch-long cut from a dagger started high on Taggart's left cheekbone and ran down into his beard line. Three evenly spaced circular scars across his upper back testified to the iron tines of a thrown pitchfork during the second attack. The foot-long line of white across his upper-right chest reminded him of the barely parried sword slash in the fourth attack.

Alina hid the loss of the tip of her right ear to a sword cut by arranging her hair carefully. For most of the year, long sleeves hid the ugly dagger cut twisting high across her left forearm. Only when she bathed did her largest scar show, a gnarled abstract in white that seemed like a jagged bite taken from her upper back. Felled by her *Iron Shark* foot sweep, a giant, bearded man wielding a pole-axe had left that one the instant before his neck vertebrae shattered against a boulder.

Such violence, Taggart thought. *So repugnant. Shameful, abhorrent reactions called forth from the depths of one's soul and forced into the light of necessity by the intentions of evil men bereft of even a hint of honor.*

For that alone I will never forgive them. For forcing me to sink to their level, for unlocking my imprisoned dark side, I despise even the memory of their faces.

With no small measure of guilt, Taggart asked, "Consider this, Ty. As you held that pitchfork to confront the wraith, was the look on your face playful? Relaxed? Or did your lovely green eyes blaze with hatred, an angry willingness to kill?"

The girl considered the possibility for a moment, recalling the boiling defiance that flooded every cell of her body. Rage had blinded her with unnatural, focused hatred for the huge predator. Yes, she would have slain the creature without mercy if she could have.

"I was the same, wasn't I, Poppy?" she ventured. "Angry and mean and hateful and . . . not myself."

Alina took the child's face in her hands and kissed her cheek. "You were still the same person, just another facet of her. Human beings are much like gemstones, Tyra. We have different facets that reflect the unique reactions of our nature. Life shines on us all in a thousand different ways, from a thousand different angles. We each reflect that light in our own ways.

"What happened in that barn last night—all of it—was one thing. What is happening right now is another. This Procession, this age-old tradition, is your time to prepare for a major reflection of Life against your gemstone. It's Poppy's and mine as well."

"I won't forget what happened, will I?" Tyra said, not really asking. "Not ever."

"No, you won't," Alina said, "nor should you be expected to. What you can do, although it is difficult, is to not carry the terrible burden upon your back. Set it down inside you and get on with the rest of whatever Life has in store for you. Do you understand?"

Tyra returned a very direct look to her grandmother. She even managed a smile as understanding began to illuminate the dark, raw memory.

"I think so, Nammy. But it takes time to set some burdens down, doesn't it? The big ones, the heavy ones, I mean."

"Yes, it does, child," Alina said, crushing her in a loving hug. "Sometimes a very long time."

"I need to get on with things then, Nammy," she said, her chin raised, her eyes intent and just a bit combative. She warred with a memory now, not a live wraith. With that, she kissed both Readers on their cheeks and turned to join her friends.

"And it's time for the rest of us to get on with things, too," Taggart said, patting Alina's shoulder.

Seven miles from the Kayne's northeastern boundary, a small trail branches northwest off Last Mission Trail into a stand of emperor spruce. The trail is thread-thin here, created solely by the passage of human boots, but unlike its larger parent, is unnamed. It begins where Last Mission loops past a pair of moss-crowned, wagon-sized boulders flanked by 200-foot-tall spruces. Passing between the towering boulders and trees, one imagines stalwart royal sentries guarding ancient castle gates.

The little trail beckons a hiker to follow, for the trees there are not as densely packed as those in dark timber. Open forest comforts the traveler. It denies ambush sites for predators.

Two hundred paces beyond the gate, the trail diffused into a hilltop clearing a hundred paces across in every direction. Today, so noticeably and unnaturally free of broken branches and nuisance stones, the clearing exuded a pristine, freshly sculpted feel. This was the Reading Theater. Wildflowers thrived here. As if out of respect, the surrounding trees blocked major windstorms, yet allowed ample sunlight to nourish swathes of scarlet, knee-high paintbrushes, and ground-hugging carpets of tiny yellow sun drops.

Taggart's critical eye for detail had made his sculptures legendary for decades. From raw blocks of marble, granite, and obsidian, he had called forth intricate details undreamed of by generations of sculptors before him. Indeed, such attention to detail had earned him a reputation as a nigh-prophetic tracker when he and Alina hunted autumn stags in mounted packs with neighbors.

"He misses nothing," Alina often said, and she was not far from the truth.

In this sacred place, Taggart's eyes swept the earth, the flowers, and the complex minutia of life at work around him.

To him, evidence of the advance Elder team was still noticeable, though already two days old. They had arrived here before the Procession had even left the academy courtyard. Their wagons, teams, and mounts were well downwind in another secluded meadow, where forest muffled even the casual neighing of a horse. No hoof impressions or wagon-wheel ruts marred the delicate palette of the clearing.

Where a single boot sole had trampled an anthill, the industrious little creatures had already rebuilt their cone of sand. To his left, a meadow gem, a small, common butterfly of brilliant yellow, lay partially impressed into the soil. A windblown branch had fallen upon the fragile insect. Broken grass blades around the insect spoke clearly to Taggart how Elders had gathered dead branches and carried them to the shallow fire pit across the meadow.

The Elders had been thorough in their grooming of the clearing, carefully skirting sprawling patches of paintbrushes, sun drops, and ankle-high clumps of purple meadow stars. Very few had been damaged. Taggart smiled in appreciation of such prudence.

"The sleeping area is over here, children," Alina said, guiding the group to the most level spot. "Pick a spot for your knapsack, bow, and blanket, and just relax for a while. We will leave you to your own thoughts for now. When it's time, bring only your blanket to cushion your stump seat around the fire."

Taggart noted the small cone of last year's kindling rising from the center of the shallow, bare-earth fire circle. Thin, bone-dry wood shavings and a handful of dry grass under the cone awaited the strike of flint to steel. A small, oiled-canvas tarp protected the wood in case of a rare autumn shower. Near the fire pit were two stump seats for him and Alina, and a large stack of seasoned wood to maintain the Reading fire.

When Alina rejoined him, they placed knapsacks, swords, his re-sheathed walking spear, and Alina's bow neatly behind their stumps. They removed the white Scroll Night robes from their knapsacks and placed the precisely folded garments atop their respective seats.

After removing the canvas tarp, they took each other's hands and drew close until the lips of each touched the left ear of the other.

"Father Creator," Taggart prayed softly, "once again we are honored and humbled for what we are about to do."

"We thank You, Great One," Alina answered in kind, "for the honor of feeling the weight of the robes once more."

Then together they intoned, "Guide our every word this night. May each word please You. Open please, the hearts and minds of the children as we bring these words to them. We ask Your blessing upon this time and upon these children, Dear Father."

As if in answer, the setting sun began to pierce itself upon the jagged spire of the highest peak in the region, Taran's Dagger.

The shadows of evening began to awaken.

Part Three:
Scroll Night

Character is the sculpture you create from the decisions you make and from the values you cherish.

Reputation is the shadow cast by your sculpture, as Life shines upon it.

—Taggart Kayne, Reader

29

Nightfall

The shadows of peak and tree and boulder lengthened subtly, growing bolder, as the sun disappeared behind the imposing Shield, deepening as they merged to shroud the earth from the waning light.

With the gathering shadows, the children lapsed into a deepening silence. Pitching their shelters in the warm sun, when light had ruled the earth, they had chattered away like birds. Now, in the cooling dusk, quiet introspection conquered nervous distraction. Anticipation grew.

In the surrounding forest, Guardians donned night stealth suits: long-sleeved, hooded parkas and loose-fitting trousers of light wool, dyed purest black. Their low, felt-soled boots were black as well. Finally, they marked each other's exposed flesh of face, hands, and neck with streaks of charcoal.

Mounts were already hobbled in a distant meadow. Once total darkness fell, the Guardians would move in to surround the Reading Theater as a tight, fully armed perimeter. They would protect the children absolutely without intruding upon the Reading, without even observing it directly. None of them would sleep this night, and only one Guardian would enter the clearing at all.

Bearach Halwyn, a potter by trade and grandfather to the Initiate Brann Halwyn, was, like Taggart and Alina, a double Dragon and veteran Picket. Simple coin tosses earlier in the afternoon had given him the honor of igniting the Reading fire.

Once Taggart and Alina donned their white robes to gather the children and lead them to the fire pit, Bearach would low crawl in as silently as a spider's shadow. When the Readers joined the children fifty paces away, he would strike flint to steel, ignite the fire, and then low crawl back into the surrounding darkness. From a distance, the fire would seem to ignite itself.

"Time," Alina said. Both Readers had been staring toward the western peaks, absorbing the gathering dusk, preparing their minds for the evening.

A pebble clacked against the little cone of kindling. *Bearach*, Taggart thought, smiling because the stealthy potter had probably crept to within a half-dozen paces of where he and Alina stood. Flat against the earth, his clothing blacker than night shadows, he was virtually invisible, even to Taggart's discerning eye.

The Readers glanced at the children before picking up their robes. Alina palmed a small stone, and as she stood up, flicked it playfully toward an oddly shaped darkness to her left. The stone just clattered in the darkness.

A voice whispered from their right front. "*Wronnnnng . . . shaaa-dow*," it hissed. Another pebble sailed in low, striking the kindling as had the first. A second one tapped the toe of Alina's boot, causing her to giggle.

"Stop that!" she whispered to the unseen potter before giggling again.

Seeing the Readers don their ceremonial robes, the children folded their blankets and rose to their feet.

Regaining her composure, Alina took her place at Taggart's right side. Solemnly, and in step, they approached the children formally now. The rounded hoods of their long, white robes reached to just above their eyebrows, nearly hiding their eyes. Their hands grasped the crooks of their opposite elbows, but the long, wide sleeves hid this. They barely smiled. The only light came from the myriad stars. Even the distant peaks were shrouded in black. The Readers and the children were barely recognizable shapes to each other now.

"It is now your time, children," Taggart said reverently. Both Readers bowed first, breaking Wraithian tradition of the younger bowing first to Elders.

"Please join us quietly, in a column of two," Alina said, before turning to face the fire pit.

As the children lined up behind her and Taggart, flames began licking up into the cone of wood in the fire pit. Their backs to the children, the Readers smiled broadly, just for a moment. No doubt the pebble-flinging potter was already back on watch somewhere in all that darkness.

Instinctively, the children fell into step with their Readers. Heartbeats increased. The heady rush of anticipation constricted throats. Each Initiate held the same thought. *At last, this is my Scroll Night. I'm really here.*

None of the children considered the symbolism of the moment when the Readers gathered them and led them toward the fire pit. For a few, it would be days. For others, it would take months or years. Eventually, they would make the connection that neither the Readers nor the children had carried lanterns, torches, or any source of light. It was, as was everything that happened on Scroll Night, a deliberate thing. The children were in darkness. The Readers sought them out in order to lead them into the light.

Slowly, as if entering an ancient, sacred temple, the little Procession made its way toward the only man-made light in a hundred square miles.

30

The Ridge

The Readers gestured for the children to take any of the nine stumps arrayed in a double arc of five and four. Five paces away, the Readers sat upon similar stumps. To the right of the Readers, the growing fire would furnish enough light to read the Scrolls but would not serve as a barrier between Readers and Initiates. All things had meaning on Scroll Night.

Full of anticipation, the children settled quickly, yet even so, one boy was unexpectedly distracted. Drystan Bradach, stocky, tow-headed middle son of the vintners Ewan and Kiera, gazed beyond the crackling fire, his thoughts drawn by Talon Ridge, swallowed by that fathomless blackness behind the white-robed Readers.

Three autumns earlier, he had been deep within that blackness. To celebrate his ninth birthday, his father had taken him on his first mounted stag hunt. Of the twenty-four-rider stag pack, twin girls and two boys were his age. Four others ranged in age from thirteen to eighteen harvests. The remaining fifteen adults were composed of Drystan's parents, his grandfather Kelwyn, and assorted uncles, neighbors, and family friends.

Wraithian stag packs are often generational in structure. To be allowed to ride with veteran hunters through the rugged high-country forests, across windswept, grassy stag parks, was considered a step toward adulthood. To be invited before his formal Reading instilled in him not just a heady blend of pride and privilege, but a breathless sense of being honored as well.

In the span of a few heartbeats, every detail of that wonderful first hunt flooded Drystan's memory. He recalled helping set up the base camp two miles from where he now sat. He and the four other youngsters spoke little to each other, silently shunning any behavior that might seem childish. Instead, they watched how the adults moved, how they communicated with little more than nods of their heads, with subtle gestures of hands and eyes. The veterans knew their places in the pack. Each moved with the efficient gait of men and women at home in rugged wilderness. Each was attuned to the stealth needed to pursue the skittish stags in their own environment.

What had surprised Drystan the most, though, was that the base camp behind Talon Ridge was a "cold" camp. He and the four other newest members had helped build the central campfire, but no one had bothered to light it. Instead, as night fell, the veterans just continued arranging equipment, grooming their mounts, and honing their stag killers or the foot-long blades of their bear lances.

No fire meant no hot food, which made little sense to the youngsters who had prepared such an excellent stack of seasoned, split torchwood pieces.

Right at sundown, Ewan slipped up behind the five bewildered youngsters and startled them with, "There's a reason we cold camp tonight, young'ns. It'll be jerky, cheese, and an apple or two for the pack."

"Why, Father?" Drystan had asked, keeping his voice just above a whisper. "We were told to stack the wood for a fire."

"For tomorrow night, lad," Ewan said with a slap of his meaty hand to the boy's shoulder. "Tonight is special. Come, let's top the ridge."

"In the dark?" Finn Caler whispered. "Without torches?"

"Especially without torches," his father answered, materializing from the darkness enveloping the camp.

The parents of the twins, Ena and Mavie Corann, joined the group as well, and despite the deepening of the evening, Drystan noticed that each set of parents carried a hard leather telescope case. That seemed as out of place as the unlit campfire that would have held the chill settling in Drystan's marrow at bay. That the parents were armed with lances and bows and that each child had been handed their own strung bows and arrows were the only things not out of place. Away from towns and villages, Wraithians never ventured outside at night unarmed.

Silently, the group followed Ewan single-file along a winding footpath leading out of camp and uphill to the crest of Talon Ridge. A half hour later, just below the flattened summit of the ridge, Ewan silently reacted to a lifetime of training. He sensed where he might "skyline" himself, had it been daylight, and dropped prone to the ground. The group mimicked him instantly, dropping as smoothly as a single organism. Without a word, the group fanned out in a skirmish line, and low crawled the remaining fifty paces.

Upon reaching the lip of the ridge, Drystan tried to pierce the darkness below, but his eyes could not distinguish valley from hill, forest from rock outcropping. The crisp, steady wind blowing unchallenged across the ridge sent tendrils of chill down his collar, whispered ineffectually against the warm woolen cap that covered his head to mid-ear. The brilliant canopy of stars blazing down through the clear, moonless sky seemed to add an even deeper chill to the night. Over the hissing wind, Drystan detected four brass telescopes being pulled from their felt-lined cases.

At his right side, Drystan's mother, Kiera, taped his shoulder and whispered, "Look down to our front. See that point of light?"

The boy noticed what was probably a hunter's campfire nearly swallowed by night and distance. "Here," Ewan whispered. "Use the scope."

All adult pack hunters carried powerful telescopes to scan potential hunting terrain. The telescope that Ewan handed his son was six generations old. As Drystan manipulated the heavy scope to locate the light source, Ewan whispered, "That's not a pack fire. That's where you will be in a few more years."

The boy didn't understand at first, but he recovered quickly as he connected "in a few years" with the campfire.

"It's a Reading, Father?" The boy kept his voice at a whisper, despite the distance to the campfire.

"Yes, probably Taggart and Alina Kayne down there. This is their sector. You'll like them, son. Your mother and I hunt with the Kayne family pack sometimes. We've gotten to know all the Kaynes over the years. Fine family. Honorable to their marrow. Taggart is as hard as the stone he sculpts, but he's still a consummate gentleman. Alina weaves some of the most beautiful tapestries anywhere, and she composes songs while she does it. Has a voice like one of the Creator's own angels."

My Readers, the boy mused. *When I reach my twelfth harvest.* He focused the scope upon two white-robed figures near the fire. The Readers. The children on the other side of the fire might have numbered two or two dozen. The distance was too great, and the darker clothing or the blankets they probably had wrapped about them against the night chill did not reflect the fire light as did the robes of the Readers.

"Why do we whisper and keep a dark camp, father? We're so far away."

"Every Reading Theater is sacred ground. Respect the experience of those on their Reading. No fires, no noise that might carry, even so far away. Never intrude on someone's Scroll Night."

"I understand, Father," the boy whispered, as his mother patted his shoulder.

Along that dark ridge, other fathers, other mothers whispered similar words to *their* children.

Alina tossed a single split log against the fire, sending a crackling shower of red sparks rising into the darkness. Drystan's reverie broke as the sound returned him to the present. He smiled toward Talon Ridge, wondering if a stag pack watched *his* Reading tonight from a cold camp. When no one was looking, he subtly waved his right hand toward the telescopes that might be trained on him that very moment.

Your turn will come, he thought, smiling.

31

Visions

"Tell me, children," Taggart began, "why are you really here tonight? After all, you've waited twelve years for this night. You've all seen friends, siblings, or neighbors go when they reached *their* twelfth harvest."

Drystan Bradach, the vintner's son, spoke first. "Our Pelanjian ancestors attended Scroll Night in the home islands, sir. They brought the tradition to the New World."

"Ah," Alina said, "tradition. We've lived as Wraithians for over two thousand years, plus another thousand in our ancestral home as Pelanjians. Any other reason?"

"We cross a threshold tonight, ma'am," Keiriam Marsali, daughter of stonemasons, said. "We become adults in some ways but remain children in others."

"Transformation then," Taggart responded. "And as a matter of distinguishing your pre-Reading condition from your post-Reading state, after tonight you will be addressed as *young man* and *young lady* instead of *child*. What else?"

"We can own land, sir," Seanna Berit, the sword smith's daughter said. "We can plan our future home site."

"Anything else?" Alina said, grinning at what was coming. "Boys?"

"We get to carry real swords!" Devyn Briac, son to the Procession's point scouts, exclaimed immediately.

"Steel ones!" Quinn Farris, the goldsmith's son chimed in. "Not wooden ones!"

"We burn our wooden ones tomorrow," Marcus Riordan, the woodcarver's son added, looking around at the other boys whose eyes were wide with anticipation of the ritual sword burning.

Leah Brenna, daughter of the tanners Cavan and Ailis and known for academic excellence, spoke up. "You will read the Orbit

Scrolls to us tonight," she said. "And tomorrow, *before* the sword burning," she emphasized sternly at the boys, "you will present us with our own set of the Scrolls."

"Also true, Leah," Taggart said, "with one distinction. We will not read both Scrolls in their entirety tonight. Rather, we will read *from* them, touching various points. In that regard, no two Readings are the same. A Reading introduces you to a vision. That vision should inspire you to delve deeper into the Scrolls on your own. To that end, each of you will be given three scrolls. Two are the true Orbit Scrolls. The third one is blank. *You* will write that one with your thoughts, observations, and impressions as you mature. Since the Reading of my youth, I've filled five scrolls so far; Alina has filled seven."

"So," Alina continued, "as Readers, we show you yourselves. We teach you your fundamental mission in Life. Tonight, we examine the nature of humankind, and of ourselves. We explore the character of the human soul."

A few children looked perplexed. Other faces reflected disappointment. Scroll Night was the most special event in a young Wraithian's life, but few had looks of anticipation now.

Just as I was at my own Reading, Taggart mused. *The thought of honing one's first steel sword with one's own whetstone is much more exciting than examining the nature of one's self.*

Alina broke the somber mood with, "Who knows what a herald is?"

Every child raised a hand.

"Outsiders use heralds when they war against each other," Brann Halwyn, the potter's son, said. "Heralds are ambassadors."

"They speak for their warring kings," Tyra added.

"Do Wraithians have heralds?" Alina asked.

"*No*," Devyn said, "Wraithians don't have kings."

"Wraithians don't make war either," Quinn stated with conviction.

Not since the Pelanjian Disappearance, Taggart mused. *Yet, our people still train The Necessary Path as if the sails of an invader might loom upon our horizon any day. Should the dark rumors brewing along Tripada's eastern coast ever degrade into reality, these children may be the last generation in over two thousand years to declare that Wraithians do not wage war.*

"So, children," Alina said, "heralds of Outsider nations bring important messages to a king from another king?" The children nodded in agreement. "Excellent, however tonight you shall learn that Wraithians have heralds too, and that they also bring important messages from a king."

The children sat up a little straighter. This was new, something not discussed at the family table, or overheard in passing. Kings? Heralds? Messages?

"Let us imagine together, children," Taggart said. "Let us truly begin your Scroll Night."

Every child perked up. What were they about to do?

Taggart's voice assumed a professorial tone—an obvious change from his relaxed baritone. "First, let us consider how humans perceive themselves. Are we accidents of Nature as some contend, or are we gleaming, created gems of the cosmos? Are we naught but hairless bipeds stumbling through Life, randomly accumulating accomplishments as well as sins? Or, are we, at our core, primordial creatures prone to invent atrocities of ever greater magnitude?

"In truth, humankind has invented so many philosophies, religions, and excuses over the centuries that only the Maker Himself knows all the varieties, or the redundancies.

"To illustrate, imagine a vast open-air theater like the one at Conclusion Bay. Picture the marble pillars, the terraced galleries. Now, imagine as ten thousand world philosophers in long, white robes take their seats. Ask them to define what a human being is. Tally their answers, then usher them out. Invite ten thousand priests representing the world's different religions to file in. Ask them the same question. Tally their responses. Repeat this process with the world's intellectuals, poets, warriors, politicians, average citizens, and tradesfolk.

"What you would find is that humanity's most consistent and common belief is the belief in a human soul. Having an *inner being* is the common thread running throughout all of humanity. Wraithians are no different."

The Readers had allowed the campfire to die to a soft glowing of reddish coals. A few children fleetingly wondered why, but like everything on Scroll Night, even the now-meager level of firelight had a purpose.

"Children," Alina said, "rise and spread your blankets out next to your seats." After they had done so, she said, "Now lie down, relax, and take in the night sky."

Cloudless, moonless, the night canopy seemed like black velvet adorned with an infinite array of silent, twinkling diamonds. The children's view of the vast expanse was unimpaired because their night vision had not been compromised by the light from a blazing campfire. Virtually all made that connection, remembering lessons taught concerning stealth and night maneuvers.

Taggart and Alina remained seated. "What do you see?" Alina asked once the children were settled.

"Stars," they all answered.

"Our Creator's home," Keiriam added a few heartbeats later.

"And what are stars?" Taggart asked.

"Suns," most answered immediately.

"Suns like ours, only far away," Marcus added.

"And what do your teachers tell you of our sun?" Alina asked. "And of those more distant above us?"

The children responded quickly. That they were flat on their backs did not hamper the ingrained give-and-take dialogue between teacher and pupil. And all were well versed in the sciences. Throughout the school year, from *Andril* through *Orctombray*, Wraithian schools hosted geologists, foresters, healers, mining engineers, astronomers, botanists, and other scientists as guest instructors. Once a month, schools loaded the children of all ages aboard "learning wagons" for field trips to working mines, orchards, vineyards, ranches, or plant nurseries. For children of *Scimitar* Province, a favorite trip was to the great telescope atop Mt. Trahern. Astronomers there taught of the distances between the stars, of meteors, of the moon, and of the solar system.

"The sun warms our planet," one said. "The seasons change because of our planet's orbit and the tilt of its axis," another added.

"Our moon causes the tides," Leah chimed in.

"And what of the moon," Alina asked, "and its orbit? Is our earth alone as it orbits the sun?"

"The moon orbits the earth, and the earth orbits the sun," Brann answered. "But other planets orbit the sun too, and those planets have moons like we do. Professor Cadell said so. He said that every star attracts something: dust or rocks or planets and moons. We just can't see it or prove it yet."

Alina nodded to her husband. The stage was set. Each child now shared a simple vision of the solar system, of the unreachable expanse of the universe.

They were ready.

"Wraithians believe that our souls are eternal," Taggart began, "that your soul is the brilliant, golden core fire of your existence. Picture your soul as miniature sun, and like all suns—and stars—things will naturally orbit it. In fact, things *must* orbit it. The power of our sun attracts space dust, comets, rock debris from unseen collisions in deep space, planets, moons, and things we are only beginning to understand."

As if to emphasize the Reader's point, a succession of meteor trails streaked overhead, causing the children to point and laugh.

"What we assume in astronomy," Taggart continued, "is that the closer something is to a sun, be it dust mote or planet, the tighter it is held in that sun's grip. Using this analogy, the tiny sun that we call your 'soul' will acquire things in orbit about it too as it matures. As Professor Cadell says, every sun, by its nature and power, will, over time, acquire the orbits of *something* large or small. Each sun matures over its lifetime and attains a certain level of completion. Our sun has a relative completion to this point in time because we know of certain planets, moons, and asteroid belts that permanently orbit it. As our scientific knowledge increases, perhaps as we build larger telescopes, we will no doubt discover that the completion, the maturity of our particular solar system is even greater than we currently understand."

"Now then, children," Alina said, "you must see yourself, your soul, in the same light. Picture the great solar system model hanging from the ceiling at the Mt. Trahern observatory. Around the yellow sun at the center, the planets and their respective moons are fixed in their orbits. Your soul is like that, only instead of planets and moons, other things will orbit you. Call them 'traits' or 'characteristics.' Those things that orbit the golden sun that is your soul determine the *quality* of your character—good or bad.

"And know this. Every human being alive has character of some kind—good or bad, high or low, as defined by which traits orbit their soul. There is no such thing as a human being without character. Character can be lofty, noble and worthy of emulation by others, just as it can be repugnant, untrustworthy, or demeaning. Our Creator gives each soul the gift of Life. The soul's mission is to build and choose the quality of its character. This Reading, *your* Reading, explains your role in the development of *your* character.

"We all have personal traits: you, your siblings, your parents and grandparents, Taggart and I. They define our character. They make each of us unique."

"Tell me the difference," Taggart said, "between character and reputation?"

"Grandfather says character is what you are inside," Keiriam said.

"Your substance," Drystan added.

"Father says character is who you are when no one is watching," Leah said with firmness.

"Ah," Taggart said with a smile, "that being the ultimate test."

The children nodded with agreement.

"Then what of reputation?" Taggart asked. "How is it different from character?"

The group was silent for a moment, each child formulating answers as if in a classroom.

"Reputation is the things that you do," Seanna answered, "the things you've done in the past. The things you are known for."

"Hmmmmm," Taggart murmured, "is that all?"

"It's *everything* we've done," Devyn emphasized.

"Our personal history then," Taggart prompted.

"Yes," Quinn said, then added, "no, not exactly."

"Well, which is it?" Taggart countered. "Yes or no?"

The boy looked perplexed but determined to answer. "It's not our personal history, because only we would know that about ourselves. It's more like what others see us do, or what they've heard that we have done. It's what people *think* we've done."

"Then reputation can be a *perception* of us, of our actions by others?" Taggart asked.

"Yes," Marcus said. "Whether they are right or wrong about us, our reputation is their *impression* of who they think we are."

"Well said, young Marcus," Taggart said with a grin and a slap to his knee. "Well said indeed. Now understand this. To Wraithians, character and reputation are deliberately created things. And of the two, character is the most solid.

"In the main studio classroom at our quarry, a sign hangs upon the north wall. Carved in oak by my great, great grandfather, it relates to my profession as a sculptor, as well as to young sculptors and stone carvers who apprentice under me. It says, in a somewhat different way, what the Orbit Scrolls say. It reads:

Character is the sculpture you create,
from the choices you make,
and from the values you cherish.
Reputation is the shadow cast by your sculpture,
as Life shines upon it.

"Now, I ask you children, what does that mean to you?"

"That even though your character is your foundation," Keiriam said, "your reputation can change over time. As Life shines upon it."

"Well said," Taggart affirmed, "and yes, reputations can sometimes change. For good *or* bad. So I ask you, of the two, which is more real?"

"Character," the children replied in virtual unison.

"And what of the shadow called '*Reputation*'?"

"The shape of any shadow depends on the shape of the thing that creates it," Drystan said.

"Yes," Taggart said, "which is absolutely why Wraithians believe in a focused, deliberate creation of one's character. Character is your true identity, the true reality of your soul. And whatever that reality is will determine the shadow of your reputation. Character is serious business. Character is a thing to be created deliberately, not a thing that creates itself randomly."

"That said, consider again the Mt. Trahern model of our solar system, complete with its central sun, and its orbiting planets and moons. Where each of us differs from the Mt. Trahern model is that we can accept or reject those influences that orbit us. We have a certain measure of ability to control the character of our *soular system*, spelled s-o-u-l-a-r."

"But how?" Brann asked. "We don't even know what those traits are," then added, "I don't think." There was a note of frustration in the boy's voice.

"That's true," Taggart agreed, "you don't. Not yet. That, my young friend, is what this Reading, what *your* Scroll Night is all about. Alina and I are about to introduce you to the League of Heralds."

"Heralds?" Seanna asked. "As in official messengers of a king?"

"Exactly," Taggart said. "And each herald is unique."

"But first," Alina said, "you must get up, cushion your backsides again, and take your seats. Formal introductions to a king's emissaries," she said with a twinkle in her eye, "simply cannot happen if one remains flat on one's back."

32

League of Heralds

The children shook their blankets clean, folded them back into cushions, and took their seats. Once settled, Marcus posed an obvious question. "This League of Heralds, sir, is it real, or a figment? It doesn't seem . . . possible, sir. I mean no disrespect."

"None taken," Taggart said, "and your question is valid. I asked the same thing at my Reading," he said, smiling in remembrance. "The League of Heralds is simply our way of illustrating something as mysterious and intangible as character. The League also helps us visualize the equally mysterious human soul."

"Consider," Alina said. "We all know what craft guilds are, do we not?" Every child nodded in assent. "Brann, your father and mother are members of the Potter's Guild. And Quinn, your parents are members of the Goldsmith's Guild, as are your grandparents, and many generations before them, correct?" Both boys answered, "Yes, ma'am."

"A guild perpetuates itself," Alina countered, "by nurturing the individual and by deliberate, continuous improvement of the craft, correct?" Again, the children nodded assent.

"Imagine that we all belonged to a particular guild," Taggart said, "and that I asked each of you to write a short essay about yourself. Each of your writings would be unique even though we all belonged to the same guild. We might tell of our age, our gender, our hobbies, who our family is, the valley or village in which we live. We might describe our eye color, our interests, our goals and ambitions in Life.

"The Orbit Scrolls are like a membership roster of a craft guild, or, in this case, a roster of the League of Heralds. Within the Scrolls is a collection of characteristics that can define the human soul—its character.

"As we read, each herald presents its case for its own existence. The herald greets you as if you are a youngster first. Then it defines itself in simple terms. It then addresses how it might influence you and what you will come to see as your orbits. Most warn you of what it means to accept or reject its orbit."

"But why," Keiriam asked, "would these heralds greet us as youngsters? For us," she said, looking around, "that would be true, but in my family, adults read the Scrolls all the time. Is there an adult version of them?"

"No," Alina said. "The Scrolls were written that way for two reasons: First, to remind us of our temporary station in Life, when compared to the lives of trees, or great mountain peaks, or the universe. Next to such as these, we are all but children."

"Secondly, though the human soul can be very complex, the individual factors that make up one's character are relatively basic. Such things—these heralds for instance—can be easily visualized *and* understood even by children. As well they should be."

"The herald *Courage,* for instance, will describe itself in such a way that you will retain an image of what *Courage* is. The herald *Love* will greet you as another individual much different from *Courage. Imagination* has its own unique story and image of itself for you to consider, as do all the others. All will describe themselves such that you will remember them as unique individuals."

Leah raised her hand at that. "Then why, Lady Kayne, has no one ever read such things to us, or even mentioned them?"

Murmurs of "yes" and "why not?" drifted from the others.

"Two reasons," Alina said. "First, all who experience their own Reading take an oath to not read the Scrolls aloud within earshot of a pre-Reading child. For millennia, that oath of silence allowed Pelanjian and Wraithian youth to enter wilderness Reading Theaters without preconceived notions of the Scroll Night experience. *Your* oath of silence is your gift to future Initiates.

"Secondly, all those around you who have experienced their own Reading, have taken a second oath—as you will also. That oath assigns each individual the mission to deliberately live their life such that their action—not their words—are an example to you. A simple mission one might think, as simple as the words of the heralds are. Yet, living the vision and applying the words of the heralds requires dedication at the core of the individual, and it demands even greater *Discipline* than *Nung-Cha*."

Taggart continued. "Do you wonder why we even come to such a remote place? Have you ever wondered why we don't just present every Wraithian child with a set of Scrolls upon their twelfth birthday? After all, is not every Wraithian expected to be literate in at least four languages by then? Wouldn't it be easier to simply instruct you to read the Scrolls on your own? And why have traditional Readers at all? In fact, why have the ritual at all?" A few children nodded in reluctant agreement. The questions made sense.

"The answer," Taggart said, "is that we come to this isolated place to distinguish *your* Reading, *your* Scroll Night, from every other experience moving forward. As with most things in Life, you will gain only as much *from* this night as you put *into* it."

"To truly benefit tonight, you must free your minds of all that is *not* this night. Open your imaginations, children. Immerse yourself in this time and place. There are no other nights—future or past. Only this one exists for you. Unshackle every sense that you have: hearing, touch, taste, smell, sight. Be with Alina and me tonight. Put aside home . . . school . . . parents . . . everything that is *not* Scroll Night. *Be . . . with . . . us*," Taggart emphasized, then gestured to the night canopy, "and with your Creator."

The expressions on the children's faces reflected more eloquently than words that they were doing just that. The atmosphere around the low firelight seemed to hug them all, children and Readers alike, with a profound sense of unity.

"If you are truly immersed in this time and place," Alina said, "you will notice everything from the warmth of the fire to the sound of the wind whispering through unseen pine needles. Shortly, you will notice something else as well. The League of Heralds is a vast band of individual traits, each with a unique personality. Each herald will sound differently as we introduce them to you. Some will seem happy, while some will exhibit anger. Some are gentle-natured, some are robust. Certain others exude aggression. Some are not true orbits at all, though most are. As with every aspect of Scroll Night, this is by design."

"Readers endeavor to assume the identity of the herald as it speaks to you. We will use different voice inflections, intensities, and tones. We will project attitudes unique to a character. Readers train this way to reinforce the message each herald brings tonight."

"Then Readers perform as actors?" Seanna asked. "Like those who bring the summer plays to the villages?"

"Yes, very much so," Alina said. "Just as performers bring life to characters in a play, Readers breathe life and a sense of identity into each herald in the League. Nothing on Scroll Night is done by accident. Scroll Night is a time of thoughtful intention, of deliberate action, and of purpose. *Randomness*," she emphasized, "does not exist here."

"We must use our imaginations then, ma'am?" Devyn said. "To understand Scroll Night? To truly *be* here?"

Alina smiled at the boy's grasp of being here. "Yes," she said, "absolutely. Now watch the sky above again for a few moments with me." As the children took in the great black expanse again, a meteor streaked from east to west. Another flashed for a few seconds from the northwest.

"See those?" Alina said, pointing as other white-hot trails appeared and faded. "The heralds in the Scrolls are like that. They appear from the dark expanse of Creation to get your attention, to introduce themselves to you. From then on, it is your responsibility to determine how long their light will last in your life. If you chose them to orbit you, they will stay. If you chose to reject them, they will darken and fade away. Is this much clear?"

The children all murmured in the affirmative. They understood—so far. In the twenty-one Readings that Taggart and Alina had performed thus far, not one child in any group had treated this question lightly. Each knew they were being addressed as thinking adults. This was not child's play. Life loomed before them as vast, as unknown, as beautifully complex as the black canopy above. As each star fit within the various constellations, so too did each sun serve its purpose to those planets and moons that orbited them. Likewise, each of these Twelfth-Harvest souls would eventually grow to fit and discover their Life's purpose.

"Now then, children," Alina said, "we've spoken much of heralds, but not of the King they serve. Let us therefore imagine one more vision."

33

Ignition

" ook at my hand, children," Taggart said, raising his open right hand skyward. The dim glow from the fire could not soften the evidence of Taggart's decades as a sculptor. Yellowed calluses from gripping mallet and chisel armored his palms and long, thick fingers. His wrist and rugged, veiny forearm were crisscrossed with countless tiny scars—cuts made by razor-sharp marble and granite shards hammered from raw quarried blocks.

Pointing heavenward, the Reader said, "Picture against that black sky, a single Great Hand as it materializes out of the darkness." A moment of silence passed before he declared reverently, "That . . . is the Hand of our Maker. Do . . . you . . . see it?"

"Yes," the children murmured, some even closing their eyes as their imaginations created the vision.

"Reach skyward with your open right hands, children, as your Maker reaches down to you." Taggart waited for them to complete the movement before saying, "Watch His Hand clench into a mighty fist." Taggart's hand mimicked his words. "Clench your own fists—slowly. Deliberately. Tightly. Thank you."

"Notice the veins pulsing in His giant wrist. Notice the nails of His fingers, thumb, the tensing of the muscles of His wrist as His fist tightens. But watch now! Something is happening inside the fist."

Even those with eyes closed strained their attention skyward.

"A faint glow of yellow inside the fist is turning part of the flesh transparent," Taggart continued. "You can make out bones in the immense fingers now. The yellow glow intensifies. Beams of brilliant golden light escape, streaming from between the tightly clenched fingers."

"Bring your fist down to chin level. Hold it there for now. Thank you."

"The Great Hand above unclenches slowly, opening palm up." Again, Taggart's hand mimicked his words. "There, floating in silence just above His palm is a single globe of boiling gold—a tiny sun. Golden flames churn silently about it in the blackness of space. See how beautiful it is . . . so magnificent a creation. An aura of purity clings to it like the scent of a rain-cleansed morning. Compared to the dark, unlimited panorama behind it, the event seems insignificant, but this cannot be. For our Creator has chosen to ignite a new soul into existence, and His souls are *never* insignificant. *You* are never insignificant—unless *you* choose to be. The people you will meet along your Life path are never insignificant—unless *they* choose to be."

"That sun is *you*," the Reader emphasized. "Created by the Father, that innocent little sun awaits His grand intention."

"Now, children," Taggart demonstrated, "open your right-hand palm up near your chin. Hear me. Listen as our Maker inhales a Great Breath against the silence of the universe. Inhale slowly with me." Taggart and Alina both held their right hands near their chins as the children now did. "Listen as He exhales against *you* there in His Hand. Exhale with me." The children all blew against their palms as their Readers did.

"The little sun floats away from the Creator's hand as delicately as thistledown," Taggart intoned. His hand disappears back into the darkness. *You* float alone in the universe, vulnerable, malleable. For nine months, you've awaited your entrance to Life, knowing inherently that you must begin an odyssey of some kind.

"And now, floating with such incandescent innocence, you await the Creator's next step, His intention for your life. So newly born, you have no idea that what you await is a passage of wanderers from the blackness surrounding you. You await the arrival of the King's heralds—the ones who will speak for the first time to the creation of that King."

"For that reason, the Scrolls are written as if the heralds are introducing themselves to you personally. Each herald that we bring to you tonight addresses the individual soul as if it had just been born, and each will follow a set protocol.

"First, each will greet you, and then define itself or its purpose in very basic terms. Each herald will give you a vision of itself, something simple yet so vivid that you will remember who and what it is. Some will warn of how their orbit might damage a soular system in some way. Each will invite you to choose it for your system, and then it will bid you farewell.

"For the most part tonight, you will be exposed to only the more positive heralds in the League. Yet, you must understand that not all in the League are positive. Negative, damaging heralds, enemies to a healthy soular system, exist within the Scrolls as well. They go by the names of *Jealousy*, *Hatred*, *Envy*, and *Greed*, to name just a few. How could they not exist? But on Scroll Night we leave such as these for your future reading and contemplation.

"Although you will meet many heralds tonight," Taggart continued, "you will not meet anywhere near the number that reside within the Scrolls. There are simply too many heralds, too many different traits of human nature to cover in our short time together.

"Nor will we even read a herald's complete commentary of itself. We will read selected high points from each one. No matter what you hear from us tonight, just know that much more remains for you to discover about each herald through your study and meditation. A single Scroll Night cannot possibly show every influence to a soul's system.

"The purpose of Scroll Night is to introduce you to the Scrolls and to paint a visual memory of the Orbit point of view. The rest belongs to you, to your discovery of truths along your journey through Life, and from your deeper reading of the Scrolls. Your first step across the threshold of adulthood is not tomorrow at the sword burning. It is right now!"

The Readers allowed the children to absorb the vision of a soul's birth, to own it personally. In the silence, Taggart reached for fresh pieces of wood to rebuild the fire. Alina poked the coals with a stick, bringing them to flame against the new wood. The fire brightened noticeably against the surrounding night.

When the flames rose to illuminate every child's face, the Readers pulled two Scrolls from their leather cases. Each lay the second Scroll atop the case at their feet. Each unrolled the first Scroll past the Pelanjian Beacons—the Wraithian Code of Honor that prefaced each Orbit Scroll. The children leaned forward, eyes wide with anticipation.

In the peripheral darkness, shadow-clad Guardians noted the change in the intensity of the campfire. Some smiled with thanksgiving that their child had reached this pivotal night. Others wept silently, joyfully, for the same reason. All raised silent prayers of gratitude to the One Whose Great Hand had just disappeared back into the dark heavens, for each remembered their own Reading. Each remembered their own vision of a soul's creation.

Upon reaching the first herald in the Scroll, Alina said reverently, "Let us begin."

34

Dawn

Silence followed as Alina opened her Scroll to the proper place. The only noticeable sounds were the crackle of the fire and the light evening wind sighing through the emperor spruces guarding them all. Taggart allowed the children to absorb the sounds before he introduced the herald that Alina was about to bring to life.

"The wanderers of the League have arrived," Taggart said, gazing skyward. Most of the children followed his gaze. Tyra and Drystan glanced heavenward, but quickly refocused their attention on Alina and this first venture into the Scrolls.

"See them as they approach in the distance. They gather about the Maker's newest creation like uncountable stars. They assemble because the scent of a newly ignited soular sun has attracted them, as it always does. *You* are that tiny sun waiting in the fathomless blackness of space. *You* have drawn the Creator's League of Heralds to you.

"Some have come in haste," Taggart continued, "others are content to appear with a kind of regal stateliness. Most will appear as individuals, while a few will present themselves as inseparable companions. A few delight in their roles as quick, unforeseen influences.

"Most bear exquisite gifts, but others are thieves of the new creation's character. The time has come for the fledgling child-sun, for you, to learn how to distinguish the difference."

Alina squirmed slightly on her stump seat in preparation. She held the Scroll in both hands and leaned toward the children until her forearms rested upon her thighs. Her eyes sparkled as she smiled, feeling, as always, the privilege of what she was about to do.

Taggart's smile matched her own. *Once again, we are blessed by the honorable weight of these robes.*

Without realizing it, the children leaned forward also. Scroll Night had finally arrived. Anticipation radiated from their little faces.

As Alina began to read, her voice assumed the friendly tone of a neighbor dropping by for a visit. Before the children's wide, expectant eyes, her voice, her persona, her very presence *became* the first member of the mysterious League of Heralds.

Good day, and welcome to Life, young one.

Call me *Awareness*, for I am always the first to greet a new soular system. Picture me as a splendid sunrise just now peeking over your personal Life-horizon. I am the first dawn of "you," the first light to illuminate your existence. I welcome each newly created soul to its Life path. I celebrate your birth. Know that I am the vanguard of many heralds who also now sense the discreet fragrance of your birth. Even now, they approach like raptors of lightning.

From incalculable distances we have come—empyrean rovers of black galactic seas. Our range is infinity, our lifetimes measured in eons. We offer powers and potentials, subtleties and refinements of endless variety. Your duty is to select those of my companions that you deem most valuable. As with any star in any galaxy, you will retain certain orbits more strongly than others. Ultimately, the character of your soular system will be determined by the orbits of those heralds you hold most firmly.

Know this beyond all else. You are a Divine creation. You belong to Father Creator. You . . . are . . . of . . . Him. Each beat of your heart, each breath you take, each blink of your eyes is His gift of life to you. Remember that. Ponder it. Be grateful each day for it. Learn of yourself, for this, I declare, is your mission in Life: To define and to refine the character of your soular system for as long as you live. Remain vigilant as your system matures. Remain cognizant of *how* it matures. Make honorable decisions. Make good Life-path choices.

Consult the Scrolls continually. Read of the heralds who bring enlightenment, nobility of being, and those qualities that invite, that *attract* respect. Read also of those heralds who might bring shadows to your life, who might erode your character. Who might weaken your system, and thus your *Reputation*. Select or reject those of the League as you will, but choose your companions well, for they will orbit you for the duration of your pilgrimage. As heralds from the King, we are but the parts. You must gather us, assemble us, and formulate the whole of your character. You and you alone are accountable for the strength of your soular system. Rationalizations are unacceptable excuses for a soul's shortcomings.

When you get older, you will ponder the meaning of Life. Most ultimately do. Remember my definition of your Life mission. Let those words define the term "meaning of Life."

At any rate, I have accomplished *my* mission. You have awakened. You are aware. I leave you to the other heralds. See them as blazing diamond comets of your future. Feel their power as they approach.

Prepare yourself, young one.

Here they come.

35

Sword and Shield

Upon completing her reading, Alina rolled her Scroll to the next herald. Taggart mimicked her. After an extended silence, Alina reverted to her naturally smooth voice and said, "After the first caress of *Awareness*, the fledgling sun begins the process of balancing, of selecting, of growing. It begins to develop as a soular system."

"Dual heralds arrive this time," she said, "as polished weapons to defend, to empower the new-born. They bolster the soul as a seasoned warrior is bolstered by sword and shield."

As Taggart took on the persona of the second arrivals, the children sensed his pleasant baritone sharpen. The voice representing these heralds was direct, clear, and precise. The tone became abrupt, almost severe. A few children held anticipatory smiles. Others dropped theirs. Taggart's clipped voice lost all trace of pleasant subtlety.

Greetings, young one. We are *Logic.* We are *Reason.* We are your power to think soundly. Picture us as your personal sword and shield. Picture equally well that which we are *not*!

We are not *Excuse*, or *Pretense*, or *Fabrication*. We are not *Rationalization*. We are inseparable twins, eternal orbits of each other. We are your means to differentiate human introspection from bestial instinct. Without our presence, free, contemplative thought cannot exist in your soular system. Without our orbits, there can be no balancing, no weighing of accumulated facts. Facts are dead stones, possessing no flame of their own. We bind the collected stones. We transform cold information into the flame of focused, *useful* thought.

Yet, we give you this warning. Incorporate us into your system with caution. In our purest form we are dangerous. Pure, stand-alone *Logic* and *Reason* transform a thinking organism into an intelligent, albeit cold machine devoid of humanity.

You must avoid descending to this condition, even though certain cultures consider supplanting the warmth of human emotion with the chill of pure *Logic* and *Reason* as a superior state of being. It is not, though the overzealous scientist, the devoted scholar of pure mathematics, even the militant devotee of a nation's legal system, might argue this point.

There must be the warmth of humanity wielding the iron-clad shield. The warmth of the human hand must grasp the cold hilt of the sword.

Temper the weaponry we offer with the heralds *Compassion*, *Understanding*, and *Intellect*. Do so to become a magnificent completion of your Creator. Invite *Love* of family, of neighbors, of community and nation, the *Love* of your Maker to join our orbits so that you might become a creation of *Balance*.

We offer a second warning very similar to the one our fellow herald, *Intellect*, will offer you. Like *Intellect*, we will atrophy and flee your system if abandoned. Yet, if you use us, if you hone us at every opportunity, you will be as perpetually armed as a seasoned warrior. Your reward for such diligence is to rise above that which is animal.

Hear and comprehend, young one. Holding the orbits of *Logic* and *Reason* close empowers you to peer over the bowed heads of multitudes of other soular systems. That is both an indictment of them and our promise of reward to you. We are a major ingredient in what your people call "deliberate thinking." We visit countless systems. We speak to all as we speak to you now. Scant few genuinely accept us for this reason. Embracing the orbits of *Logic* and *Reason* requires a healthy orbit of *Discipline* as well, and *Discipline* requires work and steadfast *Commitment*.

Be part of the elite, young one. Be an individual thinker. Choose uniqueness over those who herd-think with their fellows.

Unique thought demands *Imagination*. Unique thought demands a significant expenditure of energy for ignition. The joy of dueling against an antagonistic problem with a well-honed sword of

Reason is unknown to those who choose to dwell in comfort with the herd. The beauty of painting a unique thought with the rainbow of pigments from the pallet of pure *Logic* is denied them—by their choice! Do not deny our gifts, child-sun. Be unique unto yourself. You will never regret it, for the rewards are unique also. We offer you the armament of rational thought. Take us. Unsheathe us. Wield us. Feel the power we offer.

Grow strong with us and fear no darkened passageway. We are the strength that illuminates the darkness of *Irrationality*.

Be a mighty warrior, whose unflinching stare no danger, mystery, or superstition can withstand. We are the force behind that stare so intimidating to the fear of the unknown.

The choice is yours.

36

Torch

Readers are taught to deliberately pause after reading each herald on Scroll Night. The Master Readers who conduct the year-long training call this the "time of echoes."

"A time of silence must be allowed for the children to absorb the words, the mood and the tone of each herald," the masters remind their Elder students. "In the brief silence between heralds," they expound, "meaning will echo through the minds of the young like words tossed into a great canyon. Do not hurry the echoes. Allow them to fade deep into the young minds naturally."

Taggart allowed the echoes of his clipped words and their abrupt tone to dissipate before clearing his throat. The same words, tone and inflections echoing in the children's minds still echoed in his own. When at last he spoke again, he did so in his normal baritone, an open, friendly sound, devoid of affected implication.

"Comes now a herald closely related to those you just met. But where the sword and shield were of a somewhat colder nature, this herald—despite its closeness to the others—is, shall we say . . . warmer?"

His eyes twinkled a little at that, but not as much as Alina's. Obvious to all, she could barely contain her enthusiasm to read of the next herald.

Her soothing voice rose noticeably in pitch as her face broke into a smile. The children's eyes widened in response as the Reader's demeanor transformed from sedate to energetic. The cadence of her words was light and quick, falling upon her listeners' ears like raindrops in a brisk spring shower. Resting the Scroll in her lap, she gestured animatedly with both hands as she recited from memory.

"Some heralds arrive with exuberance," she announced with unfettered enthusiasm. "Totally aware of the value of their gift, they are anxious to be accepted."

Greetings, new one!

I applaud your birth! I celebrate your existence! May my orbit dance lifelong about your system. I doubt that any of my companions feel the same elation that I feel over a new birth.

Call me *Intellect.* I am known by other names, but this shall suffice. My fellows *Logic* and *Reason* give you the power to think. I am your capacity for knowledge, your potential for rational thought.

Envision me as a torch vigorously aflame, alive with golden brilliance, held aloft by *your* hand, thrust *by you* into the darkness of superstition, mystery, ignorance. The flames that blaze from me will illuminate paths yet to be trod, yet to be dreamed of along your Life journey. I allow you to see the world as it truly is, a world not shrouded by darkness—of any kind. And know this. What one truly sees invites rational contemplation. And what one truly understands is absorbed by the mind to guide future rational judgments.

As with any flame, the greater it is, the more energy it produces. A great forest fire rages with seemingly unstoppable energy, yet the embers of a dying campfire gradually lessen until they cool into lifeless ashes. I implore you to remember that.

Receive me as a friend, and I will give you power of incomprehensible magnitude, of intricate, enjoyable complexity. Befriend me and I will introduce you to and illuminate *for* you, vistas of knowledge and comprehension that will fill you with awe even as they delight you. I am yours forever to use, to refine, to build ever greater over time. Every new pebble of understanding your inquisitiveness discovers unveils the mountain from which it came. Every new pebble from you begets yet another mountain from me. I never tire of the game. The game *is* my joy, my reason to exist in Creation.

But I must also warn. Do not trifle with me. As powerful as I am, your system's strength of thought is totally dependent upon you. Unused, *Intellect* weakens like the embers of a dying campfire. If tested but infrequently, I begin to slip from your grasp. I will degrade to a whisper of what might have been, leaving just enough residue of myself for naught but basic animal survival and communication. Allow *Intellect* to weaken, and the heralds *Discovery, Curiosity, Comprehension,* and *Invention* will weaken as well. Intellectual darkness weakens these heralds. It destroys their orbits. Without the warmth of my flame, they might not orbit you at all.

Therefore, abuse me not, forsake me not. This is intolerable. I will not allow my mission to be so threatened. Forsaken *Intellect* is an abomination to the rhythm of Creation.

You were not created to wander aimlessly, to treat the gift of Life as if it were nothing more than a pasture to graze from at random. This is what the great herds of prey animals do. *You* are not an animal. *You* are not prey! Not to another human being. Not to a concept *or* to a culture.

You were not created to stumble through the anthem of Life. You were meant to sing it with joy, to flow with it as a living brook, to marvel at the splendor of it. You were meant to participate, to dance within it—deliberately, by will, and with *Gratitude.*

Hear me well. Turn your face from me and descend to the level of the brute, unheeded by your peers. Your mental capacity will disintegrate. You will, for all practical purposes, be rejected by Life. Not by Existence. By Life! Ponder this. Deliberate Life has meaning. Random existence does not.

Reject the power I offer, and you will find no place in Creation's song. You will have no control over your own destiny, no direction, no visions of any real depth. You will exist until your death a perpetual victim of Life's seemingly random acts and accidents.

Reject me and sentence yourself to wander this glorious universe as a blind, tattered beggar pleading for some semblance of Life to accidentally fall into your cup.

Reject me and never feel that soul-deep awe as your Creator's great constellations sing down from a boundless midnight canopy. Feel no awe of ocean tide, of soaring mountain peak.

Forsake me and never utter the question "why?"

Ignore me, fail to tend my flame and lose the joy of an answered wonderment.

The choice is yours, young one. Pursue *Intellect*. Stoke my flame, thirst for my orbit. Seek knowledge of things yet unknown to you. Seek the beauty of great works of art. Explore the history of them. Investigate the motivations of the artists who created them. Learn of your past, of your nation's past. Learn of the histories, of the trials of nations you might never visit. Learn why they rose, or why they fell.

Learn of the beauty that only the rhythm of poetry or a grand symphony can bring to the human soul. Seek the challenge, the energy of opinions different than yours. Seek out and learn of the great ideas, the great inventions, the great contributions that others have brought to Creation's song. Earn callouses from a physical skill you've never attempted before. Seek new horizons to challenge. Learn of cultures other than your own. Savor the subtleties uniquely distinct from your own.

Utilize me to your utmost. I am your friend. I am your only true power, and I can be an unconquerable source of light.

So might you be also.

Should you so choose.

37

Warrior

After a few moments of silence, Alina asked a question that seemed over the heads of the children at first. "Tell me children," she began, "can interaction with other systems—with other *people*—inspire one to absorb a desirable trait as a foundational orbit?" She spoke to them all, but her eyes sought out her granddaughter.

"I don't quite understand, ma'am," Tyra answered.

"Take *Courage*, for instance. Have you have ever seen true *Courage* displayed?" There was no doubt what the girl's answer would be.

"Yes," she replied immediately, "when the wraith came into our barn. My parents protected me and killed the beast."

"Hmmmm," Alina murmured, as if pondering the obvious. "Were they afraid?"

"They were as immovable as stones," the girl replied. "The looks on their faces frightened me more than the wraith did. Almost. The cat would have killed us all, but Father and Mother never flinched. They would have died there together—for me." Her eyes misted slightly; her voice quivered as that raw truth sunk in.

"And their *Courage* was without *Fear*?"

"Yes! I mean no! They *were* afraid . . . for *me*." Tears finally escaped the girl's eyes and ran down her face.

"Then what have we learned already?" Alina said, sounding very much like an academy teacher. "Perhaps that *Fear* can be a catalyst for personal *Courage*? That such opposites might be linked somehow? Or more to the point, can the *Courage* of other systems furnish us a visual depiction so strong, so admired, that we would desire such an influence to make up our core values?"

"But enough questions," she said. "Let us hear more of this herald, this *Courage.*"

The children had already fallen into a pattern of listening for the subtle nuances of their Readers' voices as each new herald introduced itself. That the tone and timbre of Taggart's voice seemed so normal threw them off balance initially. They relaxed at first but snapped back into the rhythm of Scroll Night within moments. Behind the easy, conversational tone of the words, something else lurked. They sensed what might be called an "aura of restraint." This herald hesitated before voicing well-chosen words.

"Certain heralds approach us with obvious . . . trepidation shall we say," Taggart said. "This one in particular knows full well the potential for misunderstanding."

Greetings, young one . . . hear me. I am the one you will call . . . *Courage.*

If you sense hesitation in my approach, there is good reason. Of all the heralds in the League, I am one of the most easily misunderstood. However, any fault of misunderstanding lies with you. I shall be every bit as concise about what I *am*, as I shall be concerning what I am *not*.

Picture me as a warrior of your people—armor clad, steel eyed, fully armed, trained and battle ready.

Let us discuss first that which I am *not*. Know this! I am not *Impetuousness*. I am not *Recklessness* or *Foolhardiness*. These heralds and *Boastfulness* roam together, but their orbits are fragile, unstable things. They claim me, but I reject them. Be clear. They are *not Courage*.

I am the resolute quality of mind that enables you to face the trials and dangers that will attempt to crush you. *Determination* is my close companion, for we are always linked. Our bond forms a solid foundation for your system. Our presence bolsters the orbits of *Confidence, Conviction* and *Honor*, as well as the orbits of other positive heralds. It is often impossible to distinguish me from *Hope*, or *Hope* from me, so closely are we linked.

Courage equips you to stride your Life-path with the composure of a warrior. Whatever vision you hold of a warrior, let that vision be what I am to you. Yet, whether you are physically imposing or outwardly frail never matters. True *Courage* comes from within you. *Boastfulness* and *Foolhardiness* are not characteristics of *Courage*. They are naught but silly trinkets to drape a fragile ego.

There is an odd universal law associated with true *Courage*—another of your Creator's amusements I suspect. It seems that when a soul exhibits *Courage* of any kind, the herald *Respect* appears. Unbidden, unexpected, *Respect* just materializes near my orbit.

Respect, when invited by pure *Courage*, clouds the eyes of your peers in one way, yet opens them in another way. *Courage*-inspired *Respect* forces peers to see your true inner being. They unwittingly judge themselves against your standard. Your outward appearance, even your relative station in Life dims in prominence. *Courage*, and the *Respect* it demands, often forces even enemies to acknowledge you. I will not make enemies love you. They may, in fact, hate you even more than before your *Courage* became obvious. Rather, I force their eyes open. I make them truly see you, the *inner* you, even if they do so begrudgingly. I delight in that.

Given that the herald Dawn has already disclosed your mission in Life as a perpetual refinement of your system and your character, you might find this amusing. Whenever friends or enemies alike notice the orbit of *Courage* in your life, they often consider the evidence of just that single herald as a mark of *Character*. At such times, the words *Character* and *Respect* seem virtually synonymous.

In speaking of *Respect*, I must also enlighten you of others as well, for their existence will help you understand me. *Courage* means conquering those things that attempt to defeat you. I am your stubborn refusal to submit to the weight of any trial you face. Personal *Dignity* plays a role as well, for a sense of one's *Dignity* is often the stimulus that not only invites but holds the orbit of *Courage* fast.

Fear plays a part as well, though that seems like a paradox. *Fear* lives eternally within the shadow of *Courage*, for logical *Fear* is necessary for survival. Equally true, *Fear*, whether logical or irrational, will always try to defeat you. That is *Fear's* mission.

Remember that. *Fear* is eternally diligent about its mission. *You* must remain eternally vigilant about yours. Know that also before judging your peers too harshly when *Fear* breaks their *Courage*. Any soul can be broken by *Fear*—*any* soul. *Courage* is never the absence of *Fear*. Quite the opposite. Without genuine *Fear* to conquer, there can be no true *Courage*. It might even be said that true *Courage* requires the existence of *Fear*, because *Courage* decides that something else is more important than *Fear*. The mature soul understands that about both heralds.

Note also that human *Courage* differs from what is perceived as *Courage* in the animal world. *Courage* in the human being, is, in part, an intellectual judgment. You visualize the particular disaster looming on your horizon, yet you decide to stand firm against the odds that *Logic* and *Reason* proclaim will destroy you. It is that very foreknowledge of personal destruction, joined with the *Choice* to persevere despite the danger that makes human *Courage* so extraordinary.

In truth, the *Courage* attributed to animals is also wonderful to behold, but it is an instinct-inspired thing, pack behavior, the reaction of a female to protect its young, the thoughtless hormonal drive of a dominate male to protect its territory.

For the human being, the blessing of *Reason* requires the burden of *Choice*. The reality of facing certain destruction yet choosing to refuse submission to it defines human *Courage*.

The ability of the human mind to foresee the possible destruction of itself, yet choosing to stand its ground, to defend family, or principle, or a personal belief, is what distinguishes human *Courage* from animal instinct. Few things in Life are more magnificent than genuine human *Courage*.

Understand something else about *Courage*, young one. Too often *Courage* is only acknowledged during noble acts of *Valor* in war, or in great events of dire proportion. These are certainly venues for *Courage*, but they are not the only ones—by far.

True, a soul can find the *Courage* during a major crisis, to exhibit a wondrous level of personal *Valor*. However, *Courage* is required in great measure during the uneventful days of your life that will comprise most of your existence. This sounds like yet another paradox of *Courage*, but it is oftentimes easier to exhibit

Courage as a dragon slayer than to do so as a farmer. The dragon slayer faces a formidable, but short term and extremely rare obstacle, while the farmer faces daily, unending obstacles of lower intensity. True *Courage* is your conscious choice to do the job at hand, whatever that might be, to accomplish the particular mission of that moment, no matter what opposes it—the monumental or the mundane.

Yes, that could mean a brave warrior exhibiting great *Valor* when staring an overwhelming enemy in the face to defend a fallen comrade in war. Yes, that could be the heroic captain who steers his ship and its passengers to safety in the midst of a murderous storm when all others had lost *Hope.* It might be the selflessness of a mother rushing back into her burning home until she rescues the last of her trapped children. These are the dragon slayers of Life.

However, *Courage* is also the selflessness of a father who grinds out a living for his family, from work that denies him recognition, which begrudges personal gratification. It is the struggling mother beset by poverty (a dragon in its own right, certainly), who awakens each day to fight for her children's wellbeing, for their daily bread. These, and millions more like them, are the farmers of Life. The *Courage* exhibited by such as these is no less magnificent than that of the dragon slayer. It is simply not as obvious or as flamboyant to surrounding observers.

You will observe many acts of *Courage* in your life, my young friend, and my simple definitions will expand as Life enlightens you. This is as it should be. Yet, remember that true *Courage* is often a quiet thing. More often than not, it will be invisible to your peers. True *Courage* actually produces a personal quietude when the *Motivation* for it is true, when the need for it is right and just. Strive, therefore, to understand my colleague *Motivation.* Only by brutally honest self-examination will you come to know the undercurrents of your true self as you journey along your Life-path.

Accept me and gain strength of foundation, of conviction. Reject me, and retain very few convictions beyond animal survival.

Without true *Courage,* you will be slave to random, impetuous attempts to achieve self-esteem. Life will be a never-ending torment of chest-pounding proclamations that will only weaken you more. Every attempt to capture recognition from your peers will addict you more. Such a path is self-destructive.

Forsake the temptation to tread the childish, clamorous paths of *Recklessness*, of *Foolhardiness*, or *Bravado.* Such as these are as meaningless as they are shallow. They are pathetic and sad despite their surface energy.

Therefore, accept me as I truly am, for I am one of the League who will not warn you of excess. You cannot possess too much true *Courage.* Life has too many variations to test you. You need me to gain access to the quiet path of *Confidence.*

Commit to the quieter path, young one. Choose the way of true strength, of true *Fortitude.* I stand in silence at your door.

Open the door, my friend.

Open it wide.

38

Undercurrent

"Children," Taggart said, breaking the required silence. "Give me your opinion. Are rituals good or bad?"

"Good," Quinn Farriss, the goldsmith's son, said quickly.

"Not always," Drystan Bradach, the vintner's son, countered after thinking about it. "They can be bad sometimes."

"Well," Alina said, "which is it? Good or bad?"

"They're good," Quinn said again, a bit more forcefully this time in defense of his point. A chorus of "ayes" rose in agreement.

"Drystan," Alina said, "rituals are bad? Is that what you believe?" Both Readers' eyes narrowed in concentration, hoping the bright lad would note Alina's misquote of him.

"No ma'am," the boy answered. "I didn't say they *are* bad, only that they *can* be."

"Ah," Alina smiled. "What makes them one way or another?"

"Meaning," Drystan answered. "They must mean something to have value."

Alina smiled. The boy's parents, Ewan and Kiera, were longtime friends of her and Taggart. Despite the work required to tend their thousand-acre vineyard and a second tract that size holding apple, peach, and pear orchards, the Bradachs were well read, and highly, but quietly intelligent.

Over the decades, the Kaynes and Bradachs had enjoyed many lively dinner conversations at each other's homes. But dialogue with the Bradachs early into a new subject tended to be . . . unburdened, as Taggart observed, by elaboration. Only deeper introspection and time spent in conversation had the power to add further Bradach embellishments to a given subject.

"Meaning," Alina said. "In what way? Don't all rituals, by their very existence, have meaning? Of some kind? By virtue of some sort of meaningful history?"

"Yes," Drystan said, "or they wouldn't exist in the first place. The problem is if the original meaning becomes shrouded or lost over time."

"So if the original intention of a ritual is forgotten," Alina said, "it becomes no more than a meaningless habit."

"Exactly," Drystan said, leaning forward for emphasis exactly as his father often did once warming to a subject. "A ritual has greater meaning if a person remembers the original purpose for it and performs it *for* that reason."

"Well said, young Drystan," Taggart said. "And what rituals do Wraithians hold dear?"

"This Reading," Leah Brenna, the tanners' daughter said.

"And?" Alina prompted.

"Children reaching their twelfth harvest have attended Readings from the time our people lived in the Pelanjian Islands. It was centuries old even then."

"And the reason for it?" Taggart asked.

"To give us a picture of Life and how character develops around our soul."

"Did you know this for a fact?" Taggart asked. "Say as recently as yesterday?"

"No sir, I did not," the girl answered. "Wraithian tradition inspires us to look forward to Scroll Night, but tradition is silent as to the experience itself."

"Any other rituals?" Alina asked.

"*Nung-Cha* practice," Seanna Berit, daughter of the swordsmiths said. "*Nung-Cha* is almost as old as the Readings are."

"And the reason behind it?" Taggart asked.

"Self-defense of the individual and the nation," she said. Without pausing, she added, "To protect the home islands from invasion by the Outsiders, the Pelanjians created *Nung-Cha*. They scoured the planet for the best warriors of empty hand, of various weapons, cavalry, and stealth techniques. They brought them, along with master archers, martial arts masters, and even skilled assassins back to Pelanjia and hired them to teach their skills. After five decades, the martial system known as *Nung-Cha*—the Necessary Path—was complete. They used *Nung-Cha* for nearly four hundred years after that to defend our home archipelago."

"Anything else?" Taggart asked.

"*Enkia-Entae,* our Prayer Stones," Devyn Briac, the farmer's son ventured. "Every household has one, and we bow before them daily at Prayer Time and before each *Nung-Cha* practice."

"Outsiders might think we pray to rocks," Taggart remarked.

A resounding chorus of "no" answered immediately. "Preposterous, sir," Keiriam Marsali, daughter of the stonemasons said. "We don't worship stones. Wraithians bow only to Creator."

"But how would you explain the ritual to an Outsider?" Taggart prompted.

"I would say that a Prayer Stone symbolizes the plight of the human being. Both are anchored to the earth, yet both reach toward our Creator. The stone reminds us of that. It's not an object of worship. Rather, the stones help focus our worship."

"Nicely stated, young miss," Taggart said. "You've been taught well to recognize distinctions, to see clearly, as it were.

"You do so because Wraithians approach Life deliberately. We leave little to chance. We actively teach the meaning behind rituals such as the Prayer Stone.

"Imagine how a meaningful ritual such as a simple bow to a granite obelisk might degrade into a meaningless religious ritual if unaccompanied by deliberate attention to detail. After centuries, a simple bow could become obscure, its meaning completely opposite the original intention."

"With that," Alina said. "Let us hear from our next herald, who just might have something to say of hidden meanings."

Alina unrolled her scroll for her turn. Her voice barely louder than a whisper, the children had to lean forward to hear. This herald seemed to lay bare a deeply hidden secret of some sort.

Greetings.

Call me *Motivation.* I am the force that causes you to act in a certain way, to plan a certain strategy, to ponder—anything, everything. I link closely with my fellow herald—*Intention* and that is an important detail to remember. Your actions, the results of your *Intentions*, are what I inspire, invite, or instigate within you. Some regard me as a spur to action, as a rider guides a mount, but given that you are of a seafaring people, it is best to imagine me as an invisible undercurrent.

Undercurrents manifest as subtle or drastic power, and this is true of oceans, rivers, or human beings. Undercurrents of *Motivation* flow within everything the human creation thinks or does. They can be noble and just, or crude and hate-filled. They can be divine with generosity or darkened by greed and avarice. *Motivations* can be coarsely driven by bestial lust, or delicately coaxed by *Love's* silken hand.

In terms of impact on your path, I am one of the most influential heralds. Our relationship is twofold: First, you must recognize my existence and my influence within you. Secondly, it is your duty to examine your behavior with others. For any thinking creature, the examination of one's motives should be a lifelong vigil. This is not an easy task that I ask of you.

Do your actions walk upright bathed in the light of *Honor*? Or do they slink about furtively, dishonorably shrouded by a dark cloak of *Envy* or *Jealousy*?

This examination of self, this duty, is uniquely human, and further widens the gulf between beast and human. Animals do not contemplate their *Motivations*, which are really just engraved instincts. Humans do ponder such things, or should, because humans have engraved in *them* the capacity to do so from their Creator.

What the human does *not* have the capacity to do is to accept or reject me as an orbit. *Motivation*, you see, exists not only at the core of the smallest, most primordial organism, but at the core of the most complex as well. I simply am.

I ignited into existence the instant that the Maker ignited you into being. I am more an ingredient in the complex recipe that equals you than a herald to choose or reject as an orbit. That does not, however, give you leave to trivialize *Motivation*, or to use me as a convenient *Justification*.

As a thinking creature, you should strive to live deliberately, to be guided by rational thought. Embracing *Discipline* empowers you to boldly examine the consequence of cause and effect. Embrace *Courage* in order to distinguish between honorable *Motivations* and those of the baser sort, those of shallow and self-serving nature.

The opposite of living deliberately as a thinking creation is to live at random. In a random state, you reject your gift of rational thought. You ignore consequence of action. You meander through Life swayed by ingrained *Motivations* strikingly similar to animal instincts. You were created for a greater existence than that. You were created to think deeper than that. Let the beast live as it does. You cannot!

Rational, introspective beings contemplate the *Motivations* flowing beneath thoughts, deeds and attitudes—their own as well as those of others. This is one way the human understands one's place in Creation, and the significance of others. To contemplate purpose behind one's actions permits one to ask the questions "why?" and "what if?"

I warn you to be wary of the word "ulterior." Ulterior motives imply a lack of purity behind one's thoughts and deeds. Ulterior motives reflect a personal dishonesty of some sort, intentionally shrouded from the light of *Truth* for reasons known only to yourself.

Examine the undercurrents behind your *Intention*s and actions. Something, however trite or base, however noble, or ritualistic, or necessary is there. In some form or another, I will always be with you.

Did you show kindness toward another because their plight broke your heart, or because you expected some form of recognition or reward? Did that kindness gain you some future advantage, or was it simply the right thing to do?

Do you *Love* for social status, for wealth, or do you *Love* because of that miraculous attraction that binds you to another person?

When angered by another, is your *Anger* born from some perceived personal insecurity, from *Jealousy* or *Envy*, or is it ignited by a genuine sense of *Justice*? Is your *Anger* righteous and honorable, or do you wield it as a weapon of power and intimidation? *Anger* has its place if the *Motivation* behind it is honorable. *Anger* fueled by ignoble *Motivations* demeans you. It degrades your *Intentions*. Your actions become suspect then. So will your *Reputation*.

And by all means, consider your children. Do you raise them deliberately? Or do you allow other influences to do so: peripheral adults, teachers, the social whims of the day, society's moral nod of the day?

Do you truly guide the child, or is there personal laziness in your stewardship of the child's path? If so, fix what is broken in your *Motivations*. Do this in every aspect of your life. The healing of flawed *Motivation* is within your power, despite the difficulty of doing so. To do so requires brutal honesty on your part. It requires perfect vision to genuinely see yourself, and the iron will that only *Honor* can give to *Discipline*.

Know yourself, for to do so is to live deliberately. Understanding your own behavior, understanding the behavior of those around you, demands that you hold fast the orbits of *Reason*, *Logic*, and *Intellect*. These heralds repel *Rationalization* and *Justification*. When such heralds orbit you, their opposites cannot.

The primal *Motivations* within you are the most powerful influences you will ever endure, listen to, fight against, or submit to. The sexual drive, hunger, *Fear*, *Greed*, the will to survive, to dominate, to flee are each strong enough in their own right to smother the recognized morals of your society. This is why I cannot, and indeed, should never orbit alone and unexamined about your system. Only animals exist governed by unexamined *Motivations*.

My advice? Be brutally honest with yourself. Boldly examine the undercurrents in your life, in your behavior. Embrace *Courage*, *Intellect*, *Reason*, *Logic*, *Discipline*, and *Honor*. Bathe me in the light of such as these to see your true self.

Understand yourself.

Improve. Your. Self.

Grow.

Then take what you have learned of others, of yourself, of me, and give it away.

Deliberately.

39

Colors

After allowing for the time of echoes. Alina said, "Let us take a moment to break from our evening routine. You are about to meet two individuals as closely related as brothers."

"But first," Taggart interjected, "we must prepare some groundwork." That got the children's attention, but it perplexed them that the Readers were closing their scrolls, as if the evening had already ended. They raised the documents toward the dark canopy above in perfect synchronization. They lowered them then lightly kissed them before placing them atop the rucksacks at their feet. The precision of the simple ritual was not lost on the children.

Without a word, Taggart twisted to his left, as Alina did to her right. They reached behind them, but the diminished fire light hid what they were doing.

Seconds later, they faced to the front again, staring stoically into the darkness. Taggart's hands rested upon his thighs. Alina now held a small canvas sack in her lap. A few moments of silence followed, then both Readers rose from their seats, took three precise steps to their left away from the campfire, and stopped. They performed a precise right face back toward the children, then bowed respectfully before easing smoothly down to their knees. Sitting back on their heels, and with backs straight, their postures mimicked the traditional *Nung-Cha* meditation pose.

The children squirmed and craned their necks—in silence—to take in each precise movement of their Readers. A common thought echoed within their impressionable minds: *Everything on Scroll Night has meaning.*

Taggart moved first. He clenched his left fist, raised it to chest level, and then bent his elbow crisply. His now-horizontal forearm faced the children. His robe sleeve hung like a sword sheath. His right hand disappeared inside the sleeve two heartbeats later, as if reaching for a sword hilt. As his right hand drew out a tight roll of tanned leather, his left hand dropped precisely to his side. He snapped the roll open smartly, showing it to be a two-foot by two-foot square. Bending forward, he lay the leather before him and Alina and smoothed it flat before resuming his meditative pose.

Tyra took special note as her grandmother then untied the sack in her lap without looking down at it. Staring into the darkness behind the children, her deft fingers loosened the knotted cords securing the neck of the sack. The grace of Alina's fingers as she uncoiled one end of the cord in one direction, and the other end in another, reminded Tyra of the precision of a harpist's strokes against the strings. It reminded her also—as it did the other children—of the exquisitely delicate ritual known as "tea for an honored guest." Tyra smiled with appreciation as her grandmother's strong, graceful fingers performed this obvious show.

Once opened, Alina placed the sack between her and Taggart. Wordlessly, the Readers pulled various items from the sack and arranged them neatly across the leather. In the faint light, the children could not identify the items. Upon finishing, Alina flattened the sack—again very precisely—arranged the neck cords just so, folded it neatly and placed it on the ground at her right knee.

Taggart then rose and walked very formally to the woodpile, to pick up a long, pre-made torch with a head of tightly woven, oiled burlap. The moment he ignited it from the fire, Alina spoke for the first time since the ritual had started.

"Arise, children and gather about me." She stood and gestured with her hands to draw them near to the leather mat and its mysterious items.

As they did, Taggart returned to hold the torch high over the mat, illuminating it clearly. "Light vanquishes the shadows of mystery, does it not?" he said with a faint smile.

Deliberately so, Tyra thought. *Especially on Scroll Night.*

What lay upon the mat were everyday items found in virtually every household in Wraithaven. Given the precise formality of the ritual, the discovery was perplexing.

A silver hand mirror lay next to a copper-plated calligraphy nib. A gray whetstone rested next to a hair comb carved from river willow and painted red. A wooden spool—light maple in color—

held yards of bright yellow yarn. Next to a simple black iron door hinge lay an intricately wrought gold bracelet and a polished steel sheath knife with a brown-and-tan stag antler grip. A brightly polished brass belt buckle lay next to several common goose-feather arrow fletches, some dyed purple, others orange or green.

The largest item, a bronze sextant, lay at one corner of the mat. Next to it, a single square of white cloth about the size of a man's outstretched hand—a survival instructor's flag—completed the collection.

The children tried to fathom meaning from the items, tried to detect a pattern, or some connection between adjacent items. Frowns of frustration furrowed the brows of most after a few minutes. Those frowns signaled the Readers to continue.

"Take one last look at each item arranged here, children," Taggart said, "for you are about to be tested." Each child renewed their concentration, burning the arrangement of the articles, the colors of each, and the purpose of each into their minds.

"Now, children," Alina said. "Here is your test." She paused deliberately, allowing the children to anticipate the question. "Select the superior color."

Not a word came from the children, but their puzzled looks spoke volumes. Marcus Riordan found voice first, asking, "Pardon me, Lady Kayne? Did you say, 'Select the superior *color*?'" The question seemed ludicrous, especially coming from a Reader. Surely they had misheard. Alina smiled at their united bewilderment.

"You heard correctly, young Marcus. I *did* say, 'Select the superior color.' And your answer is?"

"I . . . I'm afraid that I don't truly understand the question, my Lady."

"Yet!" Taggart interrupted. "There actually is an answer to this simple question. Try, please, and everyone else is free to answer anytime as well."

"Then I would have to say that the gold bracelet is by far the most valuable," Marcus ventured. "The silver mirror would be the next in value, or possibly the sextant, while the white instructor's flag would be the least."

Both Readers contemplated the answer for a moment before Taggart said, "Do the rest of you agree?" A few half-hearted shrugs of agreement met the question, but every child's face in that short interim showed obvious discomfort with the boy's answer. Except for one.

Tyra's eyes bored as straight at her Reader grandparents as if she had just drawn her bow at a target from Shadow's back. "The question wasn't about the value of any of the objects on the mat, Marcus," she said, not breaking her stare to look at the boy. "The question has nothing to do with the objects themselves, or with their value. Other Readers probably use different objects during *their* Scroll Nights."

Taggart and Alina allowed faint smiles of *Pride* at Tyra's insight to crease their faces. *She just might have the point*, they thought.

"The value of the objects isn't important," Tyra continued. "There is no pattern here, no connection between one object and another. The objects all perform different tasks. The answer to Namm . . . to Lady Kayne's question, is that there is no superior color. The red comb does what it does. It could be just as well painted blue or orange. The silver mirror has its purpose, as does the gray whetstone, the yellow yarn, or the black door hinge."

"Still, even if I'm correct, I don't know what it has to do with our Reading."

"Well said, Tyra," Alina said. "Your answer that there is no superior color is correct. As to what it means to our Reading, let us return to our seats and continue."

The moment they resumed their seats, Devyn Briac raised his hand.

"Sir and Lady Kayne," he began, "Even knowing that nothing happens on Scroll Night without purpose, I'm still confused. Until now, everything has seemed connected: our souls, the orbiting heralds, the idea that character is defined by which traits orbit us. Then you ask this question about colors. I . . . I just don't see how it all fits."

"Does anyone else feel confused?" Alina asked. "Does anyone else fail to see a connection?"

Every child raised hand reluctantly, including Tyra.

"Excellent!" Taggart exclaimed with an enthusiastic clap of his hands. "Then everything is as it should be." He laughed as if at a marvelous joke. That Alina joined him only increased the incredulous looks on the children's faces.

"You're *supposed* to be confused at this point, children," Alina said—more seriously this time. "Readers expect *all* Wraithian children to be confused at this same point in *every* Reading, in *every* province."

"If you are," Taggart said, "it means that your adult peers, indeed, the Wraithian culture itself has done its job."

The perplexity on the children's faces changed not in the least, but Keiriam Marsali, daughter of stonemasons, asked, "But what of the ritual itself? Why perform it at all?"

"We will address your concern in a moment," Taggart said. "An excellent question by the way, given our recent exposure to *Motivation*. But first things first."

"Tyra," Alina said, "you correctly surmised that asking you to select a superior color was a trick question. You said that there were no connections among the various objects. True again. All of you should hold those thoughts."

"Tyra," Taggart said. "You have green eyes, as does your mother. However, Quinn and Leah both have brown eyes. Devyn's are blue, as are Seanna's, but Brann and Marcus have gray eyes. Would anyone claim to have superior eyes because of color?"

A resounding "no" met the question.

"Of course not," Alina said, "but the same cannot be said for certain other cultures."

"Outsiders think that eye colors are superior?" Seanna Berit asked. "How silly."

"Not eye color," Taggart said. "Skin color."

The incredulous looks returned.

"Consider, children," Alina said, "our own skin color. How would you describe it?"

That the question had never been posed to the youngsters, that they had never considered the subject was obvious. They looked at each other and shrugged their shoulders at such a question. A few even pushed up their sleeves up to consider their own color before attempting to answer.

"Tan," Brann Halwyn ventured, looking at his own forearm. "I guess."

"Kind of a dark golden," Drystan Bradach added. "Spring hibiscus honey is a close color. It has a richer, darker golden hue than the lighter clover and citrus honeys of summer."

"And the son of vintners would know," Taggart said amicably. "The hives surrounding the Bradach vineyards produce wonderful honey each year."

"But, do you see where we've gone in just a few minutes? We're spending time . . . no, we're *wasting* time on a subject without any real value."

The children all agreed with nods or obvious looks of agreement. Truth be told, the triviality of the subject bored them. At least, though, words that made sense had been thrown back into the conversation.

"Children," Alina said, "understand that for the last three thousand years—two thousand as Wraithians and over a thousand as Pelanjians and Mindocean sea traders—we have kept our people deliberately separated from the Outsider nations. Certainly, we have as Wraithians, which is why we regard our Pickets so highly."

"As Mindoceans," she said, "our people deliberately married into other Mindocean tribes. Those tribes settled the eleven islands of the Pelanjian Archipelago yet maintained the tradition by marrying residents of other islands. Today, although we are a single large nation, we carry on the marriage tradition by deliberately marrying, for the most part, into the other provincial populations outside of our home province. It keeps the Wraithian bloodline strong and has resulted in such a blend of ancestry that virtually all Wraithians are of the same color."

"But Sir Kayne," Keiriam asked, "don't other nations, the Outsiders, do the same thing? Marry within their own populations?"

"Good point, Keiriam, and yes, they do, more often than not. Yet history, sea travel, worldwide commerce, and constant warfare have all left their marks as well."

"How?" Devyn Briac asked.

"The nations of northern Mascarene tend to be dark-brown skinned people," Alina said, "while the tribes and nations of southern Mascarene tend to be darker still—virtually black.

"The immense Embrican continent is a place of many different hues. The folk to the north tend to be paler, almost whitish. Nations in the extreme eastern region tend to have skin colors much like ours but with a more pronounced yellow hue. Much of the mid-continent and the western nations tend to be brown-skinned, but not as dark as the folk of northern Mascarene. The southern Embrican nations tend to be mixed colors as dark as the southern Mascarene folk to the hues of the 'pales' in the north countries."

"Then why is there such thought of superior colors?" Tyra asked. "Wouldn't the presence of other colors be of no consequence after so many centuries?"

"One would think," Taggart said, "yet just the opposite is true."

"But why?" Tyra continued. "The subject is trivial and senseless."

"Because," Alina said, "each color of the Outsiders has ample historical reasons to distrust, to even hate the others. Empires tend to be of a similar color, as do many religions. Empires are things of conquest, of power, of aggression, whether they are seeded by political intent or by religious fervor. A given color rises to prominence, becomes addicted to power, and then invades the domain of another. The invader considers the vanquished less worthy than themselves, less human, less a unique creation.

"Those invaded by the more powerful see their conquerors as savages, as destroyers of cultures. They suffer, they disintegrate as a people, as families, as individuals, and as a result, they learn to hate. They nurture revenge against the color that ruined their lives, the color that sold them as slaves to other colors, against the color that visited cruelty upon them. Despising a skin color becomes easy, yet it is the most difficult scar on the human soul to heal. Color hatred is the greatest obstacle any reasonable mind has to obtaining that emotional state we call *Balance*."

"Understand," Alina continued, "our Pelanjian ancestors defended the home islands against invaders of every color, of every political ambition, of every religious aggression masquerading as a holy crusade."

"Yet, had we remained as Pelanjians for these last two thousand years, had Admiral Balgaire not asked, *what might we become if our honor was untainted by war?* Had he not engineered *The Disappearance,* the chances are great that we too might have slid into the abyss where something as trivial as color would have tainted us as it does the Outsiders to this day."

Five children raised their hands virtually at the same instant. *Ah, here it comes*, Taggart thought, *the question. The comparison.*

Not wanting to show favoritism to Tyra, who was one of the five, Taggart pointed to Leah Brenna. "Yes? A question?"

"Sir Kayne, don't we do the same thing? Don't we look unfavorably upon non-Wraithians? We *do* call them 'Outsiders.' It seems the same as thinking one's color is superior."

"The short answer, Leah," Taggart said, "is yes, we do. In our own fashion, and for our own reasons, we favor our ancestral way of life. Our standards distinguishing right from wrong are solid, not swayed by the political wind of the day. Our Wraithian culture anchors itself to the Pelanjian Beacons. Our Maker is real to us, not just a theory. The Orbit Scrolls that we read from tonight, are a very personal reminder to each of you that building character is a deliberate act, not a thing of happenstance.

"And that, dear children," Taggart said, "is why we have dwelt so long on something that for our people is essentially a non-subject. You must know what lies beyond the Shield, in the world of the Outsiders.

"Their failings—as we perceive them at least—are human failings. Outsiders prove this every day, in a thousand ways. They prove it with every act of revenge, with every intentional slight visited upon another human different than themselves, with every war waged for some perceived or contrived justification.

"That said, we Wraithians must guard ourselves against the destructive herald *Self-Righteousness.* Yes, we *do* believe our ways are superior to Outsider ways. Consider. We do not wage war upon other nations, yet we prepare daily to defend ourselves through *Nung-Cha* practice and provincial militia maneuvers. When Outsiders practice the arts of war, it is with the intention to deliberately wage war upon another culture. A targeted culture.

"We revere our Elders, even as we actively and deliberately treasure our newborn. Sadly, many Outsider cultures consider both expendable."

"We pride ourselves that every Wraithian man, woman, and child is literate. Every one of us is steeped from birth in the *Expectation*, in the *demand* that it is necessary to read and write. We are still the only culture on this planet to create a nationwide educational system, and this creation, mind you, came from the time of our Pelanjian ancestors. It was created deliberately that long ago. Literacy in most Outsider nations is not an *Expectation*, and because it is not, there is no formal system to perpetuate it. Sadly, literacy is a privilege known, more often than not, to the wealthy, to the supposedly 'noble' classes.

"We contend that to work at a given profession, to demand skill and perfection of oneself, is a noble act. We aggressively *teach* that. To exhibit a strong work ethic toward your profession, no matter how common or lofty it might be perceived, is an act of *Honor*. We deliberately teach *Pride* of accomplishment to our children before they ever arrive for their first day at academy. Beyond the Shield, the systematic perpetuation of honorable work ethic, of *Pride* of accomplishment, is all too rare. In fairness, when Outsiders discover *Pride* of accomplishment in another's craft, they appreciate it, even praise it. Yet, Outsider cultures fail their citizens by *not* deliberately weaving *Pride* and acknowledgment into the fabric of their societies.

"All of that said," Taggart continued, "we must *Balance* our knowledge of Outsider ways with a common-sense approach as we guard our own way of life. We do not have to compromise our ways. We do not have to dilute our standards of *Expectation* of ourselves to become more like Outsider societies. But listen carefully. We also do not have to hate *them* for their differences either!"

"Two days ago," Alina said, "we saw a boy defend himself against a pine viper. He didn't hate the snake for being a viper. He just defended his own right to exist. That is what Wraithians do. Pine vipers do what they do. We don't have to hate them for their deadly poison. Yet, at the same time, we don't have to let them crawl into an infant's nursery either. They will not be allowed to do what vipers do—there!"

"With such groundwork prepared," she said, "we will now resume our Reading. With one slight change. For the next two heralds only, we will introduce them before they introduce themselves."

"This departure from our pattern tonight, Keiriam," Taggart said, nodding to the girl, "is part of the answer to your earlier question concerning the need for a color ritual at all. Understand, rituals have value only if they remind us of something truly noteworthy, if they illuminate something of true significance. This example of color, of an object's value, or to carry the illustration further, the inherent value and purpose of each human being, is worthy of significant attention. Our seemingly unnecessary ritual is performed to hammer home a reminder to us all of the place every human being has in Creation. Nothing the Father creates is inferior.

"Remember how ludicrous our question of a color's value seemed at first. Remember *not* understanding the question! But most of all, remember the lesson taught here tonight. Carry forever the vision of diverse objects lying upon a simple leather mat.

"Remember how the torchlight illuminated them. Remember how misunderstanding became enlightenment.

"Lastly, remember also that character is a sculpture created over time. Certain wines achieve superior quality as years pass. So also does the character of one's soul."

"Wraithians believe," Alina said, "as did our Pelanjian and Mindocean ancestors, that nothing is more important—after our Creator—than human *Dignity*. We believe that the greatest treasure a human being can have—and share—is personal *Honor*.

"The next heralds approach your system with a kind of inherent grace. They know that for a soul to fully achieve and appreciate their orbits requires a lifetime. They are as closely related as brothers. They are confident in the importance of the message each of them brings, but they de fine themselves carefully. Each word is steeped in deliberate thought, each one tested against some crucial standard."

With that, she cleared her throat in preparation, once again took up her scroll, and began to read with a measured, cultured tone of voice.

40

Crown

Salutations, young sun.

If my trajectory seems somewhat slower than that of many of my fellow heralds, it is true. My orbit solidifies over time once I am accepted. I admit to bringing a paradox along with me, though, because I am much easier to be *sensed* in another's system than I am to be physically *proven.* The same will apply to you. A soul might sense my orbit around you but will not be able to explain how it knows that I exist. This is due in great part to my definition.

Call me *Dignity.* To have personal *Dignity* is to deserve *Respect.* I am the absolute recognition of the *Self Worth* gifted to each new soul by the Creator. *Dignity* sees that value in self, and others. *Dignity* breaks through the obstacles of outward appearance or life accomplishments that might prevent my orbit. I change you, your posture, and your outlook on all of Creation.

Those cultures that admire, if not outright worship, wealth often bestow the mantle of what they consider *Dignity* upon only the powerful, only the wealthiest citizens among them. This is an all too human misunderstanding of what *Dignity* is. *Dignity* cannot be bestowed *upon* you by anyone. I am not a citation to be awarded. Nor am I an emblem to be worn. That said, you would do well to always assume that I orbit *others.*

To grasp that distinction, envision a small room with a single door leading to it. As you enter, you note the plain, unadorned walls, the unpainted wooden floor. A single piece of furniture, a simple wooden table, stands in the center of the room. A single object rests upon the table—a crown of pure gold. That is *Dignity.* It was created and placed there by your Creator, but He did *not, will* not place it upon your head. Only you can do that. Or not.

No one, including the Creator, can or will give you *Dignity.* No one places the crown upon your head. You do that by first recognizing that *Dignity* is a gift created and left upon the table for you. See it for the great personal treasure that it is. Indeed, see it as a unique trait that by your Creator's will, separates you from the world of the beast—both human *and* animal.

Only humankind is offered the gift of *Dignity*. Only humankind can recognize it or define it. Only humankind can take it in hand, remove it from the table, and place it upon one's head. Your sense of place in the Maker's Creation allows you the sight, the insight to wear it. Your sense of that place, of *Honor*, of *Balance*, of *Humility*, allows you to understand that every living human being has the choice to don a golden crown uniquely fitted to each person.

Be aware that just as a king's crown commands *Respect* and symbolizes his power, a soul's acceptance of true *Dignity* has the unique power to command *Esteem*, even if begrudgingly so from one's enemy.

How does this occur? By one's actions? By one's noble *Intentions*, by one's lofty goals? Yes, and more. A soul's *Dignity* lies dormant within each human soul. However, it can only be donned through personal acknowledgment of one's own value.

Note this: I am not an outward affection. I am not a contrived act on your part. I am, in fact, quite the opposite. True *Dignity* is personal nobility devoid of external trappings. To presume that all other souls created have *Dignity* should be enough to hold me in close orbit for the length of Life given to you.

Alas, I must warn that sometimes that is not enough. The human soul can forget who created it, or worse, can convince itself that it is naught but a beast. But know this. Beasts do not possess *Dignity*. Accepting one's own *Dignity* is a uniquely human form of *Gratitude* sent back to one's Maker. In essence, the human soul looks toward its Creator and says, "Father Creator, for creating me deliberately, and for Your purpose, I thank You. I will remember those I meet upon my journey, as being Your creations as well."

Interestingly, a unique cause-and-effect accompanies the orbit of *Dignity*. Once you accept my orbit it is virtually impossible to ignore the possibility of *Dignity* in others. Think about that. Such recognition changes individual lives.

True *Dignity* requires the orbit of *Self-Respect*—one of my inseparable companions. It is safe to say that without an orbit of *Self-

Respect first, there can be no *Dignity* for your system. *Dignity* in its purest definition is the acceptance of one's *Self Worth*—but not one's perceived *Superiority*! Dignity does not reign. It serves. You.

You should know that a crown of *Dignity* worn by just a single human being contains the power to change an entire culture. Yet, to do so, you must link strongly with *Courage, Conviction, Motivation*, and others. *Dignity* is not dependent upon the fortune of one's birth. Influence upon others can be considerable without the vestments of affluence. Truly, the peasant who possesses true *Dignity* will stride more imperiously in his servitude than an emperor might in his privilege. Human history is rife with examples of supposedly lowly souls rising above their perceived societal stations to greatly influence their cultures. In my opinion, this might be Father Creator's personal jest to keep the heralds *Power* and *Arrogance* in their proper places.

That said, you should ponder whether too much *Dignity* can orbit the human soul, and if so, what is "too much?"

The answer is in two parts, and the herald *Diligence* is required to grasp them both. First, you cannot have too much *Dignity*—in its purest form. *Awareness* of your unique creation by the will of your Maker, the understanding that other human beings are worthy of *Dignity* for the same reason, is, in fact, an ingredient that actually sweetens your personal song in the Anthem of Creation.

Secondly, as other heralds have warned you, so must I. *Dignity* does not overwhelm, nor is it overbearing. *Dignity* is a quiet thing, sublimely personal. Yet, it can be shouldered aside by the orbits of *Arrogance, Conceit, Vanity, Self-Glorification*, even *Rage*. None of these are *Dignity*, nor do they have *Dignity*. They are not expanded definitions of me. Such orbits are empty masks, pretenders of *Dignity* capable of exacting terrible damage upon yourself and others.

Self-Worth, without a measure of *Humility*, unchecked by *Reason* or a sense of *Balance*, can devolve into *Conceit*. In that regard, know that the power of *Conceit* is a groundless façade— despite the power that it might allow you to wield.

Vanity can beguile you with its pathetic emptiness, inflicting the pain of a thousand tiny cuts into the well-being of other systems, as well as yours.

Arrogance is simply louder about the damage it causes, more boastful in its attack.

Allow such orbits about your system and watch *Justification* replace *Reason.* Watch *Bravado* replace true *Courage.* Watch *Hope* transform from an eternal thread of gold from the Creator's own robe into a temporary thread of mist woven upon the loom of *Self-Delusion.* Watch *Honor* forsake you in disgust.

I leave you with this, young one. All living things have worth of some kind. All sing unique notes within the complex Anthem of Creation, or the Creator would not have willed them into existence.

The forest giants with roots augured deep into mountain valley soil sing, as do the stately pods of leviathans that roam the world's oceans. Uncountable creatures too small for the human eye to detect add to the Great Anthem, as does the humming and buzzing of insects. Feathered creatures—the tiny and quick, the large and the regal—all sing as do the land creatures, whether prey or predator. All sing, but only one creation sings the melody of *Dignity.* Humankind alone is capable of it. Remember that throughout the course of your Life-dance. Relish it. Cherish it. Assume I am an orbit of others at every turn in your journey, and touch your Creator with *Gratitude* and *Respect* each time you do.

Remember who *He* is, lest you forget who *you* are.

41

Robe

As with previous heralds, Taggart and Alina used the echoes to allow *Dignity*'s words time to resonate with the children.

As Alina had predicted, the next herald began without introduction. Taggart's voice deepened just enough to notice. The tone was unhurried in cadence, yet as confident and serene as the no-nonsense look he directed toward each child.

Greetings, young one.

We heralds furnish warnings of our potential, even as we define ourselves and furnish you a vision to remember. In that regard, I voice a warning early on, followed by a greater number of cautions than most heralds offer.

Call me *Honor*. As with my fellow herald *Dignity*, human cultures tend to create many definitions of me. This prompts my first warning.

Do not be distracted by the many definitions of *Honor* adrift within other cultures. In many, *Honor* is little more than a title bestowed upon another, an achievement, a form of address to authority figures. My core identity is much more than that.

Honor, as I live within these Orbit Scrolls, is not about others, not about honorific titles, or even your society, save as how you are perceived. *Honor* is about *you*. *Honor* is about *your* behavior. No one else's. That makes me the deepest, most personal treasure you possess. To put it in brutally forthright terms, you are only as valuable to Life as the depth of your sense of *Honor*. Consider that another warning.

I am the high measure of *Respect* that you might attain through the recognized quality of your behavior, through your daily acts as they match the personal beliefs you profess. Your peers will consider, then judge in their hearts if your actions are as truthful as your words. You must judge yourself even more stringently using those same criteria.

I am your good name, your reputation, the bond of your personal word. I cannot exist within your system without the herald *Respect* in orbit as well. But listen carefully. *Honor* cannot exist without a recognized code of behavior. By that I mean a code that defines your culture's definition of *Integrity*, *Dignity*, *Pride*, and acceptable moral behavior.

Such a code must exist *before Honor* can even be sought. It is imperative that your culture at large recognizes the same code of behavior that you follow—unless you follow a secret code known only by members of some society within your culture. That is not the *Honor* that lives within these Scrolls. Adherence to a secret code of honor is just elitism. That has no value here.

By your own *Discipline*, *Conviction*, and *Commitment*, you will adhere to your code, but society's perception of your *Commitment* determines whether you are ultimately judged as honorable or dishonorable. You may consider whether perception by others is necessary. It is. To deserve *Honor*, to pursue it, requires a standard by which one is measured.

If there is no acknowledged code of conduct, there can be no *Honor*. One cannot pursue, cannot adhere to that which does not exist. How then should you perceive me in your mind?

Picture *Honor* as a finely tailored, long-sleeved robe worn wherever you go. The Readers who bring you the words of these Scrolls are taught to feel the presence of their robes, to notice their weight of responsibility. So also do I teach *you*. Be ever aware of the weight of *Honor*, of the responsibility woven within the texture of its fabric.

Honor is never static. It is never a task to complete, or a goal to achieve. It is not set upon a mantle and admired while it gathers dust. Personal *Honor* is a living thing every bit as alive as you are. *Honor* is perpetual, a thing addicted to *Vigilance*, to *Discipline*. *Honor* is a true measure of self because it requires work. Work performed only by you. In that regard, I am relentless and unforgiving. Consider that another warning.

We of the League have observed humankind for eons, and one sad fact always arises. The concept of *Honor*, the very definition of *Honor*, erodes proportionately to a culture's advancement. As a culture grows technically, its *Honor* erodes. In many so-called "advanced" societies, *Honor* barely exists even as an archaic word, let alone as a disciplined choice of personal behavior, or as a guide for one's actions. Consider how sad that condemnation is.

Such societies devolve into indirection. No solid code anchors them against Life's storms. Too often, the term "modern society" illuminates its people as lacking a solid foundation of moral behavior, a people so weak that they childishly change the rules for acceptable behavior whenever the equally archaic word (to them) *Discipline* dares appear.

This is called "living at random," an existence with no focus, no *Discipline*, little true *Pride,* and one in which a culture's worst aspects are assured to be passed down to subsequent generations. Sadly, this is their choice. Yet, equally true, to a culture that lives deliberately, that does not merely graze through the pasture of Life, *Honor* can be a legacy to be passed on to one's lineage. Very few heralds can make that statement.

Know this. The characteristics that define *Honor* are, in great measure, learned from older systems that a soul respects. One sees the standard of behavior and then either emulates it or does not. I cannot be given to you, young one, except in the most superficial, titular way as some cultures do. But understand that titles do not make you honorable. It is just the opposite. The person makes the title honorable. *Honor* is learned. *Honor* is earned. But I cannot be given, bought, or legislated into existence. You cannot accidentally become honorable, nor can you assume the robe of *Honor* at the behest of another. Only you can feel the weight of *Responsibility.* Only you are responsible for your *Honor. You* earn your *Respect.* No one else can.

Even your Creator does not give you *Honor*, does not drape the robe upon your shoulders. Nor does your religion. Your profession, your family name, or your wealth cannot bestow *Honor* upon you. Social status cannot, your nation cannot, nor can your government, although all these things should create an environment where I can grow. The *individual* deliberately brings *Honor* to one's religion, to one's profession, or family name.

Nations, are naught but expanses of earth and soil, collections of valleys, streams and mountain peaks defined upon parchment maps by quill and ink and the might to hold the boundaries fast. The human beings living within such created ink scrawls furnish the nobility or the baseness, the *Courage* or the *Treachery*, the *Honor* or the *Dishonor* of a nation. In that regard, human beings should decry any loss of *Honor* in their culture, for I am a genuine treasure to both the individual and to a culture. I define both. I anchor both. I guide the present and future behavior of both.

Remember this about me:

Honor taught—lives.
Honor demonstrated—grows.
Honor ignored—dies.

Therefore, I admonish you, to consider well those heralds who will orbit you as my companions. You cannot, for instance, acquire and then maintain me without *Courage.* I assure you there are many paths much easier to take than the often rock-strewn, uncomfortable path that *Honor* demands. *Fear* will be in attendance, for it always shadows the orbit of *Courage.* You will need strong personal *Conviction*, a herald who also requires *Courage* in great measure. I have everything to do with *Choice*. I have everything to do with *Discipline*, with *Commitment*. I have everything to do with how you declare the value of the path you treasure and follow. I have everything to do with your refusal to sell the path of your *Intention* at any price. I have everything to do with your refusal to cheapen *Honor's* inherent value through *Cowardice*, or weakness of *Conviction*.

Last of all, though this might seem strange, I submit that you will need a healthy orbit of *Shame. Shame* resides within the shadow of *Honor*, just as *Fear* lurks within the shadow of *Courage.* It can be said that even the possibility of *Shame's* orbit guides the soul toward honorable behavior. To fear one's loss of *Honor* is, in itself, a measure of honorable behavior.

Shame is the prophet of *Consequence* and another herald who distinguishes Life from random existence. I warn you as does *Intellect*. Deliberate Life has meaning. Random existence does not.

Shameless souls cannot claim *Honor* because *Shamelessness* despises the value of a behavioral code.

Equally so, one eventually concludes that the most honorable souls in one's culture are those who hold the deepest insight of the consequences of *Shame*.

I leave you with those thoughts, young one. Should you choose my orbit, I offer you treasure more valuable than gemstones or the coin of your realm.

I do not offer an easy path for your Life, but if you dare to walk it, I offer you the unmeasurable treasure of *Respect*.

Choose well.

42

Ember

When the time of echoes seemed over, Drystan Bradach, son of the vintners, raised his hand. "Sir Kayne, surely Wraithians aren't the only people who believe in *Honor*, or *Dignity*, or even in the other heralds we are meeting tonight. Don't Outsiders believe in an eternal soul? Are we that unique? Are we that . . . alone on the planet in our thinking?"

The Kaynes and Bradachs had been friends for three decades. Both Readers considered Drystan the most contemplative of the five boys in this group, every bit as thoughtful and focused as Tyra. Firelight only accentuated his inquisitive frown.

A frown like that suggests a sculptor's eye for detail hiding inside the body of a vintner's son, Taggart thought with amusement. Similar, stone-dusted frowns of concentration furrowed the brows of many mallet-and-chisel-wielding apprentices in the Kayne quarry as they attacked the raw blocks of granite and marble imprisoning their visions.

"Worthy points for consideration, young Drystan," Alina said. "The answer is yes. Outsiders *do* address the same things so important to Wraithians. From large nations boasting populations in the millions to remote tribal groups of only a few dozen souls, all try to make sense of Life in their own ways. A dozen major world religions and thousands of offshoot sects prove that.

"Humankind seeks. It seeks its Creator, or *Truth*, or at the very least a philosophy to serve as an anchor against Life's trials. And if either of these are too much trouble to imagine, too inconvenient, too hard to defend, then there are always—in our Wraithian opinion—the heralds *Justification* or *Rationalization* to fall back upon. The animal world has it much easier. It bears no such spiritual burden. The only *Truth* in their world is survival. The only drive is instinct."

"But if Outsiders pursue *Truth* too, as we do tonight," Drystan persisted, "are we really any different than they are?"

Alina hesitated before answering, allowing Drystan's question time to sink into the minds of the group.

"In the realm of pursuing *Truth*, all of humankind shares a common itch—curiosity. Introspective, conceptual *Curiosity* transcends our basic senses and is yet another trait that defines our humanity, which separates us from the purely instinctive animal. We ponder, we imagine, we question, we speculate.

"However, what distinguishes Wraithians from most other peoples, religions, or intentions, is our approach. To monotonously chant clichéd mottos to a child about how hard work in a worthy profession, or honesty, or marriage, or parenthood, or faithfulness, or service to one's country will build character is worthless from the Wraithian viewpoint."

"But why, Lady Kayne?" Keiriam chimed in before Drystan could ask. "Such virtues are worthy and good."

"Indeed, they are," Alina said. "But what real connection can a young person make between tired, time-worn slogans and the concept of building character? Don't *tell* the young to build character. *Show* them by personal example. Ignite their *Imaginations*. Furnish them a vision of the human soul. Show them how traits orbit that soul. Show them how a soular system becomes more complete as it matures. Shallow clichés and platitudes only echo more faintly to the young as *Time* slips by. Make the idea of character personal. Make it real. Make it easy enough to see through the eyes of a child, but true enough to remain rooted as a clear vision deep within the adult mind. That exemplifies Wraithian *Intention* to live deeply and deliberately, rather than to merely exist as a random grazer of Life."

"Understand, children," Taggart said, taking over for Alina. "Wraithians do not let things happen. Wraithians *make* things happen. This Reading, this Scroll Night, is just one way in which we do that.

"Every Wraithian alive can recite the *Pelanjian Beacons*. We teach them to our children before the child ever sets foot in academy. We expect this of ourselves.

"Respect for our Maker, for neighbors, for the elderly, is purposely, intentionally ingrained in us from birth. We know what acceptable behavior is, and just as importantly, we know what *unacceptable* behavior is. We know what our society expects of us as individuals. Later this evening, you will learn just how powerful the herald *Expectation* is.

"We have our code of *Honor*, a herald you've already met this night. You will come to know how unique Wraithians are in simply acknowledging the worth of the word 'honor,' the actual existence of the word.

"We train ourselves to build the core of each Wraithian the same way, and part of that way is this Reading. Most Outsider societies would consider such focus an affront to personal freedom, a stifling of individuality. Fine. Let them.

"Wraithians *deliberately* teach the young to honor our Creator first. We *deliberately* teach that the very existence of peers and neighbors is reason enough to respect them. We *deliberately* proclaim that we are Divine creations that the elderly are to be revered and that the unborn and the young are to be treasured. You have all worn wooden practice swords since your seventh harvests as a reminder that we must be prepared to defend our nation if need be. There is no standing Wraithian army because each citizen, adult or child, is a trained warrior. These things chart the fundamental course for every Wraithian's life because Life should be a deliberate *squaring* of the shoulders, an act of purpose, an effort of an individual's personal will. Life is entirely too precious a gift to be taken for granted. Life is too important to be a shrug of one's shoulders. Deliberate living is our gift of *Gratitude,* our act of worship to the Creator of Life itself.

"That we actually paint a vision for our young of the human soul, that we quantify the elusive term 'character,' flies in the faces of those who dismiss such things with a nonchalant wave of their hand.

"And with that, children," Taggart said, "let us introduce our next herald."

Taking his cue, Alina cleared her throat and began to read, her voice business-like, clipped, and concise. This herald saw Life as a deliberate exercise of will.

Greetings, young one. My name is *Intention*

Define me as a course of action that you intend to follow. I am that first step taken on the journey toward the goal that you plan to achieve. I am the guide for the vision *Imagination* has painted for you. I am something you resolve to do.

Consider me a natural orbit to the human soul. For good or evil, for the lofty or the base, for that which is noble or that which is ignoble, all human beings have *Intentions*. The undercurrent *Motivation* and I are very much alike in that regard. Your responsibility is to remain aware of us both, and to understand our roles in your life.

So, hear me well and heed my words. In Life, *Intention* is the easy part. Always. During our visit, I shall remind you of that. Remember this, even if you remember nothing else of me. *Intention*. Is. The. Easy. Part.

But more of that later. For now, visualize me as a softly glowing ember, much like those pulsing faintly as breezes caress your campfire this night. That I glow *softly* is significant.

I am the next step taken past a dream, hope or plan ignited into existence by your *Imagination*. I am closely yoked with *Imagination*, but I must caution you at this point.

Imagination and the ability to dream creatively are some of the most important gifts Creator bestows upon humans. They are important distinctions between human life and animal life. The dreams and visions that your *Imagination* ignites into being give me reason to exist.

In turn, I furnish you the direction to achieve what *Imagination* has created. However, always remember that to *intend* is one thing. Anyone can do that, the slothful as well as the energetic. To actually take the first step toward achieving a goal and then to maintain the countless steps needed to complete that journey through personal *Discipline* is quite another. Students of these Scrolls often conclude that *Intention* is the easiest orbit to acquire, yet one of the most difficult to maintain. That, young one, is a conclusion worth remembering.

Intention is important because it is the first step toward declaring an objective. Without *Intention*, there is no direction! *Discipline* is the driving force that makes the objective yours.

Intentions without action are worthless—vaporous mental images, easily dissipated, mere words without power. *Discipline* and *Resolve* make *Intentions* real.

Intentions inspired by *Imagination*, empowered by *Discipline*, and driven by honorable *Motivation*, can become powerful, Life-changing accomplishments.

To put me into perspective, you must first visualize me as a softly glowing ember. *Intention* has a certain heat that you should be able to feel, but my heat is a passive thing. My glow just indicates my presence, a reminder that you must stoke the heat of the ember into a torch to light your way to an objective.

Consider. You bring a dying campfire back to full flame by adding kindling and logs, by stoking the slumbering embers awake to feed upon the new wood. You must do this with me. Stir the embers of *Intention* awake with your *Imagination.* Add the fuel of deliberate planning to your vision to speed you toward your goal. Deliberately stoke the flames with *Discipline.* Fan them with *Resolve*, with the force of your will. Only the *Courage* of personal will can ignite *Intention* into the flame of reality. And as with a campfire, the flame is your goal, is it not?

Understand this about me. You cannot intend your way to riches, to physical health, to academic achievement—or to anything else for that matter. You cannot wish a path to happiness, to victory over Life's obstacles, to success, or to *Love.*

The man who knows he should be a more involved, inspirational father, or a more devoted husband, yet spends the majority of his time each day toward his profession—and thus away from his family—fools himself. But he fools only himself. His empty *Intentions* declare him a liar to all others. Again, *Intention* is the easy part.

The woman who wishes to improve her skills at her chosen profession, or who endeavors to become a better spouse, yet fails to apply herself with tangible action, throws her credibility away. Her wishes are a waste of time. She fools only herself. *Intention* is the easy part.

The student who desires to improve academic status yet lacks the *Discipline* to apply sufficient energy and time toward study, or succumbs to frivolous distractions, might as well shout *Intentions* to the wind. Yet even the wind is not fooled. *Intention* is the easy part.

Consider.

A gatherer for a struggling tribe imagines the possibility of widely scattered edible plants existing in a single, cohesive plot of earth. A tribal hunter imagines the outlandish possibility of collecting and controlling food beasts into readily accessible herds, thus eliminating the ever-present possibility of failure of the hunt.

The *Intention* awoke. Primitive attempts to nourish seemingly dead seeds into living food plants and to gather and control wild creatures were made. Failures occurred, followed by yet more failures, yet the *Intention* lived because it linked with *Determination*, because it was fanned into flame—into action—by the wings of *Imagination*. *Motivation*, kept alive by need and desperation to achieve a goal, drove the effort of inspired dreamers.

And because it was, the concepts of both farming and ranching became realities millennia in the past.

Great stone roads that were once muddy goat paths now connect great cities, even entire civilizations one to another. When *Imagination* inspired, true *Intention* dared to take the first step. *Determination* and *Resolve* and *Motivation* constructed the journey.

Structures of precisely fitted stone and copper-sheathed roofs now shelter millions of human beings, where once only caves or dwellings of mud and straw did so.

Traders once poled their goods upon primitive rafts between river-spawned villages. Fisher folk once plied their trade in hollowed-out tree trunks. Yet, fueled by *Imagination*, directed by *Intention*, such unrefined watercraft gave way to increasingly complex vessels of wind and sail and rudder. When *Imagination* inspired human minds to ponder what lay beyond the horizon, it was *Intention*—driven by *Determination* and *Motivation*—that created the mighty ocean-spanning vessels to seek the answers. Those answers, in turn, inspired ports of trade and the civilizations that grew around them.

All of these things, and untold numbers of other human accomplishments, both great and small, exist because *Imagination* first awakened the ember of *Intention.* When that ember linked deliberately with *Determination,* when human will fanned *Determination* into flame, the visions became realities.

But just as other heralds serve their warnings, so must I. Declarations of *Intentions* devoid of action on your part eventually deafen your listeners. Family, loved ones, even your most ardent supporters of your empty *Intentions* will no longer hear you. They will not, because they *cannot.* Empty *Intentions* destroy their capacity to hear you, to believe in you. Empty *Intentions* are boasts, and boasts are nothing but empty air.

To intend is merely your announcement to begin a particular journey. If so inspired, one can actually intend to seek *Dignity,* to attain *Honor,* but as I have already cautioned, *Intention* is the easy part. Always.

Be ever watchful, for *Procrastination* will douse my glow, my fervor. So will the lack of *Discipline.* So will *Slothfulness.* So will the absence of *Logic* or *Reason.* Human *Intention* is only powerful when it is yoked with the will to act, with the *Discipline* to fight through all obstacles on the way to a goal. *Intention* is much like a link in a chain. I am only as strong or as weak as your *Will,* as your *Resolve.*

Like many heralds of the League, I can be used or misused. Misuse of *Intention* results in an endless stream of shallow daydreams devoid of substance. When my ember is unfanned, when no action is taken, no changes will occur in your life. No goals will be accomplished. This is equivalent to the directionless, random grazing of migratory herd animals. Such creatures have no true *Intentions.* They exist solely by mindless obedience to *Instinct.*

True *Intention* is an exclusively human trait. Yet equally true, *Intention* becomes valuable only when it becomes *intentional.* It becomes valuable only through deliberate action.

The human being navigates the *Realm of the Deliberate* only by sheer force of will. Change resides in this realm, because when *Commitment* is made, when *Perseverance* thrives in you, the softly glowing ember of *Intention* transforms. It blazes with power!

I am here for you, young one. Use me well. Fan the ember of *Intention.* Empower your life. Improve what must be improved in your personal life. Repair that which might be broken in your culture. Build what none but you have imagined. Blaze physical trails where only wilderness once existed. Blaze intellectual trails where the wilderness of misunderstanding once thrived. Discover *Truth* where *Ignorance* once resisted the light of *Understanding.*

Stand tall for something bathed in the light of an ember fanned into the brilliance of a firebrand.

43

Shadow

Alina allowed the weighty responsibility of the Ember's words to resonate in the minds of the children as she prepared to introduce the next herald. Rolling her scroll to the proper place, she avoided looking directly at the children. Her warm, welcoming smile deserted her, as her face clouded over like a gathering storm on the horizon.

Her shoulders seemed tense. Taggart kept silent too, but something strange emanated from the brusque way the big man maneuvered the scroll. As out of place as it seemed, Taggart looked . . . angry. No. He looked *menacing*!

"Understand, children," Alina began finally. "Not all heralds of the League bear fine gifts. There is one of darkness who swaggers into orbit bearing knowledge of things capable of tainting us all— darker things. The nature of this herald is that of the brute. Stained with *Arrogance*, with *Anger*, this herald seems to savor its aura of self-loathing."

Taggart's body noticeably tensed, as if readying itself for attack. His gray eyes glinted almost wolf-like in the yellow firelight. Even his facial features hardened.

For the first time in their lives, the children felt the *Fear* that accompanies *Intimidation* emanating from a Reader! This could not be. Readers were gentle, loving souls, dedicated to the most sacred of missions—the reading of the Orbit Scrolls on this, the most special of nights.

Not one child remembered that nothing occurred on Scroll Night by accident. Taken by the sincerity of the persona change, each just felt the ferocity of Taggart's glare as he deliberately made eye contact—as he *targeted* each of them one by one. Not even Tyra was immune. Not even she remembered. The granite-like cruelty that masked her beloved grandfather had never been seen—by anyone. When his eyes found hers, the ferocity there actually made her shrink back.

This is the face of a killer, she thought. *This is a warrior thinking of nothing but surviving or dying on a battlefield. I've never seen . . .* But of course, she *had* seen such a face, such faces before. Once. Very recently.

The man's toil-carved face was enraged then. Blood from his opponent, blood of his own, stained his killer's eyes, stained his bared teeth that seemed more like fangs. The rage on that face was frightening. Bestial intent to slay his adversary drove him to kill and kill, despite his own hideous wounds. Even here, now, Tyra remembered every hideous detail of that menacing face. The face illuminated in the Kayne barn by the pitiful light from her lantern.

The memory overwhelmed her. It drove all else from her mind, except the vision of her father's bloodied, battle-crazed face in the barn only days ago. It was that memory, so similar to Taggart's scowl right now that forced a tear down her cheek. She quickly bit her right fist to stifle the sob that tried to escape.

If the Reader's eyes glaring in the firelight noticed, they gave no indication. The cold eyes swept past Tyra to target each of the eight remaining children in turn.

The children wondered what possible Herald would require such a persona. As Taggart began reading, his normally smooth baritone grated against their ears. Harsh and combative, the threatening words snarled past teeth bared by clenched jaws.

This Herald did not even bother to greet its listeners. Every child jumped, as Taggart virtually barked the first words.

You! Harken!

Two members of the League exist whom you will pray *never* to meet. The Door is one. Prayers to avoid him are futile. *Death* meets all who live.

I am the second—and like the Door, I wait. While most systems eventually accept the Door as a begrudging reality, most assume that I will never orbit them. I cannot be, they believe. I will never arrive. My orbit is for someone else. So most presume.

Few systems believe that I even exist. A naïve mistake. The vagaries of Life will thrust my orbit upon you, one way or another. I am your dark side—your *Dark Potential.* Picture me as a shadow shaped exactly like you. I hover just outside your system, yet I can orbit you within a heartbeat. Never believe that only others have a *Dark Potential.* You will *never* escape the possibility of my orbit. I will haunt you every moment of your life from the time you first hear these words until the day you pass through the Door.

I issue my first warning by dispelling the myth that only others, not *you*, can have a *Dark Side.* Rest assured, every human being, no matter their age, gender, social status, level of wealth or poverty, has a *Dark Side.* Believe that. Or do not. I do not care. I do not love you, as do many of my colleagues. I know humanity too well, which means that I know *you*!

My greatest enjoyment, nay, my *only* enjoyment comes from those who believe themselves to be too well educated, too sophisticated, too "under control" to ever have something so crude or as primitive as a *Dark Side.* When Life provides an opening for me to such self-assured systems, I assure you, I can and do achieve orbit within the space of a heartbeat. Then I laugh, as I trample *Naiveté's* fragile orbit.

For a Shadow, you see, darkness is its own reward.

To those systems bereft of the orbit of my colleague *Balance*, to those systems ruled by the orbit of *Insecurity*, I am instant, uncontrolled anger.

To those enslaved by the orbits of *Hatred* and *Prejudice*, I am the eternal whisperer of irrational thoughts, of alleged conspiracies, of mindless violence, of plots for *Revenge.*

I am your overreaction to things that disrupt your Life Path. When unforeseen events and influences destroy your dreams, your plans, your *Intentions*, I am there. The slightest rent in your cocoon of contentment and peace invites my orbit. Nay, it *summons* me!

I appear when your survival or that of a loved one is threatened. I can make you capable of unbelievable violence at such times. I can elevate you to the level of Dragon Slayer, though you may be naught but a farmer, or a poet dedicated to peace. Love of family justifies me at such times. The love of another's life over that of your own allows, even *demands* my orbit. You will discover the orbit of personal *Courage* at such times, although the piercing reality of my darkness will silence any whisper of *Pride* in your actions. You will learn the meaning of "paradox" when *Survival, Desperation, Courage,* my Shadow and *Love* all converge at the same event.

I appear when a soul's last veneer of *Self-Delusion* is torn away on every battlefield in every war ever fought. I am the awful truth that war will teach you about yourself. I incite you to hate. I teach you *how* to hate. I reveal what *you* are capable of, not your peers, or your enemies of the moment. Every warrior, in every army, in every age, knows me. I force them to know themselves. *Pride* deserts them when I engrave their acts of darkness into the recesses of their minds.

Know this: I exist to sear you. I exist to scar the perfect, satin texture of the soul you think is immune to me. The mutilation of your soul *is* my purpose.

Yet, though I nullify *Reason* and *Honor* and *Respect*, my companions and I are not enemies. We have discoursed across the breadth of countless galaxies. Time is nothing to us. You are the temporary yelp in the anthem of Creation. We introduce ourselves and pass on our way. You shall not forget us, as we shall you.

I give you this further warning. If you choose, I can overwhelm *Balance* and *Rationality* and *Love.* Yet all of these can defeat me if you hold their orbits fast. Anchoring to a personal code of *Honor* and clinging tightly to the Golden Thread of *Hope* will rein me under control.

But even so, prepare for the sight of blood-stained hands. Yours! When the canvas of a gentle philosophy is stained, know that it can come as easily from you as from an uncouth barbarian. When *Apathy* and *Heartlessness* chill the warmth of *Love*'s orbit, I am there, invited.

My slightest touch allows *rational* anger—a thing essential for your survival. A heavier touch erodes control of hostility. I become your temper—unchecked.

Embrace me totally and I promise you eruptions of illogical anger. I promise you *Hatred.* I promise you a system devoid of all that is good and positive. I promise that *Reason* will evaporate from your orbit like mist touched by a firebrand. *Intellect* will fade as you become a system known for naught but unpredictable *Emotion.* And know that when *Intellect* and *Reason* evaporate, when only raw *Emotion* rules a system, that most valued of heralds—*Respect*—is automatically repelled. A system ruled by *Emotion* cannot invite *Respect* to orbit. *Respect* cannot be captured and held, even slightly.

Love will be repelled, yet *Self-Loathing* and *Delusion* will orbit you gladly, for they accompany me always. *Jealousy* and *Envy* will too, more often than not.

Therefore, young one, recognize the reality of my existence. Touch me but slightly and live. Embody me completely and die. No system is immune to my darkness. In all of existence, only the Creator has no *Dark Side.* All else does. Not even the belief that Life is inherently good can save you from me.

I am to be comprehended, perhaps, but I am not leaving. Try to cast me from your soul.

Just try.

44

Gem

The Shadow's mocking challenge echoed noticeably within the minds of the children. Their grim jaw lines fought the herald's arrogance that he lay in wait near each of them. Their frowns showed denial as well as defiance of the Shadow's mission.

The Readers allowed a lengthier silence this time to dissipate the gruffness of the Shadow. When Taggart finally spoke, his pleasant baritone returned. Gone was the rude, overbearing tone of the Shadow. The drastic but welcome reversal jolted the children from their stance of defiance and back to the Scrolls.

Now, each of Taggart's words touched the ears of the children without haste, without threat. He was as a grandfather might be on a spring picnic now, offering his grandchildren delicate confections he'd brought along as a surprise.

Tyra was the last to return to the present. *Poppy is back*, she thought, shrugging off remains of the battle in the barn with no little difficulty. She forced the faraway look from her face. Forced her mind and ears to open to the next herald.

"Life does not tolerate the asymmetrical," Taggart said with an engaging smile. "Negations, influences of darkness, cannot exist without the contrast from light of that which is positive and good."

"So comes the gentle one," Taggart continued, "to allow a proper weighing, to contrast the Shadow's grimness."

Alina's voice took on a sultry, earthy sweetness that only she could produce. At least so Taggart believed. She began to read of exquisite gemstones.

Greetings. Allow me to caress your cheek. Certain of the League can be somewhat . . . burdensome, can they not? Do not concern yourself. You are not the first to think that a soul's rejection and acceptance process can be a ponderous thing.

This time one comes to you without burden or prerequisite. I offer pleasantries without limit, joy enough to thaw the coldest doubt. Call me *Love* if you will. A thousand other tongues have as many other names for me, but *Love* will suffice. I am the warm, unselfish attachment that you will feel for another system, or even for many systems during your journey. My loyalty, my concern for another can withstand any trial, the most hideous disease, even the terror of war if I genuinely orbit your soul. Of all in the League, I am the most beautiful, yet at times, I can be the most deeply painful orbit you might ever encounter.

Picture me as a finely cut gem of untold value. Watch as I orbit you. Notice how sunbeams strike my many facets and radiate beauty and joy to your eyes.

Hear me and comprehend. Without my orbit, you will possess no true wealth even if you one day attain an emperor's crown. Without my caress, you will wander Life as an impoverished beggar, empty of spirit, shivering with cold, even if you clothe yourself with the most exquisite raiment. Gold and silver cannot replace the value of *Love*'s gemstone. Power cannot. Social status cannot. Cultural influence cannot.

With me, you will realize unsurpassed wealth, though you may never ascend to any great station in Life. To love and to be loved by another is the priceless jewel of one's existence.

I need no prerequisite, yet I am a prerequisite for other orbits. Accept me and not only will you know *Compassion*, *Sympathy*, and *Tenderness*, but you will project their qualities toward other systems. To hold such as these in orbit is quite impossible without first welcoming *my* orbit. Those who hold *Love* in foundational orbit give freely of themselves. They do so with joy. They do so without thought of reward.

Will you attain the physical proportions of a giant and possess the strength of ten? Will violence and war scar your countenance and turn your body as rigid as iron? It will not matter, for that is your outer shell. *Love* can soften the heart within you.

With *Love*, the scars of war may not disappear but can soften. They can lose their power to steer you from a meaningful life. With my orbit, iron can weep the gift of honest tears of tenderness at the touch of those whom you love. Such is my power.

Yet, as my fellow travelers have warned you, so also must I. Of all in the League, none possess even a portion of my capacity to link with another system. This power can be either the most exquisitely meaningful completion of your existence, or the most soul-rending time you will ever experience. Understand, there are agonies that ignore the body and attack the spirit. So terrible are these agonies, you may feel as if the satin core of your soul has been rent by razor-sharp talons. Unrequited *Love* is one.

I am a paradox requiring *Intensity* and *Commitment* balanced by fair and intelligent *Restraint*. Those whom you love should receive the strongest link that you can possibly forge. However, any such recipient must be allowed space of its own to breathe, to grow, to seek its own *Awareness* on its own path.

Hear and comprehend, young one. To smother the growth of another system ignites defensive combat from that system. This universal instinct of survival is rooted deep within the core fires of all souls—including your own.

Can a soul *Love* too much? Can one be loved too much? No. Not as long as the *Motivation*, the undercurrent for *Love* is pure and honorable.

Can I be taken to extremes? Yes, if one's *Motivation* is tainted with *Dishonor*. A sullied undercurrent nullifies me first, then it eradicates me.

Love, you see, cannot devolve into *Fanaticism*. One herald cannot become another. Our definitions are as divergent as light and darkness.

When *Love* crosses the boundary of healthy *Respect*, it becomes something else entirely. It degrades into the realm of ownership, a kind of slavery. Understand, no soul can own another. Ownership is the Father's realm. He created you.

Sense the completeness I offer, young one, for it is beyond even the combined power of the League of Heralds. I am one of the great levelers of your Life, and I am the catalyst for the greatest emotional peak that you shall ever hope to experience.

Choose well, child-sun.

I offer myself to you.

45

Dream Wings

*N*o one presents Love's words as sweetly as Alina does, Taggart thought with admiration. In the obligatory silence, the children savored her words as they might savor the scent of a freshly baked pie, or the taste of a sweet, honeyed confection.

Tyra tried to cling to the silken words of the *Gem*, but memories of the deadly battle in the barn attacked her concentration unmercifully. The calm strength of the Warrior *Courage* warred with resolute silence against the Shadow's snarling *Dark Side*. Both existed in her life now. Both fought for her attention: one to inspire her, the other to stain her soul by demanding that she acknowledge the ugliness of its existence.

Your parents showed their hidden Dark Side in that barn, the Shadow snarled in her mind with undisguised *Arrogance. They were no different than the beast they fought,* he added spitefully. *You were no different*! Shadows laugh with malice it seemed.

She fought back, holding to that blazing moment of clarity when the raging ferocity of the giant killer met the immovable *Courage* of her parents and their weapons.

Yes, she thought, *that was Courage in its purest form, summoned forth, unsheathed, unleashed. A weapon in its own right. Yes, darkness arose in them . . . and in me.*

But something else declared its presence in the barn that night as well, a silken voice injected. *A brilliant glow rose to defy such darkness and violence and absolute savagery.*

Yes, Tyra thought, *Love of family lived that night. Strong. Obvious. A violent, necessary facet of the Love Gem perhaps, but every bit as evident as the herald Courage, or the Shadow herald of the human Dark Side.*

It was her realization that such extreme opposites could balance the same event that jarred Tyra back to the introduction of the next herald.

"There are those of the League who separate imaginative, thinking life from the instinct-driven beast," Alina began. Tinged with confidence, her voice was slightly louder than the velvet subtlety of the previous *Gem*. "They come with *Pride* instead of *Bombast*, with *Self-Assurance* instead of *Boastfulness*. They bear gift casks of fine gold, and they exhibit no pretense in their introductions."

As Taggart rolled his scroll to the appropriate herald, his relaxed posture of resting his elbows on his knees changed. He sat up straight, craned his neck in preparation, and jutted his chin out slightly. His gray, now friendly eyes swept the faces of his small audience, making quick, but definite eye-to-eye contact with each child.

His voice held none of the combative intimidation that had personified the Shadow herald earlier. His baritone held no obvious threat now. But there was a kind of haughty echo that matched the restrained energy so obvious in Taggart's posture. This herald was *very* eager to speak of itself.

Greetings, child-sun. Call me *Imagination*.

I offer you the potential of true uniqueness. I am your ability to form images in your mind of things not yet real, of things that might one day be. Picture me as the powerful wings of a majestic eagle. Note the elegance of them as they reach boldly from your shoulder blades. Note how they test the air of heights never reached. See them shimmer with a limitless rainbow of colors. The wings I represent are yours, and yours alone. No other human being on earth can fly with your wings, nor can you fly with another's. I am unique to each soul who draws breath. No other herald offers the unique opportunity that I do.

Do not confuse me with *Inspiration*, however. *Inspiration* triggers me and is my closest League companion, but I produce the swirling dream colors in your mind once *Inspiration* influences you.

Certain of the League truly define your humanity. I am one of those. I divide the bestial from the introspective. *Imagination* ignites *Intellect*'s absorption of facts, and then fans it to a greater flame than can any other of the League.

With me, you can conceive abstract visions, and then build them. With me, you can stride past the drudgery of daily existence to dream of what might be. I offer a path from that which is rigid, shackled, and mundane. There is nothing more intangible than a dream, yet there is nothing more uniquely your own. I offer a gift of freedom though you may be chained in the darkest of prisons. I link with my League companion *Hope*, even in the most meaningless, the darkest of situations. No tyrant can chain *Imagination.* Thus, no soul can truly be shackled if it retains my orbit. It is, I think, the Creator's great jest at those who would incarcerate the minds and bodies of others.

Even so, I must serve you warning. I must never be forsaken or cast aside. The orbits of *Intellect, Reason,* or *Logic* are but pallets of gray shades without my dream colors. Without the brilliant hues of *Imagination's* Dream Wings, Life can be naught but a drab, machine-like existence. Yet, without substantive action, my orbit will result in another kind of meaninglessness. Inaction destroys personal flight. Inaction smothers even the powerful beat of Dream Wings. Inaction offers nothing. Remember. Inaction *is* nothing!

Never allow your dreams to stagnate. Never permit them to devolve into an empty *Intention.* I warn you just as my fellow herald *Intention* warns you. *Intention* is the easy part!

Be further warned. *Procrastination* lurks within my shadow and is your greatest adversary. *Procrastination* dissolves dreams, denying that it does so, even as it drains the life from them. *Procrastination* feeds upon inactivity, growing stronger the longer it feeds. *Procrastination* is a subtle form of the herald *Cowardice.* Its strongest ally is *Time,* and within that context, *Time* can be the greatest enemy of your dreams. *Procrastination* cunningly uses *Time* to weaken your personal *Discipline. Time* dilutes your *Resolve.* If you allow it to.

Conceptualize—yes.   Dream—absolutely.   Envision— certainly, but then build and sculpt your dreams into something of substance. Use the *Time* allotted to you for focused activity, not for shallow *Reverie* without substance.

This is my purpose, young one. This is the treasure I lay before you. I offer you Dream Wings and boundless panoramas of spirit. Remember. The Dream Wings of *Imagination* fit only the shoulders of the human creation. The creations of the animal world cannot don them. Animals cannot soar above their earth-bound state. Animals cannot envision that which does not yet exist. Only the human creation can.

Accept my wings.

Soar as your Creator intended you to.

46

The Great Race

Alina waited a few minutes before preparing for the next reading. The children focused their attention upon her. Taggart would introduce, and Alina would be the next herald.

She rolled through her scroll casually at first, but this time, Taggart imitated her. After a moment, a frown of consternation furrowed her brow. Taggart glanced at the children and tried to mimic her expression. He added an exaggerated pout for their amusement. The transition between readings would be different this time, they sensed.

Alina seemed absorbed by her scroll, moving it close to her face and squinting as if trying to read fine print, and then to arm's length as if in consternation. As Taggart tried to follow, he was always just a half-step behind. The children grinned at such unexpected but obvious play.

When Alina—still ignoring all else—began rolling her scroll rapidly backward, Taggart almost dropped his as if caught unawares. The children chuckled openly now.

"Ah-ha!" Alina exclaimed loudly in triumph. Taggart and the children all jumped in their seats. "Here we are!" Her eyes were as wide as her smile.

Taggart puffed his cheeks and blew out a big breath, taking exaggerated pains to wipe his brow with a sleeve as if exhausted. A few children playfully imitated him.

"Some heralds are more enthusiastic than others," Taggart said with a wink. "They teach us to imagine magnificent futures. They create visions in our minds of things yet to be, of ideas yet untested, yet as vivid as any reality of the moment. They see beyond obvious horizons, beyond obvious obstacles, and through all restraining shackles of the moment. They give a soul absolute, unfettered freedom of flight. Such is our next herald."

Alina set the tone of her reading subtly. As if she were now the imitator that Taggart had been moments earlier, she raised her face heavenward, smiled contentedly, and closed her eyes softly as if dreaming beyond the obvious horizons.

Her voice seemed younger somehow, but it carried an obvious confidence as well. It brought to mind the untouchable freedom the great crag lords exemplify as they soar above mountain valleys with such regal impunity.

"Let us read," she said just before opening her eyes to begin.

Welcome to life, young one. May the Creator bless you with open eyes, with a willing heart, and with long life that we might become fast friends.

Philosophers call me Life's Magnificent Quest, the human soul's Great Race. Since Great Race seems more fun, consider me that, though my true name is *Potential.*

Picture me not as a confined oval upon which human athletes or racing steeds compete. Rather, picture me as a great meandering cross-country racecourse that spans hill and valley that traverses rushing streams and rivers and mountain peaks before disappearing over the horizon to a finish. Call that completion "destiny" if you will, hidden from you as it is by distance and *Time* and by Life's ever-changing terrain.

I am your Life's possibility. I am your inherent capacity to develop into someone who does not yet exist. I am the largest member of the League, for I expand at your choosing. Simply put, I can never be fully realized while life and breath reside within you. Final, complete human *Potential* is impossible to reach, though you can reach *for* me. I tease and I frustrate. My nature is as tenuous to your grasp as a horizon is distant to your mind.

Yet, the frustrations that I offer are but sparks to bring to full flame. My teasing is merely nourishment for the seed herald *Determination.* Fan the sparks, nurture the seeds. Reach for me. Relish the Great Race that gives such meaning to Life. Revel in your own *Potential.* Delight in the concept, in the power of human *Potential.* Believe this. Your Maker created me specifically for *you.*

To run *Potential*'s course, you must utilize the strengths of many other heralds. You will need *Courage* in great measure to explore the path of your own *Potential*, for many times during your race you will deign to surrender the chase. Do not! To yield to the obstacles that *will* confront you is to stagnate. You become less than your Designer intended for you. To withdraw is to sell your soul at discount. Sell not the diamond for the price of clay! Run the race and grow; ignore it and wither. Indeed, the only way to win the race is to run it. The only way to lose it is to quit, or worse, refuse to run.

I am a race with no set course, yet one where *you* furnish the goal. *Potential* is won with every step taken forward to participate. *Potential* tests self against self, self against Life, and self against circumstances or opportunity. Glories and pitfalls inhabit *Potential*'s path. So do rewards and obstacles, satisfactions and disappointments. And be assured, that only after absorbing or overcoming them all will you grasp the value of them all.

Retain the orbits of *Reason* and *Intellect*, for they will define your strategy. Whether you seek a *Potential* level of spiritual enlightenment, of physical prowess, of intellectual power, or even the acquisition of wealth, the Sword and Shield will strengthen if you wield them wisely during your race.

Yet, be warned, for I can influence your Life-path in harmful ways if you shun *Humility*, if you neglect *Love*, if you discard *Honor* or *Dignity.*

Hold *Humility* near. Let the Liberator's whispering *Conscience* teach you control and understanding. *Humility* in proper measure tempers *Purpose* with *Discretion.* With *Humility* in orbit, *Strategy* acknowledges that other soular systems run their race as do you.

To race for one's *Potential* at the expense of the lives and dreams of others soils the very fabric of Creation. It runs contrary to the Maker's nature and it will exact a price, though you will not know when or what that price will be. Play the Great Game fairly, young one. Run Life's Race with *Integrity.* Remember who created you, so that when you look back upon your path (and one day you shall), you will feel few regrets. Run the race with *Honor* and like yourself. Run with *Dignity* and attain the most sought-after commodity in all of Creation—*Respect.*

Understand though that there is no ultimate *Potential.* Reaching the peak of an individual talent or goal is just that; one particular peak. There are so many *Potentials* of physical skill, of *Intellect,* of *Creativity* that a million lifetimes would not reach them all. Add in the opportunity to align your life ever closer with your Creator, and the idea of being first in something and then having nowhere else to go simply rings off-key and untrue. Bluntly put, such thoughts dishonor your Maker.

Run this race poorly, or not at all, and your quality of life will erode faster with each new day. Do not bother to dwell on that universal truth. Just know that such erosion affects those around you as well. Life can descend into a meaningless spiral devoid of self-esteem, a dark place where *Hope* dissolves, where the ability to dream vanishes. Essentially, the soul despises itself for its own cowardice.

Forsaking one's *Potential* negates the power of *Love*'s orbit, for if one does not love oneself, how can one *truly Love* another? Fail to seek me and lose the power to dream, for the Dream Wings of *Imagination* are only as powerful or as weak as you decide.

Fail to step upon the course of *Potential,* and your grasp on the Golden Thread of *Hope,* will weaken. perhaps even fail, for *Dreams* and *Hope* are inseparable kin. I tell you now. To lose your grasp from *Hope*'s Golden Thread is to begin your death chant. Your end becomes just a matter of time.

Live well, young one. Gaze with enthusiastic anticipation beyond the limits of your current horizons. Seek the distant, unseen horizons of your *Potential.*

Breathe deeply of the crystalline air of adventure that sweeps boldly through untrodden valleys and untainted mountain peaks.

Sense the heady challenge of stepping upon a course of unknown obstacles and rewards.

Feel the *Pride* one day of knowing you have run a great and often difficult race nobly and with personal *Honor.*

Come, race with me.

47

Phantom

The echoes of *Potential* rang clearly in the minds of the children after Alina's last words, for thoughts of distant horizons and personal dreams come easily to the young. Life has not tempered their enthusiasm with a cold dash of reality. Paths and racecourses are, to the young, free of pitfalls and obstacles.

Alina brought them back to the campfire with the gentle tone of a grandmother reading a story to her grandchildren.

"Let us begin by gazing heavenward for a moment," she said. "Out there," she pointed, "beyond the little sun, where the vast surrounding blackness seems the darkest, a silvery mist materializes. Imagine it with me. This herald, bears no resemblance to an orbiting planet or moon. Rather, it resembles a serpent of glistening fog as it writhes forth from some unseen lair in space. The graceful coils seem endless, as if they were being perpetually created. It approaches the little sun without haste, as would a serpent confident of its prey.

"This herald will not, indeed *cannot*, orbit the soul as others do, nor is it one to be invited or rejected. The instant the diaphanous tip of the silvery streamer touches the little sun, it transforms. The fog-like quality crystallizes into what resembles the hard brilliance of a perfect diamond. Uncountable, perfect facets, each a shimmering pathway for its own self-created light, reflect also the golden sheen of the soular sun itself. There is warmth, beauty, and ever-changing possibility, but then the diamond disappears."

The faces of the children frowned as they held the vision, lost it, only to regain it again. This Herald was not as easy to visualize as the others.

Alina continued, "The coils of this herald undulate through the very heart of the little sun, once again a streamer of glistening fog as it continues out the other side. Yet, the instant another coil touches the little golden sun for the first time, it too transforms into a brilliant diamond. The most tenuous of vapors becomes the ultimate substantiality, only to dissolve back into fog again as the herald slithers through the child sun. Or," Alina asks, "is it that the little sun travels *along* the vapor?

"The mist leaves in its wake the admiration of the diamond, a certain sense of loss, but oddly, a lingering doubt that the diamond ever existed at all."

With Alina's introduction complete, Taggart began. His voice assumed the matter-of-fact tone of a teacher addressing a classroom, but that was not all. Inflections of empathy and concern carried through for those who were about to meet the most difficult herald in the League to fathom.

Greetings, youngling.

Call me *Time*. I am the space where events occur in your past, present, and future. I am a non-guaranteed, nebulous measure in which you may (or may not) discover yourself, your destiny, your intended path. Beyond that, I counsel that you will never understand me, never grasp me, though you will no doubt try, as the human creation is prone to do.

It is best to envision me as a Phantom, a single entity with two very different states of being. This is difficult to grasp, certainly, but as a Phantom, I am both as insubstantial as a morning ground mist and as solid as a diamond. Allow me to illustrate.

Realize that I cannot orbit you as my colleagues do, for I am like a streamer of fog as your future approaches. I do not tangibly exist then. I am exactly the same as your past departs you. I do not tangibly exist then either, save for the importance and the priority of past memories that you allow to hold sway over you.

Yet, in the instant that you do essentially hold me, I am as crystalline pure, as solid as the most perfect diamond. I truly exist to you, for you, in that instant called "now." In that reality, be it a single heartbeat, or many extended heartbeats, I might exist to you as *Joy*, as *Awe*, as *Pride*, or *Sorrow*. I might be *Love* or *Horror*, supreme *Gratitude*, or *Despair*. Whatever I am at that moment of reality is all you have. No human being has more of me than any other human.

Know this: it is a waste of Life to ponder the concept of *Time*. In the span of such wasted moments, a seed could be planted, a poem written, a child caressed . . . or conceived. A great book could be read, or written, a great love discovered, a mountain peak could be conquered. An eagle's flight could be applauded, a night constellation could be appreciated. Your Creator could be worshipped in reverence.

Rather than dwell upon a Phantom, choose instead, to savor an elegant wine, an exquisite meal. Appreciate a craftsman's handiwork. Taste the salt spray from a rocky cape storm. Feel the pulse of an ocean's eternal tide as it caresses a shoreline. Marvel at the delicate grace of the sea birds hovering above that shore. Ponder *these* things, feel them, sense them, young one. Not me. There are more important things in your Life to ponder than *Time*, yet no herald in the League is more valuable to you. Yes, that does sound like a contradiction.

I am important but not as a concept to be dissected or defined. My value depends solely upon you. I am ignored by some, valued by others. I am used, not used. I am thrown away and wasted. I am overabundant, or stingy, yet, paradoxically, I am also the most fair and equal herald in the League. All who live have all of me. No soul, whether privileged or destitute, has more or less of me.

The king awash in his treasure has no more of me than the peasant who kneels in poverty before his throne. The devout priest has no more of me than the atheist who scorns his beliefs.

Oddly, I am the herald most dependent upon you for definition. I am never seen, never felt, but I can be despised and fretted over. I am never opaque, yet I am always in attendance. I am never tasted, never scented, yet I am always in evidence.

A dying soul has not enough of me, yet an imprisoned soul has too much. I am relative, therefore, to your recognition of my value, to your circumstances, and to your use of me. If you choose to be lazy, if you seek nothing, want nothing, care for nothing, aspire to nothing, I am of little value. *Time* without goals, purpose, direction or worthwhile ambitions is worthless. Even worse, if this is your mindset, you, not I, will relegate your Life-journey to the existence of the beast. Remember, you were created to live deliberately as only a human being can. You were not created to merely exist randomly as do animals.

Time means nothing to animals. They exist within it, but they can no more grasp the impact of *Time* than they can fathom the concept of a Creator.

Nonhuman life has no grasp of a particular day of the week, and attaches no particular value to a given month or season. Such things are the inventions of the human mind trying to quantify me. As for the seasons of giving birth, of mating or gathering in flocks, herds, schools, or pods for seasonal migrations, such things are simply instincts ingrained by the Creator. Each instinct lies silently within the creature until it is triggered in its season by Creator-endowed, invisible drives that humans are only beginning to understand.

Animals are born, they survive as the ingrained instincts of their particular species dictate, and then they die.

Humankind, on the other hand, considers *Time*, contemplates it, writes of it, and even composes songs and poetry about it. Humans create calendars to give me substance as a visual construct. Humans devise tools to quantify me: a simple stick driven into the earth to create the sun's moving shadow, a glass funneling a measure of sand grains, even complex mechanical devices of levers, and bewildering gears spinning on tiny axles.

Your philosophers, scientists, and mathematicians will author intricate theories and postulates concerning my meaning. Take comfort in knowing that their theories, despite the depth of convoluted complexity they might obtain, will grant them no more enlightenment than you have at this moment.

Ludicrously, humankind actually tries to manipulate me. Just understand that what humankind considers a manipulation of *Time* is really no more than a prioritizing of activities to be performed between one particular sunrise and another particular sunset. Such scheduling of deliberate human *Intentions*, opposes the instinctive, random existence of the animal.

That said, to souls who seek to improve their lot in life, to builders and doers of their culture, I am the most beautiful, invaluable mist-diamond possible, a Phantom by any definition.

Though you will inherently deny this, I tell you truly that your past, as well as your future, are mists, if even that! They are ground fogs burned away by the sunlight of today, of now. Just as it is impossible to hold a cloud or a mist in your hands, so also is it with the past and future. You never really have them at all, though your mind, its memories, its intentions would argue against this.

Your past retains whatever value or detriment your memories give it. Conversely, your future is only as valuable as what you dream it to be. To dwell in either place too deeply is to deny yourself the value of the diamond you hold in your hand today. It is to turn a blind eye to new experiences, to personal growth, to grand discoveries of your *Potential.*

What you have, young one, truly have, is *now*! Your Creator grants you *this* breath, *this* instant, *this* heartbeat, *this* opportunity. In return, you would do well to show Him *Gratitude* for *this* day of Life, for *this* opportunity to love your spouse one more day, to enjoy and to rejoice in the laughter of your children *one more time,* to support your family *one more day* through your profession.

Know this: your Maker does not guarantee you a future.

Strive to accept this fact young one, as difficult as that is. Learn, and keep learning how to better use your gift-moments. Cherish every opportunity, every heartbeat given to you. Relish every breath you take, every moment spent with a friend. Remember me. Learn to treasure *Time* as the nebulous mist-diamond you neither hold, keep, nor see.

Please.

48

The Door

As the children waited, Taggart prepared to introduce the next herald. Alina would read this one.

The big man quietly rolled his scroll to a certain place, then gazed toward the night sky. In the orange glow of the firelight, the set of his jaw and the contemplative look in his gray eyes gave him a mask best described as reluctant. The mood of this herald would surely be somber.

There was none of the Phantom's matter-of-fact delivery this time. There was no wide-eyed exuberance of *Potential.* There was, however, a definite light of challenge in those storm-gray eyes. The clipped brevity of Taggart's words made this the shortest introduction of the evening. His voice was a monotone, devoid of inflection or embellishment. The children sat up noticeably straighter as the curt words speared toward each of them.

"Hear this," Taggart said, making eye contact with each child. "Hear it all."

Alina delivered the words of the new herald bereft of noticeable emotion or emphasis on any particular point. With her first word, this herald commanded complete attention. This time, however, it was the subject matter, not an expressive personality that captured each child.

"That all life possesses a beginning and an end adheres to our Creator's design," she said, "to His plan of natural balance. Given that, how could Dawn's first glow of *Awareness* possibly exist without a finality to end the light?"

Young one, listen carefully. I do not greet the human soul as do my League companions. Right now, you barely sense the possibility of me. You barely understand how final my actual greeting is.

A thousand tongues have given me names: primal names, god names, outlandish names, even fanciful names. To some, I am a Final Curtain, to others a Grim Reaper. Bluntly put, I am simply *Death*. Eventually, when you finally believe in me, you will name me as well.

I may not visit you for a century, though occasionally, I arrive before a new soul even hears Dawn's first greeting. You will never be oblivious to me, for should I tarry in greeting you personally, you will sense me as I greet others around you.

Many cultures try to explain me. Some fight me, or justify me, or worship me. Some even hate me, but any of these things is a waste of the *Time* you have beyond this night. You cannot conquer me or avoid me, for I am the only herald in the League you cannot choose to reject. Your Creator chooses my arrival. *He* summons me.

I am the finality of your soular system as you understand the concept of finality. Even so, it is best to visualize me simply as a Door separating one room from another, or more aptly, as a Door closing upon one world, only to open to another. The details of your passage beyond me, the introduction of those who will greet you, are not mine to reveal. My mission, within these Scrolls, is simply to warn *you* of *me*.

Therefore, do not waste precious *Time* considering me good or evil. I am neither and such definitions are ludicrous. I am merely the last herald of the League to orbit your system.

Accept my existence but proceed on your course. Do not dwell upon me. Find worthy channels for your Life-energy, for my arrival is *always* considered unexpected, *always* considered premature. I advise you to seek those things that you do not yet know. I advise you to relish them. Relish them as the Phantom *Time* advised you to relish your diamond moments.

Heed the advice of my league companion *Potential*. Run that limitless race with enthusiasm. Seek the unseen possibilities that lie beyond untrodden horizons. Breathe the pure, crystalline air that *Potential* offers.

As long as you have breath, hold *Curiosity* in a firm, inner orbit. Never let it go. Deliberately seek out unique experiences beyond your normal routine of Life. The capacity of your mind to absorb new information and to acquire new knowledge is a treasure gift to you. Use it. Learn. Read. Acquire new skills beyond those of your station in Life.

Ponder always the magnificence of your Maker's gift of Life. Love without restraint. Sculpt your system deliberately. Do so with active *Intention* as you experience my fellow heralds. Read of my varied companions. Endeavor to understand them, so that you might achieve a wondrous *Balance* with us all. Sing in Creation's chorus. Dance in moon shadows. Dare to soar on wind currents of discovery. Relish the delicious taste of Life. And always—always give the gift of *Gratitude* back to your Maker for each savory morsel of it. For though your *Gratitude* can only scratch the surface of your Creator's gifts, it will be the most sincere form of worship that you can raise to Him.

Live to the fullest, young one, for I promise you this.

I *will* arrive to your system too soon.

You *will* feel my embrace—once.

You *will* see my face—once.

After me, there are no more orbits.

49

Tightrope

In the interim, as the children absorbed the words of the Door, Alina and Taggart leaned toward each other to exchange whispers. They seemed deliberately unhurried, deliberately relaxed. The somber words of the Door required more time to echo, it seemed. Alina's lips barely moved as she whispered near her husband's right ear. Taggart nodded silently. He whispered a few words back, and then both Readers sat up straighter as they rolled their scrolls forward to a common place.

To virtually every child, this seemed wrong. As the self-described "last herald," the Door logically should have signaled the end of the Reading, and thus, the end of Scroll Night.

Yet, the Readers showed no indication of the end of anything. They did not return their Scrolls to their pouches. Something defied *Logic* here but knowing that nothing happens without reason on Scroll Night kept the questioning hands down. Should the obvious go unexplained, however, nine hands would be raised at the end of the Reading to ask the same question.

"Tell me, children," Alina began, "what you know of *Pride*?"

"Is it good," Taggart added, "or bad?"

"It's both," Seanna Berit answered. "I mean, it can be a good thing, or it can be bad." Most of the children nodded in agreement.

"What do your parents say of *Pride*?" Alina instigated. "What do other Elders around you say?"

"Father says that *Pride* is necessary to do your job properly," Brann Halwyn said.

Both Readers smiled, knowing exactly what that meant when voiced by Brann's father. Bearach Halwyn was one of Wraithaven's master potters. As such, a long waiting list of candidates hoped to apprentice under his demanding tutelage.

Taggart had personally seen Bearach declare a novice's newly fired bowl as unworthy even to carry grain to livestock. A death knell for the offending creation, it meant chagrin for the guilty potter-to-be as Bearach's Mallet of Doom crushed the piece into worthless shards. Conversely, even the slightest praise from Master Halwyn honored the recipient.

"*Pride* is attention to detail," Brann said with finality.

I wonder where he heard that, Alina thought with a smile before continuing. "Give us another example,"

"*Pride* in your family," Quinn Farriss said.

"In your country," Keiriam Marsali added immediately.

"Hmmmmm," Alina said, "*Pride* of family, of family name. A good *Motivation* for one to maintain honorable behavior, lest one's family name be tainted, yes?" Every child either nodded or exclaimed in agreement immediately. To Wraithian children, *Honor* and family name are inseparable. Synonymous.

"A very positive kind of *Pride*," Taggart said, "could we not all agree?" Again, the children agreed with an immediate chorus of "ayes." "We will speak more of family *Pride* later," Taggart said, "but for now, just consider how such a thing might go badly. Family feuds, for instance—ones that might span generations. Consider that *Pride* can lose its way, that it can become something else."

"And if so," Alina said, "how can other forms of *Pride* become something else? Keiriam, you mentioned *Pride* in your country. Are you proud to be Wraithian?"

"Yes, ma'am, of course, I am," the girl answered defensively.

"Why," Alina prompted, "do you think so highly of Wraithaven?"

The girl's eyes flared at the personal challenge. Alina held back her smile, knowing that had she asked such a question in the daylight, she would have seen Keiriam's cheeks flush with emotion.

"Wraithaven has been at peace for over two thousand years," Keiriam declared. "No other nation in history can say that. Wraithians value peace above all else, except our Creator. We take pride in that. We despise war. Outsiders seem to love it. They continually war against each other."

"Why?" Alina asked.

"Because they're bloodthirsty brutes!" the girl answered with absolute conviction. "Texts of *their* histories prove that!"

"Anyone else agree?" Taggart asked calmly.

Most of the children raised their hands quickly, but a few hesitated, sensing something underlying his simple question.

"Children," Taggart continued, "at this very moment, do we not paint all Outsiders with a broad brush dipped in a single color called 'inferiority'? We label them 'Outsiders'—people that none of you have even met. Does not that very labeling tempt us to paint ourselves, indeed all of Wraithaven, with a brush dipped in the pigment called 'superiority'? Picture that in your minds. *Pride*, in anything, inherently fosters one's judgment of what logically must be inferior to that thing. How dare we do that?" the Reader said, his voice hard, challenging. "How dare *you*! That is another manifestation of the herald *Pride*."

"Despite their relatively short histories in comparison to ours, Outsiders can and do feel tremendous *Pride* in their own nations. Yet, as we know from our history texts," Taggart said, nodding to Keiriam, "national *Pride* in the Outsider nations has probably ignited more wars than any other cause. *Pride* of this type invites the herald *Jealousy*. It nurtures the herald *Hatred* for a neighbor. It listens to the whispers of the herald *Greed*. Like it or not, Wraithaven's *Pride* as a nation is very much akin to the national *Pride* that warlike Outsiders feel for *their* people. We absolutely must remember that."

The children's solemn silence proved how alien such a nontraditional viewpoint sounded. That the notoriously violent Outsiders might share anything in common with Wraithians who measured peace in millennia instead of mere years, jarred them. *Scroll Night. The crossing of thresholds.*

"Now," Alina said, breaking the mood, "what else besides our peaceful intentions gives us *Pride*?"

"We know who we are as a people, and where we came from," Tyra answered.

"We have a firm sense of our roots?" Taggart asked. "Our history?"

Yes," Tyra chimed in. "Our Pelanjian ancestors first settled Wraithaven two thousand years ago, and they didn't displace or kill even one other human being to do so either. No other people lived here."

"And before Wraithaven," Devyn Briac added, "our ancestors lived in the Pelanjian Archipelago for eleven hundred years, without displacing a single human being in those islands either. What they did have to do was fight to keep their islands free from invading Outsiders."

"And before that," Marcus Riordan continued, "we know that our Pelanjian ancestors were, in fact, Mindocean explorers who navigated the oceans of the ancient world centuries before any of the current nations even existed. We have records of the Mindoceans for more than three thousand years before the settling of the Pelanjian islands."

"Because they invented the first written language," Leah Brenna added.

"Well said," Alina responded, "all of you. True, we Wraithians can trace our continual ancestral roots back more than six thousand years. And as you say, no Outsider nation can do that. But that doesn't mean that Outsiders don't love their countries too, despite having much shorter histories than ours.

"Having a long history does not necessarily grant a nation superiority, any more than it would bestow honor upon its people. Does an individual who happens to achieve a long life deserve *Honor* and *Respect* simply by existing? Certainly not. Such things are earned every day of our lives, and if the individual lives Life believing that, then *Honor* and *Respect* will increase as the hair whitens. As it is with a single human being, so it is with a nation.

"*Pride* of nation, of one's history, of one's religion, or of seemingly superior cultural status are all natural human emotions and can be good, but they can be equally dangerous as well. We've taken extra time with this subject because like *Courage*, misunderstanding and unclear definitions abound with our next herald. This one approaches a soular system with a light tread, every bit as warily as *Courage* does. It knows what it is, but more importantly, it knows what it can mutate into. It knows how it can be misunderstood and more importantly, be misused."

And with that foreshadowing, Taggart's voice took on a distinctly careful tone. Turning the Scroll to better use the firelight, he began to read of the herald that furnished a rather unique vision of itself.

Greetings.

Call me *Pride* but know that I can be a variety of things to a soular system. Depending on how you allow me to orbit, I can be an overbalanced opinion of yourself. I can be exaggerated *Self-Esteem*—even *Conceit* or *Arrogance.* Conversely, I can also be a strong sense of personal *Dignity*, of *Self-Worth*, of *Self-Respect.* I can be the herald that rewards you with satisfaction for something you've worked hard to accomplish.

But because of the wide range of things that I can be to *you*, and because of the variety of perceptions I can create as *being* you to the world, you must visualize me as a Tightrope.

At village festivals, do not agile performers, with balancing poles firmly in hand, bedazzle spectators with wondrous feats of balance? So also must you.

You are the performer; I am the Tightrope. You create the balancing pole from the substance of your values. Hear that again. *You* create the balancing pole.

You already know that the character of your soul is a sculpture you create from the decisions you make and the values you cherish. So it is with *Pride*'s balancing pole. The pole can help you maintain your *Balance*, or it can topple you from the Tightrope. View me thus to hold me in a controlled, measured orbit about your system. In essence, the positive, attractive aspects of *Pride* are achieved only when one is balanced *upon* the tightrope. The negative, repellent aspects of *Pride* lurk below the rope, anxious to pull you down to them. Like *Balance*, one's *Pride* requires constant *Vigilance.*

First, consider the positive qualities of *Balance.* Consider which heralds you will need to create such balance. I will furnish a few. The rest you will discover and assimilate as you mature.

To keep *Pride*—and Life as a whole—in *Balance*, you must acquire proper *Humility*, embrace true *Introspection*, exhibit genuine *Gratitude*, and be ever watchful of personal *Motivation.*

Whether it is *Pride* of self-accomplishment, *Pride* of family, *Pride* of profession, or *Pride* of country, these fellow heralds must orbit with me as key ingredients of *Balance*.

To understand us, you must first acknowledge your own inherent worth. *Humility*, proper *Humility*, stands strong here, a reminder that you, and all who live, are creations of Father Creator. Remember. The Maker creates nothing that is without value. Nothing!

Self-Worth should never devolve into chest-pounding *Arrogance*. *Self-Worth* should invite *Introspection*—a patient, thoughtful herald whose primary function is to examine the soul. Untainted *Introspection* uncovers reasons for one's worth. It puts those reasons into *Perspective*, and proper *Perspective* leads to heartfelt, genuine *Gratitude*.

Gratitude acknowledges, for instance, that a personal *Talent* is a gift from your Creator. He bestows it. The individual develops it—or does *not*!

When *Gratitude* and *Introspection* link, other factors of *Self-Worth* are laid bare. The circumstances of one's birth cannot be denied. One's place of birth, the wealth or the poverty there, the environment of peace, of war, and of safety or danger, there are manipulative forces behind one's *Talent*. Can an environment of wealth nourish *Talent*? Certainly, just as it can starve *Talent* by shielding the individual from struggle in Life. Can poverty destroy a *Talent?* Absolutely, but it can also force *Talent* to drive roots deeper into *Determination*, into *Passion*, to thrive where *Logic* declares that it should not. A magnificent cause-and-effect choice from one's Creator, yes?

The presence of family, of a good upbringing or the lack of it, and the encouragement or the discouragement, can all be things to recognize, to examine, and indeed to express *Gratitude* for. *Gratitude* comes easily when circumstances are positive because you are shown what *to* do. Yet, *Gratitude* can be expressed from negative circumstances as well because you are taught what *not* to do.

Genuine *Gratitude* and honest *Introspection* will inspire you to disdain the shallowest of all the various forms of *Pride*—physical *Vanity*. If in *Balance* upon the Tightrope, you will recognize the pathetic shallowness of taking *Pride* in the color of your hair, or eyes, or skin for what it is—a perversion of true *Pride. Pride, without Gratitude, is self-worship and empty.*

Is your countenance considered handsome or beautiful by your culture? What of it? Your physical features were given to you at your conception. How dare you compare your physical comeliness to a perceived deficiency of such in another! How dare you look down upon them! How dare you sneer and feel superior! You did not create your physical traits. Your Maker did! You did *nothing* to earn your appearance! You can merely maintain the cleanliness of it. *Pride* devolves quickly into *Conceit* when you forget this.

Are you prideful of family wealth, of your family's social status? What of it? What did *you* do to create that wealth, to attain that lofty position? You were merely born into it. How dare you smirk at those less blessed at *their* birth! Those born into poverty did exactly the same thing you did to be born into wealth—nothing!

Do you ride upon exquisite tack adorning finely bred stallions? Do you ride in ornate carriages to purchase whatever you wish in any market you choose? Do you sneer at those afoot upon the same roads you travel? Do you laugh as your carriage wheels churn dust upon them? This is not *Pride* of family. This is *Arrogance.* Crush it every time you scent the odor of it!

Take heed. Being born to elevated social status, to generational wealth, is *not* your Creator-mandated destiny. Nor is it proof that He looks upon you, or your family, with greater favor than He does the less fortunate. Everything your Maker creates has value.

Rather, He has simply *allowed* you to be created into such a state. Wealth or poverty are both tests of the soul. The wealthy should seek to acquire the orbits of my companions, *Gratitude,* and *Introspection.* So should the poor. Again, everything your Maker creates has value.

Introspection does not leave one's *Motivations* unexamined. In all its various forms, *Motivation* is an undercurrent that manipulates all living things—both human and non-human. Examine *Motivations* under a harsh light of truth. If one's *Motivations* are dishonorable, *Balance* will be lost.

If my fellow heralds and I are in harmony, the next step is that of giving. To see the value of self, to be grateful for it, and to ultimately give back to humanity is the ultimate expression of positive *Pride*, the ultimate expression of *Gratitude* to your Maker. In this way, the created being lays a gift of one's heart at the feet of the Creator.

But what of the negative face of *Pride*? What of those unbalanced things below the Tightrope? Remember, your core values are closely linked to your *Motivations*. Is your *Pride* motivated by the desire to dominate those around you? Do you wield *Pride* as a weapon to attack the accomplishments of peers, of fellow workers, or even family? Is your *Pride* of country merely a mask hiding intended dominance on an international scale?

Be aware that there is good reason why virtually all human religions consider *Pride* to be a major sin. Negative, dominant *Pride* essentially tries to make the individual the Creator! This is *Foolishness* magnified. Such a path leads not to *Introspection*, but to *Arrogance*. And *Arrogance* pushes *Introspection* aside because true *Introspection* is deep, honorable, and patient.

Arrogance is shallow, a herald of haste, of waste, of narrow-mindedness, of incorrect conclusions drawn from *Disillusionment*. *Arrogance* is self-consuming. When *Pride* devolves into *Arrogance*, the pompous herald *Superiority* cannot be far away. Nor can *Jealousy, Conceit, Anger, Conflict,* and *Hatred*. Remember, whether for an individual, a nation, or a religion, *Arrogance* is hateful. Always! Arrogance is hurtful, mean-spirited, and demeaning. Always!

Know this about me. I am absolutely dangerous when a soul embraces me without restraint or counterbalance. I am as destructive to the individual soul as wealth can be when pursued for its own sake—as most religions rightly declare.

I can be as shallow and as evil an orbit in a system as any in the League. I can sow the seeds of the total destruction of a system if you forget how to keep me in check. I can nullify *Love*—both that of your own and that which might come from another. I can create an environment in your system so poisonous, *Respect* will wither and die. Without true *Humility* as an ingredient of your balancing pole, *Pride* will drag you from the rope and down into the abyss of *Arrogance*.

Pride can be a lie or the truth. I can be a true sense of *Self-Worth*, or a self-effacing veneer of *Arrogance* and *Bravado*. *Pride* can serve you, or make you its slave. For ill or for good, what you take *Pride* in is the image the world perceives of you.

Positive *Pride* inspires artisans to cherish perfection in their crafts. *Pride* is unfertile ground for compromise, for a "who-cares" attitude. Positive *Pride* demands expenditure of energy, demands clarity of *Intention* and *completion*. Positive *Pride* creates the environment to envision expectations, and then to exceed them. Such *Pride* produces seeming miracles. It guides you to discover the very fabric of yourself. *Pride* like this becomes a light to inspire others.

Positive *Pride* inspires parents to raise their children deliberately, to devote genuine attention to their upbringing, and to teach them manners. Positive *Pride* provides the drive to teach children how to excel, how to accomplish given tasks through a good work ethic. It teaches how to instill in them the concept of personal *Honor*.

Examine your *Values*, young sun, your *Motivations*, your *Intentions*.

Choose carefully how you *Balance* upon the Tightrope of *Pride*.

Choose the path of true, honorable, and positive *Pride* for your journey.

50

Liberator

Taggart allowed the children to absorb *Pride*'s words before continuing. The young listeners needed the time of echoes, just as the Readers did, to transition from the reading of one herald to the introduction of another.

"Quite possibly, children," he said, "the next herald will surprise you." Quizzical looks appeared on the children's faces. "Initiates often wonder why our next herald follows *Pride*. Both of us questioned it at our Readings as well."

By now, the children easily attuned to the deliberate inflections, and tones that Taggart and Alina applied to each herald. As she prepared to read this time, Alina's smooth contralto exuded a confident, open friendliness. As Taggart had predicted, Alina's voice did not seem to match this new herald's character at first. Which was exactly what the ancient Pelanjian creators of this night of such deliberate intent, had intended thirty centuries before.

Greetings.

Call me *Humility*. I approach you with certain reservations and given what you already *think* you know of *Humility,* my caution is appropriate. You no doubt expect meekness from a herald calling itself *Humility*. I assure you; my caution is similar to that of *Courage.*

Courage warned you early what it was, and what it was not. So must I, for as many misunderstandings abound with me as with *Courage.*

Yes, *Humility is* the state of being humble, a state where overt *Self-Assertion* is absent. Certain cultures, societies, or religions dilute me even more by defining me as meek, subservient, even lacking sufficient will to achieve or to participate enthusiastically in Life. This is *not* true.

To understand *Humility*, let us begin with your vision of me. Most heralds furnish you with visions of themselves that easily match their definitions. Just as they do, I will suggest a vision of myself, but you will not easily grasp the connection between vision and words—at first. I will have to convince you that my vision matches my words.

First of all, refrain from picturing me as a spineless, groveling human being too servile to stand for anything, including self. True *Humility* does not equate to weakness.

As difficult as it may seem at this moment, imagine *Humility* as a Liberator. Picture a stalwart warrior emboldened by his code of honor. Picture a great general leading his army to free an enslaved people. Envision a being of peace, a person of great intellect endowed with life-changing ideas that might transform a world. Choose your image as you will. Just accept that not all Liberators require fanfare or the pounding of war drums. Not all Liberators desire the peal of battle horns, the clash of sword against shield, or wind-fluttering pennants atop raised lances.

Equally true, *Humility* does *not* require a beaten countenance with downcast eyes. Those are the trappings of *Subjugation.* Nor is *Humility* characterized by a weak, slope-shouldered posture. *Intimidation* desires such posturing, but true *Humility* does not.

True *Humility* is a gift of insight, an agreement between you and your Creator of how Life is. You will discover that your Life-dance will be a complex array of countless available paths, of many directions to be taken or shunned. *Humility* is an important step for those who seek *Balance* in their lives.

Yet, if I am a Liberator as I say, from what do I liberate the human soul?

First, in these Scrolls, which your people hold so sacred, I immediately follow the herald *Pride.* This is not a coincidence. You must understand the Tightrope called *Pride* before you can properly understand *Humility.* Yes, that does sound like a paradox.

That said, true *Humility* breaks the burdensome chains of excessive *Pride and* of empty *Arrogance* and the myriad *Self-Delusions* that can, and do enslave a human soul. Proper *Humility* breaks the chains of *Insecurity*, which always attract the even heavier chains of *Jealousy* and *Envy*. And just how do I do that?

I remind you of your origin, of the One who ignited your soul into existence. Remember the vision of His hand opening and setting you free to drift into the Life-dance. Remember how *His* gentle breath eased you from the safety of *His* palm. Remembering this initial vision of your Scroll Night puts you on the path to understanding true *Humility*, for it is then a simple matter to remember that those you meet upon your journey have the exact . . .same . . . origin.

The ignition of your soul was a deliberate act of your Maker, done for a specific purpose. Take appropriate *Pride* in that, if you will, but remember that other *soular* systems were ignited by your Creator just as deliberately. They too were created for a unique purpose, just as you were. To remember these things is to understand how *Pride* and *Humility* can orbit the same soul. You did *not* create yourself. The universe does *not* revolve around you. The sun does *not* rise and set at your decree. Yet, you *are* a singular magnificence, as are others. Thus, the key to understanding proper *Humility* is to retain a good memory—of your own creation, and that of others.

Maintain this single memory and the herald *Self-Respect* will orbit your system as tightly as any herald in the League, for *Humility* is essentially *Self-Respect* bathed in the knowledge of one's creation by your Maker. Know also that *Self-Respect* shown *by* you invites the herald *Respect* to be awarded to you by others.

The liberation of your soul by *Humility* allows you the freedom to express genuine *Courtesy* to others, not a false *Courtesy* adulterated by *Fear* or *Subservience*. *Humility* allows you to offer the gift of genuine *Respect*, which is a form of celebration of another's existence. With *Humility*, you can achieve that elusive state of Life called *Balance*.

I allow you to sincerely praise another's accomplishments. You can offer pure, unadulterated *Appreciation*. Sincere, insightful criticism will fall from your lips, unsullied by selfish *Motivations*, unburdened by hidden agendas wallowing in *Insecurity*.

Humility allows the farmer to appreciate the talents of the swordsman, without feeling inferior to him. The warrior can wonder appreciatively at the written creation of the poet, yet not despise their physical differences. The healer appreciates the sweat of those who till the soil, and the miner nods with appreciation to the fisherfolk who brave storm-tossed seas. True *Humility* liberates the human soul because it is pure, unencumbered by weighty baggage of any kind. True *Humility* simply *is*.

I allow you to move easily among other systems. I quell the instant judgments that can ruin an initial encounter. When appreciation precedes judgment, you are free to process information about that new system unencumbered by insecure, defensive assumptions. I allow genuine acceptance of another soul, an absolute necessity toward achieving the orbit of *Balance.*

Humility in this form, used in this way, is exquisite to behold in the human character, for it illuminates others instead of self. And just as *Humility* illuminates the heralds: *Courtesy*, *Respect*, *Motivation,* and *Balance*, they in turn illuminate *you*.

Remember, Readers teach that your character is a sculpture created from your decisions and values. Do they not also teach that your reputation is the shadow cast by that sculpture as Life shines upon it? These heralds are part of that light.

Even so, I must warn you. With too little of me, a healthy level of *Pride* will distort into *Arrogance*. The herald *Arrogance* speaks for itself elsewhere in these Scrolls, but even so, I can warn you of him. His energy is as strong as it is negative because it is so repellant. Few in the League have such power to push away the orbits of *Love, Respect, Integrity, Trust, Balance,* or even *Truth*, as *Arrogance* does.

On the other side of the coin, with too much of me, the balanced orbit of *Pride* dissolves. *Humility* then degrades into a self-deprecating, head-hanging denial of *Self-Worth.* Denial of *Self-Worth* drains the life energy from your system. Once in this stage, true *Courtesy* is supplanted by *Intimidation.* True *Respect,* for self, for others, withers. Certain religious sects actually work to achieve such a state, declaring it a state of enlightenment. But is this true?

Ask yourself this. If your Creator, in His love, intentionally ignited you into existence for a specific reason, how will He look upon your use or misuse of His gift of Life? Do you actually believe that manufactured self-abasement will please Him? Will He smile at your lack of appreciation of His gift? Or will He frown at your lack of *Gratitude*?

I do not ask for an answer. I present such questions for your consideration. Then, after considering thoroughly, think again of whether my words match your vision of a Liberator.

Remember who created you.

Always remember.

51

The Gift

Alina let the words of the Liberator echo in the minds of the children for a few minutes before placing her Scroll atop the case at her feet. She whispered something to Taggart, who simply nodded in reply.

She rose from her stump seat and invited the children to do so also. "Let us take a moment, children," she said, "to stretch and give our backsides a break. She smiled as she twisted at the waist and rotated her arms in full, slow circles. The children followed gratefully, for most had long since unfolded their blanket cushions and wrapped themselves against the rapid cooling of the evening. They milled about, some imitating Alina, others raising knees high or squatting repeatedly to vanquish the stiffness.

Taggart used the time to rebuild the campfire from the woodpile a few paces away. He stoked the embers around the new wood, taking care to avoid creating too great a cloud of sparks to rise in the heady breezes still blowing. When he was satisfied that the new wood had caught and that there was enough immediate wood to last the Reading, he returned to his stump and found his place in his Scroll.

Before following suit, Alina said, "Before we resume children, place your right hand over your heart." As they did so, she asked, "And what do you feel?"

"A heartbeat, Lady Alina," Keiriam said as if chagrined to answer the obvious.

"And another, and another, and another," Alina added. "We could ask the same question as you notice each breath you inhale and exhale, with each scent and temperature variation you detect as your lungs draw air through your nostrils."

As the children nodded in understanding, she beckoned for them to resume their seats as she did. As backsides reacquainted themselves with the unforgiving stumps, and as blankets were once again pulled snuggly against the chill, Alina said, "Consider that each heartbeat in your chest is a gift. Or, said in a different way, Father Creator bestows the gift of Life upon us a single heartbeat at a time. We live by His gift of each breath we take."

Taggart cleared his throat in preparation to read. "We are about to hear from a herald who helps us understand this. One who helps put Maker and Life and other travelers on this often mysterious Life path into *Perspective*." The children tried, as they did each time now, to tune in to the demeanor of the next herald. Taggart smiled as he spoke, his face reflected happiness, but not outright exuberance as both Readers had shown in a few of the earlier heralds. *No*, the children concluded after a few moments. *There is no edge in the voice this time. This voice sounds . . . content.*

Greetings, young one.

Call me *Gratitude*. In my most basic definition, I am the state of being thankful, grateful. Human beings show *Gratitude* and demonstrate appreciation toward one another for countless reasons and in countless ways. This is well and proper, certainly, and traditional courtesy is worthy of performing oneself and for teaching the young. Yet, such a basic definition only scratches the surface of true *Gratitude*.

To understand me more fully, envision me as a personal Gift from you to someone else. Picture me as something valuable, carefully wrapped in brightly colored paper, and festooned with ribbons, such as a present you might bring to celebrate a friend's or loved one's birthday. Consider that the only Gift you have more personal than *Gratitude* is the Gift of *Love*. With that vision in mind, let us discuss true *Gratitude*.

True *Gratitude* is more than just saying "thank you." It is that certainly, and the teaching of such response should be encouraged because it carries its own kind of magnificence. However, true *Gratitude* should be an expression on a grander scale. I am the ability to offer such a Gift free of thought of personal compensation, repayment, or obligation. True *Gratitude* is pure, an expression of heart unencumbered by ego or cultural convention. Real *Gratitude* stands alone—as any free Gift should.

I am an offering of *Respect*, a personal acknowledgment of a kindness shown to you, of a blessing bestowed upon you. Expressing genuine *Gratitude* expands your personal world. It sends a direct message to your Creator that you know *you* are not the center of your universe, that *you* are not the Creator of yourself. Other creations will cross your Life path. They will orbit you as do other heralds of the League.

Expressing *Gratitude* costs you nothing. You lose nothing. Expressing *Gratitude* does not diminish you, yet the power of it often builds up another because it acknowledges the value of their contribution to you. *Gratitude* informs another that his or her existence matters in the grand, unfathomable scheme called Life.

Did a stranger help you to your feet after you had slipped and fallen crossing a stream? Were you welcomed to the warmth of a campfire as you traveled a wind-swept road on a cold winter's night? Did a tradesman skillfully and honestly complete a task for you? Did an employer acknowledge your contributions to a task? Did your grandmother prepare your favorite stew as you recovered from an illness under the quilt she lovingly tucked under your chin?

Your Life will be filled with countless great and small moments to treasure such as these. Accepting me as an orbit, opens your eyes wider each year of your existence. As your *Awareness* matures, you will recognize how often opportunities for *Gratitude* cross your path.

Can a *soular* system develop without my orbit, without *Gratitude*? Unfortunately young one, it seems so. But those souls who lack *Gratitude* are shallow and joyless, their systems claustrophobic, and dark. To focus an inordinate amount of attention upon oneself, to deny the influence and the existence of other systems is to live in a very small, unnaturally confined world. To exist without *Gratitude* in one's life is to cultivate the notion that the individual is a universe unto itself. How could such a system *not* be dark? It does not bask in the light of the Creator. Such a soul could never create a self-centered universe of any real dimension, of any significant light.

The cynic might argue that if the human soul is truly a tiny, boiling globe of golden fire as we contend, then that should be sufficient light. True enough, in a way . . . for mere existence. But remember, young one, mere existence belongs to the animal world. The world of the human being is magnified exponentially by the sheer number of layers available to it, layers beyond the mindless existence of the beast.

The soul without *Gratitude* confines itself to the shadows of its own making. It ignores the contributions of light along its path that other systems provide. Even worse, it ignores the *Potential* of others. The sheer self-centeredness of selfish, deliberate *Ingratitude* denies the value that one might be to others. *Ingratitude*, you see, is an arrogant, self-serving herald. A perversion of *Pride*.

Shall I serve warnings to you about myself as most other heralds do? Yes, I shall, but with certain conditions. First of all, you cannot have too much true *Gratitude*, any more than you can have too much *Honor* or too much *Courage*. That said, your genuineness of *Gratitude* will be dependent upon the orbits of the Liberator—*Humility*, and the Undercurrent—*Motivation*.

Let your *Gratitude* be free of hidden agendas, of selfish or contrived *Motives*. A Gift should be just that—a gift. Nothing should be expected in return, nor should it be a tool of manipulation. Consider these my subtle warnings to allow you to acquire my orbit. My most direct warning is this: You, that is your *system*, will be unable to acquire, to *achieve* the orbit of *Balance* without my orbit.

Balance can be a difficult orbit in any soul's life, but achieving it is impossible without *Gratitude*. Without *Gratitude*, *Arrogance* can force its orbit upon you. So will *Self-Centeredness*. As for personal *Pride*, without *Gratitude* to help you maintain your spiritual and emotional *Balance*, you will fall from the Tightrope.

In all fairness, all human creations are prone to experience some form of *Ingratitude* over the course of their lives. The key to countering a temporary absence of *Gratitude* is to remember that it is often just a lapse of memory. Life can sometimes become so busy that *Gratitude* is simply pushed aside or forgotten. Yet, when disease or harm befalls a friend or loved one, you will remember the blessing of health—and be grateful.

When flood or storm strikes a neighbor or another community, you will remember the blessing of personal safety—and be grateful.

When your spouse kisses your cheek for no apparent reason or snuggles against a winter's chill with you under a common blanket, you will remember the blessing of marriage—and be grateful. You will remember and appreciate that only your Maker could have created such a thing as *Love* and then given it free to His creation.

When your children are grown and return home with little ones of their own, when those little ones hug your aging neck with *Love* as their parents had once done in their youth, you will remember the blessing of family—and be grateful.

I submit that to properly interact with the magnitude of Creation, with the magnificent complexity of Life, requires that you maintain a good memory. This can be a very difficult task at times. *Gratitude* can be a difficult Gift to give on occasion—especially to one's Creator.

This can be especially true when Life strews obstacles along your path. I can be a difficult orbit to maintain when Life tests you, when it harms you, when it seems to take from you rather than give. When it takes from a loved one or friend.

Yet, true, heartfelt *Gratitude* is the ultimate expression of worship. Genuine *Gratitude* for the blessings bestowed upon you by the Creator needs no ornate temple to formalize worship. Priests and elaborate rituals are unneeded in this regard as well, for *Gratitude* directed honestly to one's Creator requires no intermediary voice, no structural context. Acknowledgements of blessings from the Creator: one's heartbeat, one's next breath, love of family, comfort of shelter, the treasure of one's profession, are things to be given back by you personally. Genuine, heartfelt *Gratitude* is the purest act of worship a human can perform.

I suggest, therefore, that you begin and end each day with *Gratitude* to your Maker. When you pray, speak to Him honestly, without routine, without formula. Your adult peers might suggest that you count your blessings. Do that. Truly count the seemingly insignificant ones as well as the grand and the obvious.

Then try to list that which you might yet need, truly need, in your life. You will discover that the list of your blessings far outweighs those things that may or may not be actual needs in your Life. You might well discover that the blessings that grace your current Life: family, good health, your profession, food upon your table, the shelter protecting that table, the influence of friends, of trusted neighbors, the safety of your nation, are all that you truly "need." All else is simply treasure heaped upon already immeasurable wealth.

Knowing that is called *Contentment*, the one herald of the League whose orbit every human soul, from monarch to servant seeks, whether they realize it or not. Read of my fellow herald in these Scrolls, for he has much to say of the simplicity, as well as the complexity, of *Contentment*.

Let this understanding influence your own conversations with your Creator. When you lift your prayers to Him, let ninety percent of them ring with words of *Gratitude*. Let only ten percent of them be respectful words of request. Let that ratio echo in your mind forever: nine expressions of *Gratitude* for every one request. Doing so reminds you that you are neither the center of your personal universe nor the creator of it.

Expressing *Gratitude* toward others puts Life into perspective. It reminds you that you alone do not create existence. You alone do not light your path. Others contribute: family, loved ones, even strangers, or brief acquaintances.

A simple "thank you," as by-rote as those two words might be as an expression of good manners in a culture, are, in fact, words capable of significant influence in another's life. A "thank you" acknowledges a person's contribution to your life, however small or great it was. It tells that person that what he or she did had value and genuine purpose in that instant of *Time*. You would do well to remember that simple fact. By acknowledging the contribution of someone else in a given instant of *Time*, *you*, in turn, contribute to that person in the same instant. "Thank you" are two words that belong in the domain of those who believe that *Gratitude* is the highest form of worship to one's Creator.

Lastly, I advise you to take nothing for granted. Nothing! May the companion orbit of my inseparable colleague *Appreciation*, teach you to cherish the wealth of your profession, your health of the moment, love of family, the presence of a trustworthy neighbor each day.

Appreciation enlightens your life's blessings, however humble or splendid they might be. *Appreciation* gives *Gratitude* the incentive for its voice. It is safe to say that without *Appreciation's* orbit, you will not be able to hold mine about your system. Allow the enlightenment of *Appreciation* to motivate your *Gratitude*.

In that vein, end each day with *Gratitude* for the gifts you have received from your Creator's Table of Life.

Then, young one, live in such a way that your path and your existence earn the Gift of *Gratitude* from others.

52

Golden Thread

"Children," Taggart said after the echoes, "we are nearing the end of our Scroll Night together. We will read two more heralds still, but you should be aware that our three thousand-year-old traditional rite of passage has had but a few rare changes in all that time. None of the substance has changed in our two thousand years as Wraithians, or in the previous thousand years when Scroll Nights were held in the Pelanjian Archipelago.

"That said, one rare change occurs at this time. The Reading order of the heralds was different for our Pelanjian ancestors. Then, a Scroll Night Reading ended with the introduction of the Door, *Death*, the herald that describes how we should treat the end of Life.

"Many of you no doubt wondered why we read of the end of Life, yet continued further with other heralds. After all, did the Door not end his message to us all with, 'After me, there are no more orbits?' Logically, it makes sense to end a Reading right there. It was just as logical to the Pelanjians. More so, perhaps, given the constant threat of invasion of their archipelago that made each generation grimmer than the one before.

"Remember, it was that descent into soul-callousing fatalism that inspired Admiral Balgaire to write his *Mirror Resolution* and then to ultimately design the Disappearance, which brought our people to Wraithaven. That casting aside of the old life, that renewing and regeneration of the power to dream—and to believe in the good and positive of Life—inspired the Council of Readers to change the order of the heralds."

"No longer would *Death* end a Reading," Alina added. "Rather, it would be relegated to a lesser role, one not so grimly final. Readings in the New World of Wraithaven would reflect the optimism of the war-weary pioneers who longed so deeply for peace and a new beginning. Starting with the first year of the Wraithaven settlement, two very special heralds were given even more special meaning by simply reordering their appearance in a Reading."

"For the first of these last two heralds," Taggart said, "we must take a moment similar to the beginning of your Scroll Night. This herald will instruct you to gaze skyward as we did then. Let us do that now." As the children raised their eyes heavenward, Taggart said, "Once again, imprint that black velvet canopy and those brilliant diamonds strewn across it in your mind.

"That vast expanse is where we all must be at this moment, children. Let us immerse ourselves in that impossible sea of blackness. Let us once again be absorbed by the immeasurable distances of Creation. Let us submit to the awe such a vision of eternity represents."

In truth, the herald describing itself as "the Door" had left an indelible impression upon the young Initiates. The grim warning, "There are no more orbits," touched them all to some degree. To those who had experienced the death of a loved one, the words had seemed to hiss from the shadows with a vile, uncaring finality.

The son of goldsmiths, Quinn Farriss, had lost his cherished great-grandfather just the month before. No longer would the hearty 119-year-old man show Quinn how to set a rabbit snare, or help him build a snow shelter in Wraithaven's rugged high country.

Tyra's loss of her beloved stallion gnawed at her heart like an open wound and would continue to do so for months and years to come. To both of the children, the Door had opened with chilling indifference. It had beckoned the loved ones to enter, and then slammed shut behind them with the same indifference it had for those who grieved alongside them. The Door was a herald who angered the living every bit as much as it saddened them.

It was that dark finality that should have logically signaled the end of the evening that had confused the children. The Door had spoken of itself as the last herald, yet the Readers had not returned their Scrolls to their leather carrying pouches. They had continued. And now the young ones once again tuned in to the character of the next herald.

Alina smoothed the sleeve of her robe with precise, exaggerated care, doing so without acknowledging the Initiates. She picked a spruce needle from one robe cuff and flicked it into the fire, before brushing a wisp of hair from her forehead. After smoothing non-existent wrinkles from the lapel of her robe, she seemed to be preparing herself for . . . what? Of all the heralds living within the Scrolls—those read tonight, and those to be read later—which two did the Council deem important enough to end a Reading?

"Children," Alina said with a radiant smile and a self-assured voice sounding decades younger. "We are about to read of a herald many Readers consider the most important of all in the League. That we asked you to once again fix the night sky firmly in your minds is significant to understanding this next herald. For much like the Phantom mist-diamond of *Time*, this herald cannot be a conventional orbit about your soular system. So, with that bit of foreshadowing stated," Alina said sweetly, "let us begin."

Greetings, young one, and welcome to Life.

Over the eons, I have been called "the source of Life," which is untrue because Father Creator is that. I have even been called "the reason for Life," which is equally as untrue. When I am called "the great intangible," though, that, at least in some measure, *is* true.

Call me *Hope*. I furnish your expectation of something yet unfulfilled. I am the reliance that what you expect and desire you will achieve. I am your wish. Just as my companion the Door is an absolute, so too am I. Yet, even as absolutes the Door and I differ. The Door is inevitable. I am not. You sense me because my essence was ingrained within you by your Creator.

In that regard, I am not an orbit as are my companions. I differ from most of them in another way as well. They introduce themselves, declare their essential definitions, and then enlighten you with warnings and affirmations. We all follow the Maker's protocol in that regard, but most heralds depict themselves as a recognizable symbol. I do as well, but with more descriptive detail that you might fully grasp what *Hope* truly is.

First, gaze at the night sky above you. Imagine me as a single thread of brilliant gold spanning that immeasurable black expanse. That thread hums with Life. You can hear it if you listen closely. The thread vibrates with power. You can feel it when you touch it. I shimmer even in such total darkness, for I am illuminated by the Creator's will. He has pulled a single thread from the hem of His robe and anchored it eternally at each end of Creation. Look at me. The Maker's Golden Thread—your Golden Thread—spans beyond the limits of your eyesight, beyond even the limits of your imagination. *Hope* cannot be severed, for I am as indestructible as the Creator is. *Hope* cannot be loosened from the immovable anchors, for it was your Maker Who tied the knots of *Hope* to those very anchors.

At this point, young one, you should be questioning my vision for you. You should be wondering why I define myself as indestructible. You should consider that if *Hope* is a brilliant, gleaming thread of gold, shimmering by the force of the Creator's will, how can it *not* be found? How can it be lost?

Good. These are worthy considerations. There are distinctions about me, about *us*, that you must understand. First, I am found merely by believing in me, and by reaching for me. Belief is strength. And yet, my young friend, does that not seem like a paradox? If *Hope* is ingrained in you as I have said, how can you reach for something that you already have? Such is the paradox of *Hope*. Here is another one.

I have painted a vision of myself, yet I have no true tangible substance. You belong to the moment called "now," while I live in a future that does not yet exist. I do, however, make the current moment livable, if not survivable in extreme cases. That is my true value. That is why your gift of free choice is so important. *Hope* exists whether you believe or not. Unbelief does not nullify either your Creator or me.

The Maker imprints within each soul the subtle knowledge that to hold the Golden Thread is to live. All human beings intuitively sense this: the sailor of a stricken ship, struggling through each battering wave that seeks to steal his last breath; the lone, poverty-stricken mother who fights each day to earn bread and shelter for her children; the father confronting a life-threatening illness, who fights on, a day at a time, then another, and another, to hold fast to his Life mission of support and leadership for his family.

Hope of future escape strengthens the captive to endure the indignities of confinement and the tortures of captors. I am the only weapon lethal to *Despair*, the only means to combat him.

But the Maker imprints something else within the human soul as well. Equally as subtle, the human soul inherently knows what will happen when one's grasp of the Golden Thread is abandoned. The soul knows that to release one's grasp of the Golden Thread is to begin dying. *Hope* is Life. The absence of it is *Death.*

Understand, therefore, that of the entire League of Heralds, I am the most important orbit to sustain Life. I give *Courage* the stimuli to act. My strength is constant, never waxing or waning. Only your belief that I exist changes. Only your grip upon the Golden Thread strengthens or weakens. And *that* is what you must always remember.

A *soular* system can exist without *Dignity*, without *Love*, without any real *Honor,* or with little or no *Imagination*, but the instant that *Hope* slips away, that soul begins to die. As inherent to your design as I am, *your* grip upon me determines my strength in your life. *You* determine how much *Hope* your life has. *You* determine if *Hope* can be "lost," or when it no longer exists.

And if a moment comes in your life when *Hope* is finally lost, then that moment is determined by you. Not by me. Not by your Creator. That is as much a fact as it is a warning. Just as a human being cannot have too much true *Courage*, one cannot have too much *Hope.* One cannot have too strong a grip upon the eternal Golden Thread.

Remember who created you, young sun.

Remember the robe of the One who created *me.*

53

Mirror

For long moments, neither Reader spoke to the group or even each other. They allowed the vision of the Golden Thread to implant itself deeply into the children's minds. In the silent interim, each child eventually raised their eyes to the night sky, imagining that shimmering, unbreakable golden line, taut as a mandolin string, linking one end of Creation to the other. Most Initiates retained a very strong vision of *Hope* long after their Reading. Alina and Taggart had.

"Children," Alina said, "let me ask a predictably biased, two-edged question. Do you believe our nation is a great one, and if so, why is it?"

"Yes," Marcus Riordan answered. "Wraithaven is great. Certainly in comparison to Outsiders."

"And you know this how?" Alina countered. "Have you ever been outside the Shield? Ever walked the streets of other nations?"

"Well . . . no," the boy answered, "but I believe the news brought back by our Pickets. They *have* walked such streets, and they are as honored as Readers."

"Yes, Marcus. A well-crafted answer by the way," she said, smiling. "Our Pickets do keep our culture informed. And yes, they do so honorably and accurately. Anyone else?"

"We leave other nations alone," Leah Brenna said. "We don't make war upon others. We never have. We've taken *Pride* in that since the time our ancestors called themselves Pelanjians. I'm not sure if that makes us great or not, but it makes us . . . *unique,*" the girl added.

"An excellent distinction," Alina said with an appreciative smile.

"Wraithians are a healthy people, Lady Alina," Brann Halwyn said. "Our healers excel in herbal remedies and perform advanced surgical techniques. Sixty years is considered ancient in Outsider cultures, but everyone here tonight knows many folk twice that age. Most are still vigorous too. They still tend farms and orchards. Still work their ranches and vineyards. They still ply their chosen crafts and still serve in militia drills every year. *Nung-Cha* masters warn, *'the grayer the hair, the deadlier the hands.'*"

"Thank you, Brann," Alina said. "Your family is not only known for your father's skill as a master potter. Many of the Halwyn line are renowned master herbalists and master healers. A nation's greatness defined by its health? *Hmm.* Interesting concept. Anyone else?"

"*Nung-Cha* makes our nation great, I think," Keiriam Marsali ventured.

"Why?" Alina asked. "It's been our people's martial art since the days of Pelanjia. But didn't we already establish that we were a great nation because we left other nations alone and avoided war?"

"Yes," Keiriam answered, "but *Nung-Cha* is more than preparation to defend Wraithaven. It unites us because the creation of it as a martial system dates back to our Pelanjian roots. It gave our ancestors the skill behind their iron will to preserve their culture. We exist today because *Nung-Cha* kept them free from domination by invaders."

"Anything else along that line?"

"*Nung-Cha* unites the nation, even as it liberates the individual," Devyn Briac said.

"Well recited, Devyn, just as *Nung-Cha* masters invoke in every training session. But what does that mean?"

"*Nung-Cha* liberates the individual from bullying," Devyn said. "In Outsider nations, the strong often intimidate the weak. It's difficult to intimidate a trained warrior. A warrior will exact a heavy price for any such attempt, and every Wraithian citizen is a trained warrior."

"Well said, Devyn. Anyone else?"

"Yes," Tyra Kayne said. "Our culture is literate. Even the poorest Wraithian can read, write, and speak multiple languages. In most Outsider cultures, literacy is available only to those of wealth, or privilege, or to the supposedly royal classes."

"True enough," Alina said, "but tell me. Why *do* we all speak and write in multiple languages?"

"It's a requirement," Tyra said. "We must speak and write two languages by our first year in academy."

"Is that all?" Alina asked the group. "Because it is a requirement?"

Most of the group nodded in the affirmative. Tyra did as well, but perplexity clouded her face. Her answer felt inadequate somehow. Something else was coming.

"I submit, children," Alina said, "that all these things are the result of the power our next herald wields. Said differently, the qualities of our culture that we so pridefully point to as signs of our greatness are the result of the power our next herald teaches us how to use."

And with that introduction, Taggart cleared his throat, rolled his Scroll to the proper place, and began to read in a clear, strong voice, brimming with confidence.

Greetings, young one.

Call me *Expectation.* Fundamentally, I am one of the easiest heralds to define. I am the act of expecting something—anything— be it good or evil, positive or negative. I am also the state of something being expected.

Stated thus, I seem like a herald without obvious power, without a worthy function, without the kind of noble cause that many of my fellows bring to orbit. In good time, you will discover the truth behind such misconceptions, and see how *Expectation* can, and indeed *should* be a powerful force.

Expectation is one of the primary forces behind the greatness of your people. For centuries, you have been driven by deliberate, precisely thought-out *Expectation.* From birth, *Expectation* is so deeply ingrained within the essence of each individual, it cannot help but permeate every aspect of your culture.

To understand, imagine me as a large wall Mirror in your home. Note the clarity of the reflective glass, and the detail of the carved and stained oak frame holding the glass.

Now visualize your image in the center of the Mirror. Note the details of your face: the color of your eyes, your hair, the frown you wear, or the smile.

Now imagine your parents behind you in the reflection. Bring forth your grandparents and other beloved family members. Add neighbors you admire. Add the teachers you respect. Make room behind your reflection to imagine the warriors who guard your culture. Note their steely sentry eyes as they wait for you to join their ranks. Behind them, all, envision the heroes of your people's history.

Now add one last set of images. In front of you, add the images of children younger than you: siblings, cousins, neighbors, newborn infants of friends. Situate them in the Mirror so that they look up to you.

Feel the weight of all those Mirror figures as they gaze upon you. Sense the confidence, the *Hope* that radiates from all those faces. Feel the power from them as it embraces you, as it bathes you in its aura. That is the power of *Expectation.* It is another liberating force that empowers you. Deliberate *Expectation* has empowered your people for millennia.

Expectation. Is. Deliberate. Power! *Expectation* is created power. *Expectation* is intentionally nurtured power. You are strong because *it* is. Your ancestors *were strong* because it is. Your children and your children's children *will be strong* because it is.

Your culture expects things of its citizens. Of *you*! And what is vitally important is that *you* know that. *Expectation* is not a prison of unfulfilled dreams, not a path of impossible aspirations. Rather, *Expectation* given to *you* is literally your permission to achieve—anything! The act of having *Expectation,* of showing *Expectation* toward another, is as deliberate an act as the unshackling of chains from a captive. *Expectation* is the act of two cupped hands opening to allow a captive sparrow the freedom to soar the winds upon wings of its own.

Listen carefully, young one. Cultures do not strengthen by expecting *less* of their citizens. Citizens do not, indeed, *cannot* tap into their *Potentials* by ignoring the power of *Expectation,* or by choosing the lazy path of spectator over that of participant.

Expectation is a powerful force in its own right. It is also a two-way responsibility.

Consider. The academic system of your culture expects you to speak and write four different languages by your twelfth harvest. And so you do. Whether you realize it or not, by doing so, you tap into the force that is *Expectation* as it flows toward you from others in that Mirror on your wall.

I submit that if your culture expected you to speak and write but one language in the span of twelve harvests, that single language would be the only one you knew.

Your culture takes *Pride*, as your ancestors did, in living deliberately. You do not, and they did not, graze randomly across Life's pastures. That said, living deliberately is not a single act of intense, but momentary focus. Living deliberately is a way of life. It is an equation of *Imagination* plus *Courage*, of *Commitment* plus personal *Intention*, of *Expectation*, and *Endurance*, and *Fortitude*.

Living deliberately requires belief in something larger than self, in something larger than one's perceived limitations. To live deliberately is to embrace personal *Potential*. Yet, the culture that chooses, that *dares* to live deliberately should have a measure of *Charity*, of *Compassion* in its overall equation.

That culture must first acknowledge the *Potential* of every human being as a Creator-given fact, a concept immune to debate. That immunity allows the culture to assume unshackled *Potential* for each individual. That is how society bestows the power of *Expectation* upon its people. That is how it creates an environment of personal liberation. And yes, this is part of the equation called "living deliberately."

But there is another side to that coin. For the power of *Expectation* to be transferred back into one's culture, for the individual to be genuinely able to live deliberately, that person must recognize that the only shackles to one's *Potential* are self-created, self-imagined ones. At least within such a liberating environment.

A culture's responsibility, therefore, is to actively *teach* and to actively *reinforce* the doctrine of *Expectation*. A well-intentioned society must nurture the concept that the power of *Expectation* exists and is real, that it flows in equal measure from society to the individual, as it does from the individual back to society.

If asked to sum up the core environment of one's culture, the best and most liberating answer would be to say that it is an environment of *Expectation.* Yet, young one, I must serve warning as most heralds do. There can be a negative side to *Expectation. Expectation* can be misused.

In certain cultures, *Expectation* is a weapon wielded to contain, not to liberate the human spirit. Within such environments, one is born into one's social station. *Expectation* is a shallow existence, despite its rigidity. When imprisoned by social hierarchy from birth, one station does not aspire to attain a loftier one.

The children of servants are "expected" to follow their parents, not to aspire to become masters of their own households. They are expected *not to* rise above their supposed Life stations. They are expected to defer to their "betters," not to dream of actually becoming better. Such cultures continually remind and actively teach the supposedly "unworthy" to *not* dream.

This is a perverted form of *Expectation,* a negative form, yet every bit as real and powerful as positive *Expectation.*

The rural peasant born to till the earth, born to generations of the same, does not, indeed dares not, aspire to acquire the skill and the *Respect* of a recognized master Tradesman. If or when such aspirations do appear, they vanish like dawn-seared ground mist in an environment ill-suited to believe, to dream, to *Hope.* At least for those born to the lower rungs of their society.

In such an environment, freedom to dream, to *Hope,* to believe in one's *Potential,* resides all too often only within the upper social ranks of royalty, hereditary wealth, or social or political power.

In such a rarified atmosphere of privilege, it is expected that the abilities to dream, to *Hope,* and to accomplish are deserved but for the worthy few. Not only do the dwellers of elevated status believe it is their inherent right to dream, but the supposed lower-ranked folk tend to believe that the worthy are right! You should know that a surprising number of long-established cultures subscribe to such a self-limiting hierarchy in one way or another. It is a tradition that is perpetually sustained by those of privilege because they benefit the most. Yet, those who accept their diminished lot with a shrug of their compliant shoulders, believing that things are as they are, and always will be, must bear at least a portion of guilt for their plight.

When those of royal houses, of houses of power or wealth, ignore rules of law in their own cultures when supposed "lesser folk" accept such behavior with slavish resignation, that too, *is* a kind of *Expectation*, but it is a perverted form. Laws do not apply equally to those of influence, but only to the "lesser folk"? One should demand to ask why that should be acceptable.

But let us dwell no longer on such negative aspects of *Expectation*. What you see in the Mirror of *Expectation* can be an extremely relative thing, determined by the positive or negative environment of a culture. In that regard, *Expectation* can either be the most cruel and soul-draining captor imaginable, or the most liberating, uplifting *Potential* possible.

Young one, I leave you with a few last considerations. *Expectation* is not necessarily just a role or cultural condition. It is often a demand, a tradition, or a duty.

For example: Your culture expects all able-bodied citizens to serve in their local and provincial militias. There is very little debate regarding one's duty to one's nation. Your nation expects you to serve, while you, in turn, expect and anticipate service. For both sides, recognized milestones of adulthood are reached with honorable service.

To be the recipient of an honorable and worthy *Expectation* is a true blessing from your culture. This is true whether the cultural *Expectation* is educational excellence or military service, whether spiritual or moral in nature, or even in adhering to simple codes of behavior with one's neighbor. Again, I remind you. Cultures do not strengthen by expecting *less* of their citizens. The individual does not strengthen by failing to tap into the power of *Potential* and *Expectation*.

All positive forms of *Expectation* give you the freedom to dream and liberate yourself from the invisible chains of soul restraint.

Consider, young one, that as I have spoken to you, I have cupped you in my hands. I open them now for you. Remember the Mirror of *Expectation* and fly from my hands.

Fly even higher than you expect you can.

54

Transition

Maintaining the pattern of the evening, the Readers allowed the meditative silence following the Mirror to linger. When Alina finally broke the silence, her words sent a subtle but delayed ripple of shock through the Initiates.

"Young *ladies*, young *men*," she said with just a hint of emphasis. "This concludes your Reading. It does not conclude your Scroll Night necessarily, unless you wish it to."

The impact of Alina's words were not immediately absorbed. They sounded different somehow. Unexpected. Then the slight emphasis took root in each of them.

Not "children," they all concluded. *We assume young adulthood tonight, not tomorrow at the sword burning. Tonight!* That dawn of understanding brought smiles to most of the faces, and to a few, a misting of the eyes. *We're here!*

Taggart waited for the dawn of comprehension to show upon the nine faces before he spoke. The time for Reader voices to match the temperament of a given Herald was now over. He resumed his smooth, natural baritone. "Tell me, young friends, does anyone feel let down right now? Perhaps even somewhat disappointed?"

A few hands reluctantly raised in answer, but the looks on the faces spoke even more eloquently in their silence. After years of *Expectation*, the abrupt ending of the much-anticipated ritual *was* somewhat disappointing. Most of the nine even managed to feel guilty for feeling so.

As if reading their minds, Alina asked, "Might you even be feeling guilty because of your disappointment?"

This time, a few more hands raised as if glad the secret was out.

"Believe it or not," Taggart said, "what you are feeling at this moment is very normal. The end of *your* Reading, and I emphasize the word 'your,' was certainly much more uneventful than you expected it to be, was it not?"

"Especially," Alina added, "given the rousing send-off your academy classmates gave you. And then there were the proud parents and grandparents and the younger siblings who so looked up to you on the eve of your big step into adulthood. Remember the tears? The hugs of encouragement? The light of *Pride* shining from all those beloved faces?"

"No doubt," Taggart said, "most of you expected some thunderous epiphany to acknowledge that you have finally arrived. Surely you would experience a flash of absolute clarity as Life kicked the door to adulthood open. Didn't happen, did it?" Taggart said, smiling at Alina as if she was in on the big joke too.

"Guess what?" Alina said, smiling just as broadly. "It didn't happen for us either. It probably didn't for your parents or grandparents either. So don't feel so disappointed."

"Know this," Taggart said, smile fading, "adulthood is a process, not an instant of ecstatic revelation. It is never a lightning-bolt transformation. Each stumble you make along your journey, each time you stand up again, dust off your knees and continue, draws you deeper along the path of adulthood. Each decision you make pulls you further off the path of childhood."

"Lady Kayne," Quinn Farriss said, "you said that *Expectation* ended our Reading, but it did not conclude our Scroll Night necessarily. What did you mean?"

"Good question," Alina answered. "And one that Readers must answer even if it is not asked out loud by an Initiate."

The boy looked puzzled, but Alina continued. "It means, Quinn, that the formal Reading for the night is finished. However, Taggart and I will answer any and all questions to the best of our ability, even if dawn finds us still talking. We are here for you tonight—and for the rest of your lives."

"Sir Kayne," Keiriam Marsali asked, "watching you and Lady Kayne move through the Scrolls tonight, there are obviously many more heralds represented than we heard tonight. Also, I could not tell if the negative heralds resided in one Scroll, while the positive ones resided in the other. Am I just imagining this?"

"No," Taggart said, "you are not. In fact, the heralds' appearances in the Scrolls are deliberately *not* arranged in any kind of logical order.

"With the exception of *Awareness*, the first herald in Scroll One, and the last two, all others are deliberately placed at random. Given our emphasis on the words 'random' and 'deliberate,' tonight, this sounds incongruous. One might think, for instance, that a positive herald should follow a negative one in interest of maintaining *Balance*. Also, it seems more logical to arrange the negative heralds in one Scroll, and the positive ones in the other.

"By design, this is not the case. Random placement stimulates discussion of cause and effect. Consider that randomly placed positives and negatives imitate Life itself."

"But what of those unread tonight versus those you've introduced us to?" Devyn Briac asked. "Are the unread considered less important? Are they too unimportant to read on our own?"

"None of the heralds are unimportant," Alina said, "even those unread so far. Each has a particular value to each of us, even those we consider detriments to a soular system. Every herald in the Scrolls can teach us something to use in our lives—even those darker ones that revel in their dire purposes. You *should* know of the darkness the heralds *Envy*, *Jealousy*, *Hatred*, *Spite* and *Revenge* have planned for you, should you embrace them. Yet, you should seek out and listen as carefully to *Balance*, *Integrity*, *Compassion*, *Discipline*, and *Human Will* as you did to *Courage* and *Dignity* and *Love* tonight.

"Read and learn of the darkness and the light found within the Scrolls. Discover the shadows as well as the warmth inside them. Read of those heralds who wound the soul, as well as those who can heal it. Know them all. Let them all illuminate the path that is uniquely your own."

"Read of the *Confidence* that true *Courtesy* brings. Learn of the inner strength needed to hold it in orbit.

"Read of the soul-draining force that is *Revenge*, but absorb the healing power that radiates in every direction when *Compassion* orbits.

"Unsheathe carefully the double-edged sword of *Ambition*.

"Discover what *Justice* is, and what it is not.

"Discover the strength that is *Duty*; hear the code of *Obligation*.

"Listen as *Cowardice* sneers at you, as *Shame* belittles you, as *Conceit* lies to you."

"That said," Taggart inserted with a conspiratorial smile, "how could such a deliberate people not consider which heralds should be read on Scroll Night? Deliberate living is what Wraithians do!

"We do not read of the exact same heralds at each Reading," he said, "but a certain few must remain in their proper place.

"*Awareness,* for instance—the Dawn of us all, must remain as the first herald brought forth from the League of Heralds.

"To *Balance* the *Dark Side* of the Shadow, the *Love* of the Gem must shine through.

"The Tightrope of *Pride* should logically be followed by the healthy liberation of *Humility.*

"Yet, where once the grim finality of *Death*'s Door ended Readings, our move to the New World inspired a break with Pelanjian Reading tradition. We did so, but Dawn remains the first herald of Scroll One, while the Door remains the last in Scroll Two."

"We of the New World, given the joyous anticipation of Initiates, their family and friends, and indeed the whole of Wraithian society for each Reading, elected to change how the heralds were presented in the Readings. Their actual order in the Scrolls remained as always.

"*Death*'s Door was relegated to a lesser role midway into a Reading. *Hope* and *Expectation* were brought forth to end a Reading in a more positive light, and to be more in keeping with the *Intentions* of our new nation, named Wraithaven.

"The unbreakable Golden Thread of *Hope* demonstrates the personal relationship we have concerning our faith in our Creator's eternal *Intention* for us.

"The Herald *Expectation* reminds us of the environment we live within. It reminds us to deliberately nourish the concept of positive *Expectation* for those who dwell with us today, as well as those who will follow after us."

"However," Alina said, "We still have one final tradition to officially end our Scroll Night. Please go now to the backside of the woodpile. You will notice a large pile of cut and very dry spruce branches. Gather a number of them as Taggart and I will, and encircle the campfire with us. After we are done, you may do as you will with your time."

Upon collecting the branches and spacing themselves equally around the campfire's glowing coals, Taggart said, "As we cast these branches upon the Reading fire, let us raise our hands in concert with the new cloud of sparks as they rise toward heaven. Let each of us send a silent prayer of *Gratitude* to Father Creator for our lives, for His uncountable blessings, and for allowing us all to experience His blessing of this Scroll Night together."

Still unseen in the darkness, the Guardians moved stealthily closer, turning their faces toward their loved ones for the first time that evening.

As the Readers and Initiates tossed their spruce branches upon the coals, the fire greedily ignited the dried fuel. Clouds of brilliant orange sparks danced heavenward as if liberated by the campfire flames. They rose quickly, crackling with joy, it seemed, to be flying toward Father Creator.

The darkness-shrouded Guardians mimicked those around the fire. Each one raised arms of praise and a silent prayer of *Gratitude* toward heaven.

The red sparks danced exuberantly heavenward, reflecting in the tears of joy streaming from the eyes of the Initiates, from their unseen Guardians, and of course, from their Readers.

55

Horizons

For Taggart and Alina, sleep would not come until they were sure that all the children were talked out. Some Readings left the Initiates in contemplative silence after the last herald. Some continued past dawn the next day, the Scrolls closed hours earlier, with Readers gamely responding to seemingly endless questions from the now young adults.

This group, Taggart thought, *will probably be like most, a mixture of the two extremes. Some of the nine will take their thoughts to sleep with them. Some will refuse sleep, preferring to sit alone in the darkness and try to absorb what they have heard. I did. Others will be too curious to withhold their questions.*

What captured Taggart's personal attention at the moment, however, was the eastern horizon, blocked from view by the nearby Keaghan's Ridge. Faint flashes of very distant lightning gave the rugged, pitch-black peaks vague shape against the briefly lit horizon. *A storm boils beyond the eastern slopes,* he mused. Various cultures believed that such phenomena often predicted some future menace. Given the Wraithian aversion to omen credibility though, Taggart attached no more meaning to the lightning flashes than the natural weather phenomenon they were.

Even so, omens and portents aside, the Reader found it impossible not to draw parallels. The weather violence, so silenced by distance, mirrored a very human, very dangerous reality beyond that same horizon.

For the last decade, Pickets returning from Tripadan tours of duty brought news of wars erupting along Tripada's eastern seaboard. Assassinations, massacres, and atrocities grew in frequency and in bestial savagery each year, it seemed. Local revolutions in many of the thirty-one small nations crowding the eastern coast arose and fell like the seasons. Regional violence ignited where peace had once reigned for centuries.

Unlike Embrica, the largest continent on the planet, where each acre was claimed and well documented on maps centuries old, Tripada's three-thousand-mile width illustrated how burgeoning civilization might collide with primeval legend, and do so poorly.

Six hundred miles west of the eastern coast, the immense Lost River sliced Tripada in two, from the icy glacier wastes of Shaitan in the north to the southern coast, where it emptied into the notoriously unpredictable and deadly Mansaro Ocean.

However, of the thirty-one nations that defined the extreme reach of Tripada's civilization, none ventured more than two hundred and fifty miles westward, essentially leaving three hundred and fifty unclaimed miles to the east bank of Lost River.

From Lost River, fourteen hundred miles of canyon-strewn desert and jagged, scrub oak-carpeted ridges continued westward to collide with the base of the highest mountain range on the planet— the Shield. Known simply as the Desolate, the unforgiving region served as a wilderness buffer zone between the recognized extent of Tripadan civilization and the border of the unknown civilization extending for a thousand miles behind the Shield to Tripada's western coast. Such was the power of myth.

Only Wraithian Pickets traveled the Desolate, to either fulfill Tripadan missions or to book passage for missions in Embrica or Mascarene. The relative scarcity of commerce between Tripada and the two other major continents meant that only Wraithians grasped the true overall political picture of the planet, such as it was.

Over the millennia, Wraithians had witnessed the cause and effect of continent-wide warfare and political struggle. Ultimately, Tripadan history would differ little from the histories of Embrica and the still savage Mascarene. Certain patterns always emerged as human beings sought dominance, or severed cooperation with their neighbors. Tripada's current pattern of turmoil had already been played out centuries ago upon the blood-drenched soil of Embrica and Mascarene, and truth be told, ubiquitous violence still erupted periodically even within those long-established civilizations.

Now, just as on Embrica and Mascarene, Tripadan alliances formed and dissolved. Hastily penned treaties were often worth less than the parchment declaring the agreement. In some cases, the ink of the signatories was literally still wet as renewed argument and hostilities ensued. The most recent Pickets brought rumors of grand confederacies forming, of slavery, of the redrawing of centuries-old borders. The sanctity of established nations, it seemed, was as tenuous as a freshly signed peace pact.

Sooner or later, Taggart thought, *a strong ruler will surface who will attempt humankind's ultimate next step—unification by the will of an iron fist. Nations bordering his own will be subjugated first, once the bloodbath of his own people dries. When the blood of his neighbors seeps into the battlefields that were once towns and hamlets and croplands, nations beyond that defeated core will be absorbed one by one. It will be then that the words "empire" and "emperor" will arise. For then the entire continent must be conquered because that is what emperors do.*

When that happens, Taggart knew, the unthinkable evil that had plagued ancient Pelanjia could return. That which inspired the Pelanjian Disappearance could theoretically march two thousand miles west to threaten Pelanjia's children's children. War existed on Tripada, and like any savage beast, the War Beast endured by feasting upon the living.

Should the War Beast now raging throughout Tripada's coastal nations ever pick up the scent trail leading west to Wraithaven, the burden to wage war against the invader would not fall upon the maniacal territorialism of the antler-crowned stags. It would not be the responsibility of any of Wraithaven's other deadly creatures: the uncannily intelligent dire wolf packs or the nightmarish saber-toothed wraiths of legend. It would fall squarely upon the shoulders of something more cunning, something even more dangerous.

The burden to wage war would fall upon those whose ancestors had led Pelanjian forces against invaders twenty centuries ago. The oldest, most deadly of Wraithians would lead Dagger formations of birth-trained citizen warriors to surgically annihilate the invader. The Elder Pickets and the Double-Dragon Readers would serve one final, albeit culturally detestable, function for the Wraithian people as ancient Pickets and Readers had once served the Pelanjians. They would lead Wraithian warriors upon *Nung-Cha*—the *Necessary Path.*

In most cultures, their age would brand them "invisible," physically and mentally inept, and scorn them as clumsy objects of little value.

But in Wraithaven, if war did come, such as these would command the maniacally focused battalions which would stop any invader cold at the foot of the Shield, or perhaps at the banks of the Lost River. Should war come, surviving invaders will echo the words of the invaders of ancient Pelanjia. They will tell of ghost armies that slew invading forces in cold, machinelike silence. They will whisper of supernatural warriors who killed without war shouts in the dead of night, in storm, in blizzard, or in open daylight. Haunted eyes, scarred minds will recall the defense-piercing formations that could not be stopped.

Survivors will learn to watch over their shoulders for the rest of their lives as had so many would-be invaders in ancient times. For in those days, Pelanjian avengers followed the enemies of their homeland long after defeating them, believing that no enemy should be fought twice. *That* was what sunk the fleeing invader ships on the high seas. *That* was what burned surviving ships in their home berths. *That* was what slew the mastermind kings, princes, admirals, and generals with seemingly supernatural stealth and cunning.

Survivors will relive battlefields of unimaginable slaughter. They will distrust darkness forever, and fear shadows forever. In their nightmares, they will hear the sighing whisper of a sword or dagger being drawn from its sheath by the unseen hand of a vengeful ghost warrior. Terror will crush the courage of even the most arrogant, the most coldblooded invader.

But what will we do if they come? Taggart pondered. *Will we abandon the Pelanjian question that brought us to this sanctuary so many centuries ago? Will Fate force us to ask instead, "What might we become if our two thousand years of honorable peace is tainted once again by the stain of war? Must our energies now be channeled for destruction, rather than for peace?"*

A breath of chilly wind whisked the ends of his hair, breaking his reverie. The first ghost-like streamer of the evening's fog-river slithered past him at knee level. *Wraithfall is a bit late for the season*, he thought, looking down, *but definitely thicker than last week.*

Another distant lightning flash reminded him of omens and of the unchained War Beast rampaging far to the east. But tonight, this man of peace forced such dark thoughts from his mind. *Tonight belongs to those of the Twelfth Harvest*, he thought, as the flowing mist of legend rose toward his chest.

Tonight, this reader of Scrolls would await the questions of the young, even as his ears strained to catch what might have been a fog-muffled snarl in that remote darkness.

In Wraithaven, he thought to himself, *nightmares are not distant things.*

The end

Glossary

Bakula:
The southern polar region. Devoid of human habitation.

Beacons:
"Pelanjian Beacons" - Twenty tenets that serve as guides for Wraithian cultural conduct.

Disappearance:
The "Pelanjian Disappearance" - Admiral Balgaire's eight-step plan to evacuate the entire population of the Pelanjian Archipelago and establish a new homeland.

Enkia-Entae:
The original name of the Prayer Stone, from Old Mindocean meaning "to reach." The name is rarely used in the current Wraithian language.

Prayer Stones are uncarved, adult-high obelisks of natural stone traditionally set at the northern boundary of *Nung-Cha* exercise arenas.

Ancient Mindoceans first set such stones out of gratitude to their Maker for allowing them to discover and settle Pelanjia, the "Beautiful Sanctuary." Over the centuries, the stones have not become sacred, but rather serve as a reminder that as a stone is anchored to the earth, so too are human beings. As the stone reaches skyward, so too should human beings reach for their Creator.

Embrica:
The largest, most populous continent in the charted world. Unending conflict has characterized the nations and would-be empires that have warred against one another for untold centuries.

Mascarene:
The least explored continent in the charted world. Despite its relatively sparse population in comparison to Embrica, the continent produces 80% of the world's exotic spices and teas. Nations here are vigorously territorial and warlike.

M.C.:
Mindocean Chronical. The oldest, most comprehensive calendar in the known world. Created by Mindocean seafarers prior to their discovery and settlement of the Pelanjian Archipelago. By year "one" of the newly created Red Sun world calendar, the Mindocean Chronical was over 2,800 years old.

Mindocean:
Ancient tribes of nomadic, seafaring folk who discovered and settled, as a united people, an eleven-island archipelago centered in the unnamed sea between the continents of Embrica and Mascarene. Centuries later, this sea became widely known as the Embrican Ocean.

Nung-Cha:
Translation: *"Necessary Path."* The term originally labeled the national defense system created from Pelanjia's Survival Quest centuries prior to the Disappearance. Over the millennia since that creation, *Nung-Cha* expanded to define more deeply the Wraithian approach to life for the individual as well as the nation.

Orbit Scrolls:
Over 3,000 years old, the scrolls illuminate the Wraithian core philosophy, which defines the human soul and the development of personal character.

Pelanjia:
The eleven-island archipelago first discovered and `settled by ancient Mindoceans. In Old Mindocean, Pelanjia meant "beautiful sanctuary."

Pickets:
Elder Wraithian citizens who volunteer to serve two-year tours-of-duty on any of the three major continents as spies. Requirements to apply for Picket training include: minimum age of sixty harvests, having achieved dual Master Dragon ranks in *Nung-Cha* empty-hands/weapons and stealth techniques. Must be fluent in at least seven languages beyond native Wraithian. Pickets are often married couples who conceal their identities by wandering as itinerant tradesfolk through their assigned "target countries."
As Pelanjia evolved into an international spice empire, the development of Picket cadres became essential to warn of impending invasions targeting the home islands. Every major invasion attempt during Pelanjia's peak years was predicted and prepared for after Pickets became a cultural necessary and tradition.

Quest:
"Survival Quest" - The deliberately designed ten-year global search by the Pelanjian people to recruit the world's most skilled military and combat experts to teach the islanders how to defend their homeland and burgeoning trading empire from increasingly aggressive Embrican nations.

Readers:
The most highly esteemed members of Wraithian culture. Readers formally present the Orbit Scrolls to Wraithian children who reach their twelfth harvest. The three-day ceremony, referred to as a Reading, is held in remote regions of Wraithaven to serve as a coming-of-age to the Initiates.

Red Sun Calendar:
At the onset of the last Red Sun Disaster, delegates of the World Trade Conference voted to replace the two major regional calendars at the time, the Valerian Record (V.R.) and the Imperial Chronical

(I.C.) to establish a single worldwide calendar reference. Designated *the Year of the Red Sun,* year "one" was shown as 1R.S.

The creation of this new, worldwide calendar was the last official act of the World Trade Conference before dissolving as the Disaster erased the civilizations of that era.

Red Sun Calendar Months:
Once completed, the new calendar utilized twelve month names common to the two superseded calendars, and arranged them as: Janobraan, Fenobraan, Mairche, Andril, Maja, Junaam, Julaam, Augustaam, Septombray, Orctombray, Novombray, and Descombray

Red Sun Disaster:
Planet-effecting volcanic eruptions which occur every few millennia to shroud the planet's skies and turn sunsets and sunrises "blood red" for years on end. Superstition declares that the event signifies eternal war in mythical Wraithaven, pitting evil "wraiths" against their jailor-gods behind the prison mountain range legend calls the "Shield."

Shaitan:
The northern polar region. Devoid of human habitation.

The Shield:
The rugged, mountainous eastern perimeter of Wraithaven that separates the nation from the uninhabitable steppes and desert lands of the "Desolate Region."

Tripada:
The third major continent, first discovered by Pelanjian fleets scouting for a new homeland necessary to implement the Pelanjian Disappearance. Located in the uncharted, unnamed expanse west of Mascarene, it was shown on navigational charts as "The Void." Ultimately, the continent was depicted on evolving charts as being bordered by the newly named Sea of Mascarene, the Mansaro Ocean, and the Western Ocean.

The Void:
Prior to the Red Sun Disaster, the Void generally showed on navigational charts as the vast, uncharted region extending from Embrica's sparsely populated, uncharted eastern coast to the unexplored, poorly charted western coast of Mascarene.

World Trade Conference:
A pre-Red Sun Disaster organization created to regulate international trade among member nations. Upon the advent of the Red Sun upheaval and planet-wide devastation, the organization's last official act was to create the Year of the Red Sun calendar. In the millennia since the disaster, no equivalent worldwide organization has been created.

Wraith:
The largest, most savage predator on the planet. The saber-tooth feline hunts from the concealment of Wraithfall as the fog rivers flow from and back up to the mountain peaks. 10,000 years ago, now long-extinct nomadic tribes roamed the plains and hills of what would one day be known as "The Desolate Region" of the continent Tripada. Terrified survivors of fog-shrouded attacks labeled the creatures "fog demons" and later "wraiths." To these primitive folk, the only thing that could control such savage creatures must be "jailer gods" dwelling high in a windswept mountain prison. Thus, was the Wraithaven legend born.

Wraithfall:
An atmospheric condition unique to Wraithaven, which describes the downward flow of dense "fog rivers" from mountain peaks to lower valleys at eventide. At sunrise, as the earth warms, the fog rises back upslope to await the cool of the evening.

Wraithaven:
The most infamous legend known to humankind. The 10,000-year-old myth has been feared but never proven. In human history, only one nation has ever had the temerity to intentionally search for the alleged "forbidden land of savage demons and their jailer-gods." Pelanjia.

Wraithian:
A citizen of Wraithaven descended from the ancient sea-faring Mindoceans 4,000 years ago. These nomads ultimately discovered the eleven-island archipelago they named "Pelanjia," and settled it as their first permanent home. Over the centuries, the settlers created the world's most influential spice trading empire. After living as "Pelanjians" for over five centuries, the people disappeared just as the Red Sun Disaster began its worldwide horrors.

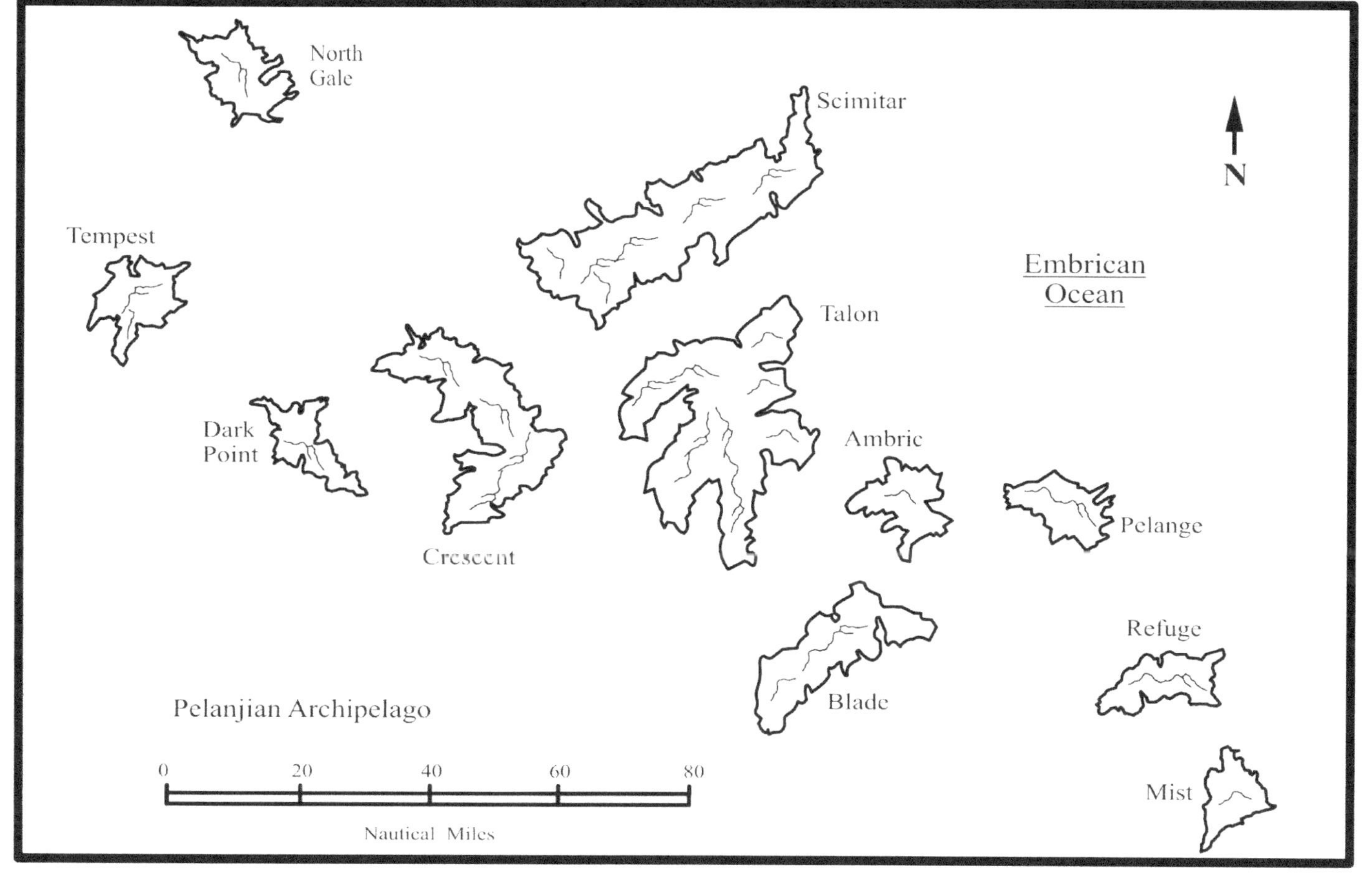

North Gale
Tempest
Scimitar
Embrican Ocean
Dark Point
Talon
Crescent
Ambric
Pelange
Blade
Refuge
Mist
N
Pelanjian Archipelago
0
20
40
60
80
Nautical Miles

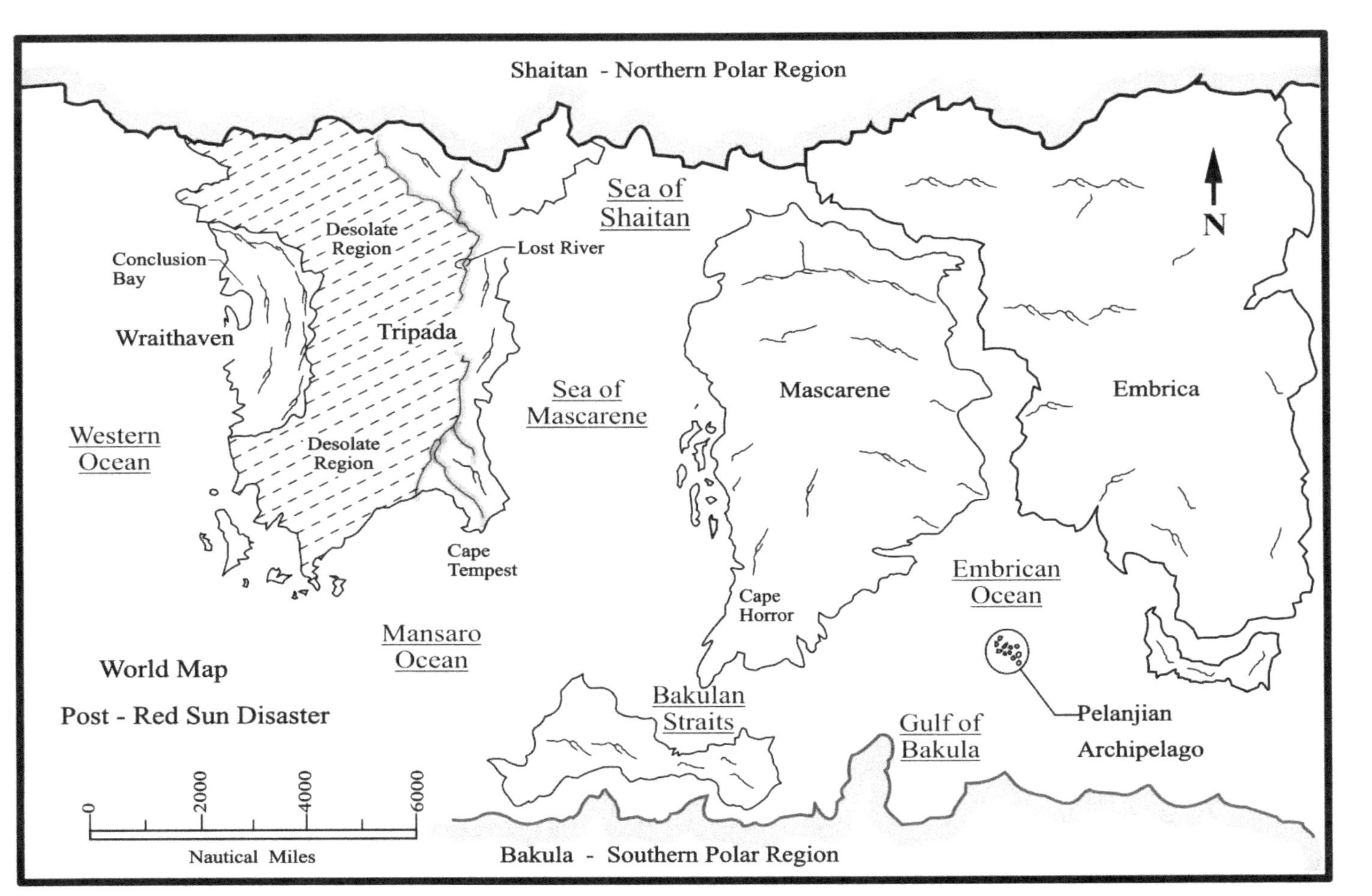

Shaitan - Northern Polar Region
N
Sea of Shaitan
Desolate Region
Lost River
Conclusion Bay
Wraithaven
Tripada
Mascarene
Embrica
Sea of Mascarene
Western Ocean
Desolate Region
Cape Tempest
Cape Horror
Embrican Ocean
Mansaro Ocean
World Map
Post - Red Sun Disaster
Bakulan Straits
Gulf of Bakula
Pelanjian Archipelago
2000
4000
6000
0
Nautical Miles
Bakula - Southern Polar Region

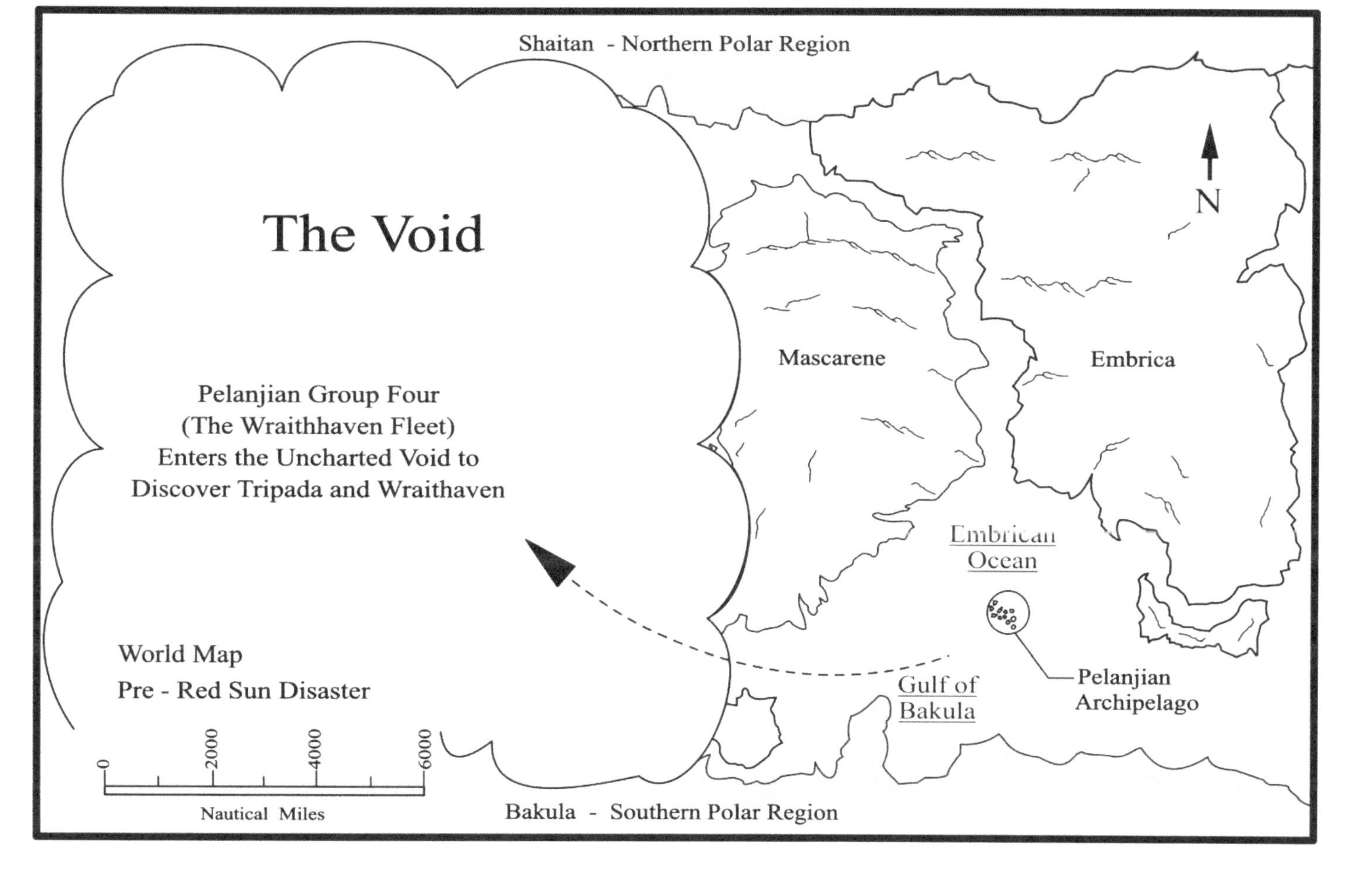

Shaitan - Northern Polar Region
N
The Void
Mascarene
Embrica
Pelanjian Group Four
(The Wraithhaven Fleet)
Enters the Uncharted Void to
Discover Tripada and Wraithhaven
Embrican
Ocean
World Map
Pre - Red Sun Disaster
Gulf of
Bakula
Pelanjian
Archipelago
0
2000
4000
6000
Nautical Miles
Bakula - Southern Polar Region

About the Author

Bruce W. Davis spent his early years in Indiana, New Mexico, and Colorado before ultimately settling in Texas. As an Eagle Scout in Colorado, his fondest memories recall majestic night canopies crowning remote mountain ranges, and the serenity of campfires flickering under countless stars.

He attended college in Colorado and Texas. He labored on steel mill maintenance gangs in East Chicago, and on longshoreman crews on the docks of the Houston Ship Channel before discovering the drafting rooms of Texas engineering companies. In Texas, he met and married Annie, the anchor of his life.

His combat tour as a Marine tank commander began with the bloody Tet Offensive in Hue City, Vietnam, and ended thirteen months later after uncountable engagements. He returned to Annie with a Silver Star commendation and that same inexpressible soul darkness all combat veterans across history have brought home from every war ever fought.

He resumed his career as a designer of electrical systems for the Alaskan pipeline, offshore platforms in the Gulfs of Mexico and Thailand, and petroleum facilities in the Middle East. While in Abu Dhabi, the word "mystical" introduced itself to him as cool desert winds slithered in from night-shrouded dunes like tan streamers of smoke. There, in the midst of those perfect, cathedral-like dunes, as sand grains sang against his boots, he recorded each and every sensation because he simply could not help himself.

The itch to write led to his discovery of Rice University's Novel Writing Colloquium in Houston, and the many accomplished writers engaged in writing passions of their own. Time eventually taught him what "catharsis" meant, after countless words had fallen free, liberated by pen and paper. Darkness dissolved under God's forgiving light, under Annie's unfading love, and from the incremental healing summoned by all those cathartic essays, impressions, and stories. How the contrast of light versus darkness, Colorado skies, and the savagery of Southeast Asian battlefields could ever coalesce with songs sung by Abu Dhabi's mystical dunes to produce *The Orbit Scrolls*, he'll never know.

But they did.

He writes from the deck of his lake house now, absorbing the scents unique to lakes and forests, and the sound of whitecaps lapping against the shoreline. He feels blessed to admire the sleek grace of otters at play, and to listen to the lonely, eerie songs that only loons can sing.

All four of his grandchildren caught their first fish from that shoreline he is proud to say. Novel chapters, essays, and short stories still fall from his soul as if summoned, but every now and then, he wonders, *"Where did that come from?"*